# JACOB
# HAVE I
# LOVED

# JACOB HAVE I LOVED

Katherine
Paterson

HarperCollins*Publishers*

Library of Congress Cataloging-in-Publication Data
Paterson, Katherine.
  Jacob have I loved.
  Summary: Feeling deprived all her life of schooling,
friends, mother, and even her name by her twin sister,
Louise finally begins to find her identity.
  ISBN 0-690-04078-4.—ISBN 0-690-04079-2 (lib. bdg.)
  [1. Twins—Fiction.  2. Brothers and sisters—
Fiction.  3. Chesapeake Bay region—Fiction]
I. Title.
PZ7.P273Jac   1980 [Fic]                          80-668

09 10 11 12 13  LP/RRDB  20 19 18 17 16 15 14 13 12

*For*
*Gene Inyart Namovicz*
*I wish it were* EMMA, *but, then,*
*you already have two or three*
*copies of that.*
*With thanks and love.*

## ACKNOWLEDGMENTS

The impetus for this book came from reading William W. Warner's *Beautiful Swimmers: Watermen, Crabs and the Chesapeake Bay*, Little, Brown and Company, 1976, which justly deserved the Pulitzer Prize it won the following year. Since then, there have been many people and books that have helped me learn more about life on the Chesapeake Bay. I should like especially to mention the Smith Island watermen I met at the Folk Life Festival at the Smithsonian: Mr. Harold G. Wheatley of Tangier Island, Virginia, and Dr. Varley Lang of Tunis Mills, Maryland. Dr. Lang, who is a writer and scholar as well as a Maryland waterman, was kind enough to read this manuscript. Any errors that remain are, of course, my fault and not his. His book about Maryland watermen entitled *Follow the Water*, John F. Blair, 1961, was also a great help to me.

# Rass Island

As soon as the snow melts, I will go to Rass and fetch my mother. At Crisfield I'll board the ferry, climbing down into the cabin where the women always ride, but after forty minutes of sitting on the hard cabin bench, I'll stand up to peer out of the high forward windows, straining for the first sight of my island.

The ferry will be almost there before I can see Rass, lying low as a terrapin back on the faded olive water of the Chesapeake. Suddenly, though, the steeple of the Methodist Church will leap from the Bay, dragging up a cluster of white board houses. And then, almost at once, we will be in the harbor, tying up beside Captain Billy's unpainted two-story ferry house, which leans wearily against a long, low shed used for the captain's crab shipping business. Next door, but standing primly aloof in a coat of fierce green paint, is Kellam's General Store with the post office inside, and behind them, on a narrow spine of fast land, the houses and white picket fences of the village. There are only a few spindly trees. It is the excess of snowball bushes that lends a semblance of green to every yard.

The dock onto which I'll step is part of a maze of docks. My eye could travel down the planking of any one of them and find at the end a shack erected by a waterman for storage and crab packing. If I arrive in late spring, the crab houses will be surrounded by slat floats that hold and protect peeler crabs in the water of the Bay until they have shed. Then the newly soft crabs will be packed in eelgrass and the boxes taken to Captain Billy's for shipping to the mainland.

More important than the crab houses, however, are the boats, tied along the docks. Though each has a personality as distinctive as the waterman who owns it, they look deceptively alike—a small cabin toward the bow, washboards wide enough for a man to stand on running from the point of the bow to the stern. In the belly of the hull, fore and aft of the engine are a dozen or so barrels waiting for the next day's catch, a spare crab pot or two, looking like a box made of chicken wire, and a few empty bait baskets. Near the winch that pulls the line of pots up from the floor of the Chesapeake is a large washtub. Into it each crab pot will be emptied and from it the legal-sized crabs—hard, peeler, and soft—will be culled from their smaller kin as well as from the blowfish, sea nettles, seaweed, shells, and garbage, all such unwelcome harvest as the Bay seems ever generous to offer up. On the stern, each boat bears its name. They are nearly all women's names, usually the name of the waterman's mother or grandmother, depending on how long the boat has been in the family.

The village, in which we Bradshaws lived for more than two hundred years, covers barely a third of our island's length. The rest is salt water marsh. As a child I secretly welcomed the first warm day of spring by yanking off my shoes and standing waist deep in the cordgrass to feel the cool mud squish up between my toes. I chose the spot with care, for cordgrass alone is rough enough to rip the skin, and ours often concealed a bit of curling tin or shards of glass or crockery or jagged shells not yet worn smooth by the tides. In my nostrils, the faint hay smell of the grass mingled with that of the brackish water of the Bay, while the spring wind chilled the tips of my ears and raised goosebumps along my arms. Then I would shade my eyes from the sun and search far across the water hoping to see my father's boat coming home.

I love Rass Island, although for much of my life, I did not think I did, and it is a pure sorrow to me that, once my mother leaves, there will be no one left there with the name of Bradshaw. But there were only the two of us, my sister, Caroline, and me, and neither of us could stay.

# 1

During the summer of 1941, every weekday morning at the top of the tide, McCall Purnell and I would board my skiff and go progging for crab. Call and I were right smart crabbers, and we could always come home with a little money as well as plenty of crab for supper. Call was a year older than I and would never have gone crabbing with a girl except that his father was dead, so he had no man to take him on board a regular crab boat. He was, as well, a boy who had matured slowly, and being fat and nearsighted, he was dismissed by most of the island boys.

Call and I made quite a pair. At thirteen I was tall and large boned, with delusions of beauty and romance. He, at fourteen, was pudgy, bespectacled, and totally unsentimental.

"Call," I would say, watching dawn break crimson over the Chesapeake Bay, "I hope I have a sky like this the day I get married."

"Who would marry you?" Call would ask, not meanly, just facing facts.

"Oh," I said one day, "I haven't met him yet."

"Then you ain't likely to. This is a right small island."

"It won't be an islander."

"Mr. Rice has him a girl friend in Baltimore."

I sighed. All the girls on Rass Island were half in love with Mr. Rice, one of our two high school teachers. He was the only relatively unattached man most of us had ever known. But Mr. Rice had let it get around that his heart was given to a lady from Baltimore.

"Do you suppose," I asked, as I poled the skiff, the focus of my romantic musings shifting from my own wedding day to Mr. Rice's, "do you suppose her parents oppose the marriage?"

"Why should they care?" Call, standing on the port washboard, had sighted the head of what seemed to be a large sea terrapin and was fixing on it a fierce concentration.

I shifted the pole to starboard. We could get a pretty little price for a terrapin of that size. The terrapin sensed the change in our direction and dove straight through the eelgrass into the bottom mud, but Call had the net waiting, so that when the old bull hit his hiding place, he was yanked to the surface and deposited into a waiting pail. Call grunted with satisfaction. We might make as much as fifty cents on that one catch, ten times the price of a soft blue crab.

"Maybe she's got some mysterious illness and doesn't want to be a burden to him."

"Who?"

"Mr. Rice's finance." I had picked up the word, but not the pronunciation from my reading. It was not in the spoken vocabulary of most islanders.

"His *what*?"

"The woman he's engaged to marry, stupid."

"How come you think she's sick?"

"Something is delaying the consumption of their union."

Call jerked his head around to give me one of his looks, but the washboards of a skiff are a precarious perch at best, so he didn't stare long enough to waste time or risk a dunking. He left me to what he presumed to be my looniness and gave his attention to the eelgrass. We were a good team on the water. I could pole a skiff quickly and quietly, and nearsighted as he was he could spy a crab by just a tip of the claw through grass and muck. He rarely missed one, and he knew I wouldn't jerk or swerve at the wrong moment. I'm sure that's why he stuck with me. I stuck with him not only because we could work well together, but because our teamwork was so automatic that I was free to indulge my romantic fantasies at the same time. That this part of my nature was wasted on Call didn't matter. He didn't have any friends but me, so he wasn't likely to repeat what I said to someone who might snicker. Call himself never laughed.

I thought of it as a defect in his character that I must try to correct, so I told him jokes. "Do you know why radio announcers have tiny hands?"

"Huh?"

"Wee paws for station identification," I would whoop.

"Yeah?"

"Don't you get it, Call? Wee paws. *Wee Paws.*" I let go the pole to shake my right hand at him. "You know, little hands—paws."

"You ain't never seen one."

"One what?"

"One radio announcer."

"No."

"Then how do you know how big their hands are?"

"I don't. It's a joke, Call."

"I don't see how it can be a joke if you don't even know if they have big hands or little hands. Suppose they really have big hands. Then you ain't even telling the truth. Then what happens to your joke?"

"It's just a joke, Call. It doesn't matter whether it's true or not."

"It matters to me. Why should a person think a lie's funny?"

"Never mind, Call. It doesn't matter."

But he went on, mumbling like a little old preacher about the importance of truth and how you couldn't trust radio announcers anymore.

You'd think I'd give up, but I didn't.

"Call, did you hear about the lawyer, the dentist, and the p-sychiatrist who died and went to heaven?"

"Was it a airplane crash?"

"No, Call. It's a joke."

"Oh, a joke."

7

"Yeah. You see, this lawyer and this dentist and this p-sychiatrist all die. And first the lawyer gets there. And Peter says—"

"Peter who?"

"Peter in the Bible. The Apostle Peter."

"He's dead."

"I know he's dead—"

"But you just said—"

"Just shut up and listen to the joke, Call. This lawyer comes to Peter, and he wants to get into heaven."

"A minute ago you said he was already in heaven."

"Well, he wasn't. He was just at the pearly gates, okay? Anyhow, he says he wants to get into heaven, and Peter says he's sorry but he's looked at the book and the lawyer was wicked and evil and cheated people. So he's got to go to hell."

"Does your mother know you use words like that?"

"Call, even the preacher talks about hell. Anyhow, this lawyer has to give up and go to hell. Then this dentist comes up and he wants to get into heaven, and Peter looks at his book and sees that this guy pulled people's teeth out just to get their money even when their teeth were perfectly good and he knew it."

"He did *what*?"

"Call, it doesn't matter."

"It don't matter that a dentist pulls out perfectly good teeth just to make money? That's awful. He ought to go to jail."

"Well, he went to hell for it."

"Pulling out perfectly good teeth—" he mumbled, pinching his own with the fingers of his left hand.

"Then the p-sychiatrist—"

"The what?"

I was an avid reader of *Time* magazine, which, besides the day-old Baltimore *Sun*, was our porthole on the world in those days, so although psychiatry was not yet a popular pastime, I was quite aware of the word, if not the fact that the p was silent. *Time* was probably the source of the joke I was laboring to recount.

"A p-sychiatrist is a doctor that works with people who are crazy."

"Why would you try to do anything with people who're crazy?"

"To get them well. To make their minds better. Good heavens." We paused to net a huge male crab, a true number one Jimmy, swimming doubled over a she-crab. He was taking her to the thick eelgrass, where she would shed for the last time and become a grown-up lady crab— a sook. When she was soft, there would be a proper crab wedding, of course, with the groom staying around to watch out for his bride until her shell was hard once more, and she could protect herself and her load of eggs on her own.

"Sorry, Mr. Jimmy," I said, "no wedding bells for you."

Now this old Jimmy didn't much like being deprived of his sweetheart, but Call pinched him from behind and threw each of them in a separate bucket. She was a rank peeler—that is, it wouldn't be more than a couple of hours before she shed. Our bucket for rank peelers was almost full. It was a good day on the water.

"Well, like I was saying, this p-sychiatrist comes up to Peter, and Peter looks him up in the book of judgment and finds out he's been mean to his wife and kids and tells him to go to hell."

"What?"

I ignored him. Otherwise I'd never get the story finished. "So the p-sychiatrist starts to leave, and then Peter says all of a sudden: 'Hey! Did you say you were a p-sychiatrist?' And the guy says, 'Yes, I did.' " I was talking so fast now, I was almost out of breath. "And Peter says, 'I think we can use you around here after all. You see, we got this problem. God thinks he's Franklin D. Roosevelt.' "

"God *what*?"

"You know when people are crazy they think they're somebody important—like Napoleon or something."

"But, Wheeze, God *is* important."

"It's a joke, Call."

"How can it be a joke? There ain't neither funny about it." He had broken into a waterman's emphatic negative.

"Call, it's funny because Franklin D. Roosevelt has got too big for his britches. Like he's better than God or something."

"But that's not what you said. You said—"

"I know what I said. But you gotta understand politics."

"Well, what kinda joke is that? Fiddle." Call's cuss

words were taught to him by his sainted grandmother and tended to be as quaint as the clothes she made for him.

When the sun was high and our stomachs empty, Call stepped off the washboards into the boat. I shipped the pole and moved up with him to the forward thwart, where we put the oars into the locks and rowed the boat out of the eelgrass into deeper water and around to the harbor.

Captain Billy's son Otis ran the crab shipping part of his father's business, while his father and two brothers ran the ferry. We sold our soft crabs, peelers, and the terrapin to Otis, then split the money and the hard crabs. Call ran home to dinner, and I rowed back around the island as far as the South Gut, where I traded oars for the pole and poled the rest of the way home. The South Gut was a little ditch of water, one of many that criss-crossed Rass, and a natural garbage dump. The summer before, Call and I had cleaned it out (it had been clogged with rusting cans and crab pots, even old mattress springs) so I could pole the skiff through it all the way to my own backyard. Rass might be short on trees, but there was a loblolly pine sapling and a fig tree that my mother had planted on our side of the gut, as well as an orphan cedar on the other. I hitched my skiff to the pine and started at a trot for the back porch, a bucket of hard crabs in one hand and a fistful of money in the other.

My grandmother caught me before I got to the door. "Louise Bradshaw! Don't you go coming in the house dirty like that. Oh, my blessed, what a mess! Susan,"

*11*

she called back in to my mother, "she's full ruined every scrap of clothes she owns."

Rather than argue, I put my crab bucket and money on the edge of the porch and stepped out of my overalls. Underneath I had on my oldest cotton dress.

"Hang them overhalls on the back line, now."

I obeyed, pinning the straps securely to the clothesline. Immediately, the breeze took them straight out, as though Peter Pan had donned them to fly across our yard toward never-never land across the Bay.

I was humming with goodwill, "Come, Thou Fount of every blessing, tune my heart to sing Thy grace . . ." My grandmother was not going to get me today. I'd had a right smart haul.

Caroline was shelling peas at the kitchen table. I smiled at my sister benevolently.

"Mercy, Wheeze, you stink like a crab shanty."

I gritted my teeth, but the smile was still framing them. "Two dollars," I said to my mother at the stove, "two dollars and forty-five cents."

She beamed at me and reached over the propane stove for the pickle crock, where we kept the money. "My," she said, "that was a good morning. By the time you wash up, we'll be ready to eat."

I liked the way she did that. She never suggested that I was dirty or that I stank. Just—"By the time you wash up—" She was a real lady, my mother.

While we were eating, she asked me to go to Kellam's afterward to get some cream and butter. I knew what

12

that meant. It meant that I had made enough money that she could splurge and make she-crab soup for supper. She wasn't an islander, but she could make the best she-crab soup on Rass. My grandmother always complained that no good Methodist would ever put spirits into food. But my mother was undaunted. Our soup always had a spoonful or two of her carefully hoarded sherry ladled into it. My grandmother complained, but she never left any in the bowl.

I was sitting there, basking in the day, thinking how pleased my father would be to come home from crabbing and smell his favorite soup, bathing my sister and grandmother in kindly feelings that neither deserved, when Caroline said, "I haven't got anything to do but practice this summer, so I've decided to write a book about my life. Once you're known," she explained carefully as though some of us were dim-witted, "once you're famous, information like that is very valuable. If I don't get it down now, I may forget." She said all this in that voice of hers that made me feel slightly nauseated, the one she used when she came home from spending all Saturday going to the mainland for her music lessons, where she'd been told for the billionth time how gifted she was.

I excused myself from the table. The last thing I needed to hear that day was the story of my sister's life, in which I, her twin, was allowed a very minor role.

# 2

If my father had not gone to France in 1918 and collected a hip full of German shrapnel, Caroline and I would never have been born. As it was, he did go to war, and when he returned, his childhood sweetheart had married someone else. He worked on other men's boats as strenuously as his slowly healing body would let him, eking out a meager living for himself and his widowed mother. It was almost ten years before he was strong enough to buy a boat of his own and go after crabs and oysters like a true Rass waterman.

One fall, before he had regained his full strength, a young woman came to teach in the island school (three classrooms plus a gymnasium of sorts), and, somehow, though I was never able to understand it fully, the elegant little schoolmistress fell in love with my large, red-faced, game-legged father, and they were married.

What my father needed more than a wife was sons. On Rass, sons represented wealth and security. What my mother bore him was girls, twin girls. I was the elder by a few minutes. I always treasured the thought of those minutes. They represented the only time in my life when I was the center of everyone's attention. From the moment Caroline was born, she snatched it all for herself.

When my mother and grandmother told the story of our births, it was mostly of how Caroline had refused to breathe. How the midwife smacked and prayed and cajoled the tiny chest to move. How the cry of joy went up at the first weak wail—"no louder than a kitten's mew."

"But where was I?" I once asked. "When everyone was working over Caroline, where was I?"

A cloud passed across my mother's eyes, and I knew that she could not remember. "In the basket," she said. "Grandma bathed you and dressed you and put you in the basket."

"Did you, Grandma?"

"How should I know?" she snapped. "It was a long time ago."

I felt cold all over, as though I was the newborn infant a second time, cast aside and forgotten.

Ten days after our birth, despite the winter wind and a threat of being iced in, my mother took Caroline on the ferry to the hospital in Crisfield. My father had no money for doctors and hospitals, but my mother was determined. Caroline was so tiny, so fragile, she must be given every chance of life. My mother's father was alive in those days. He may have paid the bill. I've never known. What I do know is that my mother went eight or ten times each day to the hospital to nurse Caroline, believing that the milk of a loving mother would supply a healing power that even doctors could not.

But what of me? "Who took care of me while you were gone?" The story always left the other twin, the stronger twin, washed and dressed and lying in a basket. Clean and cold and motherless.

Again the vague look and smile. "Your father was here and your grandmother."

"Was I a good baby, Grandma?"

"No worse than most, I reckon."

"What did I do, Grandma? Tell me about when I was a baby."

"How can I remember? It's been a long time."

My mother, seeing my distress, said, "You were a good baby, Louise. You never gave us a minute's worry." She meant it to comfort me, but it only distressed me further. Shouldn't I have been at least a minute's worry? Wasn't it all the months of worry that had made Caroline's life so dear to them all?

When Caroline and I were two months old, my mother brought her back to the island. By then I had grown fat on tinned milk formula. Caroline continued at my mother's breast for another twelve months. There is a rare snapshot of the two of us sitting on the front stoop the summer we were a year and a half old. Caroline is tiny and exquisite, her blonde curls framing a face that is glowing with laughter, her arms outstretched to whoever is taking the picture. I am hunched there like a fat dark shadow, my eyes cut sideways toward Caroline, thumb in mouth, the pudgy hand covering most of my face.

The next winter we both had whooping cough. My mother thinks that I was sick enough to have a croup tent set up. But everyone remembers that Captain Billy got the ferry out at 2:00 A.M. to rush Caroline and my mother to the hospital.

We went that way through all the old childhood diseases except for chicken pox. We both had a heavy case of that, but only I still sport the scars. That mark on the bridge of my nose is a chicken pox scar. It was more noticeable when I was thirteen than it is now. Once my father referred to me teasingly as "Old Scarface" and looked perfectly bewildered when I burst into tears.

I suppose my father was used to treating me with a certain roughness, not quite as he would have treated a son, but certainly differently from the way he treated Caroline. My father, like nearly every man on our island, was a waterman. This meant that six days a week, long before dawn he was in his boat. From November to March, he was tonging for oysters, and from late April into the fall, he was crabbing. There are few jobs in this world more physically demanding than the work of those men who choose to follow the water. For one slightly lame man alone on a boat, the work was more than doubled. He needed a son and I would have given anything to be that son, but on Rass in those days, men's work and women's work were sharply divided, and a waterman's boat was not the place for a girl.

*17*

When I was six my father taught me how to pole a skiff so I could net crabs in the eelgrass near the shore. That was my consolation for not being allowed to go aboard the *Portia Sue* as his hand. As pleased as I was to have my own little skiff, it didn't make up for his refusal to take me on his boat. I kept praying to turn into a boy, I loved my father's boat with such a passion. He had named it after my mother's favorite character from Shakespeare to please her, but he had insisted on the Sue. My mother's name is Susan. In all likelihood he was the only waterman on the Chesapeake Bay whose boat was named for a woman lawyer out of Shakespeare.

My father was not educated in the sense that my mother was. He had dropped out of the island school at twelve to follow the water. I think he would have taken easily to books, but he came home at night too tired to read. I can remember my mother sometimes reading aloud to him. He would sit in his chair, his head back, his eyes closed, but he wasn't asleep. As a child, I always suspected he was imagining. Perhaps he was.

Although our house was one of the smaller of the forty or so houses on the island, for several years we owned the only piano. It came to us on the ferry after my mainland grandfather died. I think Caroline and I were about four when it arrived. She says she remembers meeting it at the dock and following while six men helped my father roll it on a dolly to our house, for there were no trucks or cars on the island.

Caroline also says that she began at once to pick out

*18*

tunes by ear and make up songs for herself. It may be true. I can hardly recall a time when Caroline was not playing the piano well enough to accompany herself while she sang.

My mother not being an islander and the islanders not being acquainted with pianos, no one realized at the beginning the effect of damp salt air on the instrument. Within a few weeks it was lugubriously out of tune. My inventive mother solved this problem by going to the mainland and finding a Crisfield piano tuner who could also give lessons. He came by ferry once a month and taught a half-dozen island youngsters, including Caroline and me, on our piano. During the Depression he was glad to get the extra work. For food, a night's lodging, and the use of our piano, he tuned it and gave Caroline and me free lessons. The rest, children of the island's slightly more affluent, paid fifty cents a lesson. During the month each paid twenty cents a week to practice on our piano. In those days, an extra eighty cents a week was a princely sum.

I was no better or worse than most. We all seemed to get as far as "Country Gardens" and stay there. Caroline, on the other hand, was playing Chopin by the time she was nine. Sometimes people would stand outside the house just to listen while she practiced. Whenever I am tempted to dismiss the poor or uneducated for their vulgar tastes, I see the face of old Auntie Braxton, as she stands stock still in front of our picket fence, lips parted to reveal her almost toothless gums, eyes shining, drinking in a

*19*

polonaise as though it were heavenly nourishment.

By the time we were ten, it became apparent, though, that Caroline's true gift was her voice. She had always been able to sing clearly and in tune, but the older she grew, the lovelier the tune became. The mainland county schoolboard, which managed the island school more by neglect than anything else, suddenly, and without explanation, sent the school a piano the year Caroline and I were in the fifth grade, and the next year, by what could only have been the happiest of coincidences, the new teacher appointed as half of the high school staff was a young man who not only knew how to play a piano but had the talent and strength of will to organize a chorus. Caroline was, of course, his inspiration and focal point. There was little to entertain the island youth, so we sang. And because we sang every day and Mr. Rice was a gifted teacher, we sang surprisingly well for children who had known little music in their lives.

We went to a contest on the mainland the spring we were thirteen and might have won except that when the judges realized our chief soloist was not yet in high school, we were disqualified. Mr. Rice was furious, but we children figured that the mainland schools were too embarrassed to be beaten out by islanders and so made up a rule to save their faces.

Sometime before that Mr. Rice had persuaded my parents that Caroline should have voice lessons. At first they refused, not because of the time and effort it would take to get Caroline to the mainland every Saturday, but because there was no money. But Mr. Rice was determined. He took Caroline to the college in Salisbury and had her sing for the head of the music department. Not only did the man agree to take Caroline on as a private pupil, he waived the fee. Even then the two round-trip tickets on the ferry plus the taxi fare to Salisbury put an unbelievable strain on the weekly budget, but Caroline is the kind of person other people sacrifice for as a matter of course.

I was proud of my sister, but that year, something began to rankle beneath the pride. Life begins to turn upside down at thirteen. I know that now. But at the time I thought the blame for my unhappiness must be fixed—on Caroline, on my grandmother, on my mother, even on myself. Soon I was able to blame the war.

# 3

Even I who read *Time* magazine from cover to cover every week was unprepared for Pearl Harbor. The machinations of European powers and the funny mustached German dictator were as remote to our island in the fall of 1941 as *Silas Marner,* which sapped our energies through eighth-grade English.

There were hints, but at the time I didn't make sense of them: Mr. Rice's great concern for "peace on earth" as we began at Thanksgiving to prepare for our Christmas concert; overhearing a partial conversation between my parents in which my father pronounced himself "useless," to which my mother replied, "Thank the Lord."

It was not a phrase my mother often used, but it was a true island expression. Rass had lived in the fear and mercy of the Lord since the early nineteenth century, when Joshua Thomas, "The Parson of the Islands," won every man, woman, and child of us to Methodism. Old Joshua's stamp remained upon us—Sunday school and Sunday service morning and evening, and on Wednesday night prayer meeting where the more fervent would stand to witness to the Lord's mercies of the preceding week and all the sick and straying would be held up in prayer before the Throne of Grace.

We kept the Sabbath. That meant no work, no radio, no fun on Sunday. But for some reason my parents were out on the Sunday afternoon that was December 7, my grandmother was snoring loudly from her bed, and Caroline was reading the deadly dull Sunday school paper— our only permitted reading on the Sabbath other than the Bible itself. So I, bored almost to madness, had wandered into the living room and turned on the radio, very low so that no one could hear, and pressed my ear against the speaker.

"The Japanese in a predawn surprise attack have destroyed the American fleet at Pearl Harbor. I repeat. The White House has confirmed that the Japanese . . ."

I knew by the chill that went through my body that it meant war. All my magazine reading and overheard remarks fell at once into a grotesque but understandable pattern. I rushed up to our room where Caroline, still innocent and golden, lay stomach down on her bed reading.

"Caroline!"

She didn't even look up. "Caroline!" I ripped the paper from under her hands. "The Japanese have invaded America!"

"Oh, Wheeze, for pity sake." And hardly looking up, she grabbed for her paper. I was used to her ignoring me, but this time I would not allow it. I snatched her arm and dragged her off her bed and down the stairs to the radio. I turned the volume up full. The fact that the Japanese had attacked Hawaii rather than invaded the continental United States was a distinction that neither of us bothered to quibble over. She, like me, was totally caught by the tone of fear that even the smooth baritone of the announcer's voice could not conceal. Caroline's eyes went wide, and, as we listened, she did something she had never done before. She took my hand. We stood there, squeezing each other's hand to the point of pain.

That is how our parents found us. There was no remonstrance for having broken the Fourth Commandment. The crime of the Japanese erased all lesser sinning. The four of us huddled together before the radio set. It was one of those pointed ones that remind you of a brown wood church, with long oval windows over a cloth-covered speaker.

At six, Grandma woke, hungry and petulant. No one had given any thought to food. How could one think of supper when the world had just gone up in flames? Finally, my mother went to the kitchen and made plates of cold meat and leftover potato salad, which she brought to the three of us hunched about the set. She even brought coffee for us all. Grandma insisted on being served properly at the table. Caroline and I had never drunk coffee in our lives, and the fact that our mother served us coffee that night made us both realize that our secure, ordinary world was forever in the past.

Just as I was about to take my first solemn sip, the announcer said, "We pause, now, for station identification." I nearly choked. The world had indeed gone mad.

Within a few days we learned that Mr. Rice had volunteered for the army and would be leaving for the war soon after Christmas. In chorus one morning the irony of celebrating the birth of the Prince of Peace suddenly seemed too much. I raised my hand.

"Yes, Louise?"

"Mr. Rice," I said, standing and dramatically darkening my voice to what I imagined to be the proper tone for mourning, "Mr. Rice, I have a proposal to make." There were a few snickers at my choice of words, but I ignored them. "I feel, sir, that under the circumstances, we should cancel Christmas."

Mr. Rice's right eyebrow shot up. "Do you want to explain that, Louise?"

"How," I asked, my glance sweeping about to catch the amused looks of the others, "how dare we celebrate while around the world thousands are suffering and dying?" Caroline was staring down at her desk, her cheeks red.

Mr. Rice cleared his throat. "Thousands were suffering and dying when Christ was born, Louise." He was clearly discomfited by my behavior. I was sorry now that I had begun but was in too deeply to retreat.

"Yes," I agreed grandly. "But the world has not seen, neither has it heard, such a tragic turn of events as we face in this our time."

Tiny little one-syllable explosions went off about the room like a string of Chinese firecrackers. Mr. Rice looked stern.

My face was burning. I'm not sure whether I was more embarrassed by the sound of my own voice or the snorts of my schoolmates. I sat down, my whole body aflame. The snorts broke into open laughter. Mr. Rice tapped his baton on his music stand to restore order. I thought he might try to explain what I had meant, would try in some way to mediate for me, but he said only, "Now then, let's try it once more from the beginning—"

"God rest ye merry, gentlemen, let nothing you dismay," sang everyone except me. I was afraid if I opened my mouth, I might let go the enormous sob that was lurking there, right at the top of my throat.

It was nearly dark when school got out that afternoon. I rushed out before anyone could catch up with me and walked, not home, but across the length of the marsh on the one high path to the very southern tip of the island. The mud had a frozen brown crust and the cordgrass was weighed down by ice. The wind cut mercilessly across the barren end of Rass, but the hot shame and indignation inside me made me forget the wind as I walked. I was right. I knew I was right, so why had they all laughed? And why had Mr. Rice let them? He hadn't even tried to explain what I meant to the others. It was only when I came to the end of the path and sat down upon a giant stump of driftwood and stared at the sickly winter moon waveringly reflected on the black water that I realized how cold I was and began to cry.

I should not forget that it was Caroline who came and found me there. Sitting on the stump, my back to the swamp and the village, I was crying aloud, so that I did not even hear the crunch of her galoshes.

"Wheeze."

I jerked around, angry to be found out.

"It's past time for your supper," she said.

"I'm not hungry."

"Oh, Wheeze," she said. "It's too cold to stay out here."

"I'm not coming back. I'm running away."

"Well, you can't run away tonight," she said. "There's no ferry until tomorrow morning. You might as well come in and have supper and get warm."

That was Caroline. I would hope for tears and pleadings. She offered facts. But they were facts I couldn't argue with. It would be next to impossible to run away in a skiff at any time of year. I sighed, wiped my face on the back of my hand, and rose to follow her. Even though I could have walked the path blindfolded, I felt foolishly grateful for the homely bobbing comfort of her flashlight.

The watermen of Rass had their own time system. Four-thirty was suppertime winter and summer. So when Caroline and I walked in, our parents and grandmother were already eating. I expected a reprimand from my father or a tongue-lashing from my grandmother, but to my relief they simply nodded as we came in. Mother got up to bring us some hot food from the stove, which she put before us when we had washed and sat down. Caroline must have told them what had happened at school. I was torn between gratitude that they should sympathize and anger that they should know.

The school concert was Saturday night. Sunday was the only day the men did not get up before dawn, and therefore Saturday night was the only night anyone of the island would consider spending in a frivolous manner. I didn't want to go, but it would have been harder to stay away and imagine what people were saying about me than to go and face them.

The boys had helped Mr. Rice rig up footlights, really a row of naked bulbs behind reflectors cut from tin cans, but they gave the tiny stage at the end of the gymnasium a magical distance from the audience. As I stood there on the stage floor in front of the risers, I could barely make out the familiar features of my parents in the center of the second row of chairs. I felt as if those of us on the stage were floating in another layer of the world, removed from those below. When I squinted my eyes, the people all blurred like a film that has jumped the sprockets and is racing untended through the machine. I think I sang most of the program with my eyes squinted. It was a very comforting feeling thus to remove myself from the world I imagined was laughing at me.

Betty Jean Boyd sang the solo for "O Holy Night," and I hardly flinched when she went flat on the first "shining." Betty Jean was considered to have a lovely voice. In any other generation on Rass she would have been worshiped for it, flat as it was, but in my day on Rass, everyone had heard Caroline sing. No one should have had to bear that comparison. Poor Betty Jean. I was puzzled that Mr. Rice should give her this solo. Caroline had sung it last year. Everyone would remember. But this year Mr. Rice had chosen a different solo for Caroline, a very simple one. I had been angry the first time he had sung it over for us. Caroline's voice, after all, was our school treasure. Why had he given the showy song to Betty Jean and a strange thin melody to Caroline?

Now Mr. Rice left the piano and stood before us, his arms tense, his long fingers slightly curved. His dark eyes traveled back and forth, willing every eye to meet his. There were a few polite coughs from the shadowy darkness behind him. It was time. In just a few seconds it would begin. I didn't dare to shift my gaze from Mr. Rice's face to Caroline's head, two rows behind and to the right of me in the back row, but my stomach knotted for her.

Mr. Rice's hands went down, and from the center of the back row Caroline's voice came suddenly like a single beam of light across the darkness.

> *I wonder as I wander out under the sky*
> *Why Jesus the Savior did come for to die*
> *For poor on'ry people like you and like I*
> *I wonder as I wander—out under the sky.*

It was a lonely, lonely sound, but so clear, so beautiful that I tightened my arms against my sides to keep from shaking, perhaps shattering. Then we were all singing, better than we had all night, better than we ever had, suddenly judged, damned, and purged in Caroline's light.

She sang once more by herself, repeating the words of the first verse so quietly that I knew surely I would shatter when she went up effortlessly, sweetly, and oh, so softly, to the high G, holding it just a few seconds longer than humanly possible and then returning to the last few notes and to silence.

A sharp report of applause suddenly rattled the room like gunfire. I jumped, first startled by the sound and then angered. I looked from the dark noisy blur to Mr. Rice, but he was already turning to take a bow. He motioned Caroline to step down and come forward, which she did. And when she turned to go back to her place, I was disgusted to see her dimpled and smiling. She was pleased with herself. It was the same expression she wore when she had thoroughly trounced me in checkers.

When we left the gymnasium, the stars were so bright, they pulled me up into the sky like powerful magnets. I walked, my head back, my own nearly flat chest pressed up against the bosom of heaven, dizzied by the winking brilliance of the night. "I wonder as I wander . . ."

Perhaps I would have drowned in wonder if Caroline, walking ahead with my parents, had not turned and called my name sharply. "Wheeze, you better watch out walking that way," she said. "You're likely to break your neck." She had now moved beyond my parents in the narrow street and was walking backward, the better, I suppose, to observe me.

"Better watch out yourself," I snapped, annoyed and embarrassed to be so yanked away from the stars. I realized suddenly how cold the wind had become. She laughed merrily and, still walking backward, doubled her speed. She was not likely to run into anything. She never stumbled or bumped into things. That, she seemed to be saying, was what I did—often enough for both of us.

Grandma was prone to arthritis and did not go out on a winter's night, even to prayer meeting. So once home, we had to tell her all about the concert. Caroline did most of the talking, singing a snatch of this or that to remind Grandma of a carol she claimed never to have heard before.

"Did you sing the Holy Night one again?"

"No, Grandma, remember, I told you Betty Jean Boyd was doing that this year."

"Why was that? She can't half sing like you can."

"Caroline sang a different one this year, Mother." My mother was making cocoa for us and calling in a word here and there from the kitchen. "Betty Jean sounded very sweet."

Caroline gave me a look and snorted out loud. I knew she was expecting me to contradict Momma, but I wasn't going to. If Caroline wanted to be snobbish about Betty Jean, she could do it on her own.

Caroline had begun to imitate Betty Jean's singing of "O Holy Night." It was almost perfect, just a fraction flatter and shakier than Betty Jean's voice had been, the o's and ah's parodies of Betty Jean's pretentious ones. She ended the performance with a mournful shriek more than a little off pitch and looked around, grinning for her family's approval.

All the way through I had expected my parents to stop her, invoking, if nothing else, the nearness of the neighbors. But no one had. And now, she had finished and was waiting for our applause. It came in the form of a smile working at the firm corners of my father's mouth. Caroline laughed happily. It was all she desired.

Surely Momma would protest. Instead she handed Grandma a cup to drink in her chair. "Here's your cocoa, Mother," she said. Caroline and I went to the table for ours, Caroline still smiling. I had a burning desire to hit her in the mouth, but I controlled myself.

That night I lay in bed with an emptiness chewing away inside of me. I said my prayers, trying to push it away with ritual, but it kept oozing back round the worn edges of the words. I had deliberately given up "Now I lay me down to sleep" two years before as being too babyish a prayer and had been using since then the Lord's Prayer attached to a number of formula "God blesses." But that night "Now I lay me" came back unbidden in the darkness.

*Now I lay me down to sleep,*
*I pray the Lord my soul to keep.*
*If I should die before I wake,*
*I pray the Lord my soul to take.*

"If I should die . . ." It didn't push back the emptiness. It snatched and tore at it, making the hole larger and darker. "If I should die . . ." I tried to shake the words away with "Yea, though I walk through the valley of the shadow of death, I shall fear no evil, for behold, thou art with me . . ."

There was something about the thought of God being with me that made me feel more alone than ever. It was like being with Caroline.

She was so sure, so present, so easy, so light and gold, while I was all gray and shadow. I was not ugly or monstrous. That might have been better. Monsters always command attention, if only for their freakishness. My parents would have wrung their hands and tried to make it up to me, as parents will with a handicapped or especially ugly child. Even Call, his nose too large for his small face, had a certain satisfactory ugliness. And his mother and grandmother did their share of worrying about him. But I had never caused my parents "a minute's worry." Didn't they know that worry proves you care? Didn't they realize that I needed their worry to assure myself that I was worth something?

I worried about them. I feared for my father's safety every time there was a storm on the Bay, and for my mother's whenever she took the ferry to the mainland. I read magazine articles in the school library on health and gave them mental physical examinations and tested the health of their marriage. "Can this marriage succeed?" Probably not. They had nothing in common as far as I could tell from the questionnaires I read. I even worried about Caroline, though why should I bother when everyone else spent their lives fretting over her?

I longed for the day when they would have to notice me, give me all the attention and concern that was my due. In my wildest daydreams there was a scene taken from the dreams of Joseph. Joseph dreamed that one day all his brothers and his parents as well would bow down to him. I tried to imagine Caroline bowing down to me. At first, of course, she laughingly refused, but then a giant hand descended from the sky and shoved her to her knees. Her face grew dark. "Oh, Wheeze," she began to apologize. "Call me no longer Wheeze, but Sara Louise," I said grandly, smiling in the darkness, casting off the nickname she had diminished me with since we were two.

# 4

"I hate the water."

I didn't even bother to look up from my book. Grandma had two stock phrases. The first was "I love the Lord," and the second, "I hate the water." I had grown fully immune to both by the time I was eight.

"What time's the ferry due?"

"The same time as always, Grandma." I wished only to be left to my book, which was a deliciously scary one about some children who had been captured by a bunch of pirates in the West Indies. It was my mother's. All the books were hers except the extra Bibles.

"Don't be sassy."

I sighed and put down my book and said with greatly exaggerated patience, "The ferry is due about four, Grandma."

"Doubt but there's a northwest wind," she said mournfully. "Likely to be headed into the wind all the way in." She rocked her chair slowly back and forth with her eyes closed. Or almost closed. I usually had the feeling she was watching through slits. "Where's Truitt?"

"Daddy's working on the boat, Grandma."

She opened her eyes wide and sat up straight. "Not tonging?"

"Tonging's done, Grandma. It's April." It was spring vacation, and here I was sitting all day with a cranky old woman.

She settled back. I thought she might tell me not to be sassy once more for good measure, but instead she said, "That ferry of Billy's is too old. One of these days it's going to sink right there in the middle of the Bay, and no one will find neither plank of it never again."

I knew Grandma's fears were idle, but they stirred up a little fuzz ball of fear in my stomach. "Grandma," I said, as much to myself as to her, "it's got to be okay. Government's always checking it out. Ferryboat's got to be safe or it won't get a license. Government controls it."

She sniffed loudly. "Franklin D. Roosevelt think he can control the whole Chesapeake Bay? Ain't no government can control that water."

*God thinks he's Franklin D. Roosevelt.*

"What are you grinning about? Ain't nothing to grin about."

I pulled in my cheeks in an attempt to appear solemn. "You want some coffee, Grandma?" If I made her some coffee, it would distract her, and maybe she'd let me get back to my book in peace.

I slipped my book under the sofa cushion because it had a picture of a great sailing vessel on the front. I didn't want Grandma upset because I was reading a book about the water. The women of my island were not supposed to love the water. Water was the wild, untamed kingdom of our men. And though water was the element in which our tiny island lived and moved and had its being, the women resisted its power over their lives as a wife might pretend to ignore the existence of her husband's mistress. For the men of the island, except for the preacher and the occasional male teacher, the Bay was an all-consuming passion. It ruled their waking hours, sapped their bodily strength, and from time to tragic time claimed their mortal flesh.

I suppose I knew that there was no future for me on Rass. How could I face a lifetime of passive waiting? Waiting for the boats to come in of an afternoon, waiting in a crab house for the crabs to shed, waiting at home for children to be born, waiting for them to grow up, waiting, at last, for the Lord to take me home.

I gave Grandma her coffee and stood by while she noisily sucked in air and coffee. "Not enough sugar."

I whipped the sugar bowl out from behind my back. She was clearly annoyed that I'd been able to anticipate her complaint. I could see on her face that she was trying to decide how to shift to something that I wouldn't be prepared for. "Hmm," she said finally in a squeaky little tone and spooned two heaping measures of sugar into her cup. She didn't thank me, but I hadn't expected thanks. I was so delighted to have outsmarted her that I forgot myself and began whistling "Praise the Lord and Pass the Ammunition" as I returned the sugar bowl to the kitchen.

"Whistling women and crowing hens never come to no good end."

"Oh, I don't know, Grandma, we might be terrific in a circus freak show."

She was clearly shocked but couldn't seem to put her finger on my specific sin. "Thou shalt not—thou shalt not—"

"Whistle?"

"Sass!" She almost screamed. I had clearly gotten the best of her, so I sobered to an elaborate caricature of humility. "Can I get you anything else, Grandma?"

She humphed and hemmed and slurped her coffee without answering, but as soon as I'd gotten my book again and was settled down on the couch and reading, she said, "It's onto four o'clock."

I pretended not to hear.

"Ain't you going down for the ferry?"

"I hadn't thought to."

"It wouldn't hurt you to think a little. Your mother's likely to have heavy groceries."

"Caroline's with her, Grandma."

"You know full well that little child ain't got the strength to carry heavy groceries."

I could have said several things but all of them were rude, so I kept my mouth shut.

"Why do you look at me like that?" she asked.

"Like what?"

"With bullets in your eyes. Like you want to shoot me dead. All I want you to do is help your poor mother."

It was useless to argue. I took the book upstairs and hid it in my underwear drawer. Grandma was less likely to poke around in there. She considered modern female undergarments indecent and if not precisely "of the devil," certainly in that vicinity. I got a jacket, as the wind would be chilly, and went downstairs. When I reached the front door, the rocking stopped.

"Where you think you're going?"

Fury began to swoosh up inside me. I kept my voice as flat as I could and said, "Down to meet the ferry, Grandma. Remember? You said I should go and help Momma bring back the groceries."

She looked strangely blank. "Well, hurry," she said at last, beginning to rock again. "I don't favor waiting here by myself."

A small crowd of islanders had come by foot or bicycle and were already waiting the arrival of the ferry. They greeted me as I approached, pulling the red metal wagon that we used for hauling.

"Your Momma coming in?"

"Yes, Miss Letty. She had to take Caroline to the doctor."

Sympathetic looks all round. "That child has always been so delicate."

It was useless to withhold information; besides, for once, I didn't care. "She had an earache, and Nurse thought she ought to go have Dr. Walton check it."

Heads shook knowingly. "You can't be too careful 'bout the earache."

"Surely cannot. Remember, Lettice, when little Buddy Rankin come down with that bad ear? Martha thought nothing of it, and the next thing she knowed he got this raging fever. A pure miracle of the Lord the child didn't go deaf, they said."

Little Buddy Rankin was a seasoned waterman with two children of his own. I wondered idly what fixed memory they would have of me in twenty or thirty years.

Captain Billy's son Otis emerged from the unpainted crab shipping shed. That meant the boat was coming in. He walked to the end of the pier ready to catch the line. Those of us waiting moved out of the lee of the building to watch the ferry chug in. It was small and, even before it was close enough to reveal its peeling paint, seemed to sag in the water. Grandma was right. It was an old boat, a tired boat. My father's boat was far from new. It had belonged to another waterman before he bought it, but it was still lively and robust, like a man who's spent his life on the water. Captain Billy's ferry, though much larger, drooped like an old waiting woman. I buttoned my jacket against the wind and concentrated on Captain Billy's sons Edgar and Richard who had jumped ashore and were helping Otis tie up the ferry with graceful, practiced steps.

My father had walked up. He smiled at me and touched my arm in greeting. For a happy moment, I thought he'd spied me from his boat and had come on purpose to say hello. And then I saw his gaze turn toward the hatch of the under deck passenger cabin. It was Momma he had come to meet and Caroline, of course. Hers was the first head out of the opening, wrapped against the wind in a sky blue scarf. Just enough of her hair had escaped to make her look fresh and full like a girl in a cigarette ad.

"Hey, Daddy!" she called out as she came. "Daddy's here, Momma," she said back over her shoulder toward the cabin. Our mother's head appeared. She was having more trouble on the ladder than Caroline, for, in addition to a large purse, she was trying to negotiate a huge shopping bag.

Caroline, meantime, had skipped quickly around the narrow deck and jumped lightly to the dock. She kissed our father on his cheek, a gesture that never failed to embarrass me. Caroline was the only person I knew who kissed in public. It was simply not done on our island. At least she wouldn't try to kiss me. I was sure of that. She nodded, grinning. "Wheeze," she said. I nodded back without the smile. Daddy met Momma halfway round the deck and took the shopping bag. No unnecessary touching, but they were smiling and talking when they got off the boat.

"Oh, Louise. Thank you for bringing the wagon. They're still more groceries in the hold."

I smiled, proud of my thoughtfulness, conveniently forgetting it was Grandma who had sent me down to the dock.

Two other island women emerged from the cabin door, and then, to my surprise, a man. Men usually rode up top on the bridge with Captain Billy. But this was an old man, one whom I had never seen before. He had the strong stocky build of a waterman. His hair, under a seaman's cap, was white and thick and hung almost halfway down his neck. He had a full mustache and beard, both white, and was wearing a heavy winter overcoat, despite the fact that it was April. And he was carrying what I imagined one might call a "valise." It must have been heavy because he put it down on the dock as he waited quietly with the rest of us for Captain Billy's sons to hand up the luggage and groceries from the hold.

Momma pointed out her two boxes, which my father and I loaded precariously onto the wagon. They were too large to fit into the bed of the wagon, so we perched them slantwise, tilting down into the middle. I knew I would have to go slowly, for if I hit a bump, there were likely to be groceries all over the narrow street.

All the time I was watching the stranger out of the corner of my eye. Two more ancient bags and a small trunk were brought up and put beside him. By now everyone was staring. No one would have so much baggage unless he planned to stay for quite some time.

"Somebody meeting you?" Richard asked, not unkindly.

The old man shook his head, staring down at the luggage piled around him. He looked a little like a lost child.

"Got a place to stay?" the young man asked.

"Yes." He lifted his overcoat collar up as though to protect himself from the cold island wind and jerked his hat down almost to his bushy eyebrows.

By now the crowd upon the dock was positively leaning in his direction. The island held few secrets or surprises beyond the weather. But here was a perfectly strange man. Where had he come from, and where was he planning to stay?

I felt my mother's elbow. "Come along," she said quietly, nodding a good-bye at my father. "Grandma will be worrying."

I had seldom felt so exasperated—to have to go home in the middle of this unfolding drama. But both Caroline and I obeyed, leaving the little scene on the dock behind, making our slow progress up the narrow oyster-shell street between the picket fences that enclosed each house. The street was only wide enough for four people to walk abreast. The crushed oyster shells underfoot rattled the wagon so that I could feel the vibrations in my teeth.

There was such a scarcity of high land on Rass that for generations we had buried our dead in our front yards. So to walk down the main street was to walk between the graves of our ancestors. As a child I thought nothing of it, but when I became an adolescent, I began to read the verses on the tombstones with a certain pleasant melancholy.

> *Mother, are you gone forever*
> *To a land so bright and fair?*
> *While your children weep unstopping*
> *Can you hear us? Do you care?*

Most of them were more bravely Methodist in flavor.

> *God will keep you little angel*
> *Till we greet you by and by.*
> *For a moment is our sorrow*
> *Joy forever in the sky.*

My favorite was for a young man who had died more than a hundred years before, but to whom I had attached more than one of my romantic fantasies.

> *Oh, how bravely did you leave us*
> *Sailing for a foreign shore*
> *How our hearts did break within us*
> *At the thought of Nevermore.*

He had been only nineteen. I fancied that I would have married him, had he lived.

I needed to concentrate on the groceries. Momma still had the large shopping bag. Caroline could hardly bear to go as slowly as the two of us had to, so she tended to skip on ahead and then come back to share some of the details of her trip to the mainland. It was one of these times when she was walking toward us that she suddenly lowered her voice.

"There he is. There's that man from the ferry."

I looked back over my shoulder, being careful to keep my free hand on the grocery boxes.

"Don't be rude," Momma said.

Caroline leaned toward me. "Edgar is pulling all his stuff in a cart."

"Hush," Momma warned. "Turn around."

Caroline was slow to obey. "Who is he, Momma?"

"Shh. I don't know."

Despite his age the man was walking remarkably fast. We couldn't hurry because of the wagon, so he soon overtook us and walked purposefully down the street ahead as though he knew exactly where he was going. There was no longer any sense of a lost child in his manner. The Roberts' house was the last one on the street, but he walked right past it, to where the oyster-shell street gave way to the dirt path across the southern marsh.

"Where's he think he's going?" Caroline asked.

The only thing farther along the path besides the marsh itself was one long-since abandoned house.

"I wonder—" Momma began, but we were turning in at our own gate, and she didn't finish the sentence.

# 5

The stranger from the ferry offered no explanation for his presence on the island. Gradually, the people of Rass built one from ancient memory lavishly cemented with rumor. The man had gone to the Wallace place, which had been deserted for twenty years since the death of old Captain Wallace six months after his wife. He had found it without asking anyone the way and had moved in and begun to put it into repair as though he belonged there.

"He's Hiram Wallace," Grandma had announced—everyone over fifty had come to the same conclusion. "The old ones thought he was dead. But here he is. Too late to bring them neither comfort."

Bit by bit, straining my short patience to its utmost limit, the story of Hiram Wallace emerged. Call's grandmother told him that when she was a child, there had been a young waterman by that name, the only child of Captain Charles Wesley Wallace. It was back in the days when nearly every boat on the Bay was under sail, before hard blue crabs brought in much money. Captain Wallace and his son tonged for oysters in the winter, and in the summer they netted fish, chiefly menhaden and rockfish. That they had made a tidy profit was evidenced by the size of their house, which stood apart from the rest of the village. As my grandmother remembered it, their land had been large enough in those days for real grass to grow in a pasture, enough to support one of the few cows in the island's history.

What was left of the land was now all marsh, but the house, though neglected, had survived. We children had always regarded it as haunted. There were tales that Captain Wallace's ghost appeared to chase off intruders. It took me years to figure out that the purpose of the ghost story was to keep young courting couples from wandering down the path to the old Wallace place and taking advantage of the privacy.

One day I had talked Call into exploring the house with me, but just as we stepped onto the porch, a huge orange-colored tomcat came shrieking out a broken window at us. It was the only time in our lives that Call outran me. We sat gasping for breath on my front stoop. One part of my mind was saying that it had only been one of Auntie Braxton's cats. She was said to keep sixteen, and anyone who had ever been as close as her front door would have sworn by the smell that there were at least that many and more. The other part of my mind was reluctant to let it go as simply as that.

"Have you ever heard," I asked, "have you ever heard that ghosts will take an animal form when they are angry?" Now that my breath was back I let my voice glide out in a dreamy way.

Call jerked around to look me in the face. "No!" he said.

"I was reading this book," I began to improvise (of course, I'd never seen any such book). "In this book, this scientist investigated places where ghosts were supposed to be. He started out saying that there was no such thing as ghosts, but being a scientist he had to admit finally that he couldn't explain certain things any other way."

"What things?"

"Oh—" I thought fast while drawing out the syllable. "Oh—certain furry beasts that took on the personality of a dead person."

Call was clearly shaken. "What do you mean?"

"Well, for instance, suppose old Captain Wallace when he was alive didn't want any visitors."

"He didn't." Call said darkly. "My grandma told me. After Hiram left, they lived all by themselves. Never spoke to nobody hardly."

"See?"

"See what?"

"We were fixing to visit him without an invitation," I whispered. "He was yelling at us and chasing us away."

Call's eyes were the size of clam shells. "You're making that up," he said. But I could tell that he believed every word of it.

"Only one way to be sure," I said.

"How you mean?"

I leaned close and whispered again. "Go back and see what happens."

He jumped to his feet. "Suppertime!" He started out the yard.

I had done my work too well. I was never able to persuade Call to return to that old empty house with me, and somehow, I was never quite able to go there alone.

Now that the strange old man was there, the house was no longer empty, and the whole island was trying to unravel the mystery. All the old people agreed that Hiram Wallace was in his youth the hope of every island maiden's heart, but that he had left Rass with his father's money and blessing to go to college. It was an unusual enough occurrence that even someone from our island who had gone to college fifty years ago was remembered for it. People also recalled, though this point was discussed at considerable length, that he had returned home without a degree, and that he had, in some undefinable way, changed. He had never been too sociable before he left, but he was positively silent when he returned. This only made the hearts of the young girls beat the harder, and no one had suspected that anything was wrong with him until the day of the storm.

The Bay is famous for its sudden summer storms. Before they can read their school primers, watermen learn how to read the sky and to head for the safety of a cove at the first glimmer of trouble. But the Bay is wide, and sometimes safety is too far away. In the old days, the watermen would lower their sails and use them as tents to protect themselves from the rain.

This is the story that the old people told: Captain Wallace and his son, Hiram, had let down their sails and were waiting out the storm. The lightning was so bright and near that it seemed to flash through the heavy canvas of the sail, the roaring and cracking enough to wake the dead sleeping in the depths of the water. Now, a man who is not afraid at a time like this is a man without enough sense to follow the water. But to fear is one thing. To let fear grab you by the tail and swing you around is another. This, Call's grandmother said, was what Hiram Wallace had done: terrified that the lightning would strike the tall mast of his father's skipjack, he had rushed out from under his sail cover, taken an ax, and chopped the mast to the level of the deck. After the storm passed, they were sighted drifting mastless on the Bay and were towed home by an obliging neighbor. When it became apparent that the mast had been chopped down, rather than felled by lightning, Hiram Wallace became the butt of all the watermen's jokes. Not long after, he left the island for good . . .

Unless, of course, the strong old man rebuilding the Wallace house was the handsome young coward who had left nearly fifty years before. He never said he was, but then again, he never said he wasn't. Some of the islanders thought a delegation should be sent to ask the old man straight out who he was, for if he were not Hiram Wallace, what right did he have taking over the Wallace property? The delegation was never sent. April was nearly over. The one slow month of the watermen's year was coming to an end. There was a flurry of overhauling and painting and mending to be done. Crabs were moving and the men had to be ready to go after them.

"I bet he isn't Hiram Wallace," I said to Call one day in early May.

"Why not?"

"Why would a man come to Rass in the middle of a war?"

"Because he's old and has nowhere else to go."

"Oh, Call. Think. Why would a person come to the Bay right now of all times."

"Because he's old—"

"The Bay is full of warships from Norfolk."

"So? What does that have to do with Hiram Wallace?"

"Nothing. That's just it, dummy. Who would want to know about warships?"

"The navy."

"Call. Don't you get it?"

"There's nothing to get."

"Warships, Call. What better place to spy on warships than from a lonely house right by the water?"

"You read too much."

"I suppose if someone was to catch a spy they'd take him to the White House and pin medals on him."

"I never heard of kids catching spies."

"That's just it. If two kids were to catch a spy—"

"Wheeze. It's Hiram Wallace. My grandma knows."

"She *thinks* he's Hiram Wallace. That's what he wants everyone to think. So they won't suspect him."

"Suspect him of what?"

I sighed. It was obvious that he had a long way to go before he was much of a counterspy, while I was putting myself to sleep at night performing incredible feats of daring on behalf of my embattled country. The amount of medals Franklin D. Roosevelt had either hung around my neck or pinned to my front would have supplied the army with enough metal for a tank. There was a final touch with which I closed the award ceremony.

"Here, Mr. President," I would say, handing back the medal, "use this for our boys at the front."

"But, Sara Louise Bradshaw—" Franklin D. Roosevelt for all his faults never failed to call me by my full name. "But, Sara Louise Bradshaw, this medal is yours. You have earned it with your great cunning and bravery. Keep it and hand it down to your children's children."

I would smile, a slightly ironic little smile. "Do you think, Mr. President, with the life I lead, that I will live long enough to have children?" That question never failed to reduce Franklin D. Roosevelt to silence touched with awe.

In my dreams I always went it alone, but in real life it seemed selfish. Besides, I was used to doing things with Call.

"Okay, Call. First we got to work out a plan."

"A plan for what?"

"To catch this kraut in the very act of spying."

"You're not going to catch him spying."

"Why not?"

"Because he's not a spy."

What can you do with a man who has no faith? "All right. Who is he then? Just answer me that."

"Hiram Wallace."

"Good heavens."

"You're cussing again. My grandma—"

"I am not cussing. Cussing is like 'God' and 'hell' and 'damn.' "

"See!"

"Call. How about pretending? Just for fun, pretend the guy is a spy, and we've got to get the proof."

He looked uncertain. "Like one of your jokes?"

"Yes. No." Sometimes Call could be perfectly sensible and at other times you could have gotten more sense out of a six-year-old. "It's like a game, Call." I didn't wait for him to answer. "Come on." I started running for the path through the salt meadow marsh with Call puffing behind me.

If Call's family was as poor as my grandmother said they were, I could never figure out how Call got so fat. As a matter of fact, both his mother and grandmother were fat. I thought that if you were poor you were skinny. But the evidence seemed to contradict this. And Call had other problems with running besides his weight. Like all of us, his shoes came from the Sears, Roebuck catalog. To order shoes from a catalog, you stood on a piece of brown wrapping paper, and your mother drew a pencil line around both your feet. These outlines were sent to the mail-order house, and they sent you shoes to fit the brown wrapping-paper feet. But the brown paper outlines didn't tell the mail-order house how fat your feet were on the top. For that reason, poor Call never had a pair of shoes that would lace properly. The tops of his feet were so fat that once he got his shoes laced up, there was nothing left to make a proper bow. So when he ran, his shoes often came unlaced and flapped up and down on his heels.

It was low tide, so I left the path and began making my way through the marsh. My plan was to give the old Wallace house a wide berth and come up on it from the south side. The old man would never expect people from that direction.

"Wait!" Call cried out. "I lost my shoe."

I went back to where Call was standing on one leg like an overweight egret. "My shoe got stuck," he said.

I pulled his shoe out of the mud for him and tried to clean it off on the cordgrass.

"My grandma will beat me," he said. It was hard for me to imagine Call's tubby little grandmother taking a switch to a large fifteen-year-old boy, but I held my peace. I had a greater problem than that. What would Franklin D. Roosevelt say about a spy who lost his shoe in the salt marsh and worried aloud that his grandma would beat him? I sighed and handed Call the shoe. He put it on and limped back to the path.

"Sit down," I commanded.

"On the ground?"

"Yes, on the ground." What did he expect, an easy chair? Then I cleaned his shoes and mine as best I could with my handkerchief. My mother had trouble persuading me to carry one because I was a lady, but I now realized that a handkerchief was an invaluable tool for a counter-spy—to erase fingerprints, and so forth. "Now," I said, "I'm going to fix your shoestrings." I unlaced his strings and started again, skipping the second and fourth holes. This way I could make the lace long enough to provide a decent bow.

"There," I said, tying them for him as though he were a little child.

"You left out four holes."

"Call. I did it on purpose. So they wouldn't come loose all the time."

"They look dumb."

"Not as dumb as you'd look in your sockfeet."

He pretended to ignore this and stared at his shoelaces, as though trying to decide whether to retie them or to leave them be.

"Why don't you think of it as a secret signal?"

"A *what*?"

"Counterspies have to have ways of identifying themselves to other counterspies. Like secret code words. Or wearing a special kind of flower. Or—tying their shoes a certain way."

"You can't make me believe that spies tie their shoestrings funny."

"Just ask Franklin D. Roosevelt when we meet him."

"That's one of your jokes."

"Oh, come on. You can tie them again later, after the mission."

He had his mouth set to argue, but I didn't wait for a retort. Good heavens. The war would be over and he'd still be sitting there fussing about his shoestrings. "Follow me and keep low."

The cordgrass was about two feet high. There was no way, short of crawling through the mud on our bellies, that we could approach the Wallace house unseen. But there is a way of feeling invisible that makes one almost believe it's true. At any rate, I felt invisible, creeping bent over toward that great gray clapboard house. My heart was beating as fast and noisily as the motor on the *Portia Sue*.

There was no sound of life from the house. Earlier I had heard sawing and pounding. Now everything was quiet except the gentle lapping of the water on the nearby shore and the occasional cry of a water bird.

I signaled for Call to follow me to the southwest corner of the house, and then, keeping close to the side, we slipped silently to the first window facing south. Carefully, I raised my head until my eyes could peer over the sill into the room. It was evidently the room that the old man had chosen for his workshop. Weather-beaten chairs, their cane bottoms sagging and broken, were arranged to serve as sawhorses. The floor was covered with wood curls and sawdust. The sounds I had heard from across the marsh came from here, but the old man was no longer in the room. I gestured Call to stay down, that there was nothing to see, but of course he stuck his head up and peered in, just as I had done.

"No one there," he said in what he mistook for a whisper.

"Shhhhh!" I waved my hand in a violent "get down," but he was in no hurry. He gazed into the room as though it were full of great art rather than pine boards and wood curls.

I gave up trying to signal him and crept ahead to the next window. Slowly, very slowly, bracing my hand against the side of the house for support, I raised my head to the level of the window—straight into a great staring glass eye. I must have screamed. At least I did something to make Call begin to run as fast as he could around the house and in the direction of the path. I didn't run—not because I wasn't terrified, not because I wouldn't have liked to run, but because my feet had lost all power of movement.

The glass eye raised itself slowly from my face and a human voice said, "There you are. I didn't mean to scare you."

I tossed my head, trying vainly to imitate the counterspy of my imagination, hoping that a clever, careless remark would float effortlessly from my lips, but my mouth was dry as sawdust and no remark, careless or otherwise, was about to emerge.

"Would you like to come in?"

I turned frantically to find Call and located him a hundred feet away on the path toward the village. He had stopped running. I felt a surge of gratitude for him. He hadn't deserted me, not really.

"Your friend, too," the old man said, putting his periscope down on a table and smiling warmly through his white beard.

I licked my mouth, but my tongue was almost as dry as my lips. Franklin D. Roosevelt was hanging the Congressional Medal of Honor around my neck, saying, "Without regard for her personal safety, she entered the very stronghold of the foe."

"Ca-all." My voice cracked wide open on the word. "Ca-all."

He started back in a sort of zombielike walk. I could feel the presence of the man in the window above me. Call came up and stood right behind me, his breath coming from his open mouth in noisy pants. We were both fixed on the form above us.

"Won't you come in and have a cup of tea, or something?" the man said invitingly. "I haven't had any visitors since I got here except for an old tomcat."

I could feel Call stiffen like a dead fish.

"He acted like the place belonged to him. I had a time convincing him otherwise."

Call butted me in the back with his stomach. I butted him back with my behind. Good heavens. Here we were on the very trail of a spy and Call was going to get upset by a ghost—a made-up ghost, one I had made up. Annoyance drove out panic.

"Thank you," I said. My voice was a little too loud and there was a distinct quaver in it, so I tried again. "Thanks. We'd like tea, wouldn't we?"

"My grandma don't allow me to drink tea."

"The boy will have milk," I said grandly and flounced around to the front door. Call followed at my heels. By the time we got around the house, the man was there, holding the door open for us. *Without regard for her personal safety* . . .

There was very little to sit on inside the house. The man pulled a rough plank bench around for Call and me, and after he'd put a kettle on a two-burner propane stove and puttered about his kitchen a bit, he came in and sat down on a homemade stool.

"Now. You are—"

I was still in the process of deciding whether or not counterspies gave their actual names in a situation like this when Call spoke up. "I'm Call and she's Wheeze."

The man began unaccountably to laugh. "Wheeze and Call," he said gleefully. "It sounds like a vaudeville act."

How rude—to sit there laughing at our names.

59

"It would be better if it was Wheeze and Cough. Still, Wheeze and Call is pretty good."

I sat up very straight on the bench. To my utter amazement, not to say disgust, I realized that Call was giggling. I gave him a look.

"It's a joke, Wheeze."

"How can it be a joke?" I asked. I almost said *"It's not funny,"* but I stopped myself in time. Fortunately, the kettle whistled, and the man got up to make the tea. I gave Call a glare that should have stopped the tide, but he kept on laughing. I'd never heard him laugh in my life and here he was shrieking like a gull over garbage about something that was just plain insulting.

The man handed me a mug of very black tea. "I've only got tinned milk," he said to Call while returning to the kitchen.

"That's okay," Call said, wiping the tears off his face with the back of his wrist. "Wheeze and Cough," he repeated to me. "Don't you get it?"

"Of course I get it." I was trying to figure out how I was going to get down the black stuff I had been handed. "I just don't think it's funny."

The man came back from the kitchen carrying a mug. "Not funny, eh? Oh, well, I'm out of practice." He handed the mug to Call. "It's half tinned milk and half water."

Call tasted it. "Good," he said.

I waited for him to offer me something to put in my tea, but he didn't. He just got himself a mug of the black brew and sat down.

"My real name is Sara Louise Bradshaw," I said, forgetting that minutes ago I had decided against revealing my true name.

"That's a very nice name," he said politely.

"My real name is McCall Purnell, but everybody calls me Call."

"I see," he said slyly. "If I want you, I just call Call."

"Call Call!" cried Call, as though it was the most original idea as well as the funniest thing he had ever heard. "Call Call! Did you get that, Wheeze? It's a joke."

Good heavens. "I don't suppose," I said, loading my voice with significance, "I don't suppose that you would tell us your name."

The man feigned surprise. "I thought everyone on this island knew my name."

Both Call and I leaned forward, waiting for him to say more, but he didn't. I was puzzling it out, whether to press him further or to play it casually, when Call blurted out, "You don't seem like neither spy."

The old man raised an eyebrow at me. I'm sure I turned the color of steamed crab. How do counterspies keep from blushing? He stared at me unmercifully for a minute. I was shrinking into the bench. "Why," he asked accusingly, "why aren't you drinking your tea?"

"Tin—tin—tin," I stammered.

"Rin tin tin," shrieked Call.

The man laughed, too, but at least he got up and brought the tin of milk over to me. My hands were shaking with rage or frustration or exasperation, who knew which, but I managed to fill the mug to the brim with the thick yellowish milk. He waited in front of me until I had sampled the brew. I took a scalding sip. It was too hot to know how it tasted, but I shook my head to indicate that it was fine. Halfway into the mug, I realized I should have asked for sugar, but then it seemed too late.

That was the way most of our early visits to the Captain's house went. We decided, Call and I, simply to call him "the Captain." On Rass any waterman who owned his own boat was called Captain So and So after he had passed fifty. I wouldn't call him Captain Wallace, because he'd never actually claimed the name. I kept going to see him in the fading hope that he'd turn out to be a real spy and I could have a medal after all. Call kept going because the Captain told great jokes, "not like yours, Wheeze, really good ones."

At any rate, it was Call the Captain liked, not me. If I'd been a more generous person, I'd have been happy that Call had found a man to be close to. He didn't remember his own father, and if any boy needed a father it was Call. But I was not a generous person. I couldn't afford to be. Call was my only friend. If I gave him up to the Captain, I'd have no one.

# 6

It is hard, even now, to describe my relationship to Caroline in those days. We slept in the same room, ate at the same table, sat for nine months out of each year in the same classroom, but none of these had made us close. How could they, when being conceived at the same time in the same womb had done nothing to bind us together? And yet, if we were not close, why did only Caroline have the power, with a single glance, to slice my flesh clear through to the bone?

I would come in from a day of progging for crab, sweating and filthy. Caroline would remark mildly that my fingernails were dirty. How could they be anything else but dirty? But instead of simply acknowledging the fact, I would fly into a wounded rage. How dare she call me dirty? How dare she try to make me feel inferior to her own pure, clear beauty? It wasn't my fingernails she was concerned with, that I was sure of. She was using my fingernails to indict my soul. Wasn't she content to be golden perfection without cutting away at me? Was she to allow me no virtue—no shard of pride or decency?

By now I was screaming. Wasn't it I who brought in the extra money that paid for her trips to Salisbury? She ought to be on her knees thanking me for all I did for her. How dare she criticize? How dare she?

Her eyes would widen. Even as I yelled, I could feel a tiny rivulet of satisfaction invading the flood of my anger. She knew I was right, and it unsettled her. But the lovely eyes would quickly narrow, the lips set. Without a word, she would turn and leave me before I was through, shutting off my torrent, so that my feelings, thus dammed, raged on in my chest. She would not fight with me. Perhaps that was the thing that made me hate her most.

Hate. That was the forbidden word. I hated my sister. I, who belonged to a religion which taught that simply to be angry with another made one liable to the judgment of God and that to hate was the equivalent of murder.

I often dreamed that Caroline was dead. Sometimes I would get word of her death—the ferry had sunk with her and my mother aboard, or more often the taxi had crashed and her lovely body had been consumed in the flames. Always there were two feelings in the dream—a wild exultation that now I was free of her and . . . terrible guilt. I once dreamed that I had killed her with my own hands. I had taken the heavy oak pole with which I guided my skiff. She had come to the shore, begging for a ride. In reply I had raised the pole and beat, beat, beat. In the dream her mouth made the shape of screaming, but no sound came out. The only sound of the dream was my own laughter. I woke up laughing, a strange shuddering kind of laugh that turned at once into sobs.

"What's the matter, Wheeze?" I had awakened her.

"I had a bad dream," I said. "I dreamed you were dead."

She was too sleepy to be troubled. "It was only a dream," she said, turning her face once more to the wall and snuggling deep under her covers.

But it was I who killed you! I wanted to scream it out, whether to confess or frighten, I don't know. I beat you with my pole. I'm a murderer. Like Cain. But she was breathing quietly, no longer bothered by my dream or by me.

Sometimes I would rage at God, at his monstrous almighty injustice. But my raging always turned to remorse. My wickedness was unforgivable, yet I begged the Lord to have mercy on me, a sinner. Hadn't God forgiven David who had not only committed murder, but adultery as well? And then I would remember that David was one of God's pets. God always found a way to let his pets get by with murder. How about Moses? How about Paul, holding the coats while Stephen was stoned?

I would search the Scriptures, but not for enlightenment or instruction. I was looking for some tiny shred of evidence that I was not to be eternally damned for hating my sister. Repent and be saved! But as fast as I would repent, resolving never again to hate, some demon would slip into my soul, tug at the corner, and whisper,

"See the look on your mother's face as she listens to Caroline practice? Has she ever looked at you that way?" And I would know she hadn't.

Only on the water was there peace. When school let out in the middle of May, I began getting up long before dawn to go crabbing. Call went along, somewhat grudgingly, because I was unwilling to explain my great zeal for work. I had formulated a plan for escape. I was going to double my crab catch and keep half the money for myself, turning over to my mother the usual amount. My half I would save until I had enough to send myself to boarding school in Crisfield. On Smith Island to the south of us there was no high school, not even the pretense of one that we had on Rass. The state, therefore, sent any Smith Islanders who continued school after the elementary level to a boarding school in Crisfield. The prices were not out of sight. Too high, it was true, for an island family without state aid to contemplate, but low enough for me to dream and work toward. It seemed to me that if I could get off the island, I would be free from hate and guilt and damnation, even, perhaps, from God himself.

I was too clever to pin all my hopes on crabs. Crabs are fickle creatures. They always know when you need them too much and pick precisely that season to make themselves scarce. I must give the impression, therefore, despite my early risings, that I didn't much care how lucky we were. When we were on the water, poling through the eelgrass, I took pains to say at just about dawn, "This is the nicest time of day, isn't it, Call? Who cares if the crabs are here or not? Let's just relax and enjoy ourselves."

Call would give me a look that indicated that I had lost my mind, but he was smart enough not to think it out loud. I can't swear that I fooled the crabs, but our catches were good that summer. Still, I wasn't going to count too heavily on crabs. I began casting about for other ways to make money.

I found what seemed a sure thing in the back of a Captain Marvel comic book in Kellam's store. I even squandered a dime of my hard-earned cash to buy the book, which I hid with my other treasures in the underwear drawer.

WANTED: Song Lyrics
Cash for your poems!

Cash. That was a word to make the creative juices flow. The fact that most of the poetry I'd ever read came off tombstones didn't stop me. I listened to the radio, didn't I?

> *There'll be bluebirds over*
> *The white cliffs of Dover*
> *Tomorrow, just you wait and see.*
> *There'll be love and laughter*
> *And peace ever after*
> *Tomorrow, when the world is free.*

Any idiot could figure it out. Two rhyming lines, stuffed with romance, a third that neither rhymes nor makes sense right away, two more romantic ones, then the third that also rhymes with the earlier unrhymed one and sort of makes sense.

> *When the gulls fly over the Bay*
> *They cry that you're far away.*
> *But we didn't part.*
> *Though you're far across the sea,*
> *You're not far away to me,*
> *You're in my heart.*

It had all the elements—romance, sadness, an allusion to the war, and faithful love. I fancied myself the perfect lyricist—romantic, yet knowledgeable.

I tried it out on Call in the boat one day.

"What's that supposed to mean?"

"The girl's boyfriend is away at war."

"Then why are the gulls crying? Why should they care?"

"They don't really care. In poems you can't say plain out what you mean."

"Why not?"

"Then it's not poetry anymore."

"You mean a poem's supposed to lie?"

"It's not lying."

"Go on. Ain't neither gull on this Bay up there boo-hooing 'cause some sailor's gone to war. If that ain't a plain out lie, I don't know what is."

"It's a different way of talking. Makes it prettier."

"It ain't pretty to lie, Wheeze."

"Forget about the gulls. How about the rest of it?"

"The rest of what?"

"The rest of my poem, Call. How does it sound?"

"I forget."

I gritted my teeth to keep from yelling at him and then with super patience read it through again.

"I thought you's going to forget about the gulls."

"No, *you* forget them. How does the rest sound?"

"It don't make neither sense."

"What do you mean?"

"Either the guy's away or he ain't. You got to make up your mind."

"Call. It's a poem. In real life he is far away, but she thinks about him all the time, so she feels like he's real close."

"I call it dumb."

"Just wait until you fall in love."

He looked at me as though I'd proposed some indecent act.

I sighed. "Did you hear the one about the Australian who wanted to buy a new boomerang but he couldn't get rid of his old one?"

"No. What about him?"

"Get it? A boomerang. He wanted to buy a new boomerang, but he kept getting the old one back every time he threw it away."

"Why should he even want a new one? The old one's still perfectly good, isn't it?"

"Call. Just forget it."

He shook his head, the picture of patient disbelief, and I forgot I was pretending not to care about crabs and devoted my full attention to the pesky varmints. I like to recall that we netted two full baskets of rank peelers that day.

No one had told me to turn over all the money I made crabbing. I just always had. When I started, I guess, it hadn't occurred to me that it was mine to keep. We always lived so close to the edge of being poor. It made me feel proud to be able to present the family with a little something extra to hold onto. While my parents never carried on much over it, I was always thanked. When my grandmother would criticize me, I could remember, even if the laws of respect kept me silent, that I was a contributing member of the household in which she and Caroline were little more than parasites. It was a private comfort.

But no one ever said I had to turn over *every* penny I made to the stoneware pickle crock in which the household money was kept.

Why then did I feel so guilty? Wasn't it my right to keep some of my hard-won earnings? But what if Otis should say something to my father about all the crabs he was buying from us? What if Call's mother should brag to my mother about how much money Call was bringing home these days? I divided my share exactly down the middle. If there was a penny in doubt, the penny went into the crock. I was contributing almost as much as I had during the previous summer, but I wasn't taking the money proudly to Momma for her to count out and put into the crock. I was slipping it in myself and then saying later, "Oh, by the way, I left a little in the crock." And my mother would thank me quietly, just as she always had. I never said I was putting everything in. I never lied. But then no one ever asked.

If only there were some other way to make money. Call's total lack of enthusiasm for my poem had had a dampening effect. I knew perfectly well that he was as qualified to judge poetry as he was to judge jokes, which was not at all, but still, he was the only human being I could risk reading it aloud to. If only he could have said something like, "I don't know anything about poetry, but it sounds fine to me." That would have been gracious, almost honest, and would have given me a real boost when I needed it.

As it was, I waited a week or so, then pulled myself together enough to copy the poem out on clean notebook paper and mail it to Lyrics Unlimited. Even before it could have been delivered to the P.O. Box in New York, I began haunting the docks when the ferry (which also served as the mail boat) came in. I didn't have the nerve to ask Captain Billy directly if there was any mail for me, but I hoped that if I just happened to be standing there, he'd see me and let me know. I didn't know that he never opened the sack before he took it to Mrs. Kellam, who served as postmistress. But I did know that Mrs. Kellam was a noisy gossip. I dreaded the thought of her asking my grandmother about a mysterious letter arriving from New York addressed to me.

It was about that time that our day-old Baltimore *Sun* carried huge headlines about the eight German saboteurs. They had been landed by submarine on Long Island and Florida and almost immediately caught. I knew, of course I knew, that the Captain was not a spy, but as I read, it felt as though I were swallowing an icicle. Suppose he had been. Suppose Call and I had caught him and become heroes? It seemed such a near miss that suddenly it was important to me to find out more about the old man. If he was not a spy, if he was indeed Hiram Wallace, why had he come back after all these years to an island where he was hardly remembered except with contempt?

# 7

Call and I had been so busy crabbing since school let out that we'd hardly been to visit the Captain together. Call, I knew, usually went to see him on Sunday afternoons, but my parents liked me to stay closer by on Sundays. I didn't mind. The long sleepy afternoon was perfect for writing lyrics. By now I had nearly a shoe box full, just waiting for Lyrics Unlimited to write and demand all that I could deliver.

So Call was surprised when, on a Tuesday, I proposed that we wind up the crabbing an hour early and pay a visit to the Captain.

"I thought you didn't like him," Call said.

"Of course I like him. Why shouldn't I like him?"

"Because he tells good jokes."

"That's a stupid reason not to like somebody."

"Yeah. That's what I thought."

"What d'you mean?"

"Nothing."

I decided to ignore the implied insult. "You can learn a lot from someone who comes from the outside. Take

73

Mr. Rice. I guess Mr. Rice taught me more than all my other teachers put together." All two of them.

"About what?"

I blushed. "About everything—music, life. He was a great man." I talked and thought about Mr. Rice as though he were dead and gone forever. That's how far away his Texas army post seemed.

Call was quiet, watching my face. I knew he was fixing to say something but didn't quite know how to say it. "What's the matter?" I asked him. As soon as I asked, I knew. He didn't want me to visit the Captain with him. He wanted the Captain all to himself. Besides, he was suspicious of me. I decided to tackle the matter directly.

"Why don't you want me to visit the Captain?"

"I never said I didn't want you to visit the Captain."

"Well, what are we waiting for? Let's go."

He shrugged his shoulders unhappily. "Free country," he muttered. It didn't make any sense, but I knew what he meant—that if there had been a way to stop me, he would have.

The Captain was tending crab lines on his broken-down dock. I poled the boat in close before he heard us and looked up.

"Well, if it isn't Wheeze and Cough," he said, smiling widely and touching the bill of his cap.

"Wheeze and Cough, get it?" Call yelled back to me from the bow. He shook his head, smiling all over his face. "Wheeze and Cough, that's really good."

74

I tried to smile, but my face had too much basic integrity for me even to pretend I had heard something funny.

Call and the Captain gave each other a "don't mind her" look, and Call threw the Captain the bowline and he tied us up. I don't mind admitting I wasn't too keen to step out on that ramshackle dock, but after Call had jumped onto it, and it had only shuddered a bit, I climbed carefully out and walked off to the shore as quickly as I dared.

"I'm going to fix it." The Captain hadn't missed my anxiety. "Just so many things to do around here." He nodded at Call. "I tried to get your friend here to give me a hand, but—"

Call blushed. "You can't hammer on a Sunday," he said defensively.

Hiram Wallace would have known that. Nobody on the island worked on the Sabbath. It was as bad as drinking whiskey and close to cursing and adultery. I racked my brain for the next question—the one that would prove to Call beyond doubt that the Captain was no more Hiram Wallace than I was. "Don't you recall the Seventh Commandment?" I asked slyly.

He lifted his cap and scratched his hair underneath. "Seventh Commandment?"

I had him. That is, I almost had him. I hadn't reckoned on Call. Call who snorted and almost yelled, "Seventh? Seventh? Seventh don't have neither to do with hammering on Sunday. Seventh's the one," he stopped, suddenly embarrassed and lowered his voice, "on adultery."

75

"Adultery?" The Captain started laughing out loud. "Well, I'm too old to worry about that one. Now there was a time—" He grinned mischievously. I suspect Call wanted him to go on as much as I did, but the old man stopped right there. Like offering candy to a child and then yanking back your hand with some excuse about saving his teeth, I thought.

"Today is Tuesday," Call said as we started for the house.

"Tuesday! Then—then—" the Captain seemed terribly excited. "Then tomorrow is Wednesday, and after that comes Thursday! Friday! Saturday! Sunday! And Monday!!"

I thought Call would die laughing on the spot, but he managed to control himself enough to gasp, "Get it, Wheeze? Get it?"

If I couldn't smile at "Wheeze and Cough," how was I to force a laugh at a recitation of the days of the week?

"Don't mind her, Captain. She don't catch on too good."

"Too well." At least I could demonstrate proper grammar. "Too well."

"Too well. Too well," repeated the Captain chirpily, lifting his hand to his ear. "Hark? Do I hear the mating call of a feathered friend of the marshland?"

Call, naturally, collapsed. All I could think of was if we'd netted a spy like this, Franklin D. Roosevelt would have thrown him back. Good heavens.

Eventually, Call recovered from his hysterics enough

to explain to the Captain that since it was Tuesday and not yet suppertime, he and I would be glad to lend a hand fixing up the old dock or house or whatever else the Captain might want doing around the place. In fact, Call added, we could come at about this time *every* afternoon, except Sunday of course, and help out.

"I'd want to pay you something," the Captain said. My ears stretched practically to the top of my head, and I opened my mouth to utter a humble thanks.

"Oh, *no,*" said Call. "We couldn't think of taking money from a neighbor."

Who couldn't? But for once in his life Call talked faster than I could think, and the two of them snatched away my time and energy and sold me into slavery before I had breath to hint that I wouldn't be insulted by a small tip every now and then.

That was how we came to spend two hours every afternoon slaving for the Captain. I noticed grimly that he didn't mind at all ordering us around, even though we were supposed to be doing him a favor. We didn't have our tea break after the first week because tin was becoming scarce and the Captain was short on canned milk. And, as he explained, since he could no longer offer Call milk, it would have been mean for the two of us to stop for tea. I would have been glad to stop for any excuse, even that awful tea. When you're fourteen and your body is changing as mine was that summer, you just plain get tired, but I couldn't admit it. Both Call and the Captain seemed to regard me as mentally deficient, since I couldn't appreciate their marvelous humor. I couldn't let them make fun of me physically as well.

Nothing went right for me that summer, unless you count the fact that when my periods began, almost a year after Caroline's of course, they began on a Sunday morning *before* I left the house for church instead of after, but the stain went clear through my pants and slip to my only good dress. Momma let me pretend to be sick. What else could she do? I couldn't wash and dry my dress in time for Sunday school.

My grandmother kept saying things like "What's the matter with her? She don't look sick to me. Just don't want to worship the Lord." And "If she was mine, I'd give her a good smack on the rear. That'd perk her up fast enough."

I was terrified that Momma would betray me and tell Grandma the real reason I was staying home. But she didn't. Even Caroline tried to shush Grandma up. I don't know what Grandma told her old friends, but for weeks after that they'd all ask sweetly about my health, both physical and spiritual.

My spiritual health was about on a par with a person who's been dead three days, but I wasn't about to admit it and get prayed for out loud on Wednesday night by that bunch of old sooks.

# 8

I used to try to decide which was the worst month of the year. In the winter I would choose February. I had it figured out that the reason God made February short a few days was because he knew that by the time people came to the end of it they would die if they had to stand one more blasted day. December and January are cold and wet, but, somehow, that's their right. February is just plain malicious. It knows your defenses are down. Christmas is over and spring seems years away. So February sneaks in a couple of beautiful days early on, and just when you're stretching out like a cat waking up, bang! February hits you right in the stomach. And not with a lightning strike like a September hurricane, but punch after punch after punch. February is a mean bully. Nothing could be worse—except August.

There were days that August when I felt as though God had lowered a giant glass lid over the whole steaming Bay. All year we had lived in the wind, now we were cut off without a breath of air. On the water the haze was so thick it was like trying to inhale wet cotton. I began to pray for a real blow. I wanted relief that badly.

In February the weather sometimes gave us a vacation, in August, never. We just got up earlier every morning until finally we met ourselves going to bed. Call and I didn't get up quite as early as my father, who may have never gone to bed between tending to his floats and going out to crab, but we were up well before dawn, trying to sneak a fair catch of crabs from the eelgrass before the sun drove us off the water.

I had a faint hope that the Captain, not being an islander, or at least, not a regular islander, would take the heat as an excuse to slow down a bit. But Call fixed that.

"We're coming in from crabbing early these hot mornings," he blabbed. "We could come on over here and get lots more done of a day."

"I can't come before dinner," I said. "Momma expects me home to eat."

"Well, fiddle, Wheeze," Call said. "You all eat by eleven. Don't take more'n ten minutes to eat."

"We don't stuff like scavengers at our house," I said. "I couldn't possibly get here that fast. Besides, I got chores."

"We'll be here by noon," he told the Captain cheerily. I could have choked him. That meant at least four and a half hours of gut-ripping work in the heat for nothing. Nothing.

The Captain, of course, was delighted. His one concession to the temperature was that we work indoors and not on the dock in the sun. He began planning out loud all the projects the three of us could complete by the time school opened. I managed, with a lie about my mother needing me, to get away by four-fifteen. I wanted to get to the post office before supper. It would have been better perhaps if I had not, for there it was, my letter from Lyrics Unlimited. I ran with it to the tip of the island, to my driftwood stump, and sat down to open it, my hands shaking so they made a poor job of it.

Dear Miss Bandshaw:

CONGRATULATIONS!!! YOU ARE A WINNER! LYRICS UNLIMITED is delighted to inform you that your song, while not a money prize winner, is a WINNER in our latest contest.Given an appropriate musical setting, YOUR LYRICS could become a POPULAR SONG played on the radio waves all over America and even to our boys overseas. We urge you to let us set your words to music and give them this OUTSTANDING OPPORTUNITY. You might well be the lyricist of an all-time hit. You might well hear your song on the HIT PARADE. Your lyrics deserve this chance. All you need to do is send a check or money order (no stamps, please) for $25 and leave the rest to us.

We will
    Set YOUR WORDS to music
    Print the sheet music
    Make copies available to
       THE PEOPLE in the world
      of POPULAR MUSIC
And WHO KNOWS?! The next song to top the
HIT PARADE may be YOURS! ! ! !

Don't lose this chance! Time is limited! Send
in your $25 today and put yourself on the ROAD
TO FAME AND FORTUNE.

              Sincerely,
              your friends at
              LYRICS UNLIMITED

Even I, wanting so much to believe, could tell it was mimeographed. The only thing typed in was my name, and that had been misspelled. I was a fool, but I'm proud to say, not that big a fool. Heartsick, I ripped the letter down to its last exclamation point and flung it like confetti out into the water.

August and February are both alike in one way. They're both dream killers.

The next day the orange tomcat reappeared. It was the same cat, I'm sure, that had scared Call and me that time four years before when we had decided to investigate the house, and the same cat that the Captain had finally driven out after the first week or so he had lived there.

The cat marched in through the open front door as though he were the long-absent landlord popping in to check out the tenants.

The Captain was furious. "I thought I got rid of that fool thing months ago." He got his broom and took after the huge tom, who calmly jumped onto the kitchen table. When the Captain took a swing at him there, he leaped daintily to the floor, taking a cup down with his tail.

"Damn it to hell!"

I had the capacity to imagine such language, but neither Call nor I had ever really heard it spoken. I think we were as fascinated as we were shocked.

"Captain," said Call, when he recovered himself slightly, "do you know what you said?"

The Captain was still stalking the cat and answered impatiently, "Of course I know what I said. I said—"

"Captain. That's against the commandments."

He took another futile swing before he answered. "Call, I know those blasted commandments as well as you do, and there is not one word in them about how to speak to tomcats. Now stop trying to play preacher and help me catch that damn cat and let's get him out of here."

Call was too shocked now to do anything but obey. He ran out after the cat. I started laughing. For some reason, the Captain had at last said something I thought was funny. I wasn't just giggling either. I was belly laughing. He looked at me and grinned. "Nice to hear you laugh, Miss Wheeze," he said.

"You're right!" I screeched through my laughter.

"There's not—I bet there's not one word in the whole blasted Bible on how to speak to cats."

He began to laugh, too. Just sat down on the kitchen stool, the broom across his knees, and laughed. Why was it so funny? Was it because it was so wonderful to discover something on this island that was free—something unproscribed by God, Moses, or the Methodist Conference? We could talk to cats any way we pleased.

Call reappeared carrying the struggling tom. He looked first at the Captain and then at me, apparently baffled. He had never seen us laughing together, of course. Maybe he didn't know whether to be pleased or jealous.

"Who—who—" puffed out the Captain. "Who is going to take that damned animal back to Trudy Braxton?"

"Trudy Braxton!" I think both Call and I yelled it. We had never heard anyone call Auntie Braxton by her Christian name. Even my grandmother, who must have been nearly the old woman's age, called her "Auntie."

After the first shock, my feeling was one of pleasure. It really was. I no longer wanted the Captain to be a Nazi spy or an interloper. I wanted him to be Hiram Wallace, an islander who had escaped. That was far more wonderful than being a saboteur to be caught or an imposter to be exposed.

"I'll take the cat back," I said. "If the stink don't get me first."

For some reason my irreverent description of Auntie Braxton's house triggered Call. "Did you hear what she said?" he asked the Captain. " 'If the stink don't get me first.' " Then he and the Captain were laughing their heads off.

I grabbed the cat from Call just as it wriggled free. "Come along," I said, "before I call you a stinking name or two." I wasn't quite bold enough to use the forbidden curse word aloud, but I thought of it several times quite happily as I made my way up the path and to Auntie Braxton's house.

I hadn't exaggerated the smell. The windows of the house were open and the overwhelming ammonia essence of cat stood like an invisible wall between me and the front yard. The tom was scratching and struggling to get out of my grasp, leaving stinging red lines all over my bare arms. If I hadn't been afraid that he would turn and run straight back to the Captain's, I would have dropped him on the front walk and run back myself. I had, however, a duty to perform, so I marched bravely up the walk to Auntie Braxton's door.

"Auntie Braxton!" I yelled her name over unhappy cat sounds coming from the other side of the door. If I let go the tom to knock or open the door, I might lose him, so I just stood there on the dilapidated porch and hollered. "Auntie Braxton. I got your cat."

From within a cat howled in reply, but no human voice accompanied it. I called again. Still no answer from the old lady. It occurred to me that I might be able to push the cat through the torn window screen. I went over to the window. The hole was large enough if I stuffed the creature in a bit. As I stooped to do so, I saw something dark lying on the front room floor. There were cats perched on top of it and cats walking across it, so for a minute I simply stared at it, not recognizing it for what it was—a human form. When I did, I panicked. Throwing the cat down, I half tripped over it in my hurry to be gone. I raced back to the Captain's house where I nearly fell over the door stoop, panting out my terror.

"Auntie Braxton!" I said. "Lying dead on the floor with cats crawling all over her."

"Slow down," said the Captain. I tried to catch my breath and repeat myself, but after two words he was already past me and walking, almost running up the path toward the old woman's house. Call and I followed. We were both terrified, but we ran to catch up to him and stayed at his heels. No matter what terrible thing was going on, we wanted to be with him and each other.

The Captain pushed open the door. People never locked their houses on Rass. Most doors didn't even have locks. The three of us went in. No one was bothering about the smell anymore. The Captain knelt down beside the old woman, scattering cats in every direction.

Call and I hung back a little, wide-eyed and breathing fast.

"She's alive," he said. "Call, you go down to the dock. As soon as the ferry docks, Captain Billy's going to have to take her to the hospital."

Relief washed over me like a gentle surf. It wasn't that I'd never seen a dead body. On an island, you can't get away from death. But I'd never found one. Never been the first person accidentally to stumble in on death. It seemed more terrible somehow to be the first one.

"Don't just stand there, Sara Louise. Go find some men to help me carry her down to the dock."

I jumped and ran to obey. It was not until later that I realized that he had called me by my full name, Sara Louise. No one bothered, not even my mother, to call me Sara Louise, but he had done it without thinking. Strange how much that meant to me.

I got my father and two other men from their crab houses, and we raced back to Auntie Braxton's. The Captain had found a cot mattress, and he and my father gently rolled the old woman over and lifted her to the mattress. The Captain covered her with a cotton blanket. I was glad, for her thin legs seemed indecent somehow poking out from her faded housedress. Then the four men began to lift the awkward makeshift stretcher. As they did so, the old lady moaned, like someone disturbed by a bad dream.

"It's all right, Trudy, it's me, Hiram," the Captain said. "I'll take care of you." My father and the other two men gave one another funny looks, but no one said anything. They had to get her to the hospital.

# 9

"Trudy" was what did it. Simply by using Auntie Braxton's first name, the Captain confirmed himself as the true Hiram Wallace. He still didn't go to meet the ferry in the afternoon like most folks, or hang around Kellam's after supper matching water stories, or go to church. But despite these aberrations he seemed to be accepted as an islander, simply because he had called Auntie Braxton "Trudy," a name nobody had used for her since she was a young woman.

Call's life and mine took a strange turn at that time. The Captain decided that while Auntie Braxton was in the hospital, the three of us should tackle her house. I tried weakly to argue that it was like trespassing to clean up someone's house without her permission, and trespassing was something Methodists were forever bent on getting forgiveness for, so it was likely to be a fairly serious sin. The Captain just snorted impolitely at that. If we didn't do it, he said, the Ladies' Society of the Methodist Church was likely to take it on as a good deed. Although

Auntie Braxton had grown up in the church, she had, for years, been considered strange, and once her cat population had passed four or five, she had been on very strained terms with the other women of Rass.

"Would Trudy rather have them poking about her property than us?"

"She'd rather have nobody, I bet."

He sadly admitted that I was right, but since the alternative to our doing the cleaning was having it become a missionary endeavor, I had to agree that we were certainly the lesser of two evils.

The problem, of course, was the cats. Until something could be done about them, there was no hope of getting the house in any kind of order.

"How in the world did she feed them?" I asked. It had always seemed to me that Auntie Braxton was below even Call's family on the poverty scale.

"The wonder is she didn't feed them better," the Captain said. "These poor things look half-starved."

"Cat food costs a lot of money," I said, trying to remember if Auntie Braxton had ever been known to buy fish from a local waterman to feed to her cats. Anyone else would have used scraps, but anyone else would have had more people than cats in the house.

"I would have thought Trudy had more money than most people on the island," the Captain said.

Even Call was flabbergasted. "What makes you think a thing like that?" he asked. We both remembered that

Auntie Braxton got a basket from the Ladies' Society at Thanksgiving and Christmas. Not even Call's family rated a basket.

"I was here when her father died," the Captain said, as though the two of us should have known such a simple fact as that. "Old Captain Braxton had plenty, but he never let on. He let his wife and child scrimp by on next to nothing. Trudy found the money after they both died. And it scared her something silly to suddenly find all this cash, so she come running to my mother. My mother treated her like she was her own daughter. Poor Momma," he shook his head, "she never gave up hoping I'd marry Trudy. Well, anyway, Momma told her to put it in a bank, but I doubt that Trudy did. What did she know about mainland banks? What's left of it after all these years is probably hidden right here in this house, if the damn cats haven't chewed it up."

"Maybe it ran out," I said. "It's been a long time."

"Maybe. It was a lot of money." He suddenly looked at us both, changing his tone abruptly. "Look," he said, "don't say anything about any money. If she'd have wanted anyone else to know about it, she would have told them. I'm not even supposed to know. Just my mother."

Call and I nodded solemnly. Real intrigue was far more delicious than the pretend kind. The fact that there might be money hidden convinced me beyond a doubt that the Ladies' Society must not take over the housecleaning.

But the distasteful problem of the cats remained. The

Captain made both me and Call sit down in his clean, refurbished living room. He served me tea and Call some of his precious tinned milk, and then, very gently, he tried to explain to us what he believed had to be done.

"The only way to resolve the problem of the cats," he said, "is to dispose of them humanely."

Either I was a little slow or the language was too elegant, because I was nodding my head in respectful agreement when, suddenly, it hit me what he meant.

"You mean shoot them?"

"No. I think that would be hard to do. Besides it would make a mess and bring the neighbors running. I think the best method—"

"Kill them? You mean kill them all?"

"They're almost starving now, Sara Louise. They'll die slowly with no one to care for them."

"I'll take care of them," I said fiercely. "I'll feed them until Auntie Braxton gets back." Even as I heard myself say it, the words hacked at my stomach. All my crab money, my boarding school money—to feed a pack of yowling, stinking cats. I hated cats.

"Sara Louise," the Captain said kindly, "even if you had the money to feed them, we can't leave them in the house. They're a health hazard."

"A person's got the right to choose their own hazards."

"Maybe so. But not when it's getting to be a problem for the whole community."

"Thou shalt not kill!" I said stubbornly, remembering at the same time that only the day before I had been rejoicing that not one word of the blasted Bible applied to cats. He was gracious enough not to remind me.

"What are you fixing to do with 'em, Captain?" Call asked, his voice cracking in the middle of his question.

The Captain sighed, polishing his mug with the back of his thumb. Without lifting his eyes, he said softly, "Take them couple miles out and leave them."

"Drown them?" I was getting hysterical. "Just take them out and throw them in?"

"I don't like the idea, either," he said.

"We could take them to the mainland," I said. "They have places there like orphanages for animals. I read about it in the *Sun*."

"The SPCA," he said. "Yes, in Baltimore—or Washington. But even there, they'd just have to put these creatures to sleep."

"Put them to sleep?"

"Kill them as gently as possible," he explained. "Even there they can't take care of everyone's unwanted cats on and on."

I tried not to believe him. How could anything that called itself the "Society for the Prevention of Cruelty to Animals" engage in wholesale murder? But even if I was right, Baltimore and Washington were too far away to do Auntie Braxton's cats any good.

"I'll borrow a boat," he said. "One that will get us out fast. You two round up the cats." He started out the door and up the path. In a moment he was back. "There's three gunnysacks on the back porch," he said.

"You'll need something to put the cats in." Then he was gone again.

Call got off the bench. "C'mon," he said. "We can't catch neither cat sitting here on our bottoms all day."

I shuddered and got up reluctantly. It would be better not to think, I told myself. If you could hold your nose to avoid a stink, or close your eyes to cut out a sight, why not shut off your brain to avoid a thought? Thus, the catching of the cats became a sport with no consequences. We took turns, one holding the bag while the other dodged about the furniture and up the stairs in pursuit. They were amazingly lively despite their half-starved appearance, and once seized and thrown into the sack, they went after one another with ungodly shrieks. Five were in the first bag—they proved to be the hardest to get—and the bag was tied tightly with cord I found in the kitchen drawer.

By the second bag, I had become more wily. In addition to the cord, I had found some cans of tuna and sardines in the kitchen. I divided a can of sardines between the two remaining gunnysacks and then smeared the oil on my hands. I risked being eaten alive, but it worked. I lured those fool cats right to me and into those infernal sacks. We got them all, all that is but the orange tom, which was nowhere in the house. Neither Call nor I had the heart to track him down. Besides, sixteen snarling cats were more than enough.

I sneaked down to our house and got the wagon. Very gingerly we loaded the live sacks onto it. We were already scratched and bitten enough. Those claws could reach through the burlap as though it weren't there. Once one of the sacks writhed and wiggled its way off the wagon and into the street, but we got it back on and down the path to the Captain's dock. He sat there waiting for us in a skiff with an outboard. He was wearing a black tie and his old blue seaman's suit. I had the feeling he was dressed for a funeral.

Without a word, Call and I put the sacks into the bottom of the boat and climbed in after them. The cats must have exhausted themselves fighting, for the sacks lay almost quiet at our feet. The Captain yanked the starter cord two or three times and the motor finally coughed and then hummed. Slowly he turned the bow and headed for open water.

It was midafternoon and the heat closed in on us unmercifully. I was aware of the smells of cat and the awful spoiled sardine smell of my own hands. I jerked them off my lap.

Just then, a piteous little cry rose from the sack nearest my feet. It sounded more like a baby than a cat, which is why, I suppose, it suddenly tore the blinders from my mind. "Stop!" I screamed, standing up in the boat.

The Captain cut the motor abruptly, telling me to sit down. But as soon as the motor died, I jumped over the washboard and swam with all my might for shore. I could dimly hear the Captain and Call yelling after me, but I never stopped swimming or running until I was home.

"Wheeze. What happened?" Caroline jumped up from the piano at the sight of me, hair streaming, clothes dripping all over the floor. I stomped past her and my mother, who had come to the kitchen door, up the stairs to our bedroom and slammed the door. I didn't want to see anyone, but of all people in the world, Caroline was the last one I wanted to talk to. I still smelled of sardines, for goodness' sake.

She opened the door a crack and slid through, leaning on it to shut it gently behind her. There was no way, now, to get down to the kitchen and wash.

"Can't you see I'm dressing?" I turned my back to the door.

"Want me to get you a towel?"

"Don't bother."

She slid out the door and came back carrying a towel. "You're a mess," she said pleasantly.

"Oh, shut up."

"What happened to you?"

"None of your business."

She got that hurt look in her great blue eyes that always made me want to smack her. She didn't say anything, just put the towel down on her bed and climbed up and sat down cross-legged beside it, dropping her shoes neatly to the floor.

"You and Call didn't go swimming, did you?"

No one was supposed to know that Call and I sometimes went swimming together.

I tried to run my fingers through my wet knotted hair.

She slipped off her bed and came over carrying the towel. "Want me to rub your hair?"

My first impulse was to shake her off, but she was trying to be kind. Even I could tell that. And I was feeling so awful that the kindness broke down all my usual defenses. I began to cry.

She got my bathrobe for me, and then she dried my hair with those powerful fingers of hers as gently as she might coax a nocturne from our old piano. So although she never seemed to urge me to talk, I began to do so, until, finally, I was pouring out my anguish, not for the cats, but for myself as murderer. It didn't matter that I had not actually thrown them into the Bay. I had cleverly lured them to their death. That was enough.

"Poor Wheeze," she said quietly. "Poor old cats."

At last I stopped crying, dressed, and combed my hair.

"Where are you going?" she asked. It was none of her business, but she had been too nice for me to say so.

"Auntie Braxton's," I said. "We have to get it cleaned up before the Ladies' Society makes it a missionary project."

"Can I come?"

"Why would you want to come? It's a filthy stinking mess."

She shrugged, blushing a little. "I don't know," she said. "Nothing better to do."

We borrowed a bucket and mop and a bottle of disinfectant as well as a pile of rags from my mother, whose face was set in a question she did not ask. As we entered Auntie Braxton's house, I watched Caroline closely. I suppose I wanted to see some sign of weakness. "Smells terrible," she said cheerfully.

"Yeah," I said, a bit disappointed that she hadn't at least gagged.

We had hardly filled the bucket with water when Call and the Captain appeared at the front door. They just stood there, hanging back a little, like a pair of naughty kids.

"Well," I said. "Back so soon."

The Captain shook his head sadly. "We couldn't do it."

Call looked as though he were about to cry. "They sounded just like little babies," he said.

I'm sure I should have felt joy and relief. Actually, what I felt was annoyance. I had spent a lot of guilt and grief over the death of those dratted cats. They had no right to be alive. "Well," I said, the dried salt was making my skin itch and adding to my irritation, "what are you going to do with them, then? We can't keep them here. You said so yourself."

Wearily, the Captain sat down in Auntie Braxton's easy chair right on top of the pile of rags I'd left there. He scrunched around under himself and fished them out. "I don't know," he was saying. "I just don't know."

"We can give them away." It was Caroline, taking over the problem just as though someone had asked her to.

"What do you mean, 'we'?" I was furious at her.

"I—you," she said. "What I mean is, just give the cats to as many people as will take them—"

"Nobody is going to take these cats," I said. "They're wild as bobcats and half-starved to boot. Nobody in their right mind would take a cat like that."

The Captain sighed his agreement. Call nodded his Methodist preacher nod. "They're wild as bobcats," he repeated. Not that any of us had ever seen a bobcat.

"So?" Caroline was undaunted. "We tame them."

"Tame them?" I snorted. "Why don't you just teach a crab to play the piano?"

"Not permanently," she said. "Just long enough to get them new homes."

"How, Caroline?" Call was definitely interested.

She grinned. "Paregoric," she said.

Call went to his house to fetch the family bottle, and I went to our house and got ours. Meantime, Caroline had prepared an assortment of sixteen saucers, cups, and bowls, rationing out the cans of tuna fish to each container. She laced each liberally with paregoric. We set them all around the kitchen floor and then brought in the gunnysacks and untied them.

Lured by the smell of food, the cats came staggering out of the bag. At first there was a bit of snarling and shoving, but since there were plenty of dishes for all, each cat eventually found a place for itself and set itself to cleaning away every trace of the drugged feast set before it.

In the end, it was as much Caroline's charm as the paregoric that worked. She took one cat to each house along the street, leaving Call and me to mind the sacks, slightly out of sight. Nobody on Rass would dare slam a door in Caroline's face. And no matter how determined the housewife might be against taking in a cat, Caroline's melodiously sweet voice would remind her that it was no small thing to save a life—a life precious to God if not to man—and then she would hold out a cat who was so doped up with paregoric that it was practically smiling. Some of them even managed a cuddly, kittenish mew. "See," Caroline would say, "he likes you already."

When the last cat was placed, we went back to Auntie Braxton's. The Captain had put chairs on top of tables and was beginning to mop the floor with hot water and disinfectant. Call told him the whole story of Caroline's feat, house by house, cat by cat. They laughed and imitated the befuddled women at the door. Caroline threw in imitations of the happy, drunken cats while the Captain and Call hooted with delight, and I felt as I always did when someone told the story of my birth.

# 10

The blow that I had been praying for struck the next week. While not as severe as the storm of '33, which became a legend before its waters receded, the storm of '42 is the one I will never forget.

During the war, weather was classified information, but on Rass we didn't need a city man on a radio to warn us of bad weather. My father, like any true waterman, could smell the storm coming up, even before the ominous rust-colored sunset. He had made his boat fast and boarded up the windows of our house. There was not much he could do about the peelers in our floats, except hope the storm would leave him a few of the floats and spare his crab shanty for one more season.

It is a mysterious thing how cheerful people become in the face of disaster. My father whistled as he boarded up the windows, and my mother from time to time would call to him happily out the back door. She obviously was enjoying the unusual pleasure of having him home on a weekday morning. Tomorrow they might be ruined or dead, today they had each other. And then there are things you can do to prepare for a hurricane. It is not like a thunderstorm on the water or sudden illness before which you are helpless.

Just before noon Call came by and asked if Caroline or I was going down to the Captain's.

"Sure," said Caroline cheerfully. "Soon as we finish carrying the canning upstairs." High water had more than once washed through our downstairs, and my mother didn't want to take a chance on having the fruits and vegetables she had bought on the mainland and put up for the winter dashed to the floor or swept away. "You coming, Wheeze?"

Who did she think she was, inviting me to go see the Captain? As if she owned both him and Call. Call, who had always belonged to me because nobody else besides his mother and grandmother would have him, and the Captain, who finally through all our troubles and misunderstandings had become mine as well. Now, because of one afternoon of giving away a batch of drugged cats, she thought she could snatch them both for herself. I muttered something angry but unintelligible.

"What's the matter, Wheeze?" she asked. "Don't you think we ought to help the Captain get ready for the storm?"

There she was, trying to make me look bad in front of Call. Her voice had its usual sweet tone, and her face was all concern. I wanted to smack it. "Go on down," I said to Call. "We'll get there when we can."

Later the four of us boarded up the Captain's windows.

Call, Caroline, and the Captain were calling back and forth cheerfully while we worked. The Captain didn't want to move anything to the second floor, and he laughed away my fear that the water might rise higher than his front stoop. We carried our hammers and nails and boards up to Auntie Braxton's and started on her windows. Before long my father joined us, and with his help, the work was quickly done.

"Want to spend the night at our place, Hiram?" my father asked.

The Captain smiled quickly as though thanking my father for calling him by name. "No," he said. "But I thank you. Any port in a storm, they say, but I take home port if I got a choice."

"It's going to blow mean tonight."

"I wouldn't be surprised." But the Captain gathered his tools, waved, and headed for home.

I was a sound sleeper in those days and it was my father, not the wind that woke me up.

"Louise."

"What? What?" I sat up in bed.

"Shh," he said. "No need to wake your sister."

"What is it?"

"The wind's come up right smart. I'm going to go down and take off my motor and sink the boat."

I knew that to be an extreme measure. "Want me to help?"

"No, there'll be plenty of men down there."

"Okay," I said and turned over to sleep again. He

shook me gently. "I think you better go down and get the Captain. Bring him up here in case it gets worse."

I was fully awake now. My father was worried. I jumped up and pulled on my work overalls over my nightgown. The house was shuddering like Captain Billy's ferry.

"Is it raining yet?" I asked my father at the front door. The wind was so loud that it was hard to tell.

"Soon," he said, handing me the largest flashlight. "Better wear your slicker. Now you take care and be quick."

I nodded. "You, too, Daddy."

The blow came up faster than even my father had guessed. Every now and then I would grab the paling of one of the picket fences lining the street to steady myself against the wind. It was blowing from the northwest, so making my way southeast toward the Captain's house, I had the feeling that at any moment the wind might lift me off my feet and deposit me in the Bay. When I reached the last house, where the narrow street turned into a path across the marsh, I went down on my hands and knees, shoved my slicker up out of the way, and crawled. The wind seemed too powerful now to tempt with my upright body.

If our house had been shaking, protected as it was in the middle of the village, imagine the Captain's, hanging there alone so near the water. The beam of my flashlight caught for a frightening moment the waters of the Bay, which the wind had whipped into a fury. *And everyone that heareth these sayings of mine and doeth them not,*

*shall be likened unto a foolish man, which built his house*
*upon the sand: And the rain descended and the floods came,*
*and the winds blew, and beat upon that house. . . .*

I began to cry out the Captain's name. How he heard
me over the roar of the wind, I don't know, but he was
out on the porch before I reached the house.

"Sara Louise? Where are you?"

I stood up, bracing my body as best I could against
the wind. "Hurry!" I yelled. "You got to come to our
house."

He came quickly, put his body in front of mine, and
pulled my arms about his waist. He took my flashlight so
I could grasp my hands together in front of him. "Hold
tight!"

Even with his stocky waterman's body to break the wind,
our journey back up the path was a treacherous one. The
rain was coming down now like machine-gun fire, and
the water from the marsh began to swirl up around our
feet. The Captain cried out something to me, but his voice
was lost in the moaning of the wind. Like all the rest of
me, my hands were wet. Once they slipped apart. The
Captain caught my left arm and held on tightly. Even when
we got to the first picket fence, he held on. The pain in
my arm became the only real thing, a sharp point of comfort
in the midst of a nightmare. In the narrow street the dark
houses of the village gave us some shelter from the wind,
but the water of the Bay was already washing across the
crushed oyster shells.

My father was not home when the Captain and I got

there. The electricity was out. My mother, white-faced in the light from the kerosene lamp, was at the stove getting coffee. Grandma was rocking back and forth in her chair, her eyes squinched shut. "Oh, Lord," she was praying out loud. "Why don't you come down and still the wind and waves? Oh, Jesus, you told the storm on Galilee, 'Peace, be still,' and it obeyed your word. Ohhh, Lord, come down now and quiet this evil wind."

As if in defiance, the moan of the wind shifted into a shriek. We were all so startled that it took us several seconds to realize that my father had come in the front door and was now pushing the old food safe against it. The door was leeward, but we all knew that later the wind would shift. We had to be ready.

"Best douse the lamp, Susan," my father said. "And the stove. Things get banging around down here and we'll have a first-class fire."

Momma handed him a cup of coffee before she obeyed.

"Now," he said. "Best be getting upstairs." He had to shout to be heard but the words were as calm as someone telling the time. "Come along, Momma," he called to Grandma. "Can't have you floating away on your rocker." He waved his flashlight toward the staircase.

Grandma had stopped her litany. Or else the wind had swallowed it. She went to the steps and began to climb slowly. My father nudged me to follow. "Oh, my blessed," Grandma was saying as she climbed. "Oh, my blessed. I do hate the water."

Caroline slept on. Caroline would probably have slept

through the Last Trumpet. I started toward her bed to wake her up. Daddy called me from the hallway. "No," he said. "Let her sleep."

I came back to where he was. "She'll miss the whole hurricane."

"Yeah. Probably will," he said. "Better get off those wet things, now. Then you should try to get some sleep yourself."

"I couldn't sleep through this. I wouldn't want to."

Even through the shriek of the wind, I could hear his chuckle. "Nope," he said. "Probably wouldn't."

When I had changed out of my wet things and cleaned myself off as best I could, I went into my parents' room. Daddy had gone down and fetched Grandma's chair so she could rock and moan as was her custom. Somehow, the Captain had changed from his wet clothes into my father's bathrobe, which barely met at his middle. Daddy and Momma were perched on the side of their bed, and the Captain sat on the edge of the only other chair. They had lit a candle in the room, which flickered because of the wind coming through the chinks of the house. Momma patted the bed beside her. I went and sat down. I wanted to snuggle up on her lap like a toddler, but I was fourteen, so I sat as close to her body as I dared.

We gave up trying to talk. It was too hard to fight the wind screaming like a giant wounded dove. We could no longer hear the sounds of Grandma's prayers or the rain or the water.

Suddenly there was silence. "What happened?" Though as soon as I asked, I knew. It was the eye. We were in the quiet eye of the storm. Daddy got up, took the flashlight, and went to the stairs. The Captain rose, pulled the bathrobe together, and followed him. I started to get up, too, but Momma put her arm across my lap.

"You can't tell how long it will last," she said. "Just let the men go."

I wanted to object, but I was tired. It wouldn't have mattered. The men were back almost before they started.

"Well, Sue, there's two foot of Bay water sloshing about down there." Daddy sat down beside her. "I'm feared it'll make a mess of your nice parlor."

She patted his knee. "As long as we're all safe," she said.

"Ohhhh, Lord," Grandma cried out. "Why must the righteous suffer?"

"We're all safe, Momma," my father said. "We're all safe. Nobody's suffering."

She began to cry then, bawling out like a frightened child. My parents looked at each other in consternation. I was angry. What right had she, a grown woman, who had lived through many storms, to carry on like that?

Then the Captain got up and went to kneel beside her chair. "It's all right, Louise," he said, as though he were indeed talking to a child. "A storm's a fearsome thing." When he said that I remembered the tale I'd heard about him cutting down his father's mast. Was it possible that a man so calm had once been so terrified? "Would you like me to read to you?" he asked. "While it's still quiet?"

She didn't answer. But he got up and, taking the Bible from the bedside table, pulled his chair in close to the candle. As he was flipping through for the place, Grandma looked up. "T'ain't fitting a heathen should read the Word of God," she said.

"Hush, Momma!" I had never heard my father speak so sharply to her before. But she did hush, and the Captain began to read.

"God is our refuge and strength, a very present help in trouble." He read well, better than the preacher, almost as well as Mr. Rice. "Therefore we will not fear, though the earth be removed, and though the mountains be carried into the midst of the sea; Though the waters thereof roar and be troubled, though the mountains shake with the swelling thereof . . ."

Into my mind came a wonderful and terrible picture of great forested mountains, shaken by a giant hand that scooped them up, finally, and flung them into the boiling sea. I had never seen a mountain, except in a geography text. I was fourteen, and I had never even seen a real mountain. I was going to, though. I was not going to end up like my Grandma, fearful and shriveled.

They told me later that I finally slept through the worst part of the hurricane. When the eye passed, the wind came up from the south even more fiercely than before. "Grabbed this old house by the scruff of the neck and shook the bejeebers out of it," my father said. "But I couldn't wake you for nothing. Snoring away like an old dog."

"I didn't snore!" I was horrified at the thought of the Captain watching me while I snored.

"Snored so loud, you plumb drowned the wind." He was teasing me. At least I hoped my father was teasing.

It was not one of those hurricanes like the one that was to hit the Atlantic Coast in '44, not one of those hurricanes that go down in books. No island lives were lost in the storm of '42. No human lives, at any rate. The storm did accomplish without conscience what we had been too fainthearted to do. It reduced the island's cat population by at least two-thirds.

# 11

It was the bluest, clearest day of the summer. Every breath of air was delicious with just enough of a clean, salt edge to wake up all your senses. If the Captain and I had just stood on the porch with our eyes closed, it would have been a perfect day. For while our noses and lungs feasted on nature's goodness, our eyes were assaulted by evidence of her savagery.

The water had left our living room, but it was still in the yard, level with the porch. Riding the muddy surface were sections of picket fence, giant tree limbs, crab pots, remnants of floats and crab houses, boats, and . . .

"What's that?" I had grabbed the Captain's arm.

"A coffin," he said matter of factly. "These storms will dig them up sometimes. Just replant them is all." His mind was clearly not on the dead. "Look here," he said. "There's no safe walking to my place this morning. We'd best go back in and give your mother a hand."

The thought of our sodden, muck-filled downstairs dragged at me like a lead weight on a crab pot. "Don't you want to see what happened to your house?" I asked.

This was a day for adventure, not drudgery.

"Plenty of time to see later when the water's down," he said, turning to go back inside.

"My boat!" That was it. We could pole the skiff down to his house, maneuvering around the debris as we would ice floes. He cocked his head. I'm sure he doubted that my stubby little skiff could have survived the storm.

At first we couldn't tell. The gut had disappeared under the foot of water flooding the yard, bringing with it the same floating dump heap we had seen swirling about the front yard. The day before, my father had tied the boat, not just to the pine to which I usually secured her bow-line; he had run lines from her stern to the fig tree on one side and the cedar on the other. The three trees were still there, looking a bit like little boys after their summer hair-cuts, but still there. From the porch I could, at last, make out the three now taut lines, and then I caught sight of her washboards just above the water line.

"She's here!" I was half off the porch when the Captain grabbed me.

"You want lockjaw or typhoid or a combination?" He indicated my bare legs and feet.

I was too happy to be offended. "Okay," I said. "Just a minute." He waited until I fetched my father's old boots. He had worn his good ones when he left earlier to see about his own boat and the crab shanty.

We bailed out the skiff until it was bobbing merrily on the surface. The Captain loosed the lines on the house side of the still invisible gut, and then I climbed into the boat, pulled myself along the rope to the cedar tree, and loosed that knot as well. The Captain fetched the pole from the kitchen, and after he had handed it in to me in the stern, he climbed in and sat down facing me, his arms tightly folded across his chest.

He let me maneuver the skiff through the wreckage of the flood without even peeking over his shoulder to see what I might be about to hit. I poled us along what I thought might be the line of the gut. The water was too murky and trash-filled to tell. Usually my pole was only a foot or so in the water, but then suddenly it would go down three feet and I knew I had found the gut again.

The Captain looked so somber, I could almost imagine I was an Egyptian slave taking Pharaoh on a tour of the flooded Nile Delta. In fifth-grade history we had spent a lot of time worrying about the flooded river deltas of the ancient world. I would be one of those wise slaves who could read and write and dare to advise their masters. Now, for example, I would be reassuring the Pharaoh that the flood was a gift from the gods, that once it receded, the rich black earth of the delta would bring forth abundant grain. Our storehouses would be full to overflowing even as they had been when the great Joseph had been the Pharaoh's minister.

My reverie was punctured by a raucous cackling and complaining from a tiny house floating past us. "Hey!" I said. "That looks like the Lewises' chicken coop." The live occupants of the coop were squawking their unhappiness to the world as they traveled along.

The storm had been capricious. Some roofs were gone, while the next door house was not only intact but the fence and shed as well. In some yards people were already trying to collect things and clean up the debris lodged against their fences. I called out to them and waved.

They waved back and shouted greetings like, "Hey there, Wheeze. Y'all make out all right?"

And I'd answer, "Yessir. Least the house is all right." Seldom had I felt such warmth from my island neighbors. I nodded and waved and smiled. I loved everyone that morning.

I was well past and around the last house on the village street when I realized that I had lost my bearings. I should be over the marsh now. The sun was starboard, so I should have been heading straight for the Captain's house.

I made a funny squeak in my throat that startled the Captain. "What is it?" He jerked around to see what I was staring at.

I was staring at nothing. Nothing. Not a tree, not a board. Nothing was left at the spot where the Captain's house had stood the night before.

It took us both a few minutes to take it in. I circled the spot in the boat, or tried to. My pole was going down too deep for me to dare venture out too far. There was nothing to tell us if we were over the south marsh or the place where the Wallace house had stood. It was all Bay now.

At first I could do nothing but stare at the muddy water. Finally, I stole a look at the Captain. His eyes looked glazed, and he was pulling at the hair of his beard with the fingers of his left hand. He realized that I was watching him and cleared his throat.

"We used to have cows," he said. "Did you know that?"

"I heard it. Yes."

"Though the earth be removed," he was mumbling. "Though the mountains be carried into the midst of the sea."

I wanted to say how sorry I felt, but it seemed childish. I hadn't even lost my boat pole. He had lost everything.

He crossed his arms once more even more tightly across his chest. Squinting his eyes, he said in a rough voice, "Well. That's that."

As I turned the boat, I tried to read his meaning. At last I said, "Where do you want to go?"

His laugh came out something like a snort. I shipped the pole and sat down on the thwart opposite him. "I'm really sorry," I said.

He shook his head as though to shake off my concern, his eyes glittering. His hands dropped to his lap. He was wearing clothes borrowed from my father, an old blue workshirt and denim pants that were a little too tight for him. He seemed to be watching his right thumb rub the knuckles of his left hand. For all his white beard, he looked like a little boy trying not to cry. I was terrified that I might actually see tears in his eyes and so to avoid that sight more than anything else, I slipped off the thwart, crossed the narrow space between us on my knees, and put my arms around him. The rough shirt scraped my chin, and I was aware of the pressure of his knees against my stomach.

Then, suddenly, something happened. I can't explain it. I had not put my arms around another person since I was tiny. It may have been the unaccustomed closeness, I don't know. I had only meant to comfort him, but as I smelled his sweat and felt the spring of his beard against my cheek, an alarm began to clang inside my body. I went hot all over, and I could hear my heart banging to be let out of my chest. "Let go, stupid," part of me was saying, while another voice I hardly recognized was urging me to hold him tighter.

I pulled back abruptly and, putting the thwart between us, grabbed up the hard, solid pole, stood and jammed it down into the water. I didn't dare speak, much less look at him. What must he think of me? I knew that anything that made a person feel the way I felt at that moment had to be a deadly sin. But I was less concerned at the moment with God's judgment than the Captain's. Suppose he laughed? Suppose he told someone? Call or, God forbid, Caroline?

I dared a glance at his hands. The fingers of his right hand were nervously tapping his knee. I had never noticed how long his fingers were. His nails were large, rounded at the bottom and blunt and neat at the tips. He had the cleanest fingernails of any man I'd ever seen—it was the male hand in the ad reaching to put the diamond on the Pond's-caressed female hand. Why had I never noticed before how beautiful his hands were? I wanted to hold one in both of my hands and kiss the fingertips. Oh, my blessed, I was going crazy. Just looking at his hands was doing the same wild things to the secret places of my body that holding him had done.

I poled faster and tried to keep my eyes and mind totally on getting the boat back to the house. I kept banging into debris. I was sure he could tell how agitated I was. I kept waiting for him to say something. Anything.

"Well," he said. My heart went straight through my ribs at the sound. "Well." A short explosive sigh. "That's that."

*That's what?* something inside my head was crying. I rammed the boat into the back porch, leaped out, and secured the line on a post. Then, without looking back, I raced into the house up into the sanctuary of my bedroom.

"What's the matter, Wheeze?" No sanctuary. No hiding place. Caroline was there to question me as I dived onto my bed and buried my head under the pillow. "For goodness' sake, Wheeze? What on earth is going on?"

When I refused to answer, she finished dressing and went downstairs. I could hear voices, muffled as they were by the pillow. I waited for laughter. Slowly, as I calmed, I knew that the Captain would never tell my mother or my grandmother what had happened in the boat. Call and Caroline, perhaps, but not the others.

But even if he never told a soul, how was I to face him again? Just thinking of his smell, his feel, his hands, made my body go hot all over. "He's older than your grandmother," I kept saying to myself. "When your grandmother was a child, he was nearly a man already." My grandmother was sixty-three. She seemed like a hundred, but she was sixty-three. I knew because my father had been born when she was sixteen. The Captain had to be seventy or more. I was fourteen, for mercy's sake. Fourteen from seventy was fifty-six. *Fifty-six*. But then my mind would go to the curve of his perfect thumbnail, and my body would flame up like pine pitch.

I heard my father come in the front door. I jumped off the bed and tried to compose myself before our small streaky mirror. I could not pretend I had not heard him, and no one would understand any excuse for my not coming down to hear his report. I would have to be stretched out dead to remain upstairs. I ran a comb through my wild hair and banged down the steps. Everyone turned at the racket. I just caught the Captain's face. He was smiling. I'm sure I flushed all over, but no one, after that first glance, was taking notice of me. They wanted to find out what was happening at the harbor.

"The boat's all right." That was the first and only really vital thing we needed to know.

"Thank the Lord," Momma said quietly, but with a force that surprised me.

"There's plenty," Daddy went on, "that aren't so lucky. A lot of the boats not sunk are all tore up. It'll be a hard year for many." Our crab house was gone and the floats as well, but we had our boat. "The dock's tore up right smart, but folks got their homes."

"Not the Captain." Caroline said it so quickly and loudly that no one else had a chance. It didn't seem right to me that the Captain should be robbed of the chance to tell his own tragedy. He had nothing else to call his own. He should have at least had his story. But Caroline was like that, snatching other people's rights without even thinking.

"Oh, my blessed," said my father. "And here I was thinking how lucky we were. Is it clean gone?"

The Captain nodded, tightening his arms across his chest as he had earlier. "Even the fast land where she stood," he said. We were all quiet. My grandmother ceased her eternal rocking for a time. At last he said, "That whole marsh was a meadow back when I was a boy. We used to keep cows." It bothered me intensely that he should be repeating the information about the cows. I couldn't understand why it meant so much to him.

"Well," my father said. "Well." He went over to the table and sat down heavily on a chair. "You best stay with us for a while."

The Captain opened his mouth to protest, but Grandma beat him to it. "Ain't neither room for another body in this house," she said. She was right, but I wanted to kill her for saying it. Just the look on the Captain's face ripped my heart right out of my chest.

"The girls can double up for a few days, Mother," my father said. "And you can have the other bed up there."

She opened her mouth wide, but he shushed her with a look. "Louise'll help you carry up a few things now."

"I couldn't think of putting you to trouble," the Captain said. The tone was a meek, broken one I'd never heard before.

"It's no trouble," I said loudly before my grandmother could interfere again. I rushed into her room and cleared her drawers in a few swoops and carried her things upstairs on a run. Half of me was bursting with joy at the thought of having him so close, the other half was in mortal terror. I seemed to have no control over myself, I who had always prided myself on keeping the deepest parts of me hidden from view. I dumped my own things into a bag and pushed it under Caroline's bed, and then as neatly as I could, folded Grandma's things and put them in my drawers. I was shaking all over. Grandma had come thumping up the stairs. She was in a rage.

"I can't think what your daddy's up to," she said, still panting from her rush up the stairs. "Letting that heathen into our house. Into my bed. Oh, my blessed. Into my very bed."

"Stop it!" I didn't say it loudly, but I said it into her face. It may have scared her. She sniffed and backed up. She climbed up on my bed. Naturally, she assumed that I would be the one to give up a bed. "I'm resting," she said. "If anybody cares."

I slammed the drawer shut and went back downstairs. How dare she hurt his feelings? He had lost everything he had in this world. I saw his beautiful hands lovingly sanding the back of one of his old chairs. He had worked so hard on that house. We all had. He and Call and I. Not Caroline. It didn't belong to her, just to the three of us. But when I got to the living room, there was Caroline, giving him a cup of coffee, practically falling all over him while she did so. Then she got herself a cup and sat down beside him, her beautiful eyes mooning with pity.

"Would you like some coffee, Louise?"

"No," I said sharply. "Somebody's got to remember this is no picnic." There was no place to run to, no tip of the marsh where I could sit alone on a stump of driftwood and watch the water. I wanted to cry and scream and throw things. Instead, under almost perfect control, I got a broom and began savagely to attack the sand that was stuck like cement in the corner of the living room.

# 12

For the three days that the Captain lived with us, I avoided looking him in the eye. I was, instead, obsessed with his hands. They were always moving because he was intent on paying his way by helping to clean the house. By the time the water had left the yard and street, most of our downstairs, though smelling more like a crab shanty than a proper house, was at least cleaned out. We carried the stuffed chair and the couch to the front porch to let them air as best we could. Grandma's high bed had escaped the water but still smelled damp, so we put the mattress on the porch roof to sun.

The Captain treated me as though nothing had happened between us. At least I think he did. My brain was so feverish, it couldn't have judged what was natural and what was not. He called me "Sara Louise," but he had done that for some time, hadn't he? Why then did his voice speaking my name seem so heartbreakingly sweet? Tears would start in my eyes at the sound.

The second afternoon after the water was gone, he left the house for several hours. I wanted to go with him, but I couldn't trust myself. What insane thing might I do, finding myself suddenly alone with him? But after he was gone I began to worry. Would he do something foolish now that he had lost everything? I had one horrible vision of him walking straight out into the Bay until he was swallowed up. Oh, if only I could tell him that he had me—that I would never desert him. But I couldn't. I knew I couldn't.

I forgot my work and began to watch for him. Caroline and I were supposed to be putting fresh paper on the lower kitchen cabinet shelves, so that the canned goods could be brought down once more from upstairs and put away.

"Wheeze, what on earth are you doing? You've been to the front door five times in the last five minutes."

"Oh, leave me alone."

"I know what she's doing." Grandma was rocking as usual in the living room. "She's peeking around for that heathen Captain of hers."

Caroline burst into a giggle and then tried to cover it up with fake coughing. Once we were both in the kitchen and out of sight, she rolled her eyes at me and twirled her finger at her temple to indicate that she thought our grandmother was nuts.

"Yep. Yep." The voice continued from the other room. "Can't keep her eyes off that wicked man. I see it. 'Deed I do."

Caroline began to giggle in earnest then. I didn't know which one I wanted to kill more.

"I told Susan no good would come of letting that man into the house. Like letting the devil himself march in. Don't take much to bedevil a foolish girl, but still—"

My throat choked up like a swamp pond listening to her drone on and on.

"But still, they that lets the devil in cannot count themselves blameless."

I was holding a jar of string beans in my hand, and I swear, if my mother had not happened down the stairs at that moment, I might have hurled that quart at the old woman's nodding head. I don't know what my mother heard, if anything, but I suppose she sensed the hatred, the air was so thick with it. At any rate, she gently pried my grandmother from the rocker and helped her upstairs for her afternoon nap.

When she came back to the kitchen, Caroline was practically dancing across the linoleum, simply bursting to tattle. "You know what Grandma said?"

I turned on her like a red-bellied water snake. "Shut your mouth, you fool!"

Caroline blanched, then recovered. "Whosoever shall say, 'Thou fool,' shall be in danger of hell fire," she quoted piously.

"Oh, my blessed," said Momma. She didn't often resort to such a typical island expression. "Is the world so short on trouble that you two crave to make more?"

I opened my mouth but shut it again hard. *Momma, I wanted to cry out, tell me I'm not in danger of hell fire.* My childhood nightmares of damnation were rising fast, but there was no place for me to run. How could I share with my mother the wildness of my body or the desperation of my mind?

As I finished putting away the canned goods in frozen silence, my own hands caught my eye. The nails were broken and none too clean, the cuticles ragged. There was a crack of red at the edge of my index finger where a hangnail had been chewed away.

"She's lovely, she's engaged, she uses Pond's" the advertisement read, showing two exquisitely white hands with perfectly formed and manicured nails, long nails, and a diamond ring sparkling on the gracefully curved left hand. A man with strong clean hands would never look at me in love. No man would. At the moment, it seemed worse than being forsaken by God.

The five of us were already at the supper table when the Captain got back. He knocked formally at the door. I jumped and ran to the screen to open it, even though my mother had not indicated that I must. He was standing there, his blue eyes sagging with tiredness, but with a warm smile parting his lips above the beard. In his arms he was carrying the huge orange tomcat.

"Look what found me," he said, as I opened the door.

Caroline came running. "You found the old orange cat?" she cried, just as though she had had some relation to the creature. She reached out for it. I was almost glad because I figured the tom would go wild at her touch. But it didn't. The storm must have broken its spirit, for it lay purring close to Caroline's chest. "You sweet old thing," she murmured, rubbing her nose in its fur. If Caroline had been relegated to the devil, she probably would have tamed him as well. She gave the cat some of our supper fish in a bowl and set it on the kitchen floor. The cat plunged its head blissfully into the bowl.

The Captain followed Caroline to the kitchen and rinsed his hands by pouring a scant dipper of our precious fresh water over them. Then he took out a large white handkerchief and wiped them carefully before he came back into the living room to sit down at the table. I concentrated on keeping my eyes off his hands, knowing now that they were more dangerous for me than his face, but sometimes I couldn't help myself.

"Well," he said, as though someone had asked him, "I hitched a ride to Crisfield today."

Everyone looked up and mumbled, though it was evident that he was going to tell us what he had been up to whether or not we prodded.

"I went to see Trudy in the hospital," he said. "She has that perfectly good house standing there empty. It occurred to me she might not mind my staying there until I can work out something more permanent." He carefully unfolded his large cloth napkin and lay it across his lap, then looked up as though awaiting our judgment.

My grandmother was the first to speak. "I knowed it," she muttered darkly without a hint of what it was she knew.

"Hiram," my father said, "no need for you to rush away. We're proud to have you with us."

The Captain flicked a glance at Grandma, who had her mouth open, but before she got her words past her teeth, he said, "You're mighty gracious. All of you. But I could be cleaning out her place while I live there. Make it fit for her to come home to. It would be a help to both of us."

He left right after supper. He had nothing to move, so he simply walked out with the orange tom at his heels.

"Wait," called Caroline. "Wheeze and I will walk you over." She grabbed her light blue scarf and tied it loosely about her hair. She always looked like a girl in an advertisement when she wore that scarf. "Come on," she said, as I hung back.

So I went with them, my legs so heavy that I could hardly lift them. It's better, I tried to tell myself. As long as he is here I will be in danger. Even if I do not give myself away, Grandma will see to it. But, oh, my blessed, did I hate to see him go.

School opened, and I suppose that helped. With Mr. Rice gone, there was only one teacher for the whole high school. Our high school, which had about twenty students at full strength, was down now to fifteen since two had graduated the previous spring and three had gone off to war. Six of us, including Call and Caroline and me, were freshmen, five were sophomores, three juniors, and a lone senior girl, Myrna Dolman, who wore thick glasses and doggedly maintained the ambition she had harbored since first grade to become a primary schoolteacher. Our teacher, Miss Hazel Marks, used to hold Myrna up to the rest of us as an example. Apparently, the ideal pupil in Miss Hazel's eyes was one who wrote neatly and never smiled.

I wasn't smiling much that fall, but my handwriting didn't improve a whit thereby. Without Mr. Rice, all the fun of school was gone. Although he had not been our teacher when we were in the eighth grade, we had been allowed every day to join the high school for music since the chorus could not do without Caroline. Even having to acknowledge that debt could not diminish my delight in our hour of music. Now, however, there was nothing to look forward to.

On the other hand, there was a certain safety in the unrelenting boredom of each day. I heard once that there are people who commit crimes with the sole purpose of being caught and put in jail. I rather understand that mentality. There are times when prison must seem a haven.

The ninth grade was seated in the worst possible place in the classroom, at the front, and to the right, away from the window. I spent hours gazing into the disapproving face of George Washington as painted by Gilbert Stuart. This experience left me with the conclusion that our first president, besides having frizzy hair, a large red hooked nose, and apple cheeks, had a prissy, even old-ladyish mouth and a double chin. All of these would have rendered him harmless, except that he also had staring blue eyes, eyes that could read everything that was going on underneath my forehead.

"Really, Sara Louise," he seemed to say everytime he caught my eye.

My mental project that fall was a study of all the hands of the classroom. It was my current theory that hands were the most revealing part of the human body—far more significant than eyes. For example, if all you were shown of Caroline's body were her hands, you would know at once that she was an artistic person. Her fingers were as long and gracefully shaped as those on the disembodied hands in the Ponds ad. Her nails were filed in a perfect arc, just beyond the tip of her finger. If the nails are too long, you can't take the person seriously, too short, she has problems. Hers were exactly the right length to show that she was naturally gifted and had a strength of will to do something about it.

In contrast I observed that Call's hands were wide with short fingers, the nails bitten well below the quick. They were red and rough to show he worked hard, but not muscled enough to give them any dignity. Reluctantly, I concluded that they were the hands of a good-hearted but second-rate person. After all, Call had always been my best friend, but, I said to myself, one must face facts however unpleasant.

Then there were my hands. But I've already spoken of them. I decided one day in the middle of an algebraic equation to change my luckless life by changing my hands.

Using some of my precious crab money, I went to Kellam's and bought a bottle of Jergen's lotion, emery boards, orange sticks, cuticle remover, even a bottle of fingernail polish, which though colorless seemed a daring purchase.

Every morning as soon as there was enough light to see by without turning on the lamp, I'd work on my hands. It was a ritual as serious as the morning prayers of a missionary, and one which I took pains to finish well before Caroline could be expected to wake up. I carefully stashed my equipment at the very back of my bottom drawer in the bureau we shared.

Despite all my cunning, I came in one afternoon to find her generously slathering her hands with my Jergen's.

"Where did you get that?"

"From your drawer," she said innocently. "I didn't think you'd mind."

"Well, I do mind," I said. "You have no right to go poking around my drawers, stealing my stuff."

"Oh, Wheeze," she said, placidly helping herself to more lotion. "Don't be selfish."

"Okay," I screamed, "take it! Take it! Take everything I own!" I picked up the bottle and hurled it at the wall above her bed. It smashed there and fell, leaving a mixture of shattered glass and lotion to ooze down the wall after it.

"Wheeze," she said quietly, looking first at the wall and then at me, "have you gone crazy?"

I fled the house and was headed for the south marsh before I remembered it was no longer there. I stood shaking at the spot where the head of the old marsh path had begun, and through my tears, I thought I could just make out across the water a tiny tump of fast land, my old refuge now cut off from the rest of the island, orphaned and alone.

# 13

Caroline kept the Jergen's lotion incident to herself, so no one else suspected that I was going crazy. I kept the knowledge locked within myself, taking it out from time to time to admire in secret. I was quite sure I was crazy, and it was amazing that as soon as I admitted it, I became quite calm. There was nothing I could do about it. I seemed relatively harmless. After all, I hadn't thrown the lotion bottle at anyone, just the wall. There was no need to warn or disturb my parents. I could probably live out my life on the island in my own quiet, crazy way, much as Auntie Braxton always had. No one paid much attention to her, and if it hadn't been for the cats, she would have probably lived and died in our midst, mostly forgotten by the rest of us. Caroline was sure to leave the island, so the house would be mine after my grandmother and my parents died. (With only a slight chill I contemplated the death of my parents.) I could crab like a man if I chose. Crazy people who are judged to be harmless are allowed an enormous amount of freedom ordinary people are denied. Thus as long as I left everyone alone, I could do as I pleased. Thinking about myself as a crazy, independent old woman made me feel almost happy.

So since no one knew about me, the crisis demanding the family's attention centered around Auntie Braxton. She was going to be released from the hospital, which meant that the Captain would soon be homeless again.

To my father it was perfectly simple. We were the Captain's friends, we would take him in. But my grandmother was adamant. "I'll not have that heathen in my house, much less in my bed. That's what he craves. To get in my bed with me in it."

"Mother Bradshaw!" Momma was genuinely shocked. My father glanced nervously at Caroline and me. She was on the verge of laughing. I was numb with rage.

"Oh, you just think when a woman gets old no man is going to look at her that way again."

"Mother," my father said. His intenseness made her pause. "The girls—" He nodded at us.

"Oh, she's the one stirred him up," Grandma said. "She thinks he craves her, but I know. I know who he's really after. 'Deed I do."

My father turned to Caroline and me and spoke quietly. "Go to your room," he said. "She's old. You got to make allowances."

We knew we had to obey, and for once I was eager to. Caroline hung back, but I grabbed her arm and started for the staircase. I couldn't help what my parents heard, but I didn't want Caroline to hear. It was she who knew that I, not Grandma, was the crazy one.

As soon as our door was shut Caroline burst out laughing. "Can you imagine?" She shook her head. "What do you suppose is going on in that head of hers?"

"She's old," I said fiercely. "She's not responsible."

"She's not that old. She's younger than the Captain and he's not the least bit crazy." She didn't even look up to see how I was reacting. "Well," she continued in a chatty tone of voice. "At least we know he can't stay here. I can't imagine what she'd do if we invited him in again." She pulled her legs up and sat cross-legged on her bed facing toward mine. I was lying on my stomach with my head on my hands. I turned my face toward the pillow, trying not to betray myself any more than I had already. "I don't see why he can't just keep on living at Auntie Braxton's," she said.

"Because they're not married," I said. If I weren't more careful my voice alone would give me away. I cleared my throat and said as steadily as I could, "People who are not married do not live together."

She laughed. "It's not as if they'd want to do anything. My gosh, they're both too old to bother with that."

I was so hot all over at the suggestion of the Captain doing something that I could hardly breathe.

"Well?" Obviously she wanted some comment from me.

"It doesn't matter," I muttered. "It's how it looks. People don't think it looks right for people who aren't married to live together in the same house."

"Well, if people are going to be that way, they should just get married."

"What?" I swung my legs over the side of the bed and sat bolt upright.

"Sure," she said calmly, as though she were explaining a math problem. "What difference would it make? They should just get married and shut everybody up."

"Suppose he doesn't want to marry a crazy old woman?"

"He doesn't have to do anything, silly. They'd just—"

"Will you shut up about *doing* things? You have got the filthiest mind. All you can think about is *doing* things."

"Wheeze. I was talking about *not* doing anything. It would be a marriage of convenience."

"That's not the same." I'd read more than she had and knew about these things.

"Well, a marriage in name only." She grinned at me. "Like that better?"

"No. It's terrible. It's peculiar. And don't you even suggest it. It will make him think we're peculiar, too."

"It will not. He knows us better than that."

"If you mention it to him, I'll kill you."

She shrugged me off. "You will not. Honestly, Wheeze, what's got into you?"

"Nothing. It's just that he might want to marry someone else. How would it be if we made him marry Auntie Braxton and then later on, too late, he finds he's really in love with someone else?"

"What on earth have you been reading, Wheeze? In the first place, if you don't count Grandma who's really nuts, and Widow Johnson who still worships the image of her sainted captain, and Call's grandma, who's too fat, there is no one else. In the second place, we can't *make* him do anything. He's a grown man."

"Well, I think it's filthy even to suggest it."

She stood up, choosing to ignore my comment. At the door she listened for what might be going on downstairs and then, apparently satisfied that all was quiet, turned to me. "Come on," she said. "If you want to."

I jumped off my bed. "Where do you think you're going?"

"I'm going to get Call."

"Why?" I knew why.

"The three of us are going to see the Captain."

"Please stop it, Caroline. It's none of your business. You hardly even know him." I was trying to force my voice to remain calm with the result that all the unreleased shrieks were clogging my throat.

"I do know him, Wheeze. And I care about what happens to him."

"Why? Why do you always try to take over everybody else's life?" I thought I might strangle on the words.

She gave me her look which indicated that once again I had lost all sense of proportion. "Oh, Wheeze" was all she said.

It was up to Call to stop her. He would, I was sure—he and his tight little sense of propriety. But once she'd explained to him what a marriage "in name only" consisted of, he blushed and said, "Why not?"

Why not? I followed them to Auntie Braxton's house like a beaten hunting pup. Why not? Because, I yearned to say, people aren't animals. Because it is none of our business. Because, oh, my blessed, I love him and cannot bear the thought of losing him to a crazy old woman, even in name only.

The Captain was making tea and cooking potatoes for his supper when we arrived. He was uncommonly cheerful for a man who was about to be cast out on his ear for the second time straight. He offered to share his supper, but there was hardly enough for one person, so we all politely refused, insisting that he go ahead—at least, Caroline and Call were insisting. I was sitting tight-lipped on the other side of the room, but when Caroline and Call started to sit down at the kitchen table with him I dragged myself across the living room and dumped myself into the empty chair. As little as I wanted to be a part of the coming scene, I didn't want to be left out of it either.

Caroline waited until he had generously salted and peppered his potatoes, then she laid her elbows on the table and propelled herself a bit closer to it and thus to him. "We heard that Auntie Braxton is going to be back in a couple of days," she said.

"That's right," he said, taking a large bite of potato.

"We've been worried about where you're going to live."

*136*

He raised his hand to stop her talking and held it there until he had chewed and swallowed the bite. "I know what you're going to say, and I thank you, but I just can't."

See? See? I was smiling inside and out.

Caroline was not. "How do you know what I'm going to say?"

"You're going to ask me back to your house—and I'm grateful, but you know I can't come in on you again."

Caroline laughed. "Oh, I've got a much better idea than that."

All my smiles had dried up.

"Have you now, Miss Caroline?" He was spearing another piece of potato with his fork.

"I sure do." She leaned toward him with the kind of smile you see a woman give a man when she's got something more than politeness on her mind. "I'm proposing that you marry Miss Trudy Braxton."

"Marry?" he asked, putting down his fork and staring wide-eyed into her face. "You're suggesting that Trudy and I get married?"

"Don't worry," Call began earnestly, "you wouldn't have to—" at which point my bare heel slammed down on his bare toes. He stopped talking to give me a look of hurt surprise.

Caroline ignored us both. "Think of it this way," she said in her most sophisticated tone of voice. "She needs someone to take care of her and her house, and you need

a house to live in. It would be a marriage of convenience."
I noticed she didn't say "in name only." At least she
had a whiff of delicacy.

"I be damned," he said under his breath, looking from
one face to another. I pretended to study a torn cuticle
to miss his scrutiny. "You kids do beat the limit. Who
would have ever thought?"

"Once you get used to the idea, it'll make a lot of
sense to you," Caroline said. "It's not," she added quickly,
"that you couldn't find someplace else. Plenty of folks
would take you in. But no one else *needs* you. Not like
Auntie Braxton." She turned to me, then to Call for support.

By now I was biting away at the offending cuticle,
but out of the corner of my eye I could see Call nodding
his head vigorously, pumping up for a big affirmative
statement. "It'll make sense," he repeated Caroline's
theme. "It'll make plenty of sense, once you get used
to it."

"It will, will it?" The Captain was shaking his head
and grinning. "You sound like my poor old mother."
Eventually he picked up his fork and, using one side of
it, thoughtfully scraped the pepper off one of the potatoes.
"People," he said at last, no shadow of a grin remaining,
"people would say I did it for the money."

"What money?" Caroline asked.

"Nobody but you ever heard tell of no money," Call
said. "Me and Wheeze are the only ones you told. And
now Caroline."

"I wouldn't take a cent of her money, you know."

"Of course you wouldn't," Caroline said. What did she know?

"There probably isn't any," I said huffily. "We cleaned good and we never saw any."

He smiled appreciatively at me as though I had helped him. "Well," he said grinning. "It's a crazy idea." Something about the way he said it made me feel cold all over.

"You're going to think about it," Caroline said, rather than asked.

He shrugged. "Sure," he said. "No harm thinking crazy."

The next day he caught the ferry to Crisfield. He never even told us he was going. We had to get the word from Captain Billy. And he didn't come home that night or the next. We knew because we met the ferry each evening.

On the third day there he was, waving to us from the deck. My heart jumped to see him, and my body felt all over again how it was to be crushed against the rough material of his clothes, his heart beating straight through my backbone. Call and Caroline were waving back and calling out to him, but I was standing there shivering, my arms crossed, my hands hooked up under my arms and pressed against my breasts.

The boat was tied up, and now he was calling us by name. He wanted Caroline and me to see to something

*139*

in the hold and Call to come aboard and give him a hand.

Caroline, as usual, moved faster than I. "Come, look here!" she yelled. When I got to where Captain Billy's sons were handing up the freight, I saw the chair. It was huge and dark brown with a wicker seat and back and large metal wheels rimmed in hard black rubber. It took both Edgar and Richard to lift it up onto the pier. Caroline was grinning all over. "I bet he's done it," she said.

Whatever was in my look made her correct herself. "I mean," she said with an impatient sigh, "I just mean, I bet he's gone and married her."

I had no place to run to, and even if I had, it was too late. They were already emerging from the cabin. Very slowly up the ladder, first Call's head, his neck bent. Then at last the three of them, the Captain and Call carrying Auntie Braxton on a hand sling between them, she with an arm about each's shoulder. When the three of them turned around at the top of the ladder, I could see that she was wearing on her shoulder a huge chrysanthemum corsage.

"He did marry her." Caroline said it softly, but it was exploding like shrapnel inside my stomach. She ran for the wheelchair and pushed it to the end of the gangplank as proud as though she were rolling out the red carpet for royalty. Call and the Captain carefully lowered the old woman into the chair.

As he straightened up, the Captain saw me hanging

back and called to me. "Sara Louise," he said. "Come on over. I want you to shake hands with Miz Wallace here."

The old woman looked up at him when he said that, as worshipful as a repentant sinner testifying in church. When I came close, she put out her hand. Shaking her hand was like holding a bunch of twigs, but her eyes were clear and steady. I think she said, "How are you, Sara Louise?" The words were hard to decipher.

"Welcome home, Miss Trudy," I muttered. I couldn't for the life of me call her by his name.

# 14

I suppose if alcohol had been available to me that November, I would have become a drunk. As it was, the only thing I could lose my miserable self in was books. We didn't have many. I know that now. I have been to libraries on the mainland, and I know that between my home and the school there was very little. But I had all of Shakespeare and Walter Scott and Dickens and Fenimore Cooper. Every night I pulled the black air raid curtains to and read on and on, huddled close to our bedroom lamp. Can you imagine the effect of *The Last of the Mohicans* on a girl like me? It was not the selfless Cora, but Uncas and Uncas alone whom I adored. Uncas, standing ready to die before the Delaware, when an enemy warrior tears off his hunting shirt revealing the bright blue tortoise tattooed on Uncas's breast.

Oh, to have a bright blue tortoise—something that proclaimed my uniqueness to the world. But I was not the last of the Mohicans or the only of anything. I was Caroline Bradshaw's twin sister.

I cannot explain why, seeing how the storm had affected

our family's finances, I never told anyone that I had almost fifty dollars hidden away. Among the first things that had to be given up were Caroline's mainland voice and piano lessons. Even on generous scholarships, the transportation was too much for our slender resources. I suppose it is to Caroline's credit that she seldom sulked about this deprivation. She continued to practice regularly with the hope that spring would mark the end of a successful oyster season and give us the margin we needed to continue her trips to Salisbury. I might say to my own credit, as I needed every bit of credit available in those days, that I did not rejoice over Caroline's misfortune. I never hated the music. In fact, I took pride in it. But though it occurred to me to offer the money I had saved to help her continue her lessons, I was never quite able to admit that I had put it away. Besides, it was not that much money—and it was mine. I had earned it.

I went once to see the Captain after he got married. He invited the three of us—Caroline, Call, and me—to dinner. I suppose he meant it for a celebration. At any rate, he pulled out a small bottle of wine and offered us some. Call and I were shocked and refused. Caroline took some with a great deal of giggling about what would happen if anyone found out he had smuggled spirits onto our very dry little island. I was annoyed. The absence of alcohol on Rass (we never counted Momma's sherry bottle as real alcohol) was a matter of religious, not civil, law. We didn't even have a policeman, and there certainly was nothing resembling jail. If people had known about the Captain's wine, they would have simply condemned him as a heathen and prayed over him on Wednesday night. They'd been doing that ever since he arrived.

"I used to buy this kind of wine in Paris," the Captain explained. "It's been hard to get since the war." I assumed, of course, that he meant the war of the moment. Thinking back, I guess he must have meant World War I. I had a hard time keeping in mind how old he was.

With Auntie Braxton, there was no question. She sat at the head of the table in her wooden and wicker wheelchair, smiling a lopsided, almost simple smile. Her hair was white and so thin you could see the pink of her skull shining through. I suppose the strange angle of her smile was the result of the stroke, which is what had caused her to fall and break her hip. She tried to hold her glass in the tiny claw of her hand, but the Captain was there to hold it steady at her mouth. She took a sip, a bit of which dribbled down her chin. She seemed not to mind, keeping her clear, childlike eyes devoted to his face.

He patted her chin with a napkin. "My dear," he was saying. "Did I ever tell you about the time I had to drive a car across the city of Paris?"

For those of us who had lived all our lives on Rass, an automobile was almost more exotic than Paris. It irritated me that the Captain had never thought to tell, or chosen to tell Call and me about this adventure. For it was an adventure, the way the Captain told it.

Settling back in his own chair, he explained that he

had driven a car only once before in his life, and that on a country road in America, when his companion, a French seaman, suggested that they buy a car someone was hawking on the dock at Le Havre and take it into Paris. The Frenchman felt that it would be a wonderful way to pick up some girls, and the Captain, his pockets full of francs and with a week's shore leave in which to spend them, saw the car as a means to independence and excitement. He did not know until after the purchase was made that his companion had never driven a car before.

" 'But no matter,' " the Captain imitated the Frenchman. " 'Is easy.' " With difficulty, the Captain persuaded his friend to let him drive and then began their hair-raising trip from Le Havre to Paris, culminating in a cross-city ride at the busiest time of the afternoon.

"And then I came to a huge intersection—carts and automobiles and trucks coming at me from what seemed to be eight directions. If I stayed still I would be plowed under but to go forward was suicide."

"What did you do?" Call asked.

"Well—I shifted into first gear, grabbed the wheel as tight as I could with one hand, squeezed the horn with the other, jammed down on the accelerator with both feet, shut my eyes, and zoomed across."

"What?" cried Call. "Didn't you kill yourself?"

A peculiar noise, more like a chicken cackle than anything else, came from the end of the table. We all turned. Auntie Braxton was laughing. The others all began to laugh then, even Call, who knew the joke was at his expense. Everyone began to laugh but me.

"Don't you get it, Wheeze?" Call asked. "If he'd of killed himself—"

"Of course I get it, stupid. I just don't happen to think it's funny."

Caroline turned to Auntie Braxton and said, "Don't mind her." She flashed a beautiful smile at Call. "Wheeze doesn't think anything's funny."

"I do, too. You liar! All you do is lie, lie, lie."

She gave me her most pained expression. "Wheeze," she said.

"Don't call me Wheeze! I'm a person, not a disease symptom." It would have sounded more impressive if my voice hadn't cracked in the middle of the word *disease*.

Caroline laughed. She acted as though she thought I had meant to be funny. When she laughed, Call laughed. They looked at each other and hooted with pleasure as though something enormously witty had been said. I propped my forehead on my elbowed hand and steeled myself for the cackle from Auntie Braxton and the laugh, which reminded me of an exuberant tuba, that would come from the Captain. They didn't come. Instead, I felt a scratchy arm about my shoulder and a face close to my ear.

"Sara Louise," he was saying gently. "What's wrong, my dear?"

God have mercy. Didn't he know that I could stand anything except his kindness? I pushed back my chair, nearly knocking him down as I did so, and fled from that terrible house.

I never saw Auntie Braxton again, until she was laid out for her funeral. Caroline reported to me regularly how happy both the old woman and the Captain were. She and Call visited them almost every day. The Captain always asked Caroline to sing for them because "Trudy loves music so." He seemed to know a lot about this old woman that most people who had lived all their lives on the island didn't.

"She can talk, you know," Caroline said to me. "Sometimes you can't understand, but he always seems to. And whenever I sing she listens, really listens. Not with half her mind somewhere else. The Captain's right. She loves it. I never saw anyone who loved music so much, not even Momma." When she would say things like this, I'd just bury myself more deeply in my book and pretend I hadn't heard.

On the anniversary of Pearl Harbor, Auntie Braxton suffered a massive stroke and was rushed to the hospital by ferry in the middle of the night. She was dead by Christmas.

There was a funeral service for her in the church. It seemed ironic. Neither she nor the Captain had been to church for as long as anyone could remember, but the preacher in those days was young and earnest and gave her what was warmly regarded as a "right purty service." The Captain wanted our family to sit with him in the front pew, so we did, even Grandma who, I'm glad to say, behaved herself. The Captain sat between Caroline and me. While the congregation recited the Twenty-third Psalm—"Yea, though I walk through the valley of the shadow of death, I shall fear no evil; for thou art with me . . ." Caroline reached over and took his hand as though he were a small child in need of guidance and protection. He reached up with his free hand and wiped his eyes. And, sitting closer to him than I had in months, I realized with a sudden coldness how very old he was and felt the tears start in my own eyes.

Afterward my mother asked the Captain to come home and have supper with us, but when he refused, no one pressed him to change his mind. Caroline and Call and I walked him to the door of what was now his house. No one said a word along the way, and when he nodded to us at the door, we just nodded back and headed home. As it turned out, it was a good thing he had not come home with us. Grandma went on one of her worst rampages to date.

"He killed her, you know."

We all gaped in astonishment. Even from Grandma this was strong stuff.

"He wanted her house. I knew soon as he moved in there this was bound to happen."

"Mother," my father said quietly. "Don't, Mother."

"I reckon you want to know how he did it."

"Mother—"

"Poisoned her. That's how." She gazed about the table

*148*

in triumph. "Rat poison." She took a large bite of food and chewed it noisily. The rest of us had stopped eating entirely.

"Louise knows," she said in a sneaky little voice. She smiled at me. "But you wouldn't tell, would you? And I know why." She broke into a child's singsong jeer. "Nah nah nah nah *nah nah.*"

"Shut up!" It was Caroline who yelled what I could not.

"Caroline!" both our parents said.

Caroline's face was red with rage, but she pinched her lips together.

Grandma continued unperturbed. "Ever see how she looks at him?"

"Mother."

"She thinks I'm only a foolish old woman. But I know. 'Deed I do." She stared at me full in the eyes. I was too afraid to look away. "Maybe you helped. Did you, Louise? Did you help him?" Her eyes were glittering.

"Girls," my father was almost whispering. "Go to your room."

This time both of us obeyed immediately. Even behind the safety of our door we could not speak. There were no more jokes or excuses to be made for the silly, grumpy old woman we'd known from birth. The shock was so enormous that I found my own puny fear of exposure melting into a much larger darker terror that seemed to have no boundaries.

"Who knows?" the voice from *The Shadow* asks. "Who knows what evil lurks in the hearts of men?" Now we knew.

Much later, when we were getting ready for bed, Caroline said, "I've got to get away from here before she runs me nuts."

You? I thought but did not say. You? What harm can she possibly do you? You do not need to be delivered from evil. Can't you see? It's me. Me—I who am so close to being swallowed up in all that eternal darkness. But I didn't say it. I wasn't angry at her—just deadly tired.

In the light of the next day, I tried to tell myself that I had only imagined the great evil of the scene the night before. Hadn't I once tried to convince Call that the Captain was a Nazi—a U-boat delivered spy? Why, then, was I so upset over Grandma's accusation? I saw again in my mind those glittering eyes and knew it was not the same. Grandma, however, seemed to have forgotten everything. She was quite her grumpy, silly self again, and we were relieved to pretend that we, too, had forgotten.

In February, Call dropped out of school. His mother and grandmother were destitute, and my father offered to take him aboard the *Portia Sue* as an oyster culler. My father would tong, bringing up oysters with his long firwood tongs, which looked like scissors with a metal rake at the end of each shaft. He would open the rakes and drop his catch onto the wooden culling board. There

Call, his hands in heavy rubber gloves, would cull, using a culling hammer. With the hammer head he knocked off the excess shell, and with the blade at the other end he struck off the small oysters. The debris was shoved into the Bay and the good oysters forward until they could be sold to a buy boat, which would take them to market. From Monday well before dawn to Saturday night, they would be gone, sleeping all week on cramped bunks in the *Portia Sue's* tiny cabin, for the best oyster beds were up the Eastern Shore rivers, too far away for daily commuting when gas was so strictly rationed.

Of course I was jealous of Call, but I was surprised to realize how very much I missed him. All my life my father had followed the water, so it had never seemed strange to have him gone, but Call had always been around, either with me or close by. Now we only saw him at church.

Caroline made a fuss over him every Sunday. "My, Call, we sure do miss you." How could she know? Besides, it didn't seem quite ladylike to say something like that, straight out.

Each week, he seemed to grow taller and thinner, and his hands were turning more and more into the rough brown bark of a waterman's. Even his manner seemed to change. The solemnity that had always lent him, as a small child, a rather comic air, now seemed a sort of youthful dignity. You could sense his pride that he had come at last into a man's estate, the sole support of the women upon whom he had until now depended. I knew we had been growing apart since summer, but I had been able to blame that on Caroline. Now it was more painful, for the very things that made him stronger and more attractive were taking him deep into the world of men— a place I could never hope to enter.

Later that winter I began going again to see the Captain. I always went with Caroline. It wouldn't have been proper for either of us to go alone. He taught us how to play poker, which I had to be persuaded to do, but once I began it made me feel deliciously wicked. He probably owned the only deck of regular playing cards on Rass. Those were the days when good Methodists only indulged in Rook or Old Maid. We played poker for toothpicks, as though they were gold pieces. At least I did. Nothing gave me greater satisfaction than totally cleaning out my sister. It must have shown, because I can remember her saying on more than one occasion in a very annoyed tone of voice, "For goodness' sakes, Wheeze, it's only a game" as I would lick my chops and scrape all her tumbled stacks of toothpicks across the table with my arm.

One day after a particularly satisfying win, the Captain turned from me to Caroline and said, "I miss your singing now that Trudy's gone. Those were some happy times."

Caroline smiled. "I liked them too," she said.

"You're not letting down on your practicing now, are you?"

"Oh," she said. "I don't know. I guess it's all right."

"You're doing fine." I was impatient to get on to another game.

She shook her head. "I really miss my lessons," she said. "I hadn't realized how much they meant."

"Well, it's a pity," I said the way a grown-up speaks to a child to shut her up. "Times are hard."

"Yes," the Captain said. "I suppose lessons take a lot of money."

"It's not just the money," I said quickly, trying to ignore the vision of my own little hoard of bills and change. "It's the gas and all. Once you get to Crisfield, it's worth your life to get a taxi. Now if the county would just send us to boarding school like they do the Smith Island kids—"

"Oh, Wheeze, that wouldn't help. What kind of a music program could they have at that school? We beat them all to pieces in the contest last year."

"Well, we should be able to request a special school on account of special circumstances."

"They'd never pay for us to go to any school, much less a really good school," she said sadly.

"Well, they ought to." I wanted to dump the blame on the county and deal the cards. "Don't you think they should, Captain?"

"Yes, somebody should."

"But they won't," I said. "Anything dumber than a blowfish, it's a county board of education."

They laughed, and to my relief the subject was closed. It was too bad about Caroline's lessons, but she'd had a couple of good years at Salisbury. Besides, it wasn't my fault. I hadn't started the war or caused the storm.

The Captain did not come to our house. He was invited perfunctorily every Sunday, but he seemed to know that he oughtn't to come and always managed an excuse. So I was startled one afternoon a week or so later to see him hurrying up the path to our porch, his face flushed with what looked like excitement and not just the effects of his rushing. I opened the door before he had stepped up onto the porch.

"Sara Louise," he said, waving a letter in his hand as he came. "Such wonderful news!" He paused at the door. "Your father's not here, I guess." I shook my head. It was only Wednesday. "Well, please get your mother. I can't wait." He was beaming all over.

Grandma was rocking in her chair, reading or pretending to read her large leather-bound Bible. He nodded at her. "Miss Louise," he said. She didn't look up. Mother and Caroline were coming in from the kitchen.

"Why, Captain Wallace," said my mother, wiping her hands on her apron. "Sit down. Louise, Caroline, will you fix some tea for the Captain?"

"No, no," he said. "Sit down, all of you. I've got the most wonderful news. I can't wait."

We all sat down.

He put the letter on his lap and pressed out a crease with his fingertip. "There are so few opportunities for young people on this island," he began. "I'm sure, Miss Susan, a woman of your background and education must suffer to see her children deprived."

What was he leading up to? I could feel a faint stir of excitement in my breast.

"You know how much I think of you, how indebted both Trudy and I are—were—to all of you. And now—" He could hardly contain himself. He smiled at me. "I have Sara Louise to thank for the idea. You see, Trudy left a little legacy. I didn't know what to do with it, because I swore to myself I would never touch her money. There isn't a great deal, but there is enough for a good boarding school." He was beaming all over. "I've investigated. There will be enough for Caroline to go to Baltimore and continue her music. Nothing would make Trudy happier than that, I know."

I sat there as stunned as though he had thrown a rock in my face. Caroline!

Caroline jumped up and ran over and threw her arms around his neck.

"Caroline, wait," my mother was saying. Surely she would point out that she had two daughters. "Captain, this is very generous, but I can't—I'd have to talk with my husband. I couldn't—"

"We must convince him, Miss Susan. Sara Louise, tell her how you were saying to me just the other day that someone should understand that special circumstances demand special solutions—that Caroline ought to be sent to a really good school where she could continue her music. Isn't that right, Sara Louise?"

I made a funny sound in my throat that must have

resembled a "yes." The Captain took it for approval. My grandmother twisted in her chair to look at me. I looked away as fast as I could. She was smiling.

"Isn't that right, Sara Louise?" she asked in a voice intended to mimic the Captain's. "Isn't that right?"

I jumped toward the kitchen with the excuse of making tea. I could hear the Captain talking on to Mother and Caroline about the academy he knew in Baltimore with the wonderful music program. The words roared in my ears like a storm wind. I put the kettle on and laid out cups and spoons. Everything seemed so heavy I could hardly pick them up. I struggled to pry the lid from the can of tea leaves, aware that my grandmother had come in and was standing close behind me. I stiffened at the sound of her hoarse whisper.

"Romans nine thirteen," she said. " 'As it is written, Jacob have I loved, but Esau have I hated.' "

# 15

I served the tea with a smile sunk in concrete pilings.

"Thank you, Louise," my mother said.

The Captain nodded at me as he took his cup off the tray. Caroline, distracted with happiness, seemed not to see me at all. I took the cup that I had prepared for her back to the kitchen, brushing past my grandmother, who was grinning at me in the doorway. After I had put down the tray, I had to squeeze past her once more to get to the protection of my room. "Jacob have I loved—" she began, but I hurried by and up the steps as quickly as I could.

I closed the door behind me. Then, without thinking, I took off my dress and hung it up and put on my nightgown. I crawled under the covers and closed my eyes. It was half-past three in the afternoon.

I suppose I meant never to get up again, but of course I did. At suppertime my mother came in to ask if I were ill, and being too slow-witted to invent an ailment, I got up and went down to the meal. No one said much at the table. Caroline was positively glowing, my mother quiet and thoughtful, my grandmother grinning and stealing little peaks at my face.

At bedtime Caroline finally remembered that she had a sister. "Please don't mind too much, Wheeze. It means so much to me."

I just shook my head, not trusting myself to reply. Why should it matter if I minded? How would that change anything? The Captain, who I'd always believed was different, had, like everyone else, chosen her over me. Since the day we were born, twins like Jacob and Esau, the younger had ruled the older. Did anyone ever say Esau and Jacob?

"Jacob have I loved . . ." Suddenly my stomach flipped. Who was speaking? I couldn't remember the passage. Was it Isaac, the father of the twins? No, even the Bible said that Isaac had favored Esau. Rebecca, the mother, perhaps. It was her conniving that helped Jacob steal the blessing from his brother. Rebecca—I had hated her from childhood, but somehow I knew that these were not her words.

I got up, pulled the blackout curtains, and turned on the table lamp between our beds.

"Wheeze?" Caroline propped herself up on one elbow and blinked at me.

"Just have to see something." I took my Bible from our little crate bookcase, and bringing it over to the light, looked up the passage Grandma had cited. Romans, the ninth chapter and the thirteenth verse. The speaker was God.

I was shaking all over as I closed the book and got back under the covers. There was, then, no use struggling or even trying. It was God himself who hated me. And without cause. "Therefore," verse eighteen had gone on to rub it in, "hath he mercy on whom he will have mercy, and whom he will he hardeneth." God had chosen to hate me. And if my heart was hard, that was his doing as well.

My mother did not hate me. The next two days part of me watched her watching me. She wanted to speak to me, I could tell, but my heart was already beginning to harden and I avoided her.

Then Friday after supper while Caroline was practicing, she followed me up to the room.

"I need to talk with you, Louise."

I grunted rudely. She flinched but didn't correct me. "I've been giving this business a lot of thought," she said.

"What business?" I was determined to be cruel.

"The offer—the idea of Caroline going to school in Baltimore."

I watched her coldly, my right hand at my mouth.

"It—it—well, it is a wonderful chance for her, you know. A chance we, your father and I, could never hope—Louise?"

"Yes?" I bit down savagely on a hangnail and ripped it so deeply that the blood started.

"Don't do that to your finger, please."

I grabbed my hand from my mouth. What did she

want from me? My permission? My blessing?

"I-I was trying to think—we could never afford this school in Baltimore, but maybe Crisfield. We could borrow something on next year's earnings—"

"Why should Caroline go to Crisfield when she has a chance—"

"No, not Caroline, you. I thought we might send you—"

She did hate me. There. See. She was trying to get rid of me. "Crisfield!" I cried contemptuously. "Crisfield! I'd rather be chopped for crab bait!"

"Oh," she said. I had plainly confused her. "I really thought you might like—"

"Well, you were wrong!"

"Louise—"

"Momma, would you just get out and leave me alone!" If she refused, I would take it for a sign, not only that she cared about me but that God did. If she stayed in that room— She stood up, hesitating.

"Why don't you just go?"

"All right, Louise, if that's what you want." She closed the door quietly behind her.

My father came home as usual on Saturday. He and my mother spent most of Sunday afternoon at the Captain's. I don't know how the matter was settled in a way that satisfied my father's proud independence, but by the time they returned it was settled. Within two weeks we were on the dock to see Caroline off to Baltimore. She kissed us all, including the Captain and Call, who turned the color of steamed crab at her touch. She was back for summer vacation a few days before Call left for the navy, at which time she provided the island with another great show of kissing and carrying on. You couldn't doubt that she'd go far in grand opera judging by that performance.

After Call left, I gave up progging and took over the responsibility of my father's crab floats. I poled my skiff from float to float, fishing out the soft crabs and taking them to the crab house to pack them in boxes filled with eelgrass for shipping. I knew almost as much about blue crabs as a seasoned waterman. One look at a crab's swimming leg and I could tell almost to the hour when the critter was going to shed. The next to the last section is nearly transparent and if the crab is due to moult in less than a couple of weeks, the faint line of the new shell can be seen growing there beneath the present one. It's called a "white sign." Gradually, the shadow darkens. When a waterman catches a "pink sign," he knows the moulting will take place in about a week, so he gently breaks the crab's big claws to keep it from killing all its neighbors and brings it home to finish peeling in his floats. A "red sign" will begin to shed in a matter of hours and a "buster" has already begun.

Shedding its shell is a long and painful business for a big Jimmy, but for a she-crab, turning into a sook, it seemed somehow worse. I'd watch them there in the float, knowing once they shed that last time and turned into grown-up lady crabs there was nothing left for them. They hadn't even had a Jimmy make love to them. Poor sooks. They'd never take a trip down the Bay to lay their eggs before they died. The fact that there wasn't much future for the Jimmies once they were packed in eelgrass didn't bother me so much. Males, I thought, always have a chance to live no matter how short their lives, but females, ordinary, ungifted ones, just get soft and die.

At about seven I would head home for breakfast and then back to the crab house and floats until our four-thirty supper. After supper sometimes one of my parents would go back with me, but more often I went alone. I didn't really mind. It made me feel less helpless to be a girl of fifteen doing what many regarded as a man's job. When school started in the fall, I, like every boy on Rass over twelve, was simply too busy to think of enrolling. My parents objected, but I assured them that when the crab season was over, I would go and catch up with the class. Secretly, I wasn't sure that I could stand school with neither Caroline nor Call there with me, but, of course, I didn't mention this to my parents.

We had another severe storm that September. It took no lives, in the literal sense, but since it took another six to eight feet of fast land off the southern end of the island, four families whose houses were in jeopardy moved to the mainland. They were followed within the month by two other families who had never quite recovered from the storm of '42. There was plenty of war work on the mainland for both men and women at what seemed to us to be unbelievable wages. So as the water nibbled away at our land, the war nibbled away at our souls. We were lucky, though. In the Bay we could still work without fear. Fishermen off the Atlantic coast were being stalked by submarines. Some were killed, though we like the rest of the country were kept ignorant of those bodies that washed ashore just a few miles to the east of us.

Our first war deaths did not come until the fall of 1943, but then there were three at once when three island boys who had signed aboard the same ship were lost off a tiny island in the South Pacific that none of us had ever heard of before.

I did not pray anymore. I had even stopped going to church. At first I thought my parents would put up a fight when one Sunday morning I just didn't come back from the crab house in time for church. My grandmother lit into me at suppertime, but to my surprise my father quietly took my part. I was old enough, he said, to decide for myself. When she launched into prophecies of eternal damnation, he told her that God was my judge, not they. He meant it as a kindness, for how could he know that God had judged me before I was born and had cast me out before I took my first breath? I did not miss church, but sometimes I wished I might pray. I wanted, oddly enough, to pray for Call. I was so afraid he might die in some alien ocean thousands of miles from home.

If I was being prayed for mightily at Wednesday night prayer meetings, I was not told of it. I suppose people

*163*

were a little afraid of me. I must have been a strange sight, always dressed in man's work clothes, my hands as rough and weathered as the sides of the crab house where I worked.

It was the last week in November when the first northwest blow of winter sent the egg-laden sooks rushing toward Virginia and the Jimmies deep under the Chesapeake mud. My father took a few days off to shoot duck, and then put the culling board back on the *Portia Sue* and headed out for oysters. One week in school that fall had been enough for me and one week alone on the oyster beds was enough for him. We hardly discussed it. I just got up at two Monday morning, dressed as warmly as I could with a change of clothes in a gunnysack. We ate breakfast together, my mother serving us. No one said anything about my not being a man—maybe they'd forgotten.

I suppose if I were to try to stick a pin through that most elusive spot "the happiest days of my life," that strange winter on the *Portia Sue* with my father would have to be indicated. I was not happy in any way that would make sense to most people, but I was, for the first time in my life, deeply content with what life was giving me. Part of it was the discoveries—who would have believed that my father sang while tonging? My quiet, unassuming father, whose voice could hardly be heard in church, stood there in his oilskins, his rubber-gloved hands on his tongs, and sang to the oysters. It was a wonderful sound, deep and pure. He knew the

Methodist hymnbook by heart. "The crabs now, they don't crave music, but oysters," he explained shyly, "there's nothing they favor more than a purty tune." And he would serenade the oysters of Chesapeake Bay with the hymns the brothers Wesley had written to bring sinners to repentance and praise. Part of my deep contentment was due, I'm sure, to being with my father, but part, too, was that I was no longer fighting. My sister was gone, my grandmother a fleeting Sunday apparition, and God, if not dead, far removed from my concern.

It was work that did this for me. I had never had work before that sucked from me every breath, every thought, every trace of energy.

"I wish," said my father one night as we were eating our meager supper in the cabin, "I wish you could do a little studying of a night. You know, keep up your schooling."

We both glanced automatically at the kerosene lamp, which was more smell than light. "I'd be too tired," I said.

"I reckon."

It had been one of our longer conversations. Yet once again I was a member of a good team. We were averaging ten bushels of oysters a day. If it kept up, we'd have a record year. We did not compare ourselves to the skipjacks, the large sailboats with five or six crew members, that raked dredges across the bottom to harvest a heavy load of muck and trash and bottom spat along with oysters each time the mechanical winch cranked up a dredge.

We tongers stood perched on the washboards of our tiny boats, and, just as our fathers and grandfathers had before us, used our fir wood tongs, three or four times taller than our own bodies, to reach down gently to the oyster bed, feel the bottom until we came to a patch of market-sized oysters, and then closing the rakes over the catch, bringing it up to the culling board. Of course, we could not help but bring up some spat, as every oyster clings to its bed until the culling hammer forces a separation, but compared to the dredge, we left the precious bottom virtually undisturbed to provide a bed for the oysters that would be harvested by our children's children.

At first, I was only a culler, but if we found a rich bed, I'd tong as well, and then when the culling board was loaded, I'd bring in my last tong full hand over hand, dump it on the board, and cull until I'd caught up with my father.

Oysters are not the mysterious creatures that blue crabs are. You can learn about them more quickly. In a few hours, I could measure a three-inch shell with my eyes. Below three inches they have to go back. A live oyster, a good one, when it hits the culling board has a tightly closed shell. You throw away the open ones. They're dead already. I was a good oyster in those days. Not even the presence at Christmastime of a radiant, grown-up Caroline could get under my shell.

The water began to freeze in late February. I could see my culling like a trail behind us on the quickly forming ice patches. "Them slabs will grow together blessed quick," my father said. And without further discussion, he turned the boat. We stopped only long enough to sell our scanty harvest to a buy boat along the way and then headed straight for Rass. The temperature was dropping fast. By morning we were frozen in tight.

There followed two weeks of impossible weather. My father made no attempt to take the *Portia Sue* out. The first day or so I was content simply to sleep away some of the accumulated exhaustion of the winter. But the day soon came when my mother, handing me a ten o'clock cup of coffee, was suggesting mildly that I might want to take in a few days of school since the bad weather was likely to hold out for some time.

Her kindly intended words lay on me like a wet sail. I tried to appear calm, but I was caught and suffocated by the idea of returning to school. Didn't she realize that I was by now a hundred years older than anyone there, including Miss Hazel? I put my coffee down, sloshing it over the saucer onto the table. Coffee was rationed then and to waste it, inexcusable. I jumped up mumbling an apology to get a rag, but she was quicker and began sponging the brown liquid off the oilcloth before I could move, so I sat down again and let her do it.

"I worry about you, Louise," she said, mopping carefully and not looking at me. "Your father and I are grateful, indeed. I hardly know what we'd have done without you. But—" She trailed off, reluctant, I suppose, to predict what might become of me if I went on in my present manner of life. I didn't know whether to seem touched or annoyed. I was certainly irritated. If they were willing to accept the fruits of my life, they should at least spare me the burden of their guilt.

"I don't want to go back to school," I said evenly.

"But—"

"You can teach me here. You're a teacher."

"But you're so lonely."

"I'd be lonelier there. I've never belonged at that school." I was becoming, much to my own displeasure, a bit heated as I spoke. "I hate them and they hate me." There. I had overstated my case. They had never cared enough about me one way or the other to hate me. I might have from time to time served as the butt of their laughter, but I had never achieved enough status to earn their hatred.

She straightened up, sighing, and went over to the sink to wash the coffee from her cloth. "I suppose I could," she said finally. "Teach you, I mean, if Miss Hazel would lend me the books. Captain Wallace might be willing to do the math."

"Can't you do that?" Although I was no longer in love with the Captain, I did not wish to be thrown in such close company with him again—just the two of us. There was a residue of pain there.

"No," she said. "If you want to be taught at home, I'd have to ask someone else to do the math. There is no one else with the—with the time." She was always very careful not to seem to sneer at the rest of the islanders for their lack of education.

I'm not sure how my mother persuaded Miss Hazel to go along with the arrangement. The woman was very jealous of her position as the one high school teacher on Rass. Perhaps my mother argued that my irregular attendance would be disruptive, I don't know, but she came home with the books, and we began our kitchen-table school.

As for my lessons with the Captain, my mother, sensitive to the least hint of inappropriate behavior, always went with me. She would sit and knit while we had our very proper lesson, no more poker or jokes, and afterward, she and the Captain would chat across my head. He was always eager for news of Caroline, who was prospering in Baltimore as the Prophet Jeremiah claimed only the wicked do. Her letters were few and hurried but filled with details of her conquests. In turn, the Captain would share news from Call, from whom he heard nearly as often as we heard from Caroline. Between letters there was a lot of "Did I remember to tell you . . .?" or "Did I read the part about . . .?" Censorship kept Call from revealing very much about where he was or what was going on, but in what he didn't say there was enough to make my flesh crawl. The Captain, having been through naval battles before, seemed to regard the whole thing with more interest than fear.

There were only a few more days of oystering left that winter of '44. During the end of March and most of April, my father caught and salted alewives for crab bait, overhauled the motor on the *Portia Sue,* and converted it once more for crabbing. After he had caught and salted his crab bait, he did a little fishing to pass the days and even some house repairs. I crammed in as much schooling at home as possible, because once the crabs were moving, I'd be back on duty at the floats and in the crab house.

My mother heard the report of D day on our ancient radio and walked up to the crab house to tell me. She seemed more excited than I, to whom it signified only more war and killing. Besides, it was not the European war that concerned me.

# 16

Roosevelt was elected to a fourth term in the fall of 1944 without the help of Rass, which went solidly Republican as usual. And yet, when he died the following April, we shared the shock of the nation. As I heard the news, I remembered instantly the day the war had begun, Caroline and I standing hand in hand before the radio. The chill that went through me was the same coldness of that winter day in 1941 when Caroline and I had begun to grow up.

Some days after Roosevelt's death, I received the only letter I had ever gotten from Call. I was surprised to see how my hands trembled opening it, so much that I was obliged to turn my back on my mother and grandmother in the living room and go to the kitchen. It was very brief.

Dear Wheeze,
   What do you think St. Peter said to Franklin D. Roosevelt? Get it?

Call

I got it, but as was usually the case with Call's jokes, I didn't find it the least bit funny.

On April 30, the day that Hitler committed suicide, I was permitted to take the exams for graduation. I passed, much to my satisfaction, with the highest grades recorded from Rass. Not that Miss Hazel told my mother this. It was the mainland school supervisor who had graded the exams who took time to write me a note of congratulations.

When the war in Europe ended eight days later, it was overshadowed by the news from Baltimore that Caroline had been accepted by the Juilliard School of Music in New York on a full scholarship.

I looked upon this announcement with enormous relief as the end of any sacrifice I would ever be asked to make for Caroline. My parents hoped it meant that she could take a rest and come home for the summer, but she wrote at the last minute to say that she had been offered a chance to go to summer school at Peabody—an opportunity her voice teacher felt she must not pass up. I'm sure my parents were disappointed, but I was not. The war was coming quickly to a close. Soon, I felt sure, Call would be back.

Exactly what Call's return would mean to me, I could not say. I had not despised my life of the past two years, but I began to realize that it had been a time of hibernation, for I felt stirrings I had almost forgotten. Perhaps when Call came home—perhaps—well, at the very least when he came I could turn over my tasks to him. My father would be overjoyed to have a man to help him. And I—what was it I wanted? I could leave the island, if I wished. I could see the mountains. I could even take a job in Washington or Baltimore if I wanted to. If I chose to leave—there was something cold about the idea, but I shook it away.

I began to cream my hands each night, sloshing lotion all over them and sleeping in a pair of mother's worn white cotton gloves—perhaps the pair she was married in. Is that possible? It was stupid, I decided, to resign myself to being another Auntie Braxton. I was young and able, as my exams had proved. Without God, or a man, I could still conquer a small corner of the world— if I wanted to. My hands stubbornly refused to be softened. But I was determined not to give up on them this time.

Something was happening inside of Grandma, too. Suddenly that summer she decided that my mother was the woman who had stolen her husband. One afternoon I came in for supper from the crab house to find Momma trying to bake bread. I say trying, because it was a sweltering August day, which was hard enough to fight on the island, but as Momma worked, her face shining with sweat, her hair plastered against her head, Grandma was reading aloud to her, in a voice that could be heard from the street, the section in Proverbs chapter six entitled, "The mischiefs of whoredom."

" 'Can a man take fire in his bosom, and his clothes not be burned?' " my grandmother was crying out as I

*173*

came into the back door. We were used to Grandma reading the Bible to us, but the selections were not usually quite so purple. I didn't even understand what it was all about until Grandma, seeing that I had come in, said, "Tell that viperish adulteress to listen to God's Word!" And proceeded to read on into chapter seven, which details the seduction of a young man by a "strange woman."

I looked down at my poor mother, struggling to pull several loaves of bread out of the oven. It was all I could do to keep from bursting out laughing. Susan Bradshaw as a scarlet woman? It's a joke, get it? I began banging pots and pans, more to cover my giggles than to help with supper.

I looked up to see my father in the front doorway. He seemed to be waiting there, taking in the scene, before he determined what his part should be.

Grandma had not seen him. She stumbled on through the passage. " 'He goeth after her straightway, as an ox to the slaughter . . .' "

Without even removing his boots, my father walked straight across the living room to the kitchen and, pretending not to care who watched, kissed my mother on her neck where a tendril of hair had pulled loose from her bun. I blushed despite myself, but he didn't seem to notice me. He whispered something into her ear. She gave a wry grin.

" 'Till a dart strike through his liver . . .' "

"Liver?" My father mouthed the word in mock horror. Then he turned to Grandma, all teasing dropped.

"Mother. I think your supper is on the table."

She seemed a little startled by his voice, but she came to the table determined to finish the terrible passage, yet not willing to miss her supper to do so. " 'Her house is the way to hell—' " My father took the Bible gently from her hands and put it on a bookshelf above her head.

She twisted away from him like a startled child, but he took her arm and led her to the table and held her chair for her. The gesture seemed to satisfy her. She directed a triumphant look at my mother and then set herself with great energy to her food.

My father smiled across the table at my mother. She pushed her wet hair off her face and smiled back. I turned away from the sight. Don't look at each other like that. Grandma might see you. But was it only the fear of Grandma's foolish jealousies that made me want to weep?

It was, ironically, the news of Hiroshima that made our lives easier. My grandmother, catching somehow the ultimate terror that the bomb promised, turned from adultery to Armageddon. We were all admonished to fight the whore of Babylon, who was somehow identified in Grandma's mind with the pope of the Roman Catholic Church, and repeatedly warned to prepare to meet our God. A rapid scurrying through her well-worn Bible and she had located several passages to shake over our heads— telling us of the sun turning to darkness and the moon to blood. How could she know that the Day of the Lord's Anger was an almost welcome relief from her accusations of lust and adultery? There never had been any Catholics on Rass, and the end of all things was, after all, almost unimaginable, and therefore had far less power to shake one's core.

We did not take a holiday when peace was declared. There were still crabs moving in the Bay and peeling in the floats. But we ate our supper with a special delight. Toward the end of the meal, my father, turning to me as though peace had brought with it some great change to our meager fortunes, said, "Well, Louise, what will you do now?"

"Do?" Was he trying to get rid of me?

"Yes," he said. "You're a young woman now. I can't keep you on as a hand much longer."

"I don't mind," I said. "I like the water."

"I mind," he said quietly. "But I'm grateful to have had you with me."

"When Call comes back," my mother said as my heart fluttered at the words, "when Call comes back he could lend a hand and you could take a trip. Wouldn't you like that?"

A trip. I'd never been farther than Salisbury.

"You might go to New York and see Caroline." She was getting excited for me.

"Maybe," I said. I wouldn't hurt her by saying that I had no desire to see either New York or my sister. There was that old dream of mountains. Maybe I would go far enough to see a mountain.

At the tail end of the crab season Call came home. I was still at the crab house, but bored with lack of crabs to watch and pack, when suddenly the light from the doorway was blocked. The body of a large man in uniform was filling the door. There was a bass laugh that sounded vaguely familiar and a voice. "Crabby as ever, I see," it said. And then, "Get it?"

"Call!" I jumped, nearly tripping over a stack of packing boxes. He was holding out both his arms, inviting an embrace, but I was suddenly shy. "Oh, my blessed, Call. You done growed up," I said to cover my confusion.

"That's what the navy promised," he said.

I was aware of his clean, masculine smell and at the same time of the smell of salt water and crab, which was my only perfume. I wiped my hands on my pants. "Let's get out of here," I said.

He glanced around. "Can you leave?"

"Mercy, yes," I said. "I don't get more'n a boxful every couple hours."

We walked the board planking to where the skiff was tied. He handed me down into the bow as if I were a lady. Then he jumped into the stern and took up the pole. He stood there in his petty officer's uniform, tall and almost shockingly broad-shouldered and thin-hipped, his cap pushed slightly back, the sun lighting on the patch of reddish hair that showed. His eyes were bright blue and smiling down at me, and his nose had mysteriously shrunk to fit his face. I realized that I was staring at him and that he was enjoying it. I looked away, embarrassed.

He laughed. "You haven't changed, you know." If he'd

meant it as a compliment he couldn't have failed more. He himself had changed so marvelously over the past two years, surely something should have happened to me. I crossed my arms over my chest and held my hands tightly under the protection of my upper arms. They scratched like dry sand.

"Aren't you going to ask me about myself?" I had the feeling he was trying to tease me about something. I didn't like it.

"Well," I said, trying not to sound irritated. "Tell me where you been and what you saw."

"I think I seen every island in the world," he said.

"And you come home to the purtiest one of all," I answered.

"Yeah," he said, but his focus blurred for a moment. "The water's about to get her, Wheeze."

"Only a bit, to the south," I said defensively.

"Wheeze, open your eyes," he said. "In two years I've been gone, she's lost at least an acre. Another good storm—"

It wasn't right. He should have been more loyal. You don't come home after two years away and suddenly inform your mother that she's dying. I don't know what he saw in my face, but what I actually said was, "I guess you been to see the Captain already."

"No. That's why I came to get you. So we could go see him together like we used to." He shifted the pole to port side. "I guess he's gotten a lot older, huh?"

"What would you expect?"

"Crabby as ever, huh?" he repeated, trying to make it sould like a joke, to tease me out of my mood.

"He's nearly eighty," I said, and added, "I leave the skiff at the slip now. It's handier than the gut."

He nodded and steered toward the main dock.

"Miss Trudy's death took a lot out of him, didn't it?"

He was beginning to annoy me as much as he had when he was a chubby boy. "I wouldn't say that."

He squinted down at me. "Well, it did, you know. Caroline and I both remarked on it. He was never the same after that."

"Caroline," I said, so anxious to change the subject I was even willing to speak of my sister's good fortune, "Caroline is at a music school in New York City."

"Juilliard," he said. "Yes, I know."

We were at the slip now. I wanted to ask how he knew, but I was afraid to. So I jumped out and tied up the skiff, next to where my father would tie the *Portia Sue*. He shipped the pole and climbed out after me.

We walked without talking down the narrow street. When we got to our gate, I stopped. "I'd like to change my clothes before I go calling."

"Sure," he said.

I carried a pitcher of water to the washstand upstairs to bathe as best I could from the basin. Below I could hear Call's new deep voice rumbling in reply to my mother's soft alto. Every now and then a staccato interjection from my grandmother. I strained to make out the words but couldn't through the door. When I put on my Sunday dress, which I hadn't worn for almost two years, it strained across my breasts and shoulders. I could hardly bring myself to look in the mirror, first at my brown face and then at my sun-scorched hair. I dampened it with water and tried to coax it into a few waves about my forehead. I slopped hand lotion all over my hands and then on my face and legs, even my arms and elbows. It had a cheap fragrance, which I tried to fool myself would cover the essence of crab.

I nearly stumbled on the stairs. All three of them looked up. My mother smiled and would have spoken—her mouth was pursed with some encouraging comment—but I glared her into silence.

Call stood up. "Now," he said. "That is an improvement." It was not the encouragement needed at that moment.

My grandmother half rose from the rocker, "Where you going with that man, Louise? Huh? Where you going?" I grabbed Call's elbow and shoved him toward the door.

He was laughing silently as the voice followed us out onto the porch. He shook his head at me, as though we were sharing a joke. "I see she hasn't changed, either," he said at the gate.

"She's worse. The things she calls Momma . . ."

"Well," he said, "you mustn't take it to heart," dismissing the years of aggravation with a flick of his hand.

The Captain greeted me with courtesy, but he was overjoyed to see Call. He embraced him almost as though Call were a woman. Men on Rass did not hug each other, but Call returned the embrace without any sign of embarrassment. I could see tears glittering in the old man's eyes when at last he pulled away.

"Well," he said. "My. Well."

"It's good to be back," Call said, covering the old man's discomposure.

"I've saved a tin of milk," the Captain said. "Saved against this day." He started for the kitchen. "Let me just put on the kettle."

"Do you want some help?" I asked, half-rising.

"Oh, no, no. You sit right there and entertain our conquering hero." Call laughed. "You heard about Caroline?" the Captain called.

"Yessir, and she's everlastingly grateful to you."

"It was Trudy's money. Nothing would have made Trudy happier than to know she helped Caroline go on with her music." There was a pause. Then he stuck his head in the doorway. "You been keeping up with each other lately?"

"I saw her," Call said. "I stopped in New York on the way home."

My body understood long before my mind did. First it chilled, then it began to burn, with my heart thumping overtime in alarm.

They were exchanging inanities about the size and terrors of New York, but my body knew that the conversation was about something far more threatening. The Captain brought in the black tea and the tin of milk, which he had neatly poked open with an ice pick—two holes on one side, one on the other.

"I'm guessing you can take the tea now," he said, handing a chipped cup and saucer, first to me, and then to Call. "Not just the milk."

"That's right," Call said grinning. "They made me a man."

"So." The Captain seated himself carefully, and compensating for the tremor in his hands, slowly lifted his own cup to his mouth and took a long sip. "So. What's Miss Caroline got to say for herself these days?"

Call's face flamed in pleasure. It was the question he had been bursting to answer. "She—she said, 'Yes.' "

I knew, of course, what he meant. There was no need to press him to explain. But something compelled me to hear my own doom spelled out. " 'Yes' to what?" I asked.

"Let's just say," he was eyeing the Captain slyly. "Let's just say she answered her Call."

The Captain gave a great tuba laugh, sloshing his tea out onto his lap. He patted away at it with his free hand, still laughing.

"Get it?" Call turned to me. "She answered—"

"I guess it took you most of the train trip from New York to work that one out." Call stopped smiling. I suppose it was the bitterness in my tone. "She's only seventeen," I said, trying to justify myself.

*182*

"Eighteen in January." As though I needed to be told. "My mother was married at fifteen."

"So was my grandmother," I said nastily. "Great advertisement for early marriage, wouldn't you say?"

"Sara Louise." The Captain was almost whispering. I stood up so quickly that the room seemed to spin. I grabbed the arm of the chair, rattling the tea cup all around the saucer. I staggered to the kitchen and put it down, then came back into the room. I knew I was making a scene, but I didn't know how to escape it. How unjust to throw everything at me at once.

"Well," I said, "I guess you won't be culling for Daddy this winter."

"No," he said. "I've got a part-time job lined up in New York as soon as I'm discharged. With that and my GI Bill, I can go to school there."

"What about Caroline's school? Have you thought of her? What she'll have to give up to marry you?"

"Oh, my blessed," he said. "It's not like that. I'd never let her give up her chance to sing. She'll go ahead with all her plans. I wouldn't ever hold her back. Surely you know that, Wheeze." He was asking me humbly to understand. "I can help her. I can—"

"Give her a safe harbor," the Captain offered quietly.

"Caroline?" I snorted.

"She's alone in that world, Wheeze. She needs me."

You? I was thinking. You, Call? I said nothing, but he heard me anyhow.

"I guess," he was saying softly, "I guess it's hard for

you to think someone like Caroline might favor me."
He gave a short laugh. "You never did think I was much
to brag about, now did you?"

Oh, God. If I had believed in God I could have cursed
him and died. As it was, I extricated myself as quickly
as I could from them and made my way, not home, but
back to the crab house where I proceeded to ruin my
only decent dress fishing the floats.

# 17

Call was not discharged as soon as he had hoped, so it was the next year, the day before Christmas 1946, that he and Caroline were married. My parents went up for the ceremony in the Juilliard chapel, which, I gathered, was stark in word and dress, but rich in Bach and Mozart, thanks to Caroline's school friends.

I stayed home with Grandma. It was my choice. My parents spoke of getting a neighbor to stay with her, and each offered to remain and let me go instead. But I felt they were greatly relieved by my insistence. The way Grandma was or could be, we dreaded the thought of asking someone outside the family to endure even a few days alone with her. Besides, as they said later, it was the first trip of any length that the two of them had ever taken together. They left, with apologies to me, on the twenty-second. Perhaps my soul, now as calloused as my hands, could have borne such a wedding. I don't know. I was glad not to be put to the test.

Grandma was like a child whose parents have gone off and left her without making plain where they have gone or when they could be expected to return. "Where's Truitt?"

"He's gone to New York for Caroline's wedding, Grandma."

She looked blank, as though she were not quite sure who Caroline was but felt she shouldn't ask. She rocked quietly for a few minutes, picking a thread on her knitted shawl. "Where's Susan?"

"She went with Daddy to New York."

"New York?"

"For Caroline's wedding."

"I know," she snapped. "Why did they leave me?"

"Because you hate to ride the ferry, Grandma, especially in the wintertime."

"I hate the water." She dully observed the worn-out ritual. Suddenly she stopped rocking and cocked her head at me. "Why are you here?"

"You hate to be alone, Grandma."

"Humph." She sniffed and pulled the shawl tight about her shoulders. "I don't need to be watched like one of your old peelers."

The image of Grandma as an old sook caught in my mind. *Get it?* I wanted to say to somebody.

"What you cutting on?"

"Oh, just whittling." It was in fact a branch of almost straight driftwood, which I had decided would make a good cane for Grandma. I had spread out part of the Sunday *Sun* and was trimming the wood down before sanding it.

"I ain't seen that old heathen about," she said. "I guess he's dead like everybody else."

"No. Captain Wallace is just fine."

"He don't ever come around here." She sighed. "Too snobby to pay attention to the likes of me, I reckon."

I stopped whittling. "I thought you didn't like him, Grandma."

"No, I don't favor him. He thinks he's the cat's pajamas. Too good for the daughter of a man who don't even own his own boat."

"What are you talking about, Grandma?"

"He never paid me no mind. Old heathen."

I felt as though I had stumbled off a narrow path right into a marsh. "Grandma, do you mean *now?*"

"You was always a ignorant child. I wouldn't have him on a silver plate *now.* I mean *then.*"

"Grandma," I was still trying to feel my way, "you were a lot younger than the Captain."

She flashed her eyes at me. "I would've growed," she said like a stubborn child. "He run off and left before I had a chance." Then she put her head down on her gnarled hands and began to cry. "I turned out purty," she said between sobs. "By the time I was thirteen I was the purtiest little thing on the island, but he was already gone. I waited for two more years before I married William, but he never come back 'til now." She wiped her eyes on her shawl and leaned her head back watching a spot on the ceiling. "He was too old for me then, and now it 'pears he's too young. After scatter-headed children like you and Caroline. Oh, my blessed, what a cruel man."

What was I to do? For all the pain she had caused me, to see her like that, still haunted by a childish passion, made me want to put my arm around her and comfort her. But she had turned on me so often, I was afraid to touch her. I tried with words.

"I think he'd be glad to be your friend," I said. "He's all alone now." At least she seemed to be listening to me. "Call and Caroline and I used to go to see him. But—they are gone now, and it isn't proper for me to go down alone."

She raised her head. For a moment I was sure she was about to hurl one of her biblical curses at me, but she didn't. She just eased back and murmured something like "not proper."

So I took another bold step. "We could ask him for Christmas dinner," I said. "There'll be just the two of us. Wouldn't it seem more like Christmas to have company?"

"Would he be good?"

I wasn't sure what she meant by "good," but I said I was sure he would be.

"Can't have no yelling," she explained. "You can't have a body yelling at you when you're trying to eat."

"No," I said. "You can't have that." And added, "I'll tell him you said so."

She smiled slyly. "Yes," she said. "If he wants to come calling here, he better be good."

I wonder if I shall ever feel as old again as I did that

Christmas. My grandmother with her charm, gaudy and perishable as dime-store jewelry—whoever had a more exasperating child to contend with? The Captain responded with the dignity of a young teen who is being pestered by a child whose parents he is determined to impress. While I was the aged parent, weary of the tiresome antics of the one and the studied patience of the other.

But I shouldn't complain. Our dinner went remarkably well. I had a chicken—a great treat for us in those days—stuffed with oysters, boiled potatoes, corn pudding, some of Momma's canned beans, rolls, and a hot peach cobbler.

Grandma picked the oysters out of the stuffing and pushed them to the side of her plate. "You know I don't favor oysters," she said pouting at me.

"Oh, Miss Louise," said the Captain. "Try them with a bite of the white meat. They're delicious."

"It's all right," I said quickly. "Just leave them. Doesn't matter."

"I don't want them on my plate."

I jumped up and took her plate to the kitchen, scraped off the offending oysters, and brought it back, smiling as broadly as I could manage.

"How's that now?" I asked, sitting down.

"I don't favor corn pudding neither," she said. I hesitated, not sure if I should take the pudding off her plate or not. "But I'll eat it." She flashed a proud smile at the Captain. "A lot of times I eat things I don't really favor," she told him.

"Good," he said. "Good for you." He was beginning to relax a bit and enjoy his own dinner.

"Old Trudy died," she said after a while. Neither the Captain nor I replied to this. "Everybody dies," she said sadly.

"Yes, they do," he answered.

"I fear the water will get my coffin," she said. "I hate the water."

"You got some good years to go yet, Miss Louise."

She grinned at him saucily. "Longer than you anyway. I guess you wish now you was young as me, eh, Hiram Wallace?"

He put down his fork and patted his napkin to his beard. "Well—"

"One time I was too young and too poor for you to pay me any mind."

"I was a foolish young man, but that's a long time ago, now, Miss Louise."

"You had no cause to leave, you know. There was ones who would have had you, coward or no."

"Grandma? How about some more chicken?"

She was not to be distracted. "There's others who's not favored lightning, you know."

"Lightning?"

"'Course, chopping down your daddy's mast—" She tittered.

"That's just an old story, Grandma. The Captain never—"

"But I did," he said. "Took me twenty minutes to

190

chop it down and fifty years to set it back." He smiled at me, taking another roll from the tray I was offering. "It's so good to be old," he said. "Youth is a mortal wound."

"What's he talking about, Wheeze? I don't know what he's saying."

He put down his roll and reached over and took her gnarled hand, stroking the back of it with his thumb. "I'm trying to tell the child something only you and I can understand. How good it is to be old."

I watched her face go from being startled by his gesture to being pleased that he had somehow joined her side against me. Then she seemed to remember. She drew back her hand. "We'll die," she said.

"Yes," he said. "But we'll be ready. The young ones never are."

She would not leave us that day, even for her nap, but rocking in her chair after dinner, she fell asleep, her mouth slightly open, her head rolled awkwardly against her right shoulder.

I came in from washing the dishes to find the two of them in silence, she asleep and he watching her. "I thank you," I said. He looked up at me. "This would have been a lonesome day without you."

"I thank you," he said. And then, "It's hard for you, isn't it?"

I sat down on the couch near his chair. There was no need to pretend, I knew. "I had hoped when Call came home—"

He shook his head. "Sara Louise. You were never meant to be a woman on this island. A man, perhaps. Never a woman."

"I don't even know if I wanted to marry him," I said. "But I wanted something." I looked down at my hands. "I know I have no place here. But there's no escape."

"Pish."

"What?" I couldn't believe I'd heard him correctly.

"Pish. Rubbish. You can do anything you want to. I've known that from the first day I met you—at the other end of my periscope."

"But—"

"What is it you really want to do?"

I was totally blank. What was it I really wanted to do?

"Don't know?" It was almost a taunt. I was fidgeting under his gaze. "Your sister knew what she wanted, so when the chance came, she could take it."

I opened my mouth, but he waved me quiet. "You, Sara Louise. Don't tell me no one ever gave you a chance. You don't need anything given to you. You can make your own chances. But first you have to know what you're after, my dear." His tone was softening.

"When I was younger I wanted to go to boarding school in Crisfield—"

"Too late for that now."

"I—this sounds silly—but I would like to see the mountains."

"That's easy enough. Couple of hundred miles west is all." He waited, expecting more.

"I might—" the ambition began to form along with the sentence. "I want to be a doctor."

"So?" He was leaning forward, staring warmly at me. "So what's to stop you?"

Any answer would have been an excuse to him, the one I gave, most of all. "I can't leave them," I said, knowing he wouldn't believe me.

# 18

Two days after my parents' return from New York, I came the closest I ever came to fighting with my mother. Children raised as I was did not fight with their parents. There was even a commandment to take care of it, number five: "The only one of the Ten Commandments with a promise attached." I can still hear the preacher's twang as he lectured us. "Honor thy father and thy mother, that thy days may be long upon the land which the Lord thy God giveth thee."

When my mother got off the ferry, there was something different about her. At first I thought it was the hat. Caroline had bought her a new hat for the wedding, and she had worn it on the trip home. It was pale blue felt with a wide rolled-up brim that went out from her face at a slant. There was charm, both in the color, which exactly matched her eyes, and in the angle, which made her face look dramatic instead of simply thin. I could tell by looking at her how beautiful the hat made her feel. She was radiant. My father beside her looked proud and a little awkward in his Sunday suit. The sleeves had never been quite long enough to cover his brown wrists, and his huge weathered hands stuck out rather like the pinchers on a number one Jimmy.

They seemed glad enough to see me, but I could tell that they weren't quite ready to let go of their time together. I carried one of the suitcases and lagged behind them in the narrow street. Occasionally, one or the other of them would turn and smile at me to say something like "Everything go all right?" but they walked closer together than they needed to, touching each other as they walked every few steps and then smiling into each other's faces. My teeth rattled, I was shivering so.

Grandma was standing in the doorway waiting for us. They patted her as they went in. She seemed to sense at once whatever it was going on between them. Without a word of greeting she rushed to her chair, snatched up her Bible, and pushed the pages roughly and impatiently until she found the place she wanted.

" 'My son, give me thine heart, and let thine eyes observe my ways. For a whore is a deep ditch; and a strange woman is a narrow pit.' "

Momma's whole body shrank from the word "whore," but she recovered herself and went over to the umbrella stand where she carefully took the pins out of her hat. Her eyes steadily on her own image, she took off the hat, replaced the pins in the brim, and then patted her hair down with one hand. "There," she said, and taking one last look, turned from the mirror toward us. I was furious. Why didn't she scream? Grandma had no right—

"We'd best change," my father said and started up the stairs with the suitcases. She nodded and followed him up.

Grandma stood there, panting with frustration, all those words that she was bursting to say and no one but me to hear. Apparently, I would have to do. She glared at me and then began reading to herself as hastily as she could, searching, I suppose, for something she could fire at me and thus release her coiled spring.

"Here, Grandma," I said, my voice dripping molasses. "Let me help you." I'd been preparing for this moment for months. "Read it, here. Proverbs twenty-five, twenty-four." I flipped over and stuck my finger on the verse that I had memorized gleefully. " 'It is better,' " I recited piously, " 'to live in a corner of the housetop than in a house with a contentious woman.' " I smiled as sweetly as ever I knew how.

She snatched her Bible out from under my hand, slammed it shut, and holding it in both hands whacked me on the side of the head so hard that it was all I could do to keep from crying out. But at the same time I was glad that she hit me. Even while she stood there grinning at my surprise and pain, I felt a kind of satisfaction. I was deserving of punishment. I knew that. Even if I was not quite clear what I deserved it for.

But the incident didn't help Grandma. She was at my mother all the time now, following three steps behind her as she swept or cleaned, carrying the black Bible and reading and reciting to her. My father, meanwhile, seemed less than anxious to get the *Portia Sue* out on the Bay again. He spent several precious days happily tinkering with his engine, wasting lovely, almost warm, oyster weather. Couldn't he see how badly I needed to get away from that awful house? Couldn't he see that being cooped up with Grandma when she was going full throttle was driving me to the brink of insanity?

And my mother didn't help. Every waking moment was poisoned by Grandma's hatred, but my mother, head slightly bent as though heading into the wind, kept her silent course around the house with only a murmured word or two when a reply seemed necessary and could be given without risking further rancor. It would have been easier for me if she'd screamed or wept, but she didn't.

She did, however, propose that we wash the windows, a job we had done quite thoroughly at the end of the crab season. As I opened my mouth to protest, I saw her face and realized how much she needed to be outside the house, though she would never say so. I fetched the buckets of warm water and ammonia. We scrubbed and wiped in blessed silence for nearly a half hour. Through the porch window where I was working, I could see Grandma, poking anxiously about the living room. She wouldn't dare step out because of her arthritis, but it was clear that our peculiar behavior was disturbing to her. Watching her pinched face, I went through a spectrum of emotions. First a kind of perverted pride that my meek mother had bested the old woman, if only for an afternoon. Then a sort of nagging guilt that I should take such pleasure in my grandmother's discomfort. I could not forget that only the week before I had been touched by her childish griefs. This shifted to a growing anger that my clever, gentle, beautiful mother should be so unjustly persecuted, which was transformed, heaven knows how, into a fury against my mother for allowing herself to be so treated.

I moved my bucket and chair to the side of the house where she was standing on her chair, scrubbing and humming happily. "I don't understand it!" The words burst out unplanned.

"What, Louise?"

"You were smart. You went to college. You were good-looking. Why did you ever come here?"

She had a way of never seeming surprised by her children's questions. She smiled, not at me, but at some memory within herself. "Oh, I don't know," she said. "I was a bit of a romantic. I wanted to get away from what I thought of as a very conventional small town and try my wings." She laughed. "My first idea was to go to France."

"France?" I might not surprise her, but she could certainly surprise me.

"Paris, to be precise." She shook her head as she wrung out her rag over the bucket beside her on the chair. "It just shows how conventional I was. Everyone in my college generation wanted to go to Paris and write a novel."

"You wanted to go to Paris and write a novel?"

"Poetry, actually. I had published a few little things in college."

"You published poetry?"

"It's not as grand as it sounds. I promise you. Anyhow, my father wouldn't consider Paris. I didn't have the heart to defy him. My mother had just died." She added the last as though it explained her renunciation of Paris.

"You came to Rass instead of going to *Paris?*"

"It seemed romantic—" She began scrubbing again as she talked. "An isolated island in need of a schoolteacher. I felt—" She was laughing at herself. "I felt like one of the pioneer women, coming here. Besides—" She turned and looked at me, smiling at my incomprehension. "I had some notion that I would find myself here, as a poet, of course, but it wasn't just that."

The anger was returning. There was no good reason for me to be angry but my body was filled with it, the way it used to be when Caroline was home. "And did you find yourself here on this little island?" The question was coated with sarcasm.

She chose to ignore my tone. "I found very quickly," she scratched at something with her fingernail as she spoke, "I found there was nothing much to find."

I exploded. It was as though she had directly insulted me by speaking so slightingly of herself. "Why? Why did you throw yourself away?" I flung my rag into the bucket, sloshing gray ammonia water all over my ankles. Then I jumped from my chair and wrung out the rag as though it were someone's neck. "You had every chance in the world and you threw it all away for that—" and I jabbed my wrenched rag toward Grandma's face watching us petulantly from behind the glass.

"Please, Louise."

I turned so that I would not see either of their faces, a sob rising from deep inside me. I pounded on the side of the house to stop the tears, smashing out each syllable. "God in heaven, what a stupid waste."

She climbed off her chair and came over to me where I stood, leaning against the clapboard, shaking with tears of anger, grief—who knew what or for whom? She came round where I could see her, her arms halfway stretched out as though she would have liked to embrace me but dared not. I jumped aside. Did I think her touch would taint me? Somehow infect me with the weakness I perceived in her? "You could have done anything, been anything you wanted."

"But I am what I wanted to be," she said, letting her arms fall to her sides. "I chose. No one made me become what I am."

"That's sickening," I said.

"I'm not ashamed of what I have made of my life."

"Well, just don't try to make me like you are," I said.

She smiled. "I can promise you I won't."

"I'm not going to rot here like Grandma. I'm going to get off this island and do something." I waited for her to stop me, but she just stood there. "You're not going to stop me, either."

"I wouldn't stop you," she said. "I didn't stop Caroline, and I certainly won't stop you."

"Oh, Caroline. Caroline's different. Everything's always been for Caroline. Caroline the delicate, the gifted, the beautiful. Of course, we must all sacrifice our lives to give her greatness to the world!"

Did I see her flinch, ever so slightly? "What do you want us to do for you, Louise?"

"Let me go. Let me leave!"

"Of course you may leave. You never said before you wanted to leave."

And, oh, my blessed, she was right. All my dreams of leaving, but beneath them I was afraid to go. I had clung to them, to Rass, yes, even to my grandmother, afraid that if I loosened my fingers an iota, I would find myself once more cold and clean in a forgotten basket.

"I chose the island," she said. "I chose to leave my own people and build a life for myself somewhere else. I certainly wouldn't deny you that same choice. But," and her eyes held me if her arms did not, "oh, Louise, we will miss you, your father and I."

I wanted so to believe her. "Will you really?" I asked. "As much as you miss Caroline?"

"More," she said, reaching up and ever so lightly smoothing my hair with her fingertips.

I did not press her to explain. I was too grateful for that one word that allowed me at last to leave the island and begin to build myself as a soul, separate from the long, long shadow of my twin.

# 19

Every spring a waterman starts out with brand clean crab pots. Crabs are particular critters, and they won't step into your little wire house if your bait is rank or your wire rusty and clogged with sea growth. But throw down a nice shiny pot with a bait box full of alewife that's just barely short of fresh, and they'll come swimming in the downstairs door, and before they know it they're snug in the upstairs and on the way to market.

That's the way I started out that spring. Shiny as a new crab pot, all set to capture the world. At my mother's suggestion, I wrote the county supervisor who had graded my high school exams, and he was happy to recommend me for a scholarship at the University of Maryland. My first thought was to stay home and help with the crabs until September. My father brushed the offer aside. I think my parents were afraid that if I didn't go at once, I'd lose my nerve. I wasn't worried about that, but I was eager to go, so I took off for College Park in April and got a room near the campus, waiting tables to pay my way until the summer session when I was able to move into the dormitory and begin my studies.

One day in the spring of my sophomore year, I found a note in my box directing me to see my advisor. It was a crisp, blue day that made me feel as I walked across the quadrangle that out near Rass the crabs were beginning to move. The air was fresh with the smell of new growth, and I went into that building and up to that office humming with the pure joy of being alive. I had forgotten that life, like a crab pot, catches a lot of trash you haven't bargained for.

"Miss Bradshaw." He cleaned his pipe, knocking it about the ashtray until I was ready to offer to clean it for him. "Miss Bradshaw. So."

He coughed and then elaborately refilled and lit his pipe.

"Yes, sir?"

He took a puff before going on. "I see you are doing well in your courses."

"Yes, sir."

"I suppose you are considering medicine."

"Yes, sir. That's why I'm in premed."

"I see." He puffed and sucked a bit. "You're serious about this? I would think that a good-looking young woman like you—"

"Yes, sir, I'm sure."

"Have you thought about nursing?"

"No, sir. I want to be a doctor."

When he saw how determined I was, he stopped fooling with his pipe. He wished it were different, he said, but with all the returning veterans, the chances of a girl, "even a bright girl like you" getting into medical school were practically nonexistent. He urged me to switch to nursing at the end of the semester.

A sea nettle hitting me in the face couldn't have stung worse. For a few days I was desolate, but then I decided that if you can't catch crabs where you are, you move your pots. I transferred to the University of Kentucky and into the nursing school, which had a good course in midwifery. I would become a nurse-midwife, spend a few years in the mountains where doctors were scarce, and then use my experience to persuade the government to send me to medical school on a public health scholarship.

When I was about ready to graduate, a list of Appalachian communities asking for nurse-midwives was posted on the student bulletin board. From the neat, double-spaced list, the name "Truitt" jumped out at me. When I was told the village was in a valley completely surrounded by mountains, the nearest hospital a two-hour drive over terrible roads, I was delighted. It seemed exactly the place for me to work for two or three years, see all the mountains I ever wanted to see, and then, armed with a bit of money and a lot of experience, to batter my way into medical school.

A mountain-locked valley is more like an island than anything else I know. Our water is the Appalachian wilderness, our boats, the army surplus jeeps we count on to navigate our washboard roads and the hairpin curves across the mountains. There are a few trucks, freely loaned about in good weather to any valley farmer who must take his pigs or calves to market. The rest of us seldom leave the valley.

The school is larger than the one on Rass, not only because there are twice the number of families, but because people here, even more than islanders, tend to count their wealth in children. There is a one-room Presbyterian Church, built of native stone, to which a preacher comes every three weeks when the road is passable. And every fourth Sunday, God and the weather willing, a Catholic priest says mass in the schoolhouse. There are no mines open in our pocket of western Virginia now, but the Polish and Lithuanian miners who were brought down from Pennsylvania two generations ago stayed and turned their hands to digging fields and cutting pastures out of the hillsides. They are still considered outsiders by the tough Scotch-Irish who have farmed the rocks of the valley floor for nearly two hundred years.

The most pressing health problem is one never encountered on Rass. On Saturday night, five or six of the valley men get blind drunk and beat their wives and children. In the Protestant homes I am told it is a Catholic problem, and in the Catholic homes, a Protestant. The truth, of course, is that the ailment crosses denominational lines. Perhaps it is the fault of the mountains, glowering above us, delaying sunrise and hastening the night. They are as awesome and beautiful as the open water, but the valley people do not seem to notice. Nor are they grateful for the game and timber that the mountains so generously provide. Most of them only see the ungiving soil from which a man must wrestle his subsistence and the barriers that shut him out from the world. These men struggle against their mountains. On Rass men followed the water. There is a difference.

Although the valley people are slow to accept outsiders, they did not hesitate to come to me. They needed my skill.

"Nurse?" An old ruddy-faced farmer was at my door in the middle of the night. "Nurse, would you be kind enough to see to my Betsy? She's having a bad go of it."

I dressed and went with him to his farm to deliver what I thought was a baby. To my amazement, he drove straight past the house to the barn. Betsy was his cow, but neither of us would have been prouder of that outsized calf had it been a child.

I came to wonder if every disease of man and beast had simply waited for my arrival to invade the valley. My little house, which was also the clinic, was usually jammed, and often there was a jeep waiting at the door to take me to examine a child or a cow or a woman in labor.

The first time I saw Joseph Wojtkiewicz (what my grandmother would have done to that name!), the first time I saw him to know who he was, that is, he arrived in his jeep late one night to ask me to come and treat his son, Stephen. Like most of the valley men, he seemed ill at ease with me, his only conversation during the ride was about the boy who had a severe earache and a fever of 105, which had made his father afraid to bring him out in the cold night air to the clinic.

The Wojtkiewicz house was a neatly built log cabin with four small rooms. There were three children, the six-year-old patient, and his two sisters, Mary and Anna, who were eight and five. The mother had been dead for several years.

The county had sent me an assortment of drugs including a little penicillin, so I was able to give the child a shot. Then an alcohol rubdown to bring the fever down a bit until the drug had time to do its work, a little warm oil to soothe the ear, a word or two to commend bravery, and I was ready to go.

I had repacked my bag and was heading for the door when I realized the boy's father had made coffee for me. It seemed rude not to drink it, so I sat opposite him at his kitchen table, my face set in my most professional smile, mouthing reassurance and unnecessary directions for the child's care.

I became increasingly aware that the man was staring at me, not impolitely, but as though he were studying an unknown specimen. At last he said, "Where do you come from?"

"The University of Kentucky," I said. I prided myself on never letting remarks made by patients or their families surprise me.

"No, no," he said. "Not school. Where do you really come from?"

I began to tell him quite matter-of-factly about Rass, where it was, what it looked like, slipping into a picture of how it had been. I hadn't returned to the island since entering nursing school except for two funerals, my grandmother's and the Captain's. Now as I described the marsh as it was when I was a child, I could almost feel the wind on my arms and hear the geese baying like a pack of hounds as they flew over. No one on the mainland had ever invited me to talk about home before, and the longer I talked, the more I wanted to talk, churning with happiness and homesickness at the same time.

The little girls had come into the kitchen and were leaning on either side of their father's chair, listening with the same dark-eyed intensity. Joseph put an arm around each of them, absently stroking the black curls of Anna who was on his right.

At last I stopped, a little shy for having talked so much. I even apologized.

"No, no," he said. "I asked because I wanted to know. I knew there was something different about you. I kept wondering ever since you came. Why would a woman like you, who could have anything she wanted, come to a place like this? Now I understand." He left off stroking his daughter's hair and leaned forward, his big hands open as though he needed their help to explain his meaning. "God in heaven,"—I thought at first it was an oath, it had been so long since I'd heard the expression used in any other way—"God in heaven's been raising you for this valley from the day you were born."

I was furious. He didn't know anything about me or the day I was born or he'd never say such a foolish thing, sitting there so piously at his kitchen table, sounding for all the world like a Methodist preacher.

But then, oh, my blessed, he smiled. I guess from that moment I knew I was going to marry Joseph Wojtkiewicz—God, pope, three motherless children, unspellable surname and all. For when he smiled, he looked like the kind of man who would sing to the oysters.

# 20

It is far simpler to be married to a Catholic than anyone from my Methodist past would believe. I am quite willing for the children, his, of course, but also ours as they come along, to be raised in the Catholic faith. The priest frets about me when we meet, but he's only around once a month, and Joseph himself has never suggested that I ought to turn Catholic or even religious. My parents showed their approval by making the long trip from Rass to attend our schoolhouse wedding. I will always be glad that my father and Joseph met each other that once, because this year, on the second of October, my father went to sleep in his chair after a day of crabbing and never woke up.

Caroline called me from New York. I couldn't remember ever having heard her cry aloud before, and there she was weeping for the benefit of the entire Truitt village party line. I was unreasonably irritated. She and Call were going down at once and would stay through the funeral. It seemed wrong that she should be able to go and not me. I was the child who had fished his crab floats and culled his oysters, but I was so far along in my ninth month that I knew better than anyone how crazy it would be to try such a trip; so Joseph went in my place and got back to the farm four days before our son was born.

We thought he might bring Momma back with him then, but Caroline was making her New Haven debut as Musetta in *La Bohème* on the twenty-first. Our parents had planned to go before my father's death, so Caroline and Call begged her to return with them and stay on through the opening. Since she would be coming to live with us soon, it seemed the right thing for her to do. Joseph did not plead my condition. He was already learning midwifery, and I think my mother understood that he would have been disappointed not to deliver our child himself.

I suppose every mother is reduced to idiocy when describing her firstborn, but, oh, he is a beauty—large and dark like his father, but with the bright blue eyes of the Bradshaws. I swear from his cry that he will be a singer and from his huge hands that he will follow the water, which makes his father laugh aloud and tease me about our son setting sail on the trickle of a stream that crosses our pasture.

The older children adore him, and, as for the valley people, it doesn't matter how often I explain that we named the baby for my father, they are all sure that

Truitt is their namesake. Their need for me made them accept me into their lives, but now I feel that they are taking me into their hearts as well.

My work did not, could not, end with my marriage to Joseph and his children or even with the birth of Truitt. There is no one else to care for the valley. The hospital remains two hours away, and the road is impassable for much of the winter.

This year our winter came early. In November I was watching over two pregnancies, one of which I worried about. The mother is a thin, often-beaten girl of about eighteen. From the size of her, I quickly suspected twins and urged her and her husband to go to the hospital in Staunton or Harrisonburg for the delivery.

Despite his bouts of drunkenness, the young husband is well-meaning. He would have taken her, I believe, had there been any money at all. But how could I urge them to make the trip when the hospital might well reject her? And without money where could they stay in the city until the babies actually came? I counted the days and measured her progress as best I could and then sent word to a doctor in Staunton that I would need help with the births. But it snowed twenty inches the day before Essie went into labor, so when they called me, I went alone.

The first twin, a nearly six-pound boy, came fairly easily, despite Essie's slender frame, but the second did not follow as I thought it should. I had begun to fear for it, when I realized that it was very small, but in a breach position. I reached in and turned the twin so that she was delivered head first, but blue as death. Before I even cut the cord, I put my mouth down and breathed into her tiny one. Her chest, smaller than my fist, shuddered, and she gave a cry, but so weak, so like a parting, that I was near despair.

"Is it all right?" Essie asked.

"Small," I said and busied myself cutting and tying off the cord. How cold she was. It sent painful shivers up my arms. I called the grandmother, who had been taking care of the boy, to get me blankets and see to the afterbirth.

I swathed the child tightly and held her against my body. It was like cuddling a stone. I almost ran from the bedroom. What was I to do? They must give me an incubator if they expected me to care for newborn babies in this godforsaken place.

The kitchen was slightly warmer than the bedroom. I went over to the enormous iron stove. A remnant of a fire was banked in the far corner under the stove top. I put my hand on the stove and found it comfortingly warm. I grabbed an iron pot, stuffed it with all the dishrags and towels I could reach with one hand, lay the baby in it, and set it in the oven door. Then I pulled up a kitchen stool and sat there with my hand on the baby's body and watched. It may have been hours. I was too intent to keep track, but, at length, a sort of pinkness invaded the translucent blue skin of her cheek.

"Nurse?" I jumped at the sound. The young father

had come into the kitchen. "Nurse, should I go for the priest?" His eyes widened at the sight of the nurse cooking his baby in the oven, but, rather than protest, he repeated his question about fetching the priest.

"How could you on these roads?" I'm sure I sounded impatient. I wanted to be left in peace to guard my baby.

"Should I do it myself?" he asked, apparently alarmed by whatever it was he was suggesting. "Or you could."

"Oh, do be quiet."

"But, Nurse, it must be baptized before it dies."

"She won't die!"

He flinched. I'm sure he found me terrifying. "But, if it did—"

"She will not die." But to keep him quiet and get rid of him, I poured water out of the cold teakettle onto my hand and reached into the oven, placing my hand on the blur of dark hair. "What is her name?"

He shook his head in bewilderment. Apparently, everything was left for me to do. Susan. Susan was the name of a saint, wasn't it? Well, if not, they could have the priest fix it later. "Essie Susan," I said, "I baptize you in the name of the Father and of the Son and of the Holy Ghost. Amen." Under my hand the tiny head stirred.

The father crossed himself, nodded a scared-rabbit kind of thank you, and hurried out to report the sacrament to his wife. Soon the grandmother was in the kitchen.

"Thank you, Nurse. We're grateful to you."

"Where is the other twin?" I asked, suddenly stricken.

I had forgotten him. In my anxiety for his sister, I had completely forgotten him. "Where have you put him?"

"In the basket." She looked at me, puzzled. "He's sleeping."

"You should hold him," I said. "Hold him as much as you can. Or let his mother hold him."

She started for the door. "Nurse. Should I baptize him as well?"

"Oh, yes," I said. "Baptize him and then let Essie nurse him."

My own breasts were swollen with milk for Truitt. I knew his father would bring him to me soon, but there was plenty. I took my baby out of the oven and held her mouth to catch the milk, which began to flow of its own accord. A perfect tongue, smaller than a newborn kitten's, reached out for the drops of milk on her lips. Then the little mouth rooted against my breast until she had found the nipple for herself.

Hours later, walking home, my boots crunching on the snow, I bent my head backward to drink in the crystal stars. And clearly, as though the voice came from just behind me, I heard a melody so sweet and pure that I had to hold myself to keep from shattering:

*I wonder as I wander out under the sky . . .*

---

Katherine Paterson's works have received wide acclaim. Among them are *Bridge to Terabithia*, winner of the 1978 Newbery Medal; *The Great Gilly Hopkins*, a Newbery Honor Book and winner of the 1979 National Book Award; and *The Master Puppeteer*, awarded the 1977 National Book Award.

Katherine Paterson was born in China, the daughter of missionary parents, and spent part of her childhood there. She was educated in both China and the United States, graduating from King College, in Bristol, Tennessee, and later receiving her master's degree in English Bible from the Presbyterian School of Christian Education in Richmond, Virginia. She lived in Japan for four years, working for two of those years as a Christian Education Assistant to a group of eleven pastors in rural Japan.

Her four children and their friends have provided her with some of the subject matter for her sharply observant stories of family life. She lives with her family in Barre, Vermont.

"As a CEO and little league coach, I've come to see shared purpose as the best predictor of group performance. Encouraging vulnerability and connection across your team is an unlock for both. *Bring Your Whole Self to Work* is a powerful guide to this type of leadership and culture."

— **Kevin Cleary**, CEO of Clif Bar & Company

"This book is a powerful tool. The world is calling for us to step up, speak up, and bring all of ourselves to the work we do. Mike Robbins challenges us to do this in an inspiring way."

— **Gabrielle Bernstein**, #1 *New York Times* best-selling author of *The Universe Has Your Back*

"Mike Robbins is a trusted advisor to us, and has had a very positive impact on me personally, as well as on our leaders and the corporate culture at Nutanix. The ideas and principles in *Bring Your Whole Self to Work* are critical to teams that want to thrive in today's competitive business environment."

— **Dheeraj Pandey**, co-founder and CEO of Nutanix

"Mike Robbins has a unique knack for connecting personal fulfillment to business success. His important lessons of appreciation, authenticity, and empathy are universal and lead to more engaged employees. Not only do I use some of his exercises with our organization, but I even suggested one that my daughter's teacher used in class."

— **Amy Brooks**, President, Team Marketing & Business Operations and Chief Innovation Officer of the NBA

"I have witnessed the power of the principles in this book. I have seen how authentic and vulnerable leaders and teams come together and perform at a higher level and even win championships. Mike Robbins gives you the blueprint to lead and work more powerfully in this significant, pioneering, and must-read book."

— **Jon Gordon**, best-selling author of *The Power of Positive Leadership*

"The principles in Mike Robbins' *Bring Your Whole Self to Work* are important learnings, especially in today's complex business environment. Creating cultures of diverse and engaged employees is the secret to serving customers in a standout way that allows organizations to thrive, and employees to innovate and do their best work."

— **Donna Morris**, EVP, Customer and Employee Experience, Adobe

"We hear words like *integrity, authenticity,* and *empathy* kicked around these days. But what are they really? And, how do they play into our quest to contribute meaningfully to the world and to live a good life? In *Bring Your Whole Self to Work*, Mike Robbins digs into these questions and invites us to live more integrated lives and bring more of our true selves to work, so we can have the biggest impact on those around us and the world."

— **Jonathan Fields**, founder, Good Life Project® and author of *How to Live a Good Life*

# *Bring Your*
# WHOLE
# SELF
## *to Work*

# ALSO BY MIKE ROBBINS

## Books

*Be Yourself, Everyone Else Is Already Taken:
Transform Your Life with the Power of Authenticity*

*Focus on the Good Stuff: The Power of Appreciation*

*Nothing Changes Until You Do: A Guide to
Self-Compassion and Getting Out of Your Own Way\**

## CDs

*The Power of Appreciation*

\*Available from Hay House
Please visit:

Hay House USA: www.hayhouse.com®
Hay House Australia: www.hayhouse.com.au
Hay House UK: www.hayhouse.co.uk
Hay House India: www.hayhouse.co.in

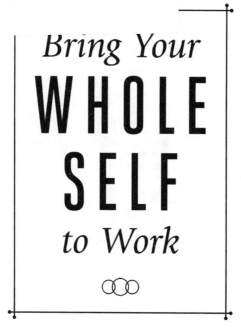

*Bring Your*

# WHOLE

# SELF

*to Work*

How Vulnerability Unlocks Creativity,
Connection, and Performance

# MIKE ROBBINS

**HAY HOUSE, INC.**
Carlsbad, California • New York City
London • Sydney • New Delhi

*Published in the United States by:* Hay House, Inc.: www.hayhouse.com® • *Published in Australia by:* Hay House Australia Pty. Ltd.: www.hayhouse.com.au • *Published in the United Kingdom by:* Hay House UK, Ltd.: www.hayhouse.co.uk • *Published in India by:* Hay House Publishers India: www.hayhouse.co.in

*Cover design: the*BookDesigners • *Interior design:* Nick C. Welch

### Library of Congress Cataloging-in-Publication Data

Robbins, Mike.
Title: Bring your whole self to work / Mike Robbins.
Description: Carlsbad, California : Hay House, [2018]
Identifiers: LCCN 2017060611 | ISBN 9781401952358 (hardcover : alk. paper)
Subjects: LCSH: Employee motivation. | Employee morale. | Job satisfaction. |
Performance. | Organizational behavior.
Classification: LCC HF5549.5.M63 R622 2018 | DDC 650.1--dc23 LC record available at https://lccn.loc.gov/2017060611

Hardcover ISBN: 978-1-4019-5235-8

11 10 9 8 7 6 5 4 3 2
1st edition, May 2018

Printed in the United States of America

*This book is dedicated to my sister,*
**Lori Dempsey Robbins.**
*Thank you for teaching me so much.*
*I love you and I miss you.*

# CONTENTS

# INTRODUCTION

For us to truly succeed, especially in today's business world, we must be willing to bring our *whole selves* to the work that we do. And for the teams and organizations that we're a part of to thrive, it's also essential to create an environment where people feel safe enough to bring all of who they are to work. The lines between our personal and professional lives have blurred more than ever in recent years, even inside the most structured and traditional companies.

Bringing our whole selves to work means showing up authentically, leading with humility, and remembering that we're all vulnerable, imperfect human beings doing the best we can. It's also about having the courage to take risks, speak up, ask for help, connect with others in a genuine way, and allow ourselves to be truly seen. It's not always easy for us to show up this way, especially at work. And it takes commitment, intention, and courage for leaders and organizations to create environments that are conducive to this type of authenticity and humanity.

My research and experience have shown me that when we bring our whole selves to work in this way, not only are we more likely to create success and fulfillment for ourselves, but we are able to have the greatest impact on the people around us. And creating a culture that encourages us to show up fully allows us collectively to do our best, most innovative work together.

I decided to write this book because I wanted to share some of what I've witnessed, experienced, and learned through my own work over the past 17 years. I've partnered with many different leaders, groups, and companies, and have seen some remarkable things—both positive and negative—in terms of what creates (or hinders) the success and fulfillment of individuals, teams, and organizations as a whole. Of course every work environment is unique. Working at Google in the heart of Silicon Valley is quite different from working for the City of San Antonio in Texas. Working for ourselves out of our spare bedroom in Ohio is also very different from leading a global team at Microsoft while being based in Europe and traveling internationally all the time.

According to Gallup, however, only 32 percent of people in the United States are engaged in their jobs, and worldwide the number is a staggeringly low 13 percent. This means that the vast majority of us are not fired up about or fulfilled in the work that we do. Lack of engagement leads to a whole host of problems for us personally— decreased performance, diminished fulfillment, increased stress, and greater likelihood of well-being issues. And for our teams and organizations, the impact of disengaged employees is significant, and often leads to a lack of results, collaboration, and innovation; it is also a primary cause of turnover. A study conducted by the human capital management company ADP estimated the real monetary cost at $2,246 per disengaged employee per year. The total economic impact of employee disengagement in the U.S. easily runs into billions of dollars each year—by one estimate, over $400 billion.

As I've seen and learned through my research and experience, one of the most important aspects of being engaged, fulfilled, and successful in our work is the ability to be ourselves. Organizations that have environments where people are more likely to engage, collaborate, and perform, do what they can to encourage people to fully show up and be all of who they are at work.

This book will offer you insights, ideas, and tools to inspire you to bring your whole self to the work that you do—regardless of where you work, what kind of work you do, or with whom you do it—thus allowing you to be more satisfied, effective, and free. And if you're an owner, leader, or just someone who wants to have influence on those around you, this book will also give you specific techniques for how to build or enhance your team's culture in such a way that encourages others to bring all of who they are to work—which will unlock greater creativity, connection, and performance for your group and company.

## My Recent Journey

As often happens for me with my work when I take on a new project, particularly a book, I see it reflected back to me in many areas of my life. Such was the case when I pitched the idea for this book to my publisher in December 2015. I was excited about this topic, looking forward both to refining some of the key principles I'd discovered and to exploring these ideas more deeply. I was also grateful to have a new creative project on which to focus. But I wasn't quite prepared for how soon after agreeing to write this book that the circumstances of my life would test my *own* ability to bring my whole self to my own work.

My sister Lori had been diagnosed with stage 3 ovarian cancer in April 2012, just 10 months after our mom died of lung cancer. Lori's diagnosis was shocking and scary—to her, to me, and to all of us around her. She was

42 years old at the time and her daughter was just seven. After almost a year in remission, Lori's cancer returned in the fall of 2014. She went back into treatment and it seemed to be going well at first, but by the middle of 2015 things took a turn for the worse.

I was with Lori at her house just a few days after New Year's in 2016. Her situation had worsened quite rapidly in the previous few weeks—we had gone from checking in on her regularly, to rotating shifts of being with her overnight, to her needing 24-hour professional care.

Before I left her bedroom that afternoon, I kissed her on the forehead and said, "I'm flying down to Orlando in the morning for a speaking engagement on Wednesday. I'll be back to see you on Thursday. I love you."

"I love you too," Lori whispered as she closed her eyes to get some rest.

The hospice nurse followed me out, and I turned, meeting her gaze before asking in a hushed tone, "How long do you think she has left?"

"It's hard to know for sure," the nurse said, "but she's pretty strong. I'd say at least a month, maybe longer."

My trip to Orlando was a bit of a blur. I was speaking at an event for a client that I love working with, OneMain Financial. It was the annual kickoff meeting for all their branch managers and field leaders in the eastern half of the country—about 700 people total. Given what was going on with Lori, I found it very difficult to focus on my client, their event, and my speech. Yet, at the same time, I was grateful for the distraction. While I'm usually pretty open and transparent about what's going on in my life, even with my clients and when I speak publicly, I decided not to talk about Lori, but just to show up, be as present as possible, and put my attention on the people in that audience. Even when intense things are going on in our lives, we still have to show up for work and do the best we can, which is what I tried to do that day.

At the airport in Orlando on my way back home, I got a call from Lori's hospice nurse letting me know that things had taken another turn for the worse. "I know I told you on Monday that I thought she had a month or more left; I think it's probably more like a week now." Hearing her say this as I stood in the boarding area, I doubled over, trying to catch my breath.

The flight home that night seemed to take forever. I got back late and tried to get some sleep, which wasn't easy. The next morning I went over to Lori's house, planning to spend much of the day there before heading to San Francisco for an event I was scheduled to speak at that night. When I got to her house, the energy was much different than it had been just a few days earlier—it felt quiet and sad, yet calm. There was a reverence and sacredness in the air. A few of Lori's close friends were there, along with her nurse. There were some hugs and tears as we greeted each other. We didn't speak much, but a lot was said in the unsaid.

Throughout the day we took turns going into Lori's bedroom and spending time with her one-on-one. She was sleeping a lot. She seemed peaceful but wasn't verbally responsive, and her breathing was labored. I held her hand, touched her face, and let her know I loved her. I figured I would have more conversations with her in the coming days, but I felt compelled to talk to her at that moment about some of the ups and downs, joys and pains, twists and turns of our relationship over the years. Even though she wasn't verbally responsive and her eyes were opening and closing as I spoke to her, it felt like she could hear me.

As the time for my event in the city neared, I began to feel very uncomfortable about leaving. Even though I was scheduled to lead an evening workshop that people had signed up and paid for, I decided to contact the event organizers and let them know I couldn't make it. They were shocked, but thankfully very understanding and compassionate. It felt scary, and seemed somewhat irresponsible of me, to make this call just a few hours before I was scheduled to speak; but it felt like the right thing to do. Keeping my word and showing up for work are important to me. And in that moment, being there with and for Lori felt *much more important.*

A few hours later, and just three days after the hospice nurse told us Lori had at least another month, she passed away peacefully. As we stood around her bed, holding hands, praying, crying, and hugging, many different emotions raced through me all at once.

In the days and weeks that followed I continued to feel a slew of emotions—shock, sadness, and disorientation, to name a few. We knew from the time she got diagnosed that Lori might die. And once the cancer returned and her condition worsened, it seemed likely that she would die. But the way things unfolded so fast in the final days and weeks of her life took me by surprise and knocked me off my feet.

I was also challenged by how to navigate all of this and still do my work. My life and schedule weren't set up for me to take time off to grieve, process everything, and take care of all that needed to be handled. Thankfully, as is often the case in situations like this, many amazing people showed up with love and support.

Since speaking is the primary way I make money and support our family, I continued to speak and travel a lot. It was challenging, but it also felt good to work and to focus on inspiring others, even as I was reeling in my own grief.

I spoke about Lori, her death, and my grief from time to time, but out of respect for her and her privacy I hadn't talked much publicly about her cancer before she passed. My close friends and family all knew she was sick, but I had chosen not to directly acknowledge it in my work. After she died, I did open up about it publicly, but due to the intensity of my emotions and the whole experience, I was discerning about when, where, and how. When I did feel compelled to speak about Lori and my loss, I was amazed by the response—so many people had their own grief stories to share. I continued to get a lot of support from my friends and family members, and also from some amazing counselors and therapists who helped me grieve and heal.

What I didn't have much space or energy for was writing—at least not for publication. I continued to journal, and I shared some of my grief experience in a series of Facebook posts over that first month or two, which actually felt both safe and healing. But sitting down to write blog posts, articles, and especially this book didn't feel good, right, or even possible at that time. I felt like I had a great deal to say and nothing to say, all at the same time. I wanted to write about Lori and about my grief, but also didn't want to, and I was scared it would be too intense for people to relate to, understand, or want to read about. But writing about anything else seemed weird and inauthentic to me.

Now here I am—just at the point where I'm ready and willing to write, with a lot to say and share about showing up, being real, and bringing our whole selves to work. Lori's death was a painful but important reminder to me that life is short and uncertain, and that it's a waste of time for me—for any of us—to worry about doing or saying the wrong thing, being "too much" for people to handle, or not having everything figured out. I think we're all just doing our best, given the resources we have and the circumstances we're facing. The irony was not lost on me that, through one of the greatest losses of my life, I had to go even deeper within myself and practice how to bring all of me to work in a new way, before I could write this book.

As Sheryl Sandberg, Chief Operating Officer of Facebook, wrote about the sudden death of her husband, Dave, in 2015 and in her wonderful book, *Option B*, which is both about her experience of grief and about ways we can all face adversity and build resilience, "If I believed in bringing my whole self to work before Dave died, what I learned after is that I have no choice. If my whole self is going through adversity and tragedy, that whole self comes to work."

I agree with Sheryl. Hiding who we are and what we're going through doesn't serve us or the people we work with, and in many cases it isn't even possible. We're all dealing with being human. Some of us may be experiencing significant pain, loss, or stress. Others of us may be going through incredibly exciting and wonderful times in life. In most cases, it's a mixed bag. And we're always dealing with ups, downs, and the inherent uncertainty and vulnerability of human life, all while having to show up at work and do our jobs.

## Learning from Others

In addition to all that I've learned both personally and professionally, and much of what I've been speaking about, writing about, and teaching to my clients for the past 17 years, I'm excited about the different types of research I've done for this book. In the summer of 2016, as a way to immerse myself more deeply in this topic and learn from the wisdom of others, I decided to interview some of the most interesting business and thought leaders I know—asking them about their lives and careers, and about the twists and turns of their own journeys. I also wanted to inquire into what bringing their whole selves to work meant to them, and how they, as leaders, approached creating a culture conducive to this. I decided to record the interviews, and launched the *Bring Your Whole Self to Work* podcast. It has been fun to produce this show, and I've been amazed by the openness and different perspectives of my guests, as well as by all that I've learned from them and from going through this process.

Many of the people I've interviewed have been touched by loss, like me, and have also been forced to make changes, take risks, and recover from failure. I'm constantly amazed, although no longer surprised, to learn that even people who seem on the surface to "have it all together" still deal with some of the same self-doubt, fear, and insecurity that the rest of us do. These interviews have continued to remind me that although we're all unique individuals, with our own stories, we're much more alike than different. The insight I've gained from these conversations has enhanced the way I think, operate, and show up in my own life and work.

Chip Conley, founder and former CEO of Joie de Vivre Hospitality and current Strategic Advisor for Hospitality and Leadership for Airbnb, shared this pearl of wisdom during our interview: "Holding things back about ourselves is hard and actually takes energy. If we're willing to do the inner work of more fully understanding who we are and what truly matters to us, we'll have more clarity about if where we're working and what we're doing is the right fit for us."

And Melissa Daimler, Senior Vice President of Talent at WeWork and former Head of Learning at Twitter, said in our podcast conversation, "I've always been interested in thinking about work as our learning lab. We can use work to grow and learn as human beings. There are so many opportunities to leverage every single day. I look at my job as helping people develop so that they can bring their whole selves to work."

## Looking at Compelling Studies and Data

In addition to all the interviews I've done, I've taken a look at some of the most interesting and up-to-date studies and data on such things as employee engagement, company culture, leadership, mindfulness, well-being, emotional intelligence, and growth mindset. What's really exciting is that, over the past decade or two, many really smart people—in academia, science, and business—have become more interested in these important topics, which some people dismiss as "soft skills." But as we all know, soft skills are hard. And as leadership expert Peter Drucker famously said, "Culture eats strategy for breakfast." These "soft" things drive the success (or failure) of our careers and of most businesses, and science and research are now backing this up in many ways.

A Harris Interactive study conducted for Deloitte found the following to be true:

- 83 percent of executives and 84 percent of employees rank having engaged and motivated people as the top factor that substantially contributes to a company's success.

- There is a correlation between employees who say they are "happy at work" and feel "valued by their company" and those who say their organization has a clearly articulated and lived culture.

In the 2016 Edelman Global Trust Barometer survey of more than 33,000 people worldwide, only 27 percent of leaders were seen as behaving in open and transparent ways. In that same report in 2013, 82 percent of workers said they did not trust their bosses to tell the truth. Another study found that 85 percent of employees admitted to withholding important concerns about critical issues from their manager.

These statistics and so many others point to the fact that the ability (or inability) for us and others to bring our whole selves to and engage in our work has a huge impact on our success, well-being, and fulfillment (or lack thereof). And the willingness of leaders and organizations to create the conditions for trust, connection, and a positive culture make a significant difference in the loyalty and productiveness of their people.

## How to Use This Book

In this book, I share stories from my own life and work, as well as many stories and examples from the people I've interviewed and the companies I've worked with over the years. I also share some of the latest studies, along with ideas, techniques, and best practices I've learned from various experts, clients, and my own research.

The book is organized into five principles:

1. **Be Authentic.** The foundation of bringing our whole selves to work is authenticity, which is about showing up honestly, without self-righteousness, and with vulnerability. It takes courage to be authentic, and it's essential for trust, growth, and connection.

2. **Utilize the Power of Appreciation.** Appreciation is fundamental both to building strong relationships and to keeping things in a healthy and positive perspective. Bringing our whole selves to work is about being willing to be seen, and also about seeing and empowering the people around us, which is what appreciation provides.

3. **Focus on Emotional Intelligence.** Our emotional intelligence (EQ) is often more important than our skills, IQ, and experience—in terms of our ability both to manage our relationships and to bring our whole selves to work. EQ is both about us (self-awareness and self-management) and about how we relate to others (social awareness and relationship management).

4. **Embrace a Growth Mindset.** Growth mindset is a way of approaching our work and our life with an understanding that we can improve at anything if we're willing to work hard, dedicate ourselves, and practice. It's also about looking at everything we experience (even, indeed especially, our

challenges) as opportunities for growth and learning, which is fundamental to bringing our whole selves to work.

5. **Create a Championship Team.** The people we work with and the environment around us have a significant impact on our ability (or inability) to fully show up, engage, and thrive. And at the same time, the more willing we are to bring our whole selves to work, the more impact we can have on others. Creating a championship team is about building a culture that is safe and conducive to people being themselves, caring about each other, and being willing and able to do great work together.

These ideas and concepts are fairly easy to understand on the surface. But like many important aspects of life, growth, and business, it's not the understanding of them that makes the biggest difference, it's their *application*. Chapter by chapter, I lay out what each of these principles mean, why they can be difficult, and how to implement them both individually and in groups. The final chapter of the book focuses on how to bring the key elements of these five principles together and put them into action for yourself, your team, and all the people you work with.

I'm excited and honored that you've chosen to read this book. I look forward to leading you on this journey, and I hope you find it helpful, enlightening, and empowering. Here we go . . .

# PRINCIPLE #1—
# BE AUTHENTIC

Have you ever been in a meeting where you were nervous but pretending not to be? Most of us have. I've been in this situation many times in my life and career, and a memorable one for me was a meeting I had with my publisher about a decade ago. My first book, *Focus on the Good Stuff*, had come out the previous year. My publisher for that book was Jossey-Bass, a San Francisco–based imprint of a large publishing company called John Wiley & Sons, located in Hoboken, New Jersey (right outside of New York City).

I was scheduled to meet with them in the San Francisco office to pitch an idea for what I was hoping would be my second book, this one on authenticity. I was both excited and nervous, but I felt pretty comfortable because my understanding was that the meeting would be with Alan, my editor for my first book, and a few of the members of his team with whom I'd previously worked.

When we got into the conference room, Alan said, "Mike we're going to wait a few minutes before we start the meeting."

"Why?" I asked.

"Because Debra's coming to the meeting," Alan said.

Debra, the president of Jossey-Bass, was someone I'd not yet met.

"And," Alan added, "her boss from Wiley flew in from New York to hear your pitch."

"Oh, great!" I said.

Except that's not actually what I was thinking. *Dude you're going to screw this up. You should've prepared more. Don't blow it.*

But since I'm pretty good at pretending I'm not nervous when I really am, I just smiled and acted confident.

A few minutes later, Debra and her boss walked into the room. They were quite warm and friendly, and not all that intimidating, but given who they were and the positions they held, I was now a nervous wreck.

"Mike, why don't you tell us about your new book idea?" Debra asked.

I launched into my pitch. Usually in meetings like this, I'm most nervous at the beginning, but once I get into it my anxiety diminishes. This time, that wasn't happening. In fact, the more I talked, the worse it got. While I wasn't forgetting what I wanted to say or making a complete fool out of myself, I felt my fear level going up, and found that I was pushing really hard emotionally, trying to impress them. After a few minutes, I couldn't stand it, so I just stopped.

I looked right at Debra and said, "I know I mentioned this a few minutes ago when you came into the room, but it's really an honor to meet you and I appreciate you coming to this meeting." I turned to her boss. "And you flew all the way out here from New York to hear my pitch." Then I added, "I notice that I'm feeling really nervous and I'm trying hard to impress you. Can I stop doing that now and just be myself?"

As this last comment came out of my mouth, the voice in my head shouted, *Don't say that out loud! What's the matter with you?*

There was a long, awkward pause. The looks on people's faces around that table seemed to be asking, *Did he really just say that out loud?* Then something interesting happened: Debra laughed, as did her boss and everyone else in the room.

I laughed too, took a deep breath and said, "Here's what I know about authenticity: it's important. It's important to me and just about everybody I know. It's important in all types of relationships. It's important to the organizations I work with, and to their leaders and teams. It's important in most areas of business and life. And authenticity is challenging. It's much easier to say I want to be authentic than it is to actually operate authentically. I want to write a book about that. Why is it so difficult? What can we do to make it a little easier?"

At that moment I stopped "pitching" my book idea, and we just had a conversation. We talked about some of the things that make authenticity challenging for me, for them, in business, for their company, in relationships, for my clients, in our society, and in life in general. It was a fascinating discussion, and I left the meeting feeling excited, but still nervous for different reasons. I really wanted them to publish this book. Alan told me he would give me a call as I left, but didn't give me any specific indication of their level of interest.

As I drove home, I began to second-guess myself. *Maybe I should've talked more about the specific content of the book, or the marketing and promotion plan. Maybe I shared too much and was too transparent about my feelings and insecurities. I wonder if I came across as credible and if they're going want to work with me on this project? When are they going to call me and let me know?*

Late that afternoon I got a call from Alan. He said, "Mike, I wanted to get back to you by the end of the day and let you know that we'd like to publish your book. After you left, we talked about you. We all agreed that was one of the strangest pitch meetings we'd ever been in, but we appreciated your openness and candor. We're excited to work with you on this project."

I learned something very important that day, and I've learned a lot over the last decade through my study and teaching of authenticity. The specific lesson of that day for me was the importance of being real, even when I'm in a high-stakes situation where the outcome matters. I've spent a lot of my life doing my best to be prepared, especially for big moments like that. But sometimes in life and in business, as important as it is to be prepared, it's even more important to be present and show up fully in the moment.

What I then learned as I researched and wrote that book (*Be Yourself, Everyone Else Is Already Taken*) and as I've more deeply explored this topic in my work and life over the past decade, is that authenticity, particularly in the workplace, can be incredibly challenging and complex, but it's essential to many aspects of success, trust, leadership, credibility, business culture, and more.

In this chapter, which is the first and foundational principle of bringing our whole selves to work, I'm excited to share some of the key ideas I've learned about authenticity since writing and publishing that book back in 2009, and some of the latest research that points to the importance of authenticity to the success of individuals, leaders, teams, and organizations.

In a 2016 article for the *Harvard Business Review*, researchers James Detert from the University of Virginia's Darden School of Business and Ethan Burris from the McCombs School of Business at the University of Texas at Austin wrote:

In a number of studies we've found that when employees can voice their concerns freely, organizations see increased retention and stronger performance. At several financial services firms, for example, business units whose employees reported speaking up more had significantly better financial and operational results than others. And at one national restaurant chain, managers were able to persuade senior leaders to make improvements that reduced employee turnover by 32 percent and saved at least $1.6 million a year.

In study after study, we see data that shows the connection between authenticity and job satisfaction, engagement, and performance. However, for us to more fully utilize the power of authenticity at work for ourselves, and to enhance the environment of authenticity in which we work, it's important for us to understand and embody it at a deeper level.

## The Authenticity Continuum

When I'm speaking about the core principles of authenticity, one of the first questions I often ask the audience is, "What does authenticity mean to you?" I usually have people pair up and discuss this with a partner, and then we talk about it. Some of the answers I hear are "honesty," "integrity," "transparency," "realness," "originality," and "truthfulness." All these words, and others like them, are aspects of authenticity, for sure. But I think we sometimes have a misunderstanding of what authenticity actually means, especially at work.

Some years ago I delivered a keynote speech on the power of authenticity, and right as I walked offstage a man came up to me, got right in my face, and said, "I'm authentic. I'm authentic all the time!" He seemed upset.

So I asked him, "What's the problem?"

"Well," he said, "I've lost some jobs because of this."

"Really?" I asked.

"Yeah. Not everyone can handle it."

I didn't know him, but I was getting a pretty strong sense of his personality in that moment. I'm not quite sure what prompted me to ask him this somewhat provocative question, but I did: "Now tell me the truth, is it 'authentic' or 'obnoxious'?"

He was a bit taken aback by my question.

I myself was surprised I'd asked this—it just kind of flew out of my mouth. *Wow, I really just said that?*

After a moment of shock, his face softened and he laughed. Given his intense personality and directness, I think he appreciated my quick response and comeback. He then said, somewhat sheepishly, "Well, maybe a little bit of both."

"I appreciate your honesty and self-awareness," I said. "I don't know for sure, but if I had to guess, I bet it was the 'obnoxious' that got you fired, not the 'authentic'."

He laughed, nodded, and walked away with a look on his face that said, *You know what, that's probably true.*

Authenticity is about being real, not "right." It's also not about always "speaking our mind" or "telling people how it is." It has more complexity, depth, and nuance.

Authenticity is not a static thing; rather, it exists on a continuum. And it's an in-the-moment phenomenon. As my mentor and counselor, Eleanor, likes to remind me, "Mike, the truth can't be rehearsed." Understanding this Authenticity Continuum and where we find ourselves on it in any given moment is essential to our ability to be more authentic ourselves, and to influence the authenticity of others and the environments in which we work.

There are three main aspects of the Authenticity Continuum—Phony, Honest, and Authentic:

**Phony————Honest————Authentic**

## Phony

We all know what it's like to listen to, watch, or interact with someone who is being phony or inauthentic. It can be off-putting, frustrating, and even disrespectful. We don't like it, and as a culture we love to point fingers at and judge people who are being phony. We do this with politicians, celebrities, business leaders, and people in our own lives. We can understandably be skeptical of the people around us and in the world, sometimes questioning the authenticity of those we communicate, interact, and work with. Most of us have been lied to or deceived by people we believed in. This can create a certain level of mistrust and even cynicism within us and around us. This skepticism is stronger for some of us than others, and in some situations and relationships, based on a variety of factors, personality traits, and past experiences, among other things.

But given what we're looking at here in this chapter and this book, the best place for us to inquire into phoniness is within ourselves. While it may be fairly easy to point out the phoniness in others, looking at it within ourselves can be a bit more challenging. Where, when, with whom, and in what situations do you find yourself being phony? It's usually not malicious. It's not like we wake up in the morning and say to ourselves, *You know what I'm going to do today? I'm going to lie and manipulate people.* No, it's much subtler than that. And, in most cases when we find ourselves being inauthentic, we're either unconscious of it or we justify and rationalize it.

Here are a few common situations in which we might find ourselves being phony:

**Social or cultural norms.** There are many things we do and say simply because the people around us do them and say them. For example, what's the first question that we often ask when we greet each other? "How are you?" Or, "How's it going?" Or some other version of that question. And what's the usual response? "Fine," "Good," "Awesome," or something like that. It's usually some simple, one-word answer (mostly positive), and then we ask in return, "And how are you?" To which the response is, again, one of those positive one-word answers.

This, however, is an inauthentic interaction most of the time. It's friendly, sure, but it's also often phony.

Here's how you know. Have you ever asked that question as a greeting and someone answered honestly by letting you know that things weren't going well for them? It can catch us off guard. It's not that we don't care how they are—we just don't usually mean it when we ask, because it's merely a way of saying hello in our culture. On the other side of the interaction, responding by saying we're "fine" or "good" usually doesn't come anywhere close to encapsulating how we're truly feeling in that moment. We often respond that way just because it's easier and it's what's expected. These are the rules of this simple social norm, and we tend to play by these rules.

How many other things do we do or say at work or in life simply because that's the social norm? While these things are usually benign, they show up a lot at work, and being more aware of them can help us and those around us not fall into the unconscious trap of allowing these norms to dictate how we interact, communicate, and show up.

**When we don't know or understand something.** Do you ever find yourself in a conversation or meeting where you have no idea what someone's talking about but you pretend that you do because you don't want to seem like an idiot? I catch myself doing this from time to time. Typically we can get away with this without people knowing. But it can cause us stress and unnecessary pressure. What if we had more courage and the confidence to simply admit, "I'm sorry, I don't know what that means—could you explain it to me?" In the moment it often seems easier to just pretend and hope it doesn't become an issue. In addition to doing this in meetings and conversations, we sometimes do it in larger ways in other areas of work and in life—pretending we know, understand, or can do things we can't (or at least haven't done yet). Most of us have painted ourselves into a corner by pretending to know or be able to do something we really don't. Or at the very least, we've made it seem like we've got it all figured out or taken care of, when in reality we've needed a lot of help and guidance.

**When we don't agree with a decision or with the group consensus.** This often happens at work with a team we're a part of, or in other group settings. A discussion is taking place or decisions are being made, but we don't feel comfortable with the way it's going although everyone else seems to be onboard. Maybe we want to speak up. Maybe we want to ask questions. Maybe we want to disagree with what's being said or decided. But in some cases, it may feel too risky to do so. Or we fear we'll be seen as an outlier or not a team player. So, we go along with what's being discussed and decided, even though it doesn't sit well with us. Then we end up frustrated, either with ourselves for not speaking up or with the group for making a bad decision.

**Conflicts or difficult conversations.** One of the situations in which inauthentic behavior shows up most often in my own life, and in many of my clients', is when there are conflicts. When we're faced with a difficult or potentially uncomfortable conversation we need to have with someone, we often try to avoid it, or at least delay it a bit. At some point we can't put it off any longer. So we finally sit down with the person to give them feedback or to let them know we need to talk to them about something important. In these situations, it's very common that somewhere between our brain and our mouth things get a little mixed up. The other person might get defensive or say things we weren't prepared to hear. We might get flustered and, in the middle of the conversation, realize it's not going well. We then might decide to just stop and somehow figure out a way to get out of the conversation before things get much worse. Then we might walk away feeling uncomfortable, and realize we had only part of the conversation we wanted to have with them. At that point we might be stuck in the difficult position of either pretending to let it go or deciding to go back to the person the next day and say, "Hey, remember that awkward conversation we had yesterday? Yeah, well, there's more . . ."

Conflicts and conversations like these, while usually uncomfortable, are essential to building trust and creating a healthy and positive work environment. However, most of us don't like engaging in these types of discussions, and we tend to avoid them or, when we do have them, we find it difficult to be authentic. I often find myself avoiding such conversations, and when I do have them I find it challenging to really speak the truth, and to do so in a way that's conducive to resolution, connection, and trust, rather than just trying to make my case, win the argument, protect myself, or "make nice" (in an inauthentic way) so the problem "goes away" or "gets better." Although I've gotten better at these conversations over the years, they're rarely easy for me, even though I know how important they are.

As a mentor of mine said to me years ago, "Mike, you know what stands between you and the kind of relationships you really want to have with people? Probably a ten-minute, sweaty-palmed conversation you're too afraid to have. If you get good at those ten-minute, sweaty-palmed conversations, you'll have fantastic relationships—you'll resolve conflicts, build trust, and be able to work through things. But if you avoid them, as most of us do, because they're uncomfortable, you'll simply be a victim of whomever you live with, work with, and interact with in life."

Acknowledging our phony tendencies and behaviors is essential. We're not weak, wrong, or bad for operating in inauthentic ways—we're just human. But if we have enough self-awareness to notice when we're being phony, we can then make different choices. Authenticity is a choice, and in some cases not an easy one. But when we show up in phony ways and we either aren't willing to see it or we blame it on other people or the environment, we give away our power. People often say things to me like, "I *can't* be authentic with my boss (or my client, or my mother-in-law, etc.)," or "You *can't* really be authentic like that here—that's not how people operate or communicate." My response is usually, "Listen, I may not know what that person or this environment is like specifically, and I do understand that it can be hard to be authentic—especially with certain people, in certain situations, and at work in general. But the issue isn't that you *can't*, it's that you *won't*. And maybe choosing not to be authentic is what you believe right now to be the best, most self-preserving choice to make. Just own it as a choice." Seeing and owning our inauthenticity gives us the awareness and sometimes the motivation to move along the continuum toward authenticity.

## Honest

Halfway down the Authenticity Continuum we get to honesty. My mom would often say, "Honesty is the best policy." This simple saying contains a lot of wisdom. But have you ever had a situation in life, particularly at work, where you were honest about something and it caused a problem? Have you ever been honest about something and it hurt someone's feelings? Have you ever created or escalated a conflict by being honest? Have ever you put your foot in your mouth when your honesty ended up being inappropriate, offensive, or embarrassing? For most of us, the answer to these questions is, "Yes, many times."

While on the surface honesty seems straightforward, universally encouraged, and positive, it's a bit more complicated than that. Over the course of our lives, and particularly in our careers, most of us learn how to tactfully "massage" the truth. We end up saying to ourselves, *I don't want to be phony, I want to be honest—but "mostly" honest. I want to be honest in a way that makes me look good, doesn't get me into trouble, and has the people I work with respect, admire, and trust me.* Or as someone shouted out from the audience a few years ago when I was speaking at their department's all-hands meeting, "You mean like

'HR honest'"—at which everybody roared in laughter, even some of the HR folks.

We end up spending a lot of time and energy on this side of the Authenticity Continuum, trying to figure out how honest we can be with certain people and in certain situations. Although this makes sense and is how most of us are trained to operate, especially at work, it's exhausting. Some of us are more comfortable being direct and telling the truth—based on our personality, cultural background, where we grew up, how we were raised, and other factors. Others have a harder time being direct and telling the truth, based on these same factors, on the feedback and experience we've had throughout our lives and careers, and on our position and environment at work.

This is where honesty can get confusing. For those of us who do have the courage to be honest, but sometimes get pushback that we're too abrupt or too direct, and could soften it up a little bit, we tend either to question ourselves or, more often, to dig in and judge the people giving us that feedback or the environment we're in—thinking they're "too soft." For those of us who have a harder time speaking up, telling the truth, and being direct, we tend to have fears and recollections of times we've done this and it hasn't gone well for us, thus justifying our hesitancy to be more forthcoming.

Unfortunately, we think of honesty as this binary black-and-white thing. In some respects this is the case: We're either telling the truth or we're not. We're either showing up honestly or we're not. And yet honesty does not equal authenticity. It does take real courage, particularly in our professional lives, for some of us to speak up and tell the truth. But the reason why honesty sits just at the midway point on the Authenticity Continuum is that it's only the entry point into being truly authentic.

Where there's real freedom and power for us is on the other side of honesty. Yes, we must be honest, which takes courage in and of itself; but in order for us to get to authenticity, we have to remove something from our honesty and add something to it. The thing we have to remove is our **self-righteousness**. And what we have to add is **vulnerability**.

## Removing Self-Righteousness

Self-righteousness can be a bit tricky for us to fully identify, understand, and own within ourselves. When I'm speaking to a group about this, I often ask these two questions:

1. How many of you, like me, have a lot of opinions?

2. And how many of you, like me, think your opinions are *right*?

Usually most of the hands go up in the audience in response to both of these questions, and there is often some knowing laughter, especially after the second question. Many of us are quite opinionated, which is fine, and some of us are more than happy to share our opinions openly. In today's world, we have more ways and platforms than ever before to express our opinions, which can be wonderful—but also problematic, for a variety of reasons. But the issue isn't with our opinions or even our willingness (or lack thereof) to express them; it's the self-righteousness with which we hold our opinions. When we hold an opinion with self-righteousness, whether or not we express it, we are coming from a place of *being right*. And if I'm *right* about something and you don't agree with me, what does that make you? *Wrong.* Now we have a problem.

Self-righteousness separates us from others. In certain relationships, situations, and environments, we might be open and honest enough with other people to let them know directly that we think they're wrong. We might be able to say straight to their face something like, "I think that's a bad idea, I totally disagree with you, and I think it's wrong." More often than not, however, and especially at work, we bite our tongue in such situations, or say something ambiguous that doesn't agree or disagree. We may say, "Thanks for your input and feedback; I'll take that into consideration." And then we might leave the room, find someone we agree with, and say, "There's no way we're doing that; that's a ridiculous idea, and he's an idiot"—or something to that effect.

Self-righteousness negatively impacts us, our relationships, and the teams we belong to or lead. It also undercuts our ability to influence those around us. As Dr. Martin Luther King, Jr., said, "You have very little morally persuasive power with those who can feel your underlying contempt."

Identifying our self-righteousness can be challenging because often when you and I are being self-righteous, we don't think we're being self-righteous, we think we're *right*.

At an event a few years ago, I delivered a keynote address on authentic leadership in which I spoke about, among other things, the Authenticity Continuum. Afterward, a man approached me and said, "Hey Mike, thanks for your speech. I got a lot out of it." He reached out to shake my hand. "I'm Dan."

"Thanks, Dan," I said, shaking his hand.

"I know your talk this morning was about leadership," he said, "and while I was thinking about my team and how I lead, I couldn't help but think about my mom, especially when you were talking about self-righteousness."

"What specifically made you think about your mom?" I asked.

"Well," Dan said, "my dad died a few years ago, and my mom's getting older. I'm the oldest of four. We all agree that she should sell her house and move into a condo. Doing this would definitely make her life easier, and ours as well—since we're constantly having to help her with so many things around the house that she's getting too old to take care of, or that my dad managed when he was around. But she can be so stubborn. It's hard to get through to her. My siblings have all stopped trying, but not me. I try to talk to her about it, but we end up fighting, which drives me crazy. It never occurred to me until today that maybe one of the reasons that she doesn't listen to me is because I'm so incredibly self-righteous with her."

I could see that Dan was starting to get emotional as he talked about his mother and their situation. I said, "I'm sorry to hear about your father's death. I know every situation is unique. But both my mom and dad have passed away, so I do have some understanding of the emotional and practical challenges involved with losing a parent. I can tell how much you love your mom. You wouldn't have come up to talk to me about her and this situation if you didn't love her so much." I paused before asking, "How do you really feel?"

"How do I really feel about what?" asked Dan.

"About everything going on with you, your mom, and your family?" I asked.

"Well," he said, "I guess I feel scared."

"What do you feel scared about?"

"My dad took care of her and of so many things. Even though I have a family of my own and have a lot of responsibility at work, I'm not used to taking care of my mom like this. I worry about her—worry that it will continue to get harder as she gets older. And I just want to do what's best."

"That all makes sense to me," I said. "Have you had this conversation with your mom?"

"No, not specifically."

"It's up to you, of course, but you might want to let her know how you really feel. I bet she would hear you and understand," I said. "The natural human response to self-righteousness is defensiveness. Your mom is just defending and protecting herself, which is what we almost always do when we feel self-righteousness coming at us. Being self-righteous doesn't make you a bad son or a bad person; it just means you're human. You could apologize to her for it. And I bet you have some good ideas and suggestions that might help her and her situation. If you can let go of your self-righteousness, she might actually be able to hear some of them."

Like Dan, most of us can be self-righteous at times, and we often aren't aware of it because we're so focused on being right. It takes quite a bit of self-awareness to notice our self-righteousness, and it takes willingness and maturity to let it go, or to at least look at things from a different perspective. It can also be helpful to have people around us whom we trust to point out when we're being self-righteous but may not be aware of it.

## The Distinction Between
## Self-Righteousness and Conviction

Removing self-righteousness does not mean watering down our opinions or decreasing our passion. Believing strongly in our opinions, as well as in our values and beliefs about life, work, and everything else, is important. However, understanding the difference between conviction and self-righteousness is essential. When we're coming from a place of *conviction* about something, we believe it to be true, we think it's "right," and we're often willing to speak up about it, to defend our position, and to engage in healthy dialogue or debate about it. But we must also have enough humility, awareness, and maturity to consider we might be wrong—or that, at the very least, there may be other ways to look at it, even if we can't see or understand them. We've all had experiences when we were convinced we were 100 percent right about something, only to realize we were wrong. As humbling as this can be, keeping it in mind can help keep us from crossing the line over to self-righteousness and give us the perspective to stay in a place of healthy conviction.

When we do cross over into self-righteousness, we're no longer interested in hearing what anyone else has to say if they disagree with us or have a different perspective. We're *right* and anyone and everyone who doesn't see it our way is *wrong*.

Look at the tenor of the political discourse in our country and our world. Many of us, myself included, have very strong political opinions, and there are serious issues that divide us. Instead of engaging in healthy and productive debates about these things, there is so much intense self-righteousness we seem unable even to listen to one another, which is almost as scary and dangerous as any of the important issues we're facing. We end up demonizing people who don't agree with us, refusing to talk or listen to them—or, when we do, we make our case in such a self-righteous way that we create more separation and disconnection. Turn on cable news, or read the comments section of many news websites or blogs, and you'll see the intensity of self-righteousness playing out right in front of you.

And this doesn't happen just with politics; it happens right in our own lives, families, and work environments. We separate ourselves from those who don't think like we do or hold the same ideas, opinions, or beliefs. At work our self-righteousness leads to disconnection, unresolved conflicts, and factions within teams and organizations. Lines get drawn between departments, offices, regions, and levels within the company, making it more difficult to make decisions, collaborate, and get things done.

Self-righteousness is one of the most damaging energies we carry as human beings. If we want to connect with those around us in an authentic way, and create an environment of authenticity, trust, and collaboration, we must be willing to recognize, own, and remove our self-righteousness.


## Adding Vulnerability

Vulnerability is fundamental to relationships, trust, and, of course, authenticity. However, it's often misunderstood. Most of us have a strange relationship to vulnerability. Over the past decade, as I've researched, studied, and traveled around the world exploring authenticity—and specifically vulnerability—I've learned a lot and been inspired by the work of others. Dr. Brené Brown is a research professor at the University of Houston who studies human emotions, including vulnerability. Her research has had a big impact on both my work and my personal life. In her book *Daring Greatly*, she defines vulnerability as "uncertainty, risk, and emotional exposure." This succinct definition is spot on, yet like many important things in life, being vulnerable is easier said than done, for a variety of reasons.

I got invited to speak at an event for Gap in Japan a few years back. This event, a three-day leadership academy, was similar to a number of events I'd done for them, which had all taken place in the United States. As with these previous events, I was asked to deliver the opening keynote address. The big difference this time was that my presentation would be translated into Japanese. They were going to do what's called a simultaneous translation. In other words, I would get up on stage and speak in English, but the people in the audience who don't speak English would wear an earpiece, and a person sitting in a booth at the back of the room would translate what I say into Japanese.

I had a few calls with the team from Gap to go over the details and logistics of the event, as well as to discuss some of the cultural dynamics, since this would be my first time to Japan. In preparing my speech, I tried to be as mindful as possible. Whenever I travel outside the U.S., I usually feel a mixture of excitement and fear—especially if it's a country I've never been to before. I try to be as culturally sensitive as possible, although I'm almost always confronted with my own bias and how incredibly limited my worldview can be.

I wanted to get to the ballroom early so I could meet with the team from Gap and, specifically, talk to the translator. There are two things that often make it challenging for translators to work with me. First, I talk pretty fast, so it can be hard to keep up with me. Second, I don't usually use slides and I speak fairly extemporaneously, which can make it challenging to follow me and translate what I say into another language.

When the translator and I met, we discussed some of the key points of my keynote, and I said, "One of the most important things is how I define authenticity. It's honesty, without self-righteousness, and with vulnerability."

"Vulnerability?" she asked, somewhat surprised.

"Yes, vulnerability."

"Vulnerability?" she asked again, now seeming almost agitated.

"Yes, vulnerability."

She gave me a strange look and, after a long pause, she said, "There's no word for that in Japanese."

"Really?" I asked.

"Well," she said, "there is a word, but it's a *bad* word."

Now I was fascinated. "What is it?"

"It means 'weakness.'"

"Actually," I responded, "people often think that's what it means in English, as well."

"Why would you tell people to be vulnerable?" she asked, in a somewhat argumentative way.

"Well," I said, "my research and experience have taught me two important things about vulnerability. First, it's fundamental to human trust and connection. So for these three hundred leaders who will be here this afternoon, if they want to build trust with the people on their teams and connect with them in a genuine way, it's important for them to embrace vulnerability. Second, vulnerability is essential for creativity, innovation, change, risk, and anything new or different. If these leaders want to be able to innovate, grow, or inspire risk-taking in themselves and others, vulnerability is necessary."

She stood there staring at me like I was crazy. I could tell she didn't agree with what I was saying. Adding to my nervousness and my own vulnerability about giving this presentation in a place I'd never been and an environment I assumed would be challenging, I was now having a standoff with the translator.

After an awkward pause, I said, "Listen, do me a favor: just translate what I say as best you can. If it doesn't make sense or doesn't resonate with the group, I'll figure it out."

She nodded and walked back toward the translation booth. I didn't really know how I was going to figure it out; I just knew I wanted to be done with that conversation, because it was stressing me out.

When I got up onstage to deliver my keynote, my heart was racing and my hands were shaking. As I got rolling, some of my anxiety dissipated. But when I began to talk about authenticity I noticed my heart rate going back up. *Maybe I shouldn't mention vulnerability. Maybe it won't make sense or translate. What if it's culturally insensitive or even offensive?* As I got closer to that point in my presentation, I realized there was no way for me to talk about authenticity without talking about vulnerability, so I decided just to go for it. As I began to explain vulnerability, I looked back into the translating booth. *What is she telling them right now?* I realized in that moment she could be saying anything she wanted to say, and I would have no idea what it was. Was she saying, "Don't listen to this crazy American," or "Vulnerability is bad," or something else?

Yet it seemed like what I was saying was resonating with the group, although in that environment and given the language and cultural differences it was hard to tell.

I even decided to lead the group through a paired vulnerability exercise, which I often do if I have time and the environment is conducive. Although it was a little challenging to facilitate this exercise, given the size of the group and the language barrier, it felt important to me that they have an experience of vulnerability, not just a concept.

As my presentation ended and I walked offstage, I felt excited that it seemed to have gone well but also relieved that it was over. I walked to the back of the room to take off my microphone and saw the translator coming out of the booth.

She walked right up to me, bowed, and said, "Thank you for your presentation."

"You're welcome," I said.

"I didn't understand what you meant about vulnerability when we spoke before your speech. But after hearing you talk about it and watching the group do that exercise, I think I understand it now. Vulnerability isn't bad, it's just hard."

"That's right. It's hard."

Being vulnerable takes courage. Unfortunately, all too often we relate to vulnerability—especially in certain environments, relationships, and situations (particularly at work)—as something we should avoid. But it's vulnerability that liberates us from our erroneous and insatiable obsession with trying to do everything "right"—thinking that we can't make mistakes, have flaws, or be human. Embracing vulnerability allows us to let go of the pressure-filled perfection demands we place on ourselves.

In addition to liberating us, being vulnerable gives other people permission to be vulnerable as well; and in doing so, we open up the possibility of real human connection. The natural human response to vulnerability is empathy. And with empathy, we can create deeper trust, connection, and understanding with those around us.

## The Authenticity Equation

As we move along the Authenticity Continuum from phony, to honest, and then to authentic, we can think of authenticity as an equation:

*Honesty – Self-Righteousness + Vulnerability = Authenticity*

By noticing our own phony tendencies, challenging ourselves to be honest, being self-aware enough to remove our self-righteousness, and having the courage to be vulnerable—we're able to be truly authentic.

Understanding the Authenticity Equation and practicing it with ourselves, at work, and in life allows us to show up and connect with others in a real way. It's not easy, and it takes significant self-awareness and courage, but when we do this it's both liberating for us and inspiring for those around us. At the core, bringing our whole selves to work is based on our ability to be authentic. And, being authentic has a profound impact on how we connect with others and build relationships, as well as how we engage in our work and produce results.

In a study conducted by Dan Cable, of London Business School, and Virginia Kay, then of the University of North Carolina at Chapel Hill, recent M.B.A. graduates were surveyed four months into their jobs. The ones who felt they could express their authentic selves at work were, on average, 16 percent more engaged and committed to their organizations than those who felt the need to hide.

In another study, Cable and Kay surveyed 2,700 teachers who had been working for a year, and reviewed their performance ratings given by their supervisors. The teachers who said they could express their authentic selves received higher ratings than the teachers who didn't feel they could do so.

## Lower the Waterline on Your Iceberg

The metaphor I like to use when talking about authenticity is the iceberg. In life, and especially in our work, most of us feel comfortable showing just the tip of our iceberg—the professional, appropriate, and put-together aspects of ourselves. But who we really are, what we really think, how we really feel, and what's really going on in our lives is below the waterline. How we show up more authentically and create an environment around us conducive to this is by lowering the waterline on our iceberg.

The exercise I facilitate that encourages people to lower their waterline is called "If you really knew me . . ." I learned this exercise many years ago from my friends and mentors, Rich and Yvonne Dutra-St. John. They are the co-founders of a wonderful nonprofit organization called Challenge Day. This powerful exercise gives people the opportunity to be real and vulnerable with others, and allows groups and teams to connect with each other in an authentic way.

I've led this exercise hundreds of times over the past decade. We do it in big groups, small groups, and with intact teams of people who work together on a daily basis, which is one of my favorite ways to do the exercise.

I am going to explain in detail how I set up, lead, and facilitate this exercise because it's a fairly simple yet incredibly powerful way to engage the people you work with in an authentic conversation, and in the process build a deeper level of trust and connection within your group. This exercise encourages us to get real with each other, and gives people a real-life, visceral experience of authenticity that can be profound. And introducing and facilitating this exercise is something you can do with the people on your team and others you work with.

If the group is large, like the one at the event in Japan, I usually have people pair up for the exercise. If the group is a bit smaller, but has more than 15 people, as in a workshop or seminar setting, I will often put people into small groups of 4 or 5. And, if the group is small enough (15 people or fewer), and we have the time, we'll do the exercise all together as one group.

I set up the exercise by explaining the Authenticity Continuum and the Authenticity Equation, acknowledging that being honest takes commitment and skill, that removing self-righteousness takes self-awareness and humility, and that being vulnerable takes courage and faith. None of these things are easy, and in certain situations they can be very difficult. Then we talk about the iceberg and the importance of lowering the waterline. I tell everyone that when we lower our waterline, we liberate ourselves, give other people permission to do the same, get to know each other in a more real way, build trust and connection, and embody the essence of authenticity. I then explain that we're going to do an exercise where we get to practice being authentic and challenge ourselves to step out of our comfort zones by lowering the waterline on our icebergs.

At this point I put people into pairs or groups, if that is necessary, and explain that I'll let everyone know exactly how the exercise will go, that then I'll go first (as a way to model it and set the tone), and that then we'll do it all together as a group (or in pairs or small groups).

I say, "When it's your turn, you'll have about two minutes to talk. You'll just repeat this phrase: 'If you really knew me, you'd know . . .' And then you'll share whatever you're willing to share." Then I let them know, "You don't have to say anything you don't want to say."

At this point, I often joke, "This is not like 'shock-the-group time'," at which people usually laugh—both because it's funny and because some people are feeling nervous and uncomfortable hearing what they're being asked to do. Then I usually say, "This is an opportunity for you to be authentic in a vulnerable way with your colleagues. Again, it's totally your choice about what you choose to share, although I do encourage and challenge you to step out of your comfort zone. In order for this exercise to be as safe as possible, it's important that we not talk when someone else is talking, and that we agree to confidentiality. That means that when people are talking we don't make comments, give feedback, ask questions, or make any jokes. It also means that whatever people share, we keep it to ourselves." Then I ask, "Can we all agree to these things?"

Once the exercise is set up, people are clear, and there aren't any more questions, I start by lowering the water-line for myself and sharing whatever is true for me in that moment. I don't prepare it or think about it too much; I just open my mind, my heart, and my mouth—and share about how I'm feeling, what's going on in my life, or whatever's real for me right then.

After I'm done sharing, I open it up to the group and we go around in some understandable order that depends on whether we're doing the exercise as a full group, in a small group, or even in pairs. If we do the exercise in the full group, I find it often works best for the leader of the team to go right after me, and then for us to go around the table in one direction from there. If the group is broken up into smaller groups, I usually ask for one person in each group to raise their hands so that we have volunteers to go first; and then the rest of the people follow in one direction in their small group. I also find it helpful to ask one person in each group to be a timekeeper. They usually use the timer on their phones, and set it for two minutes. Having the timekeeper allows everyone to have the same amount of time, and also allows me to manage the overall time of the exercise for the whole group. For pairs, we pick an A and a B . . . and I usually have person B go first, just to give the group another laughter release when I mention that. It's important to give everyone about the same amount of time, so that things are balanced as well as possible. I remind them that there is no right or wrong way to do the exercise—the main goal is just to lower the waterline and allow themselves to be authentic. Sometimes people get emotional; it's not uncommon for there to be tears in this exercise, although that's not necessary for it to have impact and it's never something I'm trying to force or manufacture. It's just that when we're given the opportunity to get real, what sometimes comes out of people is some emotion they've been holding on to that wants to be expressed.

Once everyone involved has had a chance to lower their waterline and share, then we get to discuss it. In pairs or small groups, I often ask people to share anything they want to say in response to what people revealed, and to talk a little bit about what it was like to have that conversation.

Every group is unique, and I've seen, heard, felt, and shared lots of different things over the years in this exercise. However, there are some universal aspects. Often I'll have people in the room who love this exercise and others who hate it. Most people have a mixture of feelings about it. Sometimes I hear things like, "Wow, I had no idea this was going on for people." They're often amazed by the courage displayed in what people share, and how much stuff is going on below the waterline that we mostly don't know or talk about. There are two questions I usually ask the group as we debrief:

1.  How many of you now know a little more about the person or people you just did this exercise with?

2.  How many of you can relate to what was said by others in this exercise?

Almost everyone's hands go up in response to both of these questions. This exercise and follow-up conversation serve as an important way for people and teams to connect with one another and get to know each other in a deeper way, even and especially if they work together regularly. And the second question speaks to something that is very important about authenticity, specifically vulnerability. As I said earlier, the natural human response to vulnerability is empathy. The irony is that often the more personal we're willing to be, the more relatable we are to the people around us. In some cases we may be able to relate to the specific circumstance, situation, or experience a person is talking about. Even if we can't relate specifically, however, we can almost always relate emotionally.

Deep down below the waterline, we get to some pretty basic and important human experiences and emotions—fear, joy, sadness, gratitude, anger, hope, hurt, uncertainty, risk, and, ultimately, vulnerability. I've done this exercise with groups of all kinds; in different industries, cities, and countries; and facing all kinds of circumstances. What I'm constantly reminded of when we have this conversation is that we're way more alike than we are different. One of the great paradoxes of life, and in working with other people, is that while we're diverse in many important ways, we also have much common ground as human beings. As simple of a realization as this is, it's important for us to remind ourselves and each other, to remember, and to create opportunities as often as we can to experience this type of genuine human connection. Authenticity is an in-the-moment phenomenon, and lowering our waterline and encouraging others to do the same, even and especially at work, is how we build more authentic relationships and enhance the environment around us.

## If You Really Knew Me . . .

As a way of practicing and modeling this, right here and right now (as I would do if I were facilitating this exercise with a group), I'll share . . .

If you really knew me right now, you'd know that I have lots of self-criticism going on in my brain as I write this—the voice in my head won't stop chattering. *You've written about this before, and have been speaking about it for years. You're a one-trick pony who doesn't really have anything unique to share. This is lame and nobody cares.*

If you really, really knew me you'd know that even after more than 20 years of being in therapy, seeing hundreds of practitioners of all kinds, doing as many workshops and seminars as possible, reading tons of books, and teaching what I've been teaching—I still get stuck in deep, dark places of self-doubt and self-judgment, especially about my body and appearance, my fatherhood, and my career.

And, if you really, really, *really* knew me, you'd know that while my many experiences of loss and grief have taught me a great deal and given me incredible perspective, they've also freaked me out in a way I don't like to fully acknowledge. I pretend like I'm okay, but there are times when my fear of death get really intense—worrying about my own death or about people close to me dying. I also find that I judge myself harshly—thinking that these experiences of loss should have taught me more and given me even more perspective and peace than I actually have. I still waste way more time and energy than I'd like worrying about stuff either that I can't control or that I know doesn't really matter in the scheme of things.

These are some of the things you'd know about me right now if you really knew me. How about you? What would people know about you if they really knew you? Specifically, what would the people you *work* with know about you, if they really, really knew you? Of course, you don't have to share this with anyone, and certainly not everyone, but what would it be like to have more freedom to lower your waterline, especially in your work and with the people you interact with professionally? How might it liberate you and connect you with others?

It takes a lot of energy to keep our waterline up. We tend to carry around a big shield, erroneously thinking it will protect us. We've all been hurt, taken advantage of, disappointed, let down, and manipulated in the past—at work and in life. These experiences can be painful, and do have impact. Sadly, however, we use them as justification to build up our shield to be even bigger. And we can't understand why we're so exhausted and stressed out, especially at work. Our stress and exhaustion is not as much from all the meetings, demands, and goals as we think it is. In fact, much of it comes from trying to be how we think we're "supposed" to be, instead of how we really are. What if we put down the shield? What if we stopped trying to protect ourselves all the time? Will we get hurt? Yes. Will we get taken advantage of from time to time? Yes. Might we make a fool of ourselves or put our foot in our mouth? Of course. Will these things be painful or embarrassing? Yes, some of them. But guess what? These things will probably happen from time to time no matter how much we try to "protect" ourselves.

As another mentor of mine said to me years ago, "Mike, you're living your life as though you're trying to survive it. You have to remember something very important: nobody ever has." What are we really afraid of? What are we trying to shield ourselves from anyway? The mortality rate is holding strong at 100 percent.

I once heard Sheryl Sandberg share a poignant story about an experience she had about a year after her husband, Dave, died. She was at her son's music concert at school one afternoon. Seeing all the other families there, especially all the other dads, made her very sad.

"Seeing all the fathers watching their children," she said, "was a stark reminder of what my children and I lost—and what Dave lost. As soon as I got home, I ran upstairs in tears. Unfortunately, my work day wasn't over. I was hosting a dinner at my house for Facebook's top clients from around the world." She went on to say, "As people started to arrive, I still couldn't pull myself together. My son was with me, and I told him that I needed to stop crying and go downstairs. He held my hand and said,

'You should just go. It's okay if you're crying. Everyone knows what happened to us.' Then he added, 'Mom, they probably have things they cry about too, so you should just be yourself."

## Lowering the Waterline with Your Team

As I mentioned above, one of my favorite environments in which to do the "If you really knew me" exercise is with an intact team of people who work together regularly. I've seen some incredible things with this exercise over the years in those team environments. A number of years ago, I got a call from Aditi Dhagat, a director at Adobe at the time. She was someone I'd had a chance to partner with a few times, and Adobe is a longtime client. Aditi had just gotten a new role leading a new team, and wanted me to come in and do a half-day session with them in the morning of a day-long kickoff meeting she'd put together. She's a leader who embodies authenticity, which I really appreciate. When she called me, she said, "I want the team to get to know me and each other in an authentic way. Let's start right away with lowering the waterline on the iceberg and do the 'if you really knew me exercise.'"

When I met with Aditi's new team, we dove right into authenticity, as she had requested. I set up the exercise just as I mentioned above, and kicked things off by lowering the waterline on my own iceberg. I was sitting at one end of the table and Aditi was at the other end. Usually, as I mentioned earlier, I will ask the leader to go second, right after me, but on that particular morning I decided just to turn directly to my right and ask the person sitting there to go next. I realize this can often be difficult, especially for the first few people—they sometimes feel put on the spot and, in a case like this, they're still in that getting-to-know-each-other phase with their team and their new boss, which adds to the challenge. The first few people did engage in the exercise, but it was clear they were being cautious, which was understandable.

When it came to Aditi's turn, she smiled and said, "If you really knew me, you'd know that I'm not sure I should've taken this job." There was a gasp, and I looked around the table at the people on the team: most of them had their eyes and mouths wide open. This isn't the kind of thing you usually say to your new team. She continued: "If you really, really knew me, you'd know that I'm having a hard time letting go of my old team. Even though this job is a good opportunity for me, I've worked really hard with my previous team and I'm worried I might be making a mistake taking on this new role." The truth, openness, and vulnerability of what she was saying and how she was saying it was palpable. Then she said, "If you really, really, really knew me, you'd know I'm feeling nervous about being your new leader; and I'm not sure how you all feel about me or if you think I was the best person for this job, which makes me feel a bit insecure stepping into this role."

I thanked her for sharing, as I do after everyone shares during the exercise. And I was struck by her courage and authenticity. What she said and how she said it created openness, space, and safety in that room for the rest of the people on the team to really open up. Every person who went after her was able to lower their waterline even further, because she had modeled it so beautifully and made it even safer for people to let down their guard. The conversation deepened as we completed the exercise, and, more importantly, as the team began to discuss how they wanted to communicate and collaborate. Aditi had not only talked about the importance of authenticity, she had modeled it in a courageous and vulnerable way. Not only was this a great way for her to kick things off and set the tone in her new role with her new team, but her commitment to authenticity and her team's willingness to engage with each other served them very well in the subsequent months and years they worked together. They built a culture of trust, connection, and collaboration that was based on authenticity.

## Two Types of Credibility

One of the things that makes authenticity challenging, and why we cling to our self-righteousness and avoid vulnerability, is that we worry about damaging our credibility. We erroneously think that somehow being right and covering up any perceived weakness, flaw, or insecurity will give us credibility with others, especially at work. But this is a superficial understanding of credibility. There are really two types of credibility:

**Professional Credibility.** This is about our résumé, our track record, our title, where we went to school, the results we've produced in the past, our skills, and other tangible things. Professional credibility is important: most of us have our jobs or careers owing in part to our professional credibility. When I'm speaking to a group, particularly leaders, I often say, "You wouldn't be sitting in this room or have this role if you didn't have the professional credibility for it. I wouldn't be here speaking to you right now if I didn't have the professional credibility for it." Professional credibility is important. In many cases, however—especially for the purpose of building trusting relationships, strong teams, and a positive culture—personal credibility is much more important.

**Personal Credibility.** This has to do with people being able to relate to us, trust us, understand us, and find common ground with us—and with our ability to do these things with them in return. We build personal credibility with others by listening to them, opening up with them, sharing about ourselves, caring about them, apologizing when necessary, and being willing to lower the waterline on our iceberg. Self-righteousness damages our personal credibility, and vulnerability enhances it. The best way for us to build personal credibility with others is to be authentic. When we have personal credibility with others, there is more connection, loyalty, and understanding. We can give and receive feedback, work through challenges, and navigate the ups and downs of business and life together. We see each other as real people, not just as titles or résumés.

Understanding and separating out these two types of credibility can allow us to let go of our attachment to being right, and encourage our willingness to be more vulnerable—both of which are required for us to be authentic.

Authenticity is the foundation of bringing our whole selves to work. When we have the courage to be authentic (honest, without self-righteousness, and with vulnerability), not only does it liberate us, but it also gives us the ability to inspire and empower others. Authenticity is also a key factor both in creating a safe, healthy, and strong culture around us, and in ensuring that people and teams are engaged and performing at the highest level.

PRINCIPLE #2—

# UTILIZE THE POWER OF APPRECIATION

A few years ago, I spoke at an annual recognition event put on by Charles Schwab to celebrate the winners of their "Chairman's Club" award. The winners, who are Schwab employees from across the entire company, are nominated by their manager and, if selected, receive the award and public recognition, and get to invite a guest to join them for the event, which is held each year at a luxury resort in a beautiful location. It's a big deal and a prestigious award within the company.

At the start of my speech, I asked the winners in the room, "What was it about receiving this award that made you feel appreciated specifically?" I had them break into pairs to discuss this question. After a few minutes, I asked for volunteers who would be willing to share with the rest of us what they talked about with their partners. A number of hands went up in the room of about 250 people. I called on a man who was sitting near the back.

He stood up and said, "My wife and I don't get away very often, just the two of us; so to come on a trip like this and to stay at a place this nice is fantastic." He shook his head in amazement. "I've never won this award before and never thought I would. When you asked us to reflect on what it was that made us feel appreciated in receiving it, for me it was when I came home and told my family that I'd won." He paused and his voice cracked with emotion as he said, "My son told me he was proud of me. That was the moment of appreciation for me. As great as this trip and this honor are, I didn't really need anything after my son said that to me."

I appreciated his poignant and heartfelt story—it elicited an emotional response from me and many other people in that room, and it underscored a simple but important distinction I've learned over the many years I've studied and researched appreciation. There's a big difference between **recognition** and **appreciation**. Unfortunately, we often use these words interchangeably and think of them as the same thing, especially in the business world. They're both important; however, they're distinct. For us to bring our whole selves to work and create an environment around us where people can do the same, it's important for us to understand and act upon this key distinction.

## Recognition

Recognition is positive feedback based on results or performance. When we produce a particular result, we hope to get recognized for it. Sometimes recognition is given in a formal way—an award, a bonus, a promotion, a raise, an official announcement, a gift, public acknowledgment, a trip like the one given to the award winners at Charles Schwab, etc. Sometimes recognition is given more informally—a thank-you, a literal or figurative pat on the back, a note, or something simple letting us know we've done a good job. These things can be important, especially if they're done in a timely, generous, and genuine way. They're also often motivating and exciting.

Even if we get a little embarrassed, there are very few of us who don't like to be recognized for doing a good job. And, getting a bonus, a raise, or an award is something that most of us enjoy very much. As author and leadership expert Tom Peters says, "Celebrate what you want to see more of."

But there are some limits to and issues with recognition. First, it's performance based—so it's conditional. Second, it's based on the past, so it's about what we've already done. Third, it's scarce. There's a limited amount of recognition to go around, and in some cases it can be stressful when many people are vying for a finite amount of recognition. Finally, although many organizations have set up internal recognition programs that allow peers to recognize one another, the major forms of recognition (promotions, raises, bonuses, significant awards, etc.) usually have to come from the top.

## Appreciation

Appreciation, on the other hand, is about acknowledging a person's inherent value. It's not about recognizing their accomplishments; it's about appreciating who they are as a human being. In simple terms, recognition is about what we do; appreciation is about who we are. This is important for many reasons, but mainly because even when we have success, individually and collectively, there may be failures and challenges along the way. And even if there aren't, there may not be tangible results to recognize. If we focus solely on positive outcomes, we miss out on lots of opportunities for connection, support, and appreciation. What most of us truly yearn for at work and in life is to be appreciated for who we are, not just what we do.

Oprah Winfrey spoke about this in a powerful way when she gave a commencement speech at Harvard in 2013. She said, "The single most important lesson I learned in 25 years talking every single day to people on television, is that there's a common denominator in our human experience. The common denominator I found in every single interview is we want to be appreciated and understood. I've done over 35,000 interviews in my career. And as soon as that camera shuts off, inevitably in their own way everyone asks this question: 'Was that okay?' I heard it from President Bush. I heard it from President Obama. I've heard it from heroes and from housewives. I've heard it from victims and perpetrators of crimes. I even heard it from Beyoncé in all her Beyoncé-ness. They all want to know, 'Was that okay?' Really what they're asking is 'Did you hear me?' 'Do you see me?' 'Did what I say mean anything to you?'"

Appreciation is about hearing people, seeing them, and letting them know that not only what they say, but who they *are* matters.

## Understanding the Distinction Between Recognition and Appreciation

The best way I know to illuminate the difference between recognition and appreciation is to give you an example from my baseball career. As I've written about in my previous books, and often talk about when I speak, I spent a good part of my childhood, adolescence, and young adulthood playing baseball. I started playing when I was seven years old. I got drafted out of high school by the New York Yankees, but chose instead to play baseball at Stanford University. Out of Stanford I was drafted by the Kansas City Royals and signed a pro contract. I went into the Royals' minor-league system and tried to work my way up to the major leagues. Unfortunately, in my third season in the minors, at the age of 23, I tore ligaments in my pitching elbow. I had a series of surgeries, but wasn't able to play again. The injury to my arm ended my baseball career.

One of the biggest things I do *not* miss about playing baseball is what would happen when I wasn't pitching well. Whether or not you're a baseball fan, you probably know what happens to the pitcher when he doesn't perform well. It's brutal. They stop the game, and the manager comes out onto the field and takes the ball from you; then you have to leave—right in the middle of the game. Another pitcher then comes in and takes over for you. Imagine if you were at work and in the middle of an important project when you made a big mistake. Now imagine that your boss burst into the room and said, "Stop right there. Please leave." And you had to get up and walk out. Then some other person came into the room, sat down in your chair, and picked up right where you left off. Oh, and imagine thousands of people were watching this happen. You'd probably feel a little embarrassed, right? This is what it's like to be taken out of the game as a pitcher.

There were different situations in which I would get taken out. But let's say it was late in the game, like the eighth inning, and the score was close. Maybe a runner or two had gotten on base and my pitch count was getting high. My manager might come out to get me and say something like, "Hey Robbins, you did a good job, battled hard, and kept us in the game. We're going to get someone in here to relieve you now, because it seems like you're running out of gas. Good work." The competitive part of me would usually be angry and want to stay in.

But if I'd pitched that deep into the game, I could walk off the mound with my head held high, knowing that I'd done my job, kept us in it, and performed pretty well. I'd walk into the dugout and my teammates would give me high fives and tell me I'd done well. In other words, they'd recognize me for my performance.

But let's say it was the second inning and we were already losing 7–0. That would usually mean I'd pitched poorly—really poorly. My manager would come out to get me and wouldn't say anything; or if he did, it wasn't very positive or helpful. In that situation, I'd walk off the mound upset, embarrassed, and frustrated. And, if we were on the road (in the other team's ballpark) it was worse, because there would often be some foul-mouthed fans heckling me, adding to my embarrassment and frustration. The worst part of all was that I would get into the dugout, sit on the bench, and no one would talk to me.

Even if you don't watch baseball much, turn on a game sometime and watch what happens when the pitcher doesn't perform well and gets taken out. Although things have gotten a little better in the past 20 or so years since I stopped playing, there still seems to be an unwritten rule about how to treat a pitcher who has had a bad game and gets removed: *Leave him alone, he's upset.*

Of course I would be upset and disappointed with myself and the outcome whenever I found myself in this situation. But you know what I could have used if I was sitting on the bench after just giving up seven runs in the second inning?

Some appreciation.

Not recognition.

I would not have wanted, needed, or deserved any recognition in that situation. What were they supposed to say? "Hey Robbins, way to go . . . seven runs in the second inning, not so bad."

No.

I would have failed—not just for myself, but for the entire team. We were probably going to lose the game and much of that was my fault. Appreciation is not inauthentic recognition; it's not about blowing smoke or sugarcoating the situation. What I would have needed in that moment was some appreciation—not for what I'd done, but for who I am.

What could they have done to show me some genuine appreciation? They could have said, "Hey man, that was rough, but you're an important part of this team. We believe in you." They could have done or said things that let me know they appreciated me as a person, not just as an athlete. In hindsight, knowing what I know now about myself and about human behavior, I wish someone had asked me this simple but important question in that moment: "Is there anything you need or any way I can support you right now?" Each of us is wired differently, so not everyone would respond to this question the same way. But if anyone had been thoughtful and aware enough to ask me this in that situation, and I'd had the courage to answer honestly, I probably would have said, "Yes, there is. Could you sit down right next to me, put your arm around me, and talk to me for a while? Hopefully that will help this awful feeling in my gut to go away, and also interrupt the voice in my head that's calling me a loser right now." When we fail or things aren't going well, what we often need more than anything else is to know that the people around us still appreciate us and have our backs. We want to know that we're valued, cared about, and included—regardless of our performance.

Appreciation is about *people*; recognition is about *results*. Great leaders have to be good at both. And all of us benefit from understanding this distinction in business (and in life). Recognition is appropriate and necessary when it's earned and deserved. Appreciation, however, is important all the time.

## Appreciation Matters

According to a study conducted by Glassdoor, a company whose website allows employees and former employees to anonymously review companies and their management, 53 percent of people said they would stay longer at their company if they felt more appreciation from their boss. The same survey found that 81 percent of employees said they were motivated to work harder when their boss showed appreciation, compared to only 38 percent who said they were motivated to work harder when their boss was demanding and 37 percent who said they were motivated to work harder when they feared losing their job.

In another study, done at the Wharton School of the University of Pennsylvania, researchers randomly divided university fund-raisers into two different groups. One group made phone calls to solicit alumni donations in the same way they always had. The second group, who were assigned to work on a different day, received a pep talk from the Director of Annual Giving, who told them she appreciated their efforts. During the following week, the university employees who heard her message of appreciation made 50 percent more fund-raising calls than those who did not.

Appreciation matters. And more than just the warm fuzzy feelings it often elicits, it actually has a direct impact on retention, morale, productivity, and results. I've seen this many times over my years of partnering with leaders, teams, and companies of all types and sizes, and in various industries.

A few years ago, I got an e-mail from a leader named Maria, who had seen me speak at a conference. She's a district manager for a large bank, responsible for a number of retail branches in a particular area of the country. Her e-mail said,

> Dear Mike,
>
> Thank you for the speech you gave at our leadership conference two weeks ago. I found the distinction you made between recognition and appreciation interesting. I've always thought of them as essentially the same thing, so hearing you separate them out the way that you did caught my attention and made me think. I'm someone who focuses a lot on numbers and results, and I push my team pretty hard. When the numbers are good, I get excited and recognize them—individually and as a team. But, when the results aren't that good, I tend to get upset and try to figure out what's wrong and how we can fix it. In reflecting on your presentation, I realized that I don't do a very good job appreciating my people.
>
> I have a short conference call with my branch managers each morning, to check in with them, go over the numbers from the day before, and share any updates or announcements they need to know. At the beginning of last week, we had a couple of rough days right in a row, and I was frustrated with the low numbers. Before our morning

call last Wednesday, I remembered some of what you talked about and decided to take a different approach with my team that morning. I got on the phone and said, "Listen, I know we've had a few tough days in row. I'm not happy with the results. I'm sure you're not happy either. But I want you all to know how much I appreciate you. You work hard, take good care of your people, and so often go above and beyond the call of duty. I appreciate your effort and your commitment."

After I said this, there was stunned silence on the phone. No one said anything for quite a while—I actually wondered if the call had dropped or something happened to the phone line. Finally, one of my managers said, "Uh, thanks. Are you feeling okay today?" Then they all laughed, and so did I.

This approach was obviously a bit out of the ordinary for me. However, I was able to then share a little with them about what I'd learned from you at the conference about the difference between recognition and appreciation. It was an important discussion for us to have—for me as their leader, and also for them as leaders of their branches.

The most amazing thing happened that day— we ended up having our second-best day, numbers-wise, over the past year. And for the past few days since then, our numbers have been really good, on the heels of a stretch when they hadn't been very good at all. I'm going to continue to focus on expressing my appreciation for the people on my team, regardless of the numbers.

Thanks,

Maria

## Why Expressing Appreciation at Work Can Be Challenging

As important as appreciation is, it can also be challenging to express authentically—particularly at work. Here are some of the reasons why:

- We don't feel appreciated ourselves.

- We're too busy.

- The results aren't what we want them to be.

- We're more focused on what's wrong or what needs improvement.

- We don't want to send mixed messages to someone we find difficult to deal with, or someone who isn't performing the way we'd like.

- We don't know the best or most appropriate way to do it.

- It can sometimes be awkward or make us feel vulnerable.

- The culture where we work isn't conducive to the expression of appreciation.

- People act goofy when they receive appreciation or turn it into a joke.

- We spend more time complaining, criticizing, or gossiping than expressing appreciation for others.

- Appreciation is sometimes perceived as "soft."

- We worry that if we focus too much on appreciation it will lead to complacency—both in us and others.

These things and others can get in our way. It takes commitment, skill, and courage to express appreciation at work effectively.

In a survey conducted by the John Templeton Foundation, nearly all 2,000 respondents reported that saying "thank you" to colleagues "makes me feel happier and more fulfilled." However, only 10 percent acted on that impulse on a given day. And a stunning 60 percent said they "either never express appreciation at work or do so only about once a year."

Ironically, even something as positive as expressing our appreciation for the people we work with is often below the waterline on our iceberg. It can be scary or uncomfortable to do. And even if we want to do it, it's not always encouraged or remembered in our work environments. We have to be willing to be vulnerable and to step past a certain amount of discomfort and/or cultural resistance in order to do it. To do this, we have to be willing to bring our whole selves to work and to the relationships we have with one another.

### The Appreciation Seat Exercise

One of my favorite exercises to do with teams is what I call the "Appreciation Seat." I'm going explain how I set up, facilitate, and debrief this exercise in detail because it's something that can have a big impact on you and the people you work with, similar to the "If You Really Knew Me" exercise we talked about in the previous chapter.

For the "Appreciation Seat" exercise, it's best to do it with your full, intact team if you can—ideally 15 or fewer people. If the group has more than 15, or I'm facilitating this exercise in a workshop setting with people from an extended team or from multiple teams or departments,

I usually break people up into smaller groups of four or five, depending on the overall size of the group and the room setup. To set up the exercise effectively, it's important to discuss the distinction between recognition and appreciation so that people understand the difference and know that this activity is about appreciating one another's value as people, not about recognizing one another's specific skills or results.

I then let everyone know that we're going to do an important exercise that will allow us to have an experience of both giving and receiving appreciation in a heartfelt, genuine way. I explain that each person will have a turn in the Appreciation Seat, and when it's their turn, all they'll have to do is sit there and receive the appreciation being expressed to them. They don't even have to move from where they're sitting, and I encourage them not to say anything other than "thank you." One of the specific, interpersonal reasons that expressing appreciation can be challenging is that most of us aren't all that comfortable with *receiving* appreciation from others. We often feel awkward when someone appreciates us, and as a social-norm reaction we tend either to give them a compliment right back or to deflect their appreciation with self-deprecation, self-criticism, or humor. While these reactions are normal, they get in the way of our ability to really take in the appreciation, and thus make it harder for people to express it to us. Getting a compliment is like being given a gift: our job is to receive it graciously and gratefully, not to give a quick gift back or somehow diminish the gift—which unfortunately is what we do much of the time. In the exercise I remind everyone of these things and encourage them to listen, breathe, and really take in the appreciation that's being offered to them.

I pick someone in the group to start—usually someone I think will be fairly open to receiving appreciation from his or her teammates. It's often a little uncomfortable for everyone at first, but that usually subsides within a few minutes. As I've learned so many times with this exercise, it's a good idea to use a timer with a chime if possible: even though it may start slow, once people get into it, they tend to have a lot to say and everyone wants to jump in. Depending on how much total time we have and the size of the group, I usually plan for about three minutes per person, although it often goes longer than that. Anyone is welcome to start, and people who feel moved to share some appreciation for the person in the Appreciation Seat can jump in as we go; there's no particular order we have to follow. Once the chime on the timer goes off, that is the signal for the person who is currently speaking to wrap up their appreciation so we can we move on to the next person.

Although we don't go in any particular order in terms of the people giving appreciation, I find it's best simply to go counterclockwise around the group for who is next in the Appreciation Seat. Most of the time the group will be sitting around a table or in a circle, so this makes sense and works pretty naturally. We continue going counterclockwise until everyone has had a chance to receive appreciation from some of the people in the group. I usually remind the group that it's not necessary (and usually not even feasible time-wise) for every person in the group to express appreciation for every other person. This eliminates both the pressure people can feel to say something to everyone and any concern someone might have about another person in the group not expressing appreciation for them.

By the time we're a couple of people into the exercise, however, it's very common for a few more people to demand that they be allowed to express their appreciation for the person in the Appreciation Seat even after the chime sounds. This is usually fine, as long as there will be enough time to get to everyone.

If I'm facilitating this exercise with a larger group, and we have split up into smaller groups of four or five, it's even more important to use the timer (or have a timekeeper in each group) and encourage each group to move on to the next person when the chime goes off—so that all the groups finish around the same time. In those smaller groups, there is sometimes enough time for everyone to get a chance to express appreciation for everyone else. But to manage the expectations and pressure, I still remind the groups that it's not required that everyone express appreciation for every other person.

It's not uncommon in this exercise for people to get emotional as they express and receive appreciation. It never ceases to amaze me how simple yet profound this exercise can be. As the facilitator, my job is to set it up, model appreciation (which sometimes involves me going first and expressing some appreciation for the first few people), hold the space (especially at the beginning when people feel most vulnerable), and to gently keep things on track both in terms of time and in case people start deflecting, making jokes, or doing other things that we human beings sometimes do when we feel uncomfortable.

Once the exercise ends and everyone has had a chance to be appreciated, I thank the group and ask them to reflect on how it was. Sometimes it makes sense to have people pair up to talk about it, even if we did the exercise as one group, because of the personal and emotional nature of the activity; also because some people are less likely to speak up in a group than others, so having them initially talk in pairs gives them a chance to speak and be heard as they reflect on their experience. If they're separated into small groups, it's definitely best to have them discuss their experience in their small groups before we have a larger discussion.

There are two questions I usually ask the group as we debrief:

1.  What was it like to express appreciation for the people in the group?

2.  What was it like to receive appreciation from the people in the group?

After they're done discussing these questions in their pairs or small groups, we discuss their experience of the exercise as a full group. The conversation that follows is almost always fascinating. Here are some of the common themes I've heard from people over the years:

*   It's easier and more comfortable to give than to receive appreciation.

*   It's not all that easy to just say "thank you" and let in people's appreciation.

*   It feels good and is fun to express appreciation.

*   It's nice to be appreciated (even if appreciation is a little challenging to receive).

*   We should do this more often.

*   It's simple but powerful.

*   We feel more connected to each other as people and as a team.

I love this exercise. I often end it by reminding the group that, on the one hand, what we just did was forced and artificial: I told them to say positive things to each other and they did that. But given that in most cases they know each other, work together, and care about each other, finding things to appreciate about one another is usually easy and quite fulfilling; it just takes awareness, commitment, and courage. And even when it's "forced" like this, it can still be meaningful and genuine. I also let them know that they probably won't forget anytime soon what their team-mates said to and about them. Finally, I encourage them to find simple and practical ways to express appreciation for one another (and for others, such as cross-functional part-ners, clients, senior leaders, and even friends and family) on a more regular basis. Appreciation has impact.

## Appreciation in Action

I was invited to lead a multi-day offsite for the executive leadership team of one of my clients, a global technology company with 25,000 employees worldwide. They were having this retreat to discuss a variety of issues and challenges facing them as a leadership team and as a company. The offsite was intense—lots of difficult discussions, conflicts, and hard decisions. The team and the company were in a tough spot and their future was uncertain. They had a lot of pressure on them to turn things around and get the company back on the right track.

On the final day of the offsite, I introduced the "Appreciation Seat" exercise. I was nervous about how it might be received. As I suspected, they weren't all that into it at first. I have a lot of experience with this, so I navigated through their resistance and discomfort, and we did it anyway. Whenever there is resistance like this— people sometimes laugh, make jokes, or seem like they might shut down and not engage—I try to do my best to acknowledge the resistance (either directly or just to myself), and at the same time make sure I'm more committed to the process, and to the power and impact of people giving and receiving appreciation, than I am worried about the discomfort of the group.

Once we got past the initial reluctance and some of the awkward joking, they started to get into it. As we went around the table, they began to disregard the timer, and just about every person took time to appreciate every one of the 12 other people on their team. These were highly educated and well-established executives, with years of experience, success, and accomplishment under their belts. And, like Oprah said, they all wanted to know that they were seen, heard, and that they mattered to each other—not just for what they do, but for who they are. We spent close to two hours doing that exercise on the final day of their offsite, giving us just enough time to do a final wrap-up and to come up with some action steps for them to take as a team.

I stayed in touch with them over the course of the next year. And they invited me back to their annual leadership-team offsite the following year. As we kicked things off for the meeting, their CEO, Bill, got up to speak for a few minutes before turning it over to me. He said, "Last year at this time, we were in a really difficult spot as a team and as a company. And while we aren't completely out of the woods yet, we've made incredible progress over past 12 months. I think our time together at this meeting a year ago set the course for us to make the progress we did. Specifically, the appreciation we expressed for one another on that final day of last year's retreat has stayed with me all year."

We had another intense but productive meeting over the next few days. On the final day, I wasn't planning to do the "Appreciation Seat" exercise again, but they insisted. An hour and a half later, we were done, and they were able to both express and receive appreciation for one another in a heartfelt and genuine way once again.

Another great example of a leader and a team putting appreciation into action is Chris Mauger, the Principal of Cottonwood Elementary School in Hesperia, California (about an hour and a half east of Los Angeles). I initially met Chris a number of years ago when I spoke to him and his fellow administrators in the Hesperia Unified School District. Over the past few years, he has made a real commitment to appreciating the staff, parents, and students in his school community, which has had a positive impact on the morale and performance of Cottonwood Elementary. Here are a few things Chris told me that they do:

- "Every Friday, I leave a note in the box of three to five of our staff members, asking them to come see me and my assistant principal at the end of the day. Naturally they get nervous about 'the note,' but the real reason we call them in is to let them know how much we appreciate all they do for our students and community. We put some real thought into it, so it's genuine and specific, not just a random 'Hey, good job.' We find this sends them off for the weekend on a high note. And as an unintended (but awesome) consequence, my assistant principal and I get to leave school on Friday energized as well after having these positive conversations."

- "Toward the end of each school year we invite the families of some of our sixth-graders (we're a K–6 school) to come in for a meeting with me, my assistant principal, and their child. Often they bring the student's siblings, grandparents, and anyone else they choose. During this meeting we express our appreciation for the student, and thank them for giving us the opportunity to work with them and their family. We also let them know that even though their child won't be with us moving forward, we're always happy to hear about how they're doing and provide any support we can."

- "We encourage our teachers to call parents often to appreciate their children. We also make calls from the office for this reason. Parents aren't used to getting calls from school for good things. Typically, when they hear from the principal, it's not about something positive. We're doing our best to change that perception, and parents are always happy to hear about the good stuff. There have been some tears of joy on these calls. And we feel that it is helping to build a strong and healthy relationship between our staff and our parents. Too often parents are viewed as adversaries, which is definitely not the relationship we want to have in education."

Whether it's an executive leadership team expressing their appreciation for one another, a school that encourages appreciation in its community, or any leader or team that makes a commitment to caring about the people around them and letting them know, the act of appreciating others is fairly simple—but the impact on the people and environment in which we work can be huge. Appreciation allows our heart and soul to connect with the hearts and souls of others, which is ultimately what bringing our whole selves to work is all about.

## Gratitude

The foundation of appreciation is gratitude. If you Google the word *gratitude*, the first definition that comes up is "The quality of being thankful; readiness to show appreciation for and to return kindness." Gratitude is the mindset and perspective that is necessary to foster an environment of appreciation—within ourselves, with our co-workers, and for life in general. However, given the pace and nature of life and business today, it's easy to get so caught up in the stress, worry, negativity, and intensity of our lives and jobs, that we forget to focus on what we're grateful for, or don't prioritize it. We're often so focused on challenges, issues, or goals that we miss out on all the good stuff around us. Sometimes it takes something big (or small) to intervene and remind us to be grateful.

It was just before 3 A.M. when I heard my wife, Michelle, let out a little scream. I woke up with a start, saw her jump out of bed, and felt the house shaking. Having grown up and spent most of my life in the San Francisco Bay Area, I knew exactly what was happening—it was an earthquake. I too jumped out of bed and followed Michelle out of our bedroom. She ran into our older daughter Samantha's room, while I ran into our younger daughter Rosie's room. This was the first earthquake I could remember since we'd had the girls. Samantha was eight and Rosie had just turned six. The quake was over very quickly, as they usually are. I heard Samantha crying in the other room as Michelle was trying to calm her down and explain what happened. When I reached Rosie's bedside, I was amazed and impressed to find that she was still asleep. She'd slept right through it. I stood there for a moment staring at her with my heart racing. It always blows me away how beautiful and peaceful they are—especially when they're asleep. I gently picked her up out of bed, trying not to wake her, and carried her back into our bedroom. She stayed asleep and I laid her down in our bed, next to Michelle.

Samantha was also in our bed. She was still crying a bit and was somewhat disoriented from being woken up in the middle of the night with the house shaking. Michelle and I were doing what we could to calm Samantha down and soothe her, while trying not to wake up Rosie. Within a few minutes, Samantha fell back asleep. I lay there in bed for a while, but couldn't fall back to sleep myself. My heart rate had come down a bit, but my mind was racing. Even though our house and neighborhood seemed fine, I couldn't help but think, *Was that the "big one"? Was there a lot of damage? Is everything okay?*

I finally surrendered to the fact that I probably wasn't getting back to sleep, and I got up quietly (so as not to disturb Michelle and the girls), went downstairs, and opened my laptop. I started searching the Internet for information about the earthquake. Given that it was now only about 3:30 A.M., there wasn't a ton of news yet. But from what I could gather, the epicenter of the quake was in Napa, about 30 miles from where we live. It looked like there had been some property damage in downtown Napa, but all in all, from the initial reports, it didn't seem too serious. I felt a sense of relief—but my relief quickly turned into sadness.

As scary and disruptive as it was to be woken up in the middle of the night by the earthquake, and to be sitting at my kitchen table surfing the Internet in the wee hours of the morning trying to figure out how much damage had been done, I realized that this type of thing almost never happens to me. I began to think about all the people around the world, and even in our community, who often wake up in the middle of the night worried about their safety or that of the people they love. I felt deep sadness and empathy for what that must be like.

As I began to look around our house and reflect on my life, my sadness turned into gratitude. *Wow, I'm so fortunate. What an amazing life I have. Michelle and the girls are upstairs sleeping. They're healthy and happy. We're safe. I'm healthy. I get to do work that I love. We live in this beautiful home. We have so many privileges, and so many blessings in our lives.* As I continued to reflect on all that I was grateful for, I was reminded of the profound impact gratitude can have.

Gratitude is actually a generating emotion. Being in a state of gratitude impacts us mentally, emotionally, and even physically. It sends positive chemicals into our nervous system. The hypothalamus (the part of our brain that controls basic bodily functions, such as eating and sleeping) and dopamine (the "reward neurotransmitter"), are both significantly affected by gratitude. In an article for *Psychology Today*, Dr. Alex Korb wrote, "Gratitude can have such a powerful impact because it engages your brain in a virtuous cycle." Feeling grateful can increase our wellness, improve our sleep habits, increase our metabolism, and lessen our stress. These aspects of personal well-being are vital for our success and our relationships at work, especially given the pace and intensity of the way we work these days.

## Gratitude at Work

A few years ago, I was talking to Erica Fox, who at the time was the Head of Learning Programs at Google. I had partnered with her and her team quite a lot over the years, delivering seminars for Google employees around the world. After attending one of my seminars, she came up with an idea of how to engage her direct reports in a positive way. Since she was leading a remote team of people who were located in various cities, it was challenging for them to connect in a personal way. Even with the use of Google's state-of-the-art video-conference technology, there's nothing quite like being in the same room. And as anyone who leads or is part of a team that is distributed across multiple locations knows, it can be difficult to connect effectively and personally via conference call or video conference.

During her next weekly meeting, Erica asked each of her team members to share something they were grateful for from the previous week—it could be something work related or something personal, so long as it was something that they genuinely felt grateful about. She asked them not only to share this verbally with their teammates, but also to write down what they were grateful for on a Post-it note and stick it somewhere out of sight in their workspace (like inside a folder or desk drawer). She thought it would be fun for them to find the Post-it note again sometime later and be reminded of the positive thing they were grateful for that they shared with the team.

The exercise was fun and set a nice tone for their weekly team meeting that day. It allowed people to connect with one another in a more personal and positive way, even though they weren't all sitting in the same room together. It went so well the first time she tried it, she decided to do it again the following week. Some of the people on her team were more into it than others, which is often the case for things like this. She did it a third time in their next weekly meeting. She decided not to do it the following week because she thought it might be getting a little old, and she wasn't sure if the people on her team were all that into it. But when she started that next meeting without doing the gratitude exercise, to her surprise a number of her people got upset. They had been ready with their Post-it notes and had already planned what they were going to share. So she decided to do the exercise again that week and made it a standard practice for her subsequent weekly team meetings, which helped improve their personal connection and team culture even though they didn't all work together in the same location.

Erica later told me, "In addition to generating a practice/routine of appreciation, it also allowed us to share more about ourselves (in small bits) with each other, which ultimately led us to more openness, vulnerability, and safety within our team. And these things invariably led to better work results as well." She continued, "An unintended outcome of this gratitude practice was that people became more comfortable sharing small flops eventually. We had a standing team-meeting agenda item that was called 'milestones, celebrations, and fantastic flops.'"

These types of activities and practices matter for teams. Kim Cameron and some of his colleagues at the

University of Michigan published a research article in *The Journal of Applied Behavioral Science* that found that a workplace characterized by positive practices like the one Erica did with her team at Google can help people excel in a variety of ways.

Cameron and his colleagues theorized that the three main reasons these types of practices benefit teams and companies are that they

- **Increase positive emotions** that broaden people's resources by improving their relationships with their colleagues and by amplifying their creativity

- **Buffer against negative events** like stress or failure, improving people's ability to bounce back from challenges

- **Attract and bolster employees,** making them more loyal and bringing out their best

There are also benefits to the bottom line. Cameron et al. summarized their findings by saying, "When organizations institute positive, virtuous practices they achieve significantly higher levels of organizational effectiveness—including financial performance, customer satisfaction, and productivity."

Another great example of this is what Cindy Elkins did with her team at Genentech, where she was Vice President of IT for the Americas and the site leader for IT at Genentech's main campus in South San Francisco. Genentech is one of the world's leading biotech companies; they discover, develop, manufacture, and sell medicines to treat patients with serious or life-threatening medical conditions, such as cancer. My sister Lori received drugs developed by Genentech when she was going through her cancer treatment. They are a company that prides themselves on what they do and how they do it, and on their culture. Genentech has been listed on *Fortune* magazine's "100 Best Companies to Work For" list for 19 consecutive years (10 times in the top 10).

Cindy and her team put on an annual event called Full Spectrum for her entire technology group of over 600 people. When I interviewed Cindy about this on my podcast, she told me, "This event is like an annual national sales meeting where we look back at how things went the previous year, introduce our rallying cry for the coming year, and get folks pumped about what's to come. However, since it's called 'Full Spectrum' we introduce ideas that go way beyond technology and work—topics that appeal to developing our whole selves, personally and professionally."

Leading up to their event in 2015 they came up with the theme of Attitude of Gratitude. Cindy had been fascinated by some of the research on gratitude, and wanted to introduce it to her organization. They had also been through quite a journey over the previous few years since she took over as VP. The company, and her team in particular, had navigated lots of change and challenge—especially after being acquired by Roche. The organization continued to succeed and the culture remained strong, but as is often the case with big integrations, there were bumps in the road, people who left, and things that were difficult. She wanted to both to express her appreciation for her team members and to encourage them to adopt gratitude as a way of being, thinking, and communicating. Cindy said, "I wanted our 2015 event and this 'Attitude of Gratitude' theme to be something that impacted our culture at work, and also benefited us in our lives outside of work."

The gratitude theme really resonated with the team at the event. Cindy told me, "I didn't want it to be a onetime thing; I really wanted to infuse our community with gratitude. And at the end of the day, we're a business, so it had to be tied to a business objective." Connecting gratitude to their engagement and wellness scores on the annual employee survey, which the company takes very seriously, gave them the business focus they needed. After the event they conducted surveys, shared some of the latest scientific studies on gratitude, communicated about it consistently, encouraged the leaders in the group to model and express gratitude as much as possible, and suggested various practices and exercises for people to bring gratitude to life in daily activities, interactions, and meetings at work.

Some of the many things they did to infuse their culture and community with gratitude were as follows:

- The Attitude of Gratitude logo, signage, and staging that they created for their initial event were used throughout the year—on T-shirts and signs, and at all their follow-up all-hands meetings.

- They launched a "60-day gratitude challenge"—encouraging everyone in their IT community to take time each day to "Say it, Write it, Express it."

- They created a special "gratitude" section on their Google+ collaboration group where people could publicly express their gratitude.

This gratitude initiative was led by a group of employee volunteers called the Community Champions. Over 100 people, more than 20 percent of the entire organization, volunteered to be a part of this group.

As they were planning their next Full Spectrum event in 2016, they decided that the Attitude of Gratitude theme was resonating so well with everyone that they wanted to use it again, so they did. They called it "Attitude of Gratitude—The Sequel," because they were looking at gratitude not as a word but a practice.

In their first year focusing on gratitude as their cultural theme, the Genentech IT organization went from #10 to #3 on *Computerworld's* "Best Places to Work in IT" list, and they saw improvements in their engagement and wellness scores. This commitment to gratitude impacted the way they thought and interacted with one another, and also had tangible results in how they operated and performed as a team.

## What Are You Grateful For?

One of my favorite questions to ask is "What Are You Grateful For?" I ask it all the time. About once a week I post this simple question on social media, and the response is usually immediate and abundant. The outgoing voice mail message in my office says to "leave a message, and in your message, let us know something you're grateful for." People leave us great messages. Sometimes someone will call trying to sell something and their message will go something like this, "Oh, wow, I wasn't quite prepared for that question. Let me see . . . I'm grateful for my family." Or, "I'm grateful for my job." Or, "I'm grateful for my health." It always makes me smile.

Not only is it nice to learn what people are grateful for when they post it on social media or leave it in a voice mail message, but it also encourages me to stop and reflect on what I'm grateful for myself. The pressures of life and work today can be intense. Most of us are expected to get more done in less time than ever before. Many of us are facing stressful situations and circumstances—some big, some small—at work and at home. The challenges we face, especially in our professional lives, can be complex and even overwhelming. However, there is always much for us to appreciate and be grateful for—if we choose to stop and pay attention. And when we do this, not only does it benefit us—mentally, emotionally, and physically—but it also impacts the people around us and our ability to work together in a positive way. Appreciation and gratitude are access points to connecting us with the people we work with, and to reminding us about what matters most.

# PRINCIPLE #3 —
# FOCUS ON EMOTIONAL INTELLIGENCE

A few years ago I was invited to give a talk on emotional intelligence to a group of leaders at Adobe. Jeff Vijungco, then Adobe's VP of Global Talent, introduced me by saying, "Mike's here to talk to us today about emotional intelligence, also known as EQ. I've always believed that IQ gets you your job, but EQ gets you promoted."

I'd never heard someone say that, and found it both succinct and relevant. I got up onstage, thanked Jeff, and said, "Well, what Jeff just said is basically the point of my entire presentation." The group laughed and so did I.

In today's fast-paced, diverse business environment, emotional intelligence is more important than ever. And organizations who understand this and create an environment conducive to the emotional awareness and development of their people are more likely to thrive.

## What Is Emotional Intelligence?

For generations, it was thought that our intelligence quotient (IQ) was the primary determinant of our success, especially in business. In 1990, however, professors Peter Salovey of Yale University and Jack Mayer of the University of New Hampshire coined the term "emotional intelligence" (now also referred to as the "emotional quotient" or EQ). Salovey and Mayer described EQ as "a form of social intelligence that involves the ability to monitor one's own and others' feelings and emotions, to discriminate among them, and to use this information to guide one's thinking and action."

In 1995, psychologist and author Daniel Goleman built on this work and brought it to a much wider audience with his international best-selling book, *Emotional Intelligence: Why It Can Matter More Than IQ*. And in 1998, Goleman wrote a classic article for the *Harvard Business Review* in which he shared the research he'd done on EQ at nearly 200 large, global companies. This was the first significant and mainstream application of emotional intelligence theory in business. Goleman found that the most effective leaders are distinguished by a high degree of EQ. Without it, he argued, a person can have first-class training, an incisive mind, and an endless supply of good ideas, but still won't be a great leader. According to Goleman, EQ was even more important to our success than IQ.

This was a radical notion at the time, and in some circles it still is. But we've all worked with people who were incredibly smart and talented but struggled to deal with the emotional stress and complex demands of work, or had difficulty dealing with the "people dynamics" of their jobs. This is especially true of leaders. There are many smart people in high levels of business leadership who lack social and emotional skills, which creates a host of challenges for them and everyone they work with.

Today, most of us understand the importance of emotional intelligence in business, and the research on and awareness of this topic has grown exponentially in the past two decades. Many companies have formal programs that train employees, managers, and executives in EQ skills. And during the recruiting process for many jobs, companies try to assess not only the interviewee's IQ, experience, qualifications, and skills but also his or her emotional intelligence. But although EQ gets talked about a great deal in today's business world, it's important for us to first discuss its primary components, so that we can then go deeper and explore how to both increase our own emotional intelligence and influence the people around us and our work environment.

## The Four Components of Emotional Intelligence

**Self-awareness** is about being able to recognize and experience our own thoughts, feelings, and physical sensations. This can be challenging, not least because of the lightning-fast pace of work and life these days. Self-awareness is about paying attention to ourselves and noticing what's going on inside of us. It's about more deeply understanding who we are and what makes us tick, as well as what we're feeling and why we're feeling it, both in general and in a given moment.

**Self-management** is about being able to manage our thoughts and feelings as best as we can, as well as to motivate and discipline ourselves. In order to have some ability to manage what's going on inside of us, we of course have to be aware of what we're thinking and how we're feeling. It's also important that we pay attention to what works and doesn't work for us as we make our way through life. This is about being able to intervene and direct ourselves when we get stuck in negative loops of anxiety, apathy, stress, or worry. It's also about being able to channel our energy in directions that are the most positive and productive for our work and relationships. Self-awareness and self-management are intricately connected to each other. They're like the "1" and "1a" of emotional intelligence. The first of them is about noticing (awareness) and the second is about taking action (management).

**Social awareness** is about paying attention to other people and tapping into what's going on for them emotionally. Another way to think of social awareness is "other awareness." If self-awareness focuses on how we're thinking and feeling, social awareness focuses on what the people around us might be thinking or feeling. Of course we can't read their minds or feel their feelings, but we can pay attention to others with curiosity, compassion, and interest. Social awareness has a lot to do with our ability to empathize with others and use our instincts and intuition to sense where people are coming from, to pick up on body language, to pay attention to social cues, and more.

**Relationship management** is about how we engage with and relate to other people, and how we manage the different relationships we have. This has to do with our ability to connect with different types of people, understand the context and intention of each unique relationship, and navigate the complexity and diversity of our interactions. Not everyone is like us, of course. For us to be effective in managing our relationships, especially at work, we have to tap into our social and relational skills, which are sometimes referred to as social intelligence. Relationship management is also about building trust, connecting, and motivating others. Similarly to the first two aspects of EQ, social awareness and relationship management are like the "2" and "2a" of emotional intelligence, the first of them again being about noticing (social awareness) and the second being about taking action (relationship management).

## Emotions at Work

Although we've made progress on this front in recent years, there still seems to be a stigma about expressing certain emotions at work. It's like we're supposed to check many of our feelings at the door when we walk into the office. I've always found this phenomenon to be strange. Most organizations and leaders want their people to be excited, engaged, passionate, and motivated about their work, the products and services they offer, the mission of the company, and the customers they serve. Yet at the same time, in many organizations there are clear (albeit unwritten) rules about which emotions are appropriate to express at work. In many cases, expressing feelings like sadness, fear, jealousy, hurt, anger, doubt, and insecurity is seen as "inappropriate" or "unprofessional." According to the research of Dr. Brené Brown, however, "the problem is that we cannot selectively numb emotions. When we numb those hard feelings, we also numb joy, gratitude, and happiness." If we want to be excited and engaged at work, and we also want the people around us to feel the same way, we have to make space for a wider range of emotions, even the uncomfortable ones. This takes courage, commitment, skill, and, of course, personal and collective emotional intelligence.

A beautiful example of this popped up in the media just as I was writing this chapter. Madalyn Parker, a web developer at a company called Olark Live Chat in Ann Arbor, Michigan, sent out an e-mail to her team that said,

Hey Team,

I'm taking today and tomorrow off to focus on my mental health. Hopefully I'll be back next week refreshed and back to 100%.

Thanks,

Madalyn

Later in the day, the CEO of her company, Ben Congleton, responded with an e-mail back to her saying,

Hey Madalyn,

I just wanted to personally thank you for sending e-mails like this. Every time you do, I use it as a reminder of the importance of using sick days for mental health—I can't believe this isn't standard practice at all organizations. You are an example to us all, and help cut through the stigma so we can all *bring our whole selves to work.*

(Sidenote: I love that he used the phrase "bring our whole selves to work" in his note back to her.)

Madalyn shared a screen shot of the e-mail exchange on Twitter and said this in her post:

When the CEO responds to your out-of-office e-mail about taking sick leave for mental health and reaffirms your decision 100%.

Very soon after she posted it, Madalyn's tweet was retweeted more than 16,000 times, was liked more than 45,000 times, and received hundreds of comments and responses. Her viral tweet was also picked up by several news outlets. When Ben was asked about his response to Madalyn for an article in *Money* magazine, he said, "I sort of felt like this was just something that should be normal. It's just business as usual for us, not something new." He went on to say, "We built this organization with a culture where this kind of talk is no big deal. So many people live in fear of disclosing mental health issues at work. In many ways that fear makes those mental health issues worse."

In response to Madalyn's tweet, however, some Twitter users shared negative reactions to their requests for mental health days at work. One woman said she left a job after "HR wanted to know in advance when I'd have a panic attack."

According to the aforementioned article in *Money* magazine, one in five adults in America experience depression, anxiety, or some other kind of mental or emotional disorder. The American Psychiatric Association provides information for companies to better understand mental health in the workplace, ranging from detailing how anxiety disorders are "not a sign of personal weakness" to reporting that 80 percent of employees treated for mental illness showed improved levels of work efficiency.

As someone who comes from a family with a lot of mental illness—my dad suffered from bipolar disorder for most of his adult life, which caused significant difficulties in his career—I'm keenly aware of the challenges associated with mental illness and the stigma that often surrounds it. My own struggles with depression in college and throughout my early twenties helped me to understand that mental illness is as debilitating as any other illness. But it's often accompanied by intense judgment and shame from ourselves and others, which adds to its difficulties and makes it harder for us to admit to and, for people who haven't experienced it, to understand.

This isn't just about particular mental health issues; it's more about understanding, appreciating, and acknowledging the overall significance of our mental and emotional state at work. Checking our emotions at the door as we walk into work is not only unhealthy, it's almost impossible. We humans are emotional creatures, and it's our feelings that connect us to ourselves and each other. The more open and courageous we are about feeling and expressing our emotions, the more access we have to our own power and the more permission we give to the people around us. Our emotions are a big part of our "whole selves," and if we suppress them, it holds us back in many detrimental ways and keeps us from performing at our best.

Madalyn Parker exhibited self-awareness and self-management in knowing that she needed to take a few days off to manage her mental and emotional well-being. She courageously chose to share this publicly with her team, which made her vulnerable. Ben's response exemplified his social awareness. And the empathy and appreciation he expressed for Madalyn not only positively impacted his relationship with her, but also reinforced a cultural and relational norm for the company that he as the CEO believed to be important. Their interaction displayed both personal and collective EQ.

Being emotionally intelligent takes awareness, commitment, and skill. As Dr. David Caruso of the Yale Center for Emotional Intelligence says, "It is important to understand that emotional intelligence is not the opposite of intelligence, it is not the triumph of heart over head—it is the unique intersection of both." Dr. Caruso points to the fact that for us to be successful at work, we have to integrate our IQ and our EQ.

A manager named Susan reached out to me a few years ago and told me that after hearing me speak about the importance of emotional intelligence she realized she wanted to do a better job of checking in with her team on an emotional level. She said that she started asking each of her direct reports in their weekly one-on-one meetings, "Are you happy?" The first time she asked this of her team, a few of them burst into tears. Susan told me, "I guess some of the people on my team weren't very happy and were much more stressed out than I'd realized. Those conversations were hard, but important." Emotional intelligence is about paying attention to and managing our own internal state *and* wanting to understand the internal states of those around us, so that we can connect with them more deeply, build stronger relationships, and know how to best collaborate with them.

## Crying at Work

Speaking of bursting into tears, crying is something that many of us have resistance to and judgment about, especially at work. Why is this? A lot of us have been shamed or criticized for doing it, or simply coached *not* to do it. Some of this can be specific to our background, culture, age, industry, position, and other unique factors. And our gender definitely plays a role: most of us men were taught at a young age that "boys don't cry." We were also told to "suck it up" and "be a man." Such messages—which I myself heard often growing up, especially in sports—can be emotionally damaging.

From a very early age, I was an incredibly sensitive and emotional kid, but from what I could tell that wasn't a good thing. I didn't get much emotional support or encouragement from my friends, teachers, coaches, or even at home. So like most of my male peers, I did what I could to shut off that emotional part of me. For a lot of men, it's not just crying at work that's an issue—it's crying in general. Many of us have trained ourselves not to cry much, if at all, and we worry that if we do, we'll be seen as weak.

As for women, many I've talked to about this issue have told me about receiving clear messages to "keep it together," especially at work. "There's no crying in the boardroom" is a saying that many women have quoted to me when talking about this. The feedback they get is that if they allow themselves to be emotional at work, and especially if they cry, they won't be taken seriously and will be labeled as "too emotional" or "too sensitive," damaging their professional credibility.

As we discussed in Chapter 1, when we were talking about being authentic, crying at work entails definite risks. It makes us vulnerable and is almost always below the waterline of our iceberg. But one of the many things tears can do is remind us of our humanness, our connection to one another, and that there are things much bigger than the particular circumstances we're facing. While some of us cry more easily than others, it's an involuntary act. We cry for different reasons and from different emotions. Sometimes we shed tears of pain, sorrow, loss, disappointment, sadness, anger, frustration, embarrassment, or grief. Other times tears show up because of love, joy, inspiration, hope, celebration, or kindness. Regardless of the underlying emotions, and even when the reason for our tears is painful, crying often makes us feel better and is one of our most authentic expressions of emotion as human beings. And it's a healthy thing for us to do. According to a study by Dr. William H. Frey II, a biochemist at the St. Paul-Ramsey Medical Center in Minnesota, there are both physical and psychological benefits to crying. Tears help release toxins from the body. And according to Dr. Frey's research, 88.8 percent of people feel better after crying, whereas only 8.4 percent feel worse.

Even though crying is natural and healthy, we still have to grapple with the stigma associated with it, especially at work. I see this a lot in my own work, and I'm often fascinated by how people react when tears show up, which is a fairly regular occurrence when I speak and especially when I'm working with teams.

I delivered a workshop for a leadership team at the Lawrence Livermore National Lab and we did the "If You Really Knew Me" exercise. As we went around the table and people lowered the waterline on their icebergs, a few of the people in the group were moved to tears. When the exercise was complete, I had them pair up with a partner to talk about their experience. After a few minutes, I asked the group as a whole, "How was that for you?"

A woman named Judy spoke up right away and said, "That was awful!"

"What was so awful about it for you, Judy?" I asked.

"I hate crying at work. I'm too sensitive and I cry easily. I've worked really hard to control it, especially in this role and on this team, because I want to be taken seriously. And then you make us do this exercise and I'm a mess," Judy said.

"Yes, sometimes being emotional and crying can be intense and get a little messy," I said. "You weren't the only one who got emotional during the exercise, though. What was it like when other people shared and even cried when they were talking?" I asked.

"I actually liked that," said Judy. "I appreciated their courage, openness, and could relate to a lot of what they shared. I was also happy to know that I wasn't the only crier on this team." As she said this, Judy laughed, and so did everyone else around the table. The laughter lightened the mood in the room. I was about to respond to her when Judy got that wide-eyed, lightbulb look on her face, and blurted out, "Oh my gosh! It never occurred to me until just now that when I break down and cry it feels messy and like I'm being weak, but when other people do, it usually seems courageous to me and I appreciate it."

Judy's insight that day was profound for her, the team, and for me. She identified an interesting but important paradox about crying and vulnerability in general. When we do it, it often seems like weakness to us. When we see others do it, however, it often seems like courage.

I've seen tears (and other expressions of emotion and vulnerability at work) dramatically shift people's perspectives, change the dynamics of a conflict, and bring teams together. It has a way of breaking down emotional walls and mental barriers we put up within ourselves and toward others. Crying is natural, and a great human equalizer. As Sheryl Sandberg's son reminded her (and all of us) in that story I shared in Chapter 1, we all have things that make us cry. Remembering this and giving ourselves and others permission to cry if necessary, or to express ourselves in other vulnerable ways, allows more emotional space in which to connect with one another as human beings, which is a big part of what bringing our whole selves to work is all about.

## Wisdom 2.0

A great example of the evolution of emotional intelligence in the business world is Wisdom 2.0. In February 2011 I attended the second annual Wisdom 2.0 conference in Redwood City, California. The event was put together by Soren Gordhamer, author of *Wisdom*

*2.0: Ancient Secrets for the Creative and Constantly Connected.* Soren was interested in the intersection of ancient wisdom traditions, particularly meditation, and the digital world, which at the time was exploding with social media, smartphones, and a whole new level of interconnectivity.

The event was incredibly stimulating. There were about 400 people there, and the presentations and panels consisted of founders, leaders, and investors from tech companies like Google, Facebook, Twitter, and eBay, as well as authors and teachers with decades of experience teaching meditation and mindfulness. They were talking about both the importance of mindfulness and how to integrate it into how we work and how companies operate.

Mindfulness is one of the most powerful ways for us to deepen our self-awareness and to expand our capacity for self-management. And the more mindful we are, the more empathy we tend to have for others and the better we become at managing the relationships we have. So mindfulness is, of course, a key practice in the evolution and deepening of our emotional intelligence.

Aside from loving the conference, I was excited to meet other like-minded people and to find out there were so many other folks interested in both of these things. It felt a bit like my two worlds colliding, and although it was a little disorienting at first, it was inspiring. Being at this event reinforced a few important things that I'd been aware of before, but not in such a profound way. First, the personal and the professional aren't really all that separate, especially in today's world. Second, there is a deep desire that many of us have to connect with ourselves and each other, especially as things continue to speed up and we have more devices to distract us. Third,

I was selling out myself and my clients, and not bringing my whole self to the work I'd been doing in the corporate world for many years, because I had too many stories in my head about some of the things I was interested in, like meditation, and about some of my deeper personal and spiritual beliefs being too "out there," too "woo-woo," too "touchy-feely" for me to bring them into the companies where I was speaking and consulting. The truth was I was simply too scared and didn't believe or trust that there was an interest. And in a practical sense, I needed to find a way to make the case that these things were important to the success and fulfillment of my clients. The connection between mindfulness and emotional intelligence became clear to me, and it was exciting to realize that there were a lot of smart and successful businesspeople and companies that were seeing this and starting to embrace it.

Over the past seven or eight years, I've continued to attend the annual Wisdom 2.0 conference and some of the other regional conferences they've offered. I'm honored and grateful to have been invited to speak at and participate in a number of their events and to connect more deeply with the Wisdom 2.0 community and the larger mindfulness movement that has emerged. The annual event has grown from a few hundred to a few thousand each year. The speakers at these events have included such notables as Tony Hsieh (CEO of Zappos), author-teacher Eckhart Tolle, Congressman Tim Ryan, singer-songwriter Alanis Morissette, Evan Williams (co-founder of Twitter), author-teacher Jon Kabat-Zinn, Arianna Huffington (founder of the Huffington Post), Pete Carroll (head coach of the Seattle Seahawks), Bill Ford (Executive Chairman of Ford Motor Company), and author-teacher Byron Katie. The attendees are from companies of all types and sizes, as well as people who work in the education, nonprofit, and philanthropic worlds. It's wonderful to see the expansion of interest in mindfulness in business—both through the Wisdom 2.0 community and in the country and the world at large.

## Mindfulness at Work

The Wisdom 2.0 community has been both an example of and a catalyst for the expansion of mindfulness in the business world. Following on the growing understanding of emotional intelligence over the past few years, interest in and research about mindfulness, and programs to bring it into the workplace, have exploded. According to the American Mindfulness Research Association, between 1980 and 2000 there was a total of 58 studies of mindfulness in scientific or medical journals. By 2007, the number of journal articles on mindfulness had grown to 69 in just that single year. And for the year 2016, it had increased almost tenfold, to 667.

The evolution of mindfulness in the West, and its penetration into the business world, are key to understanding how to embrace it more deeply in our professional lives. Many of us were introduced to meditation in a personal or spiritual context. For me, my meditation practice has been an important part of my spiritual journey for almost 25 years. There are, however, many forms of meditation, and mindfulness is just one of them. While it can be a part of someone's spiritual practice, as it is for me, mindfulness isn't necessarily spiritual or religious in nature.

Jon Kabat-Zinn has arguably played the most significant role in establishing the scientific credibility of mindfulness in the West. Although he studied with various Buddhist teachers and has drawn on many

Buddhist techniques, he's not a Buddhist himself, and his approach to mindfulness is not religious in nature. Jon has a Ph.D. in molecular biology from MIT and became fascinated with the health benefits of mindfulness. In 1979 he created the Mindfulness-Based Stress Reduction (MBSR) program at the University of Massachusetts Medical Center.

To this day, MBSR programs, which usually consist of an eight-week series of two-hour classes each week, a one-day retreat (six-hour mindfulness practice), and daily homework of 45 minutes, are delivered all over the world by certified teachers. Much of the modern interest in and research behind the benefits of mindfulness started with the work of Jon Kabat-Zinn and MBSR.

Building upon that, his own meditation practice, and his interest in emotional intelligence at work, Google engineer Chade-Meng Tan wanted to create a program that would train people to be more mindful in their personal lives and at work. He was interested in putting together a course that would help people become more aware of their emotions, more compassionate toward others, and more able to build sustainable and harmonious relationships at work. In other words, he wanted to teach the fundamentals of mindfulness and emotional intelligence in a way that would benefit and resonate with his colleagues at Google. He assembled a group that included some consultants, a scientist from Stanford, and Marc Lesser, a Zen teacher with an MBA, who worked together to create the "Search Inside Yourself" program, which launched in 2007. It very quickly became the most popular training program at Google, and drew lots of attention from the corporate world given the impact it was having and the fact that Google had established itself both as a worldwide leader in business success and company culture. Google has been ranked #1 on the Fortune 100 Best Companies to Work For list eight out of the last 11 years.

The interest in this program became so significant that Tan and Lesser created the Search Inside Yourself Leadership Institute (SIYLI) in 2012, and the following year Tan's book *Search Inside Yourself,* which was endorsed by former president Jimmy Carter and the Dalai Lama, became a *New York Times* bestseller. SIYLI delivers programs for companies and businesspeople all over the world. According to their website, as of mid-2017, 13,000 employees had participated in their programs, with some noticeable results: 36 percent reduction in stress levels, 62 minutes in increased production per week, 7 percent reduction in health-care costs, and $3,000 saved per year per employee owing to gained productivity.

The success and awareness of programs like this one at Google have led many other companies to create or institute mindfulness programs for their employees in recent years. In the same way that organizations a decade or two ago realized they could reap benefits by encouraging their employees to exercise and eat better—even creating on-site resources and incentives for these healthy activities—this has been happening in the past few years with mindfulness.

And while this "mindfulness movement" may have started in Silicon Valley, it has quickly spread to companies and industries outside of the tech world. There are now mindfulness programs at Aetna, Ford, Schwab, BlackRock, General Mills, Dow Chemical, and many other companies. We're also seeing mindfulness programs for members of the military and law enforcement, and in schools.

## Mindfulness and Performance

At the 2015 Wisdom 2.0 conference in San Francisco, I had the honor of being on a panel with Dr. Michael Gervais and George Mumford. We talked about mindfulness and peak performance. Michael is a sports psychologist who works with the Seattle Seahawks; George is a mindfulness teacher who worked with Michael Jordan and the Chicago Bulls in the 1990s, and with Kobe Bryant and the Los Angeles Lakers in the 2000s.

While we were onstage together, Michael said, "In our culture we focus a lot on mastery of task or mastery of skill. If you're really good at something in business, sports, or the arts, you get recognized and rewarded for that. However, what it ultimately takes to be really good at something is mastery of *self.* Unfortunately, we don't talk about or focus on that as much." He's right. As a culture we're so outcome focused that we tend to overlook the process and what it truly takes to create the result. Mindfulness enhances our self-awareness and our focus, which can allow us to respond more effectively when we need that "mastery of self" to achieve a goal, accomplish a task, or simply remain calm in the face of adversity or uncertainty. It's about self-management at the highest level.

George's story and background blew me away. In 1970 he sustained a career-ending injury while playing in a pickup game with the varsity men's basketball team at the University of Massachusetts. His roommate at UMass was Hall of Famer Julius ("Dr. J") Erving. The end of George's basketball career ultimately led him to a severe drug addiction. Meditation and mindfulness helped him get clean and sober, and also helped him manage his chronic pain. He completed an internship in

Jon Kabat-Zinn's MBSR program, and together they created the Inner-City Stress Reduction Clinic in the early 1990s. In 1993 Phil Jackson, then coach of the Chicago Bulls, contacted Jon looking for someone who could teach mindfulness to his players. Jon recommended George, and George went on to help Phil Jackson and the Bulls win their second set of three consecutive NBA championships in the late '90s; George later worked with Jackson's Los Angeles Lakers when they won five NBA titles between 2000 and 2010.

During our panel discussion at the 2015 Wisdom 2.0 conference, George said, "I feel like I can come out of the shadows now. Back in the 1990s when I was working with the Bulls, and even just a few years ago when I was working with the Lakers, it didn't seem like it was okay to talk openly about mindfulness. But now it's become cool; and people in sports, business, and other areas of our culture are understanding the importance mindfulness plays in our ability to perform at a peak level."

George is right on both fronts. It has become way more "cool" to talk about and practice mindfulness. When I was playing pro baseball in the mid-90s, I would never tell my teammates that I liked to meditate. In those days it was just starting to become socially acceptable for athletes to talk about working with sports psychologists, and even that was considered a bit "out there."

As we're now learning from brain scientists, mindfulness plays an important role in our ability to operate at the highest level. In a study conducted by Adrienne Taren and Peter Gianaros of the Center for Neuroscience at the University of Pittsburgh, and J. David Creswell of the Department of Psychology at Carnegie Mellon University, MRI images showed that after 155 healthy adults underwent an eight-week course of mindfulness practice, the "primal" part of the brain known as the amygdala appeared to shrink. The amygdala, also known as the "fight or flight" center of the brain, is associated with our feelings of fear and our instincts for survival. It initiates the body's response to any stress or threat to one's safety by causing the arteries to harden and thicken, enabling them to handle the increased blood flow from a fight-or-flight response. As the amygdala shrinks, the newer "rational" part of the brain known as the prefrontal cortex, grows. The prefrontal cortex is associated with our higher functions and acts as the control center for our thoughts, words, and actions. The Taren-Gianoros-Creswell study demonstrated that mindfulness practices not only cause the amygdala to shrink, but they weaken the "functional connectivity" between the amygdala and other parts of the brain, meanwhile strengthening the neural networks between the higher-functioning prefrontal cortex and the rest of the brain. In other words, practicing mindfulness is good for our brain and nervous system, and helps us stay calm and focused.

Similarly, participants in Google's aforementioned Search Inside Yourself program reported 34 percent less emotional drain after the program, a 32 percent greater ability to focus and be more effective, and a 29 percent improvement in their ability to maintain calm and poise during challenges.

Mindfulness has gained a great deal of attention in recent years for a number of reasons: it's important, lots of successful people and teams are talking about it, it has impact, and we have scientific proof of its benefits. By learning to be more mindful, we can train our brain and our nervous system to relax, focus, and be more open. This is a practical way to enhance our EQ and our ability to perform at our best. And as the practice of mindfulness becomes much more socially acceptable, especially at work, it allows us to expand our capacity for being present and connecting with others—which is the essence of emotional intelligence.

## My Mindfulness Practices

As a way of demystifying mindfulness a bit and giving you practical examples, I thought I'd share some of my own mindfulness practices. These practices are important for a few reasons. First, like anything positive or healthy, the more we practice, the better we get; and doing something on a consistent basis turns it into a habit, allowing it to have the most impact. Second, mindfulness practices are practical ways for us to enhance our emotional intelligence—by increasing our self-awareness we can also expand our capacity for self-management, social awareness, and even relationship management (all four components of EQ). And third, these types of practices can help us keep things in perspective, disconnect from the daily stress and drama of life and work, and enhance our well-being—thus setting us up for increased success, joy, and fulfillment.

Following are some of the main practices I use nowadays, and which have evolved quite a bit over time. I'm more consistent with some than others, and most are fairly simple—but they have a big impact on my life, my outlook, my mental and emotional state, my overall well-being, and my ability to operate effectively and bring my whole self to work.

**Morning meditation.** I like to meditate in the morning when I have time. My meditation practice transformed a few years ago when I gave myself permission (with the help of my counselor Eleanor) to just meditate in bed right after I wake up. I've always found it easiest for me to relax my body and my mind when I lie down, but I struggled for years with the idea that lying down in bed didn't count as "official" meditation. While there are certain types of meditation practices that involve sitting in particular postures, I find it works best for me to just lie in bed and meditate. I've trained myself not to fall asleep, which is one of the biggest practical challenges to meditating in this position. For people who find this difficult, getting up, using the bathroom, and splashing some water on your face before lying back down can help ensure that you stay awake. I meditate sometimes for as little as five minutes, and sometimes for as long as an hour. On average I do it for about 20 minutes. I start by counting down from 10 to one, focusing on the lower part of my body and moving up toward my head. I sometimes just focus on my breath and relax, but most often I do a guided-imagery meditation technique where I visualize myself going through a particular process— walking through the woods, lying down in a field, flying through the air, and so forth. I've learned a number of these visualizations over the years from various teachers and recordings. Two of my favorites are ones that I talked about in detail in my book *Nothing Changes Until You Do*; they are called "Fulfilling Your Own Needs" and "Embracing Powerlessness." I still use these, along with others. I've even recorded audios of these two visualizations; you can download them for free from my website at Mike-Robbins.com/Meditations. I also sometimes listen to other meditation audios; or I simply visualize activities, conversations, or events that are coming up that day or that week for me—playing them out in my mind in a positive way. I find meditating in the morning works best for me and sets the tone for my day.

**Journaling.** While I was in college I started writing in a journal and carrying it around with me all the time. These days I actually have two journals. The first is my regular journal, in which I write about how I'm feeling, where I'm at, what's going on, where I'm struggling, what I want, and more. It's a safe place for me to write anything and everything—about myself, my life, my work, and my internal process. I go through stretches when I write in my regular journal every day, and others when it will be a week or two between entries. I like to write in this journal first thing in the morning after I meditate, or if I can at the very end of the day—sometimes both. Sitting on airplanes or in waiting rooms I also find to be good times for me to journal (if I can remember to put down my phone). My second journal is a gratitude journal, which morphed recently into a gratitude/self-forgiveness journal. I try to write in this journal each day—three things I'm grateful for and three things for which I forgive myself. I've been doing this daily (well, almost daily) gratitude off and on for many years, and love it. It helps keep me grounded and focused on the many blessings in my life. The self-forgiveness part of this is something I started recently as a way to practice more forgiveness and compassion for myself. I've been enjoying this, and it's helping me be a little more kind to myself and a little less self-critical.

**Music meditation.** As part of a workout and eating program that Michelle and I were introduced to a few years ago called The Happy Body, based on a book with the same name by Aniela and Jerzy Gregorek, I started to do a short five-minute meditation at the conclusion of my workouts. According to Aniela and Jerzy's research, doing this allows the body to relax, recover, and burn fat—thus enhancing the impact of the workout. Instead of rushing right into the next activity or checking my phone, I lie down on the floor and listen to a five-minute piece of classical music they recommend called "Thaïs: Meditation." It's a piece from the opera *Thaïs* by French composer Jules Massenet. I downloaded it from iTunes, and when I'm done working out I turn it on and allow myself to relax. It's one of my favorite parts of my workout. And if I didn't get a chance to meditate in the morning (or even if I did), it's a nice little break that allows me to stop, breathe, and take inventory of how I'm feeling physically, mentally, and emotionally. And if it actually helps burn a little extra fat too, that's awesome.

**Visualization.** As I've already said, I like visualization. Given that I'm more auditory (than visual or kinesthetic), when I visualize I don't usually see vivid images in my mind. During my days as an athlete, however, I learned about the power of positive visualization, and I still use this practice. I find it most helpful when I have a meeting, speech, event, or project that I'm feeling nervous about and that I want to go well. I'll often take a little time in my office, my car, my hotel room, or wherever I can before I head out for the meeting or event to ground myself. If I'm feeling really nervous about it I might take out a piece of paper and write down some of my biggest fears, doubts, or insecurities—not to freak myself out, but just to get them out of my head. After writing them out, I rip up the piece of paper and either throw it in the trash or flush it down the toilet—to give myself a clear message that I'm letting go of those limiting thoughts and beliefs. I'll then close my eyes and visualize how I want things to go, how I want to feel, and what I want the experience to be like. Sometimes I also write this down in my journal or on a piece of paper. I find that doing this can change my perspective on whatever it is I'm about to go do. And, I find that this practice helps me prepare myself emotionally and is a great self-management technique.

**Leaving my phone out of the bedroom.** This is one I just started doing, and it's making a big difference in how

I sleep. I had gotten into the habit of bringing my phone to bed with me—using it to read, listen, or watch stuff right before going to sleep. I knew it wasn't the healthiest thing for me, my marriage, or my sleep, but I had gotten somewhat addicted to it, thinking that because so much of my life runs through my phone, I needed to have it close to me at all times. I've started to leave it downstairs in the kitchen and it has really helped me relax more, sleep better, and wake up more refreshed. If I do bring it into the bedroom because, for instance, I want to listen to a meditation audio in the morning, or I'm in a hotel room and I can't leave it somewhere else, I try to remember to at least put it on airplane mode, so that in both a practical and an energetic way it can't distract me or suck me into something that will keep me awake or get me all amped up. I find this practice is becoming more and more challenging, and at the same time more and more important. My love/hate relationship with my phone continues to evolve, and this self-management practice is helping me deal with it in a more healthy and mindful way.

These are some of the simple things that I do to practice being more mindful, which has had a positive impact on my life, my work, and my well-being. They also enhance my emotional connection to myself and to others. I'm sure you have certain practices that you do that focus on your well-being and mindfulness (whether or not you think of them this way). It's not about being fanatical about them. I know a thing or two about this, and have learned the hard way that even when we do "healthy" things too intensely, it sometimes defeats the purpose. The goal is for us to find simple practices that we enjoy and that put us in touch with our minds, hearts, and bodies in a healthy and open way. This is what emotional intelligence and mindfulness are all about. Many of these are things we can do at work or in conjunction with our work. And all these things help us bring more of ourselves to the work that we do.

## Empathy

Empathy is one of the most important aspects of emotional intelligence and building strong relationships. Social awareness and relationship management, the two components of EQ that focus on other people, are predicated on our ability to empathize. Empathy is our ability to understand and share the feelings of another. We could also say that it's "walking in other people's shoes." There are many situations in which empathy is essential to our success and fulfillment at work. And like a lot of things we've been discussing, it's also something that can seem a little "soft." But even in the most competitive environments, empathy is an asset. Being able to understand and relate to people is important regardless of what we do, where we do it, and with whom. If we manage other people, empathy is essential to relating to the people on our team. If we're in a role where we sell or promote a product or service, being able to empathize with both customers and colleagues allows us to be more effective. If we're in a service role of any kind, empathy is vital to our ability to respond appropriately, anticipate what's needed, and communicate successfully with those we serve and support.

Whether we work for ourselves, run a large company, manage a team of people, or have just started our career as an entry-level individual contributor, empathy is crucial to our success. For a variety of reasons, it's a more important business skill than ever before.

The Center for Creative Leadership studied data taken from 6,731 managers in 38 countries. The study showed a positive correlation between empathy and job performance. Managers who were rated by their direct reports as showing more empathy received consistently higher job-performance ratings.

Having empathy for the people we work with is something we can both exhibit and increase in simple ways. It's about opening our minds and our hearts, and choosing to pay attention and care about the people around us. When we do this, we're often motivated to perform small acts of kindness and compassion that go a long way to building stronger relationships at work and creating a positive environment in which to operate.

Dr. Kelsey Crowe is the co-author of *There Is No Good Card for This: What to Say or Do When Life is Scary, Awful, and Unfair to the People You Love* and the founder of an organization called Help Each Other Out. Her organization is a growing collective of people who are embracing the idea that being there for others is often easier than we think, that it can be learned, and that it matters. Through social-science research, storytelling, and art, Kelsey and her team deliver "Empathy Bootcamp" workshops for groups and organizations of all kinds, giving people the skills to be supportive in all types of relationships and situations.

When I interviewed Kelsey on my podcast, she told me, "Empathy is our ability to imagine what someone else might be going through. This requires that we tap into some other kind of core experience that we've had, even if we can't relate to specifically what they're going through. For example, maybe you've never lost your job, but you may know what it's like to have your confidence shattered. And with that understanding, imagine approaching someone who has lost their job." She continued, "We can reach out to others, especially at work, with a light touch. A woman I worked with described mentioning to a colleague that today would have been her due date if not for her miscarriage. And then after lunch, there were flowers on her desk. Sometimes just small gestures that don't even require a lot of conversation show that you notice and that the person's life matters." Kelsey's wisdom and insight are so important. Having empathy for the people around us doesn't take a lot of effort, but it can have a profound impact.

Another example, which is actually more of an example of a *lack* of empathy, is the United States Congress. Tim Ryan is an eight-term Congressman from Ohio's 13th district and is the author of two books, including *A Mindful Nation: How a Simple Practice Can Help Us Reduce Stress, Improve Performance, and Recapture the American Spirit.* I've gotten to know Tim in recent years, and have heard him speak on several occasions about a simple but profound change that has taken place in Washington, DC, over the past few decades. He said, "A generation ago, most of us in Congress would move our families to DC when we were elected. This meant that people on opposite sides of the political divide had kids at the same schools, saw each other at the grocery store, and interacted with one another as members of the same community. Today, most of us live in our home districts because the pressure to be at home and to constantly raise money is so intense, we simply commute back and forth to DC, which means we no longer live in the same community with our colleagues on the other side of the aisle. It would be a lot harder to go onto the House floor or on cable TV and say nasty things about each other if we knew we're going to have to see each other at our kid's soccer game over the weekend."

When I first heard Tim talk about this, it made total sense to me and wasn't something I'd ever thought about before. And while the state of politics in Washington, DC, is challenging for a number of reasons, one of the simplest may be a lack of empathy.

This happens all the time in business, especially in large companies with multiple locations. The people in the other offices or departments can easily turn into "them," and we lose our understanding of one another. Empathy is about remembering the connection we have with each other and tapping into our common humanity.

## Listening

Listening is a fundamental and practical element of emotional intelligence. It's a very specific manifestation of social awareness and relationship management in action. It also happens to be the key to communication—which is a pretty important element of our business relationships, don't you think? Although we all know how important listening is, many of us still struggle with it. And even if we don't (or think we don't), we definitely work with people who do, right?

What makes listening so challenging? What gets in the way for you when you're listening to others? There are three main categories of things that usually get in the way for us when we're listening to other people:

**Practical.** The practical barriers to listening have to do mainly with not paying attention or being distracted. This is more pronounced than ever nowadays, with all our devices. I've been in team meetings with my clients recently where people will be sitting around the table with their laptops open and their phones either in their hands, in their laps, or faceup on the table right in front of them. I've even seen people with not one but two phones (which I assume means one is for work and the other one personal). It's hard to pay attention to someone speaking when we're staring at a screen. And let's be honest about our phones: in addition to being somewhat addicted to them, most of us are total hypocrites about them. When we're talking to someone and they're looking at their phone, what do we call that? Rude, right? But when *we* look at *our* phone, it's *important*. In addition to distractions, time constraints get in the way of listening. According to a 2015 Accenture survey of 3,600 business professionals from 30 countries, 64 percent of respondents said that listening has become significantly more difficult in today's digital workplace; 98 percent reported that they multitask at work; and 80 percent said they multitask during conference calls. We can't effectively listen to people and do something else at the same time.

**Informational.** Sometimes it's hard to listen to people because we just don't understand the information they're sharing. They may be communicating it in a way that doesn't make sense to us, or is hard to follow. Or we may not be interested in what they have to say, or don't think it's relevant to us, or simply don't care. We're often asked to be on conference calls or in meetings where some (if not all) of the information being presented isn't relevant to us. And sometimes we don't agree with the speaker, which also makes it hard to listen. We might feel compelled to argue, which isn't always smart or politically correct, so we might just sit there and stew.

**Personal.** Sometimes it's not about the message, it's about the messenger. If we don't like, respect, or trust the person speaking, it can be challenging for us to listen to what's being said. We may agree completely, it may be super relevant to our job and our life, and we may need to pay close attention to every word that is being said, but if the individual conveying the message is someone we have unresolved issues with or don't particularly care for, it's often hard for us to listen effectively. We also tend to hear different things based on who is speaking and how we feel about them.

So whether it's practical, informational, or personal, listening can be difficult for us. But listening to others is crucial to the success of our relationships and our work. How can we enhance our capacity for listening? By understanding the three *challenges* of listening I just mentioned, as well as the three *levels* of listening listed directly below.

**1) Listen to what's being said.** This means we have to slow down, put down our phone or turn away from our computer, and actually pay attention to the speaker and the information they're sharing. This is no small thing, especially in today's fast-paced world. If you start paying attention to your ability to pay attention, you'll probably notice that you check out a lot when people are talking. It's not because you're selfish or don't care; it's usually because there are so many things inside your brain and out in the world that can distract you. Our attention spans seem to be getting shorter and shorter, and the pressure on us to be checking our various devices, accounts, and messages is increasing all the time. If you don't listen to what people are saying, you'll not only miss important information, you'll also diminish your ability to connect to, understand, and empathize with them. Listening to what people are saying is actually a great mindfulness practice, and is something that can enhance your EQ. Noticing when you check out or get distracted is a great way to practice being more present and bringing yourself back to the conversation. Just as in meditation noticing that our mind wanders enables us to come back to our breath; so too in listening it enables us to come back to the present moment.

**2) Make an emotional connection.** The second level of listening is making an emotional connection to the person who is talking—whether that is one-on-one or in a group. We can't make an emotional connection to the person speaking if we're not actually listening to what they're saying. So in order to get to the second level, we first have to pay attention to them. Making an emotional connection is about listening to and tapping into the emotion behind the words. It's about empathy. Sometimes people say one thing, but they mean something else. If we're really listening to them, we can hear not only what they're saying but what they may be communicating nonverbally. Making this emotional connection is especially important when we're coaching someone, wanting to more deeply understand where they're coming from, working through a conflict, trying to influence or motivate them, or offering support. This second level of listening is essential to social awareness and relationship management.

**3) Clean out our filter.** When we listen to people, we don't usually hear what they say. We hear a filtered version of what they say. This filter is based on our judgments, opinions, assessments, and evaluations—of the person and of what they're saying. We are, of course, entitled to our opinions, and in some cases part of our job is to evaluate people and what they say. But oftentimes these filters are filled with our biases—conscious and unconscious—and, as we discussed in Chapter 1, a degree of damaging self-righteousness. When we have conflict with or disconnection from someone we work with, it's usually because our filter has gotten clogged up with negative, self-righteous judgments. It's kind of like the filter in the dryer: it needs to be cleaned out regularly, because if it isn't, there's a ton of buildup that accumulates. If we continue to neglect it, it can blow up the dryer and set the house on fire. Something analogous is what can happen in our relationships if we don't clean out our own filter.

After a speech I gave on emotional intelligence and communication at a managers' conference for one of my clients, a man came up to me and said, "Hi, my name's Chris. I appreciated your presentation and resonated with much of what you talked about, except for the part about the filter."

"Really? What didn't resonate with you specifically about the filter?" I asked.

"Well," Chris said, "I think I understood the concept, I'm just not sure it fits with my boss. He's a jerk. That's not a 'filter'; it's the truth."

"Okay," I said. "I can tell you have a very strong opinion about your boss."

"He's awful. He doesn't care about people, doesn't communicate, ridicules us in front of each other, and is sometimes downright cruel. I tried to talk to him about it, which only made it worse. I even tried to talk to his boss about it, but they like him because he's smart and our team puts up big numbers for the company."

I could tell by his passion and genuineness that he was really frustrated. I asked him, "Would you like this situation with your boss to improve?"

"Yes."

"I have two suggestions. The first one will handle it completely, but the second one will take more effort and commitment," I said.

"What's the first one?" Chris asked.

"You could quit your job," I said.

"I've thought about that," he said. "But I really like my job and love the company; I don't want to leave. What's the second suggestion?"

"You could clean out your filter. In other words, you could change how you relate to your boss," I said. He looked at me like I was crazy, so I continued. "Let's imagine that for some reason, a year from today you're no longer working for him. Is that a realistic scenario?"

"I suppose it's possible," Chris said. "I mean there are no plans, but things change around here from time to time, so it could happen."

"Okay, so a year from today you're no longer working for him—maybe because one of you gets another job within the company or something like that. But let's say that starting today you decide that instead of getting upset, annoyed, and offended by his behavior, you're going to challenge yourself to think of him as a very important 'teacher' for you."

"A teacher?" he asked, looking confused.

"Yes, a teacher," I said. "And what's he teaching you? How to deal with difficult people more effectively. I don't think this is the last difficult person you'll ever work with, and maybe not even the last boss you don't particularly care for either. Imagine if you called me one year from today to tell me that he left the company or took another role. And let's also imagine that you could honestly say that you were less stressed out and more effective, not only in dealing with him, but in dealing with any difficult person at work or in life." Then, after a pause, I asked, "Would that be a valuable relationship for you?"

"Well, when you put it that way, I guess it would be."

"Look, I realize that it's easy for me to give you this advice and then walk out that door. I don't have to go back to work and deal with a boss that I can't stand. It may not be easy and probably won't be all that fun, but if you really take it on and challenge yourself, it can have a big impact. I'm not sure what you'll do specifically—maybe you'll practice not getting offended so easily, or you'll stop gossiping about him with your co-workers, or complaining about him to your wife. There are lots of different things you can do and try. I trust that you'll figure out what to do if you're really committed to things changing."

Chris looked at me with a hopeful yet still somewhat skeptical expression and said, "Thanks."

Listening is not always easy—we first have to commit ourselves to being present, paying attention, and putting down our phone or turning away from our computer. We then have to care enough to make an emotional connection with the person speaking—to use our emotional intelligence to empathize with them as best as we can. And finally, we've got to be aware of and take responsibility for our bias, judgments, and the filter through which we listen, and be willing to clean them out if we want to connect with people in an authentic and open way.

There are really only two ways to clean out our filters. We can either deal with the conflict, issue, and person directly, until things change and get resolved. Or we can simply let it go and choose to change our perspective, as I challenged Chris to do. Both of these things take commitment, courage, and quite a bit of emotional intelligence. However, we all have experience doing both of these things, even though they can be challenging.

Emotional intelligence is a pretty easy concept to understand. Self-awareness, self-management, social awareness, and relationship management—all are fairly simple terms and ideas. The practice of emotional intelligence, like many of the other themes of this book, is a bit more difficult to integrate as we go deeper below the surface. When we do, however, the rewards are huge for us and our co-workers. It's our EQ that allows us to connect with who we really are so we can both bring our whole self to work, and also connect with the whole selves of the people around us.

# PRINCIPLE #4–
# EMBRACE A
# GROWTH MINDSET

My friend Brian took me out to lunch many years ago, not long after my baseball career ended. He was worried about me. Although I was doing my best to move forward in my life and put on a good face, he knew I was still struggling to figure out who I was and what I was going to do, now that my childhood dream had come to a sudden end.

"Mike, when we go through something difficult in life, like you just have, there's a tendency to ask ourselves a very simple but dangerous question." Brian paused and took a sip of his water. "The question is 'Why is this happening to me?'" He paused again, and said, "While this question makes sense and most of us ask it, you want to be careful about it. I'm sure you've been asking yourself this question since you got hurt and your baseball career ended. If I were you, I'd be asking it over and over again."

Brian was right, I had been asking myself this question a lot.

"However," he continued, "the problem with asking this question is that the only answers we get in response are reasons, justifications, and rationalizations for why it's not fair and why we're a victim. This doesn't usually leave us empowered or inspired. But if you change one word in that question, it will fundamentally change the way you're relating to this challenge—and *any* challenge, big or small, you face in life." After another sip of water, Brian said, "Change the word *to* to the word *for*. Ask yourself, 'Why is this happening *for* me?' That's a completely different question. It doesn't necessarily mean you like what's happening or even understand it. It's not about sugarcoating the pain, difficulty, or confusion of the situation. It's about challenging yourself to find the value, the lesson, and the opportunity in what you're facing, instead of simply reacting to it or complaining about it. It's not easy, but if you can do this, not only will it help you navigate your way through this process, but you can learn and grow while you're doing so."

Brian's wisdom was spot on, especially given my situation and how I was feeling at that moment in my life. I took his advice to heart and started asking myself, "Why is this happening *for* me?" I soon began to see some real lessons and opportunities, even in the midst of my uncertainty, disappointment, and grief. In hindsight, I can now see many blessings and much growth that came out of the painful end of my baseball career, even though I didn't particularly like it or understand it while it was happening. I can also see that Brian was introducing me to a concept that many years later I would more fully understand to be what's known today as "growth mindset." This notion has had a profound impact on me. And for people, teams, and organizations who embrace a mindset of growth, the benefits are enormous—in terms of learning, navigating change, dealing with failure, embracing feedback, personal growth, achieving success, and more.

## What Is Growth Mindset?

The concept of growth mindset was initially developed by Stanford professor and research psychologist Carol Dweck, and made popular by her best-selling book, *Mindset: The New Psychology of Success*. According to her decades of research on learning, achievement, and success, we all have a "mindset"—a perception we hold about ourselves. Our mindset has a significant effect on our ability to learn and acquire new skills, as well as on our personal relationships, our professional success, our ability to navigate change, our resilience, and many other important aspects of work and life. The fundamental distinction that Dweck developed is what she calls the difference between a "fixed" and a "growth" mindset.

With a **fixed mindset**, we believe our basic qualities, like our talent or intelligence, are simply fixed traits. We spend our time documenting our intelligence or talent, instead of developing them. We also believe that talent alone creates success—without effort. With a **growth mindset**, on the other hand, we believe that our most basic abilities can be developed through dedication and hard work—brains and talent are just a starting point. This view creates a love of learning and a resilience that is essential for great accomplishment.

Many companies have embraced this idea, and are using it both to empower their employees and to enhance their cultures. In a 2016 article for *Harvard Business Review*, Dweck wrote:

> Individuals who believe their talents can be developed (through hard work, good strategies, and input from others) have a growth mindset. They tend to achieve more than those with a more

fixed mindset (those who believe their talents are innate gifts). This is because they worry less about looking smart and they put more energy into learning. When entire companies embrace a growth mindset, their employees report feeling far more empowered and committed; they also receive far greater organizational support for collaboration and innovation. In contrast, people at primarily fixed-mindset companies report more of only one thing: cheating and deception among employees, presumably to gain an advantage in the talent race.

Our mindset has a big impact on how we learn and work as individuals and on how we collaborate with others. And according to the research, our mindset exists on a continuum, from "fixed," to "mixed," to "growth." We're not static human beings and none of us have a mindset that is all fixed or all growth, although we may have a tendency to be more on one side of the continuum than the other. The good news is that we can always move in the direction of growth if we choose. It also turns out that in some situations and some relationships we might have more of a growth mindset, and in others more of a fixed mindset. It's important for us to be aware of our fixed mindset "triggers"—the things that can pull us from the growth-mindset side of the continuum back toward the fixed-mindset side. These triggers can be things such as receiving criticism, facing challenges, faring poorly compared to others, dealing with change or uncertainty, and failing. These are things that can push us into places of insecurity or defensiveness, which can inhibit our growth and learning.

As I've been researching, thinking about, and writing this book (and this chapter in particular), I've been clearly seeing some of my own triggers that take me into a fixed mindset. One example is comparison. I've been reading articles and studies, listening to interviews, and watching TED talks and other videos as I've been working on this book. There are times when I read about someone or their work, or listen to them talk about it, and I find myself feeling jealous. *Wow, they're super smart, innovative, and creative. Their ideas and their work are profound and have real impact. I just don't have what they have and could never be like that.*

If I'm not mindful about it, my tendency to compare myself to others can trigger a whole self-critical spiral where I start discounting myself, my work, and my life. It's amazing how fast it can happen, almost unconsciously. These and other triggers can move me from a growth to a fixed mindset in a hurry. A few other ways to say or think about this are that these triggers can take me from abundance to scarcity, from possibility to resignation, or from trust to fear. We all have these types of triggers. The more aware of them we are, the more compassion we can have for ourselves when we notice them, and the easier it can be for us to shift to a more positive and growth-oriented direction. This is about self-awareness and self-management, which we covered in the previous chapter.

Adopting and expanding our growth mindset takes awareness, commitment, and courage. Being interested in growth means risking failure and being willing to look bad, which is not always easy for us—or more specifically, for our ego. But this is an important part of true success, and essential to bringing our whole selves to work.

In addition to the beneficial effects that embracing a growth mindset has on our own work and success, it also plays a major role in our perception of others and our work environment. Dweck's research found that employees with growth mindsets are

- 47 percent more likely to say their colleagues are trustworthy than their fixed-mindset peers

- 34 percent more likely to have a strong sense of commitment to their organization than their fixed-mindset peers

- 65 percent more likely to say their organization supports risk-taking than their fixed-mindset peers

- 49 percent more likely to say their organization fosters innovation than their fixed-mindset peers

Growth mindset is an attitude, a perspective, and a commitment we make to our development. It's about consciously choosing to look for the potential growth and learning in any and every situation, and to lean into those opportunities even if they're uncomfortable. It's also the best possible approach we can take if we're interested in our own development and that of the people around us. In the rest of this chapter, we'll take a look at examples and situations in which growth mindset is important, as well as when and where it can be challenging. And, we'll explore ways we can enhance our ability to learn, grow, and be successful by deliberately embracing a growth mindset.

## Change

Change is an essential and inevitable part of work and life, one that can be complicated and upsetting, fun and exciting, or a combination of all these things and more. There are, of course, all different types of changes that we experience. Some are big and some are small. Some are personal and some are professional or organizational. Some impact only us, while others impact many people. Some we choose deliberately, and others are given to us without much, if any, warning or preparation. And most significantly, some we consider "good," and others we consider "bad"—although in many cases that assessment can itself *change* over time as we gain more perspective and hindsight. "Good" change usually comes in the form of new things we want—relationships, opportunities, experiences, accomplishments, and so on. "Bad" change usually shows up as rejections, losses, disappointments, failures, and any other number of things not going the way we think they should.

Clearly, getting a new job, moving to a new city, achieving a big goal, or falling in love are very different from losing our job, getting divorced, failing miserably at something important, or having someone close to us die. Regardless of the circumstance or situation, however, all these things (and others) are changes and as the Greek philosopher Heraclitus is supposed to have said, "The only constant is change."

One of the things that make change so complicated emotionally is that most of us seek it and fear it at the same time. More precisely, we could say that it's our growth mindset that seeks change, and our fixed mindset that fears it. Change can be really exciting, and often gives us opportunities to learn new skills, have new experiences, and grow in all kinds of new ways. Change can also be scary, because we often can't control it, it usually forces us out of our comfort zone, and it tends to involve uncertainty. Even change we consider to be positive can be scary and upsetting, especially at first.

Almost all changes, even the biggest and best, involve discomfort of some kind. And the fear that often accompanies change is normal. If the circumstances of the change are more challenging, the likelihood of us feeling pain and loss are increased. As the author Haruki Murakami said, "Pain is inevitable. Suffering is optional." We don't have to suffer as we go through change—we can embrace it, be real about how we feel, and reach out to those around us to support us as we face any anxiety or discomfort we may experience as we go through it, regardless of the circumstances. The suffering we may experience while going through change isn't usually due to the pain, fear, or loss itself; it's most often a result of our avoidance of these feelings, as well as our mindset about the change.

Growth mindset isn't a superficial, Pollyanna, "look on the bright side" approach to life. It's a challenging but necessary commitment to taking ownership, looking for the value in all of our experiences, and being open to learning and growing through whatever we face. Doing this doesn't magically protect us from dealing with or going through difficulties, however; rather, it empowers us and reminds us that we can consciously choose to grow, no matter what.

## Change at Work

Change at work, as in any area of life, can be exciting or painful, and sometimes both. Oftentimes changes at work are ones that we don't choose—they are offered to us or even mandated. Given the nature of business today, there are constant changes with technology and how we do our work. Organizational changes often impact the scope of our role, the people we work with, and the nature of our job. With a number of my tech-company clients, it's not uncommon for people to have a new manager every six months to a year, or to change roles themselves. And according to the Bureau of Labor Statistics, people born between 1957 and 1964 held an average of 11.7 jobs between the ages of 18 and 48. This means that the youngest baby boomers had almost 12 jobs each between 1975 and 2012. More important, this means that the vast majority of us will change jobs many times over the course of our careers. Dealing effectively with change at work is essential to our success and that of our co-workers. And growth mindset plays a crucial role in this.

A change experience at work that can be quite challenging is when there is a merger or acquisition. I've worked with many clients over the years who went through this experience. While it can often end up being a great thing for the companies and people involved, the integration process can be long and difficult for a variety of reasons—changes in leadership, differences in culture, changes in process, duplication of roles, changes in brand, differences in philosophy, among others. In such situations people often fear for their jobs, wonder what it will mean for them personally, and can feel like all the time, energy, and equity they have built in their work and relationships are in jeopardy.

Wells Fargo has been a client of mine for 15 years. They acquired Wachovia at the end of 2008 and went through a massive integration process over the next few years. These were two of the biggest banks in America at the time they merged, which also happened to be right in the middle of a massive recession and a major change in financial regulations. In addition, both of these companies had over 100,000 employees each and were set up very differently. Wells Fargo, which is based in San Francisco, had a de-centralized organizational structure, whereas Wachovia, which was based on the other side of the country in Charlotte, North Carolina, was very centralized. For these and many other reasons this merger was quite complicated.

A few years into their integration process, I was invited to speak at one of their leadership meetings. My contact, Cindy, was really excited to introduce me to one of the leaders in the group, whose name was Robert. Cindy said, "Mike, I hope you can meet Robert. He's one of our best leaders—he and his team have performed incredibly well through the transition process. He's been amazing at communicating with them, coaching them, and keeping them on track through all the change, stress, and uncertainty of this process. His team has some of the highest engagement scores in the entire company." Given what Cindy said about Robert, I was looking forward to meeting him and asking him some questions.

When we had a chance to chat after my keynote, I said, "Robert, Cindy had great things to say about you as a leader and the success of your team over the past few years during the integration."

"Thanks, I'm just doing my job, nothing special," he said in an "aw-shucks" kind of way.

"Listen," I said, "I appreciate your humbleness and humility, but I could tell by what Cindy said that you've done a remarkable job in the midst of a challenging time. That's no small thing. I'd love to know a bit about what you've been doing and what you think the key to your success has been."

As Robert began to answer, his face turned red. I sensed he was embarrassed by my praise; but since people sometimes get funny about receiving compliments, as we discussed in Chapter 2, I totally understood. He said, "Well, I think part of it has to do with the fact that I really love my job and love my team. I feel genuinely grateful to work for this company and to get to do what I do, even when things get stressful. I had a boss many years ago whom I admired a great deal. One of the things he did that I really liked was that he asked for and gave a lot of feedback—so I always knew where I stood and how I could improve; I was also allowed to let him know what I thought and what I needed from him. In our one-on-one meetings, he would ask us three questions: First, 'What can I *start* doing to make your job easier or that you think will help me be more successful?' Second, 'What can I *stop* doing that is making your job more difficult or that you think is getting in the way of my success?' Third, 'What can I continue doing that is making your job easier or that you think is helping me be successful?'"

"He wanted us to give him honest answers to these three questions. And he expected us to ask the same three questions of him, so he could give us honest answers in turn. At first this process was a little uncomfortable, even scary, but over time I got to really appreciate it. The lines of communication with him were open and they flowed honestly in both directions, which I found really healthy and helpful. My boss was really smart and talented, but he was also humble and open enough to solicit and take in the feedback we gave to him. We even got to the point where we would have this feedback conversation collectively as a team. We created a culture of feedback and it helped us all to learn, grow, and be more successful."

As Robert was telling me this story there was a twinkle in his eye, and I could feel his passion and excitement, as well as his appreciation for his former boss and mentor. One of my own growth-mindset practices is to ask people like Robert about their keys to success or their philosophies about life, business, leadership, and more. It's a great way to learn from the wisdom and experience of others.

Robert continued, "When I got my first job as a manager, I decided to use the 'Start, Stop, Continue' questions with my team—both because I liked working for someone who did that with me and our team, and because I needed a lot of feedback, given my lack of experience. I didn't really know how to manage people, and I wanted to learn as much as I could from them. I found it helped me not only to improve as a manager, but to more effectively coach them, build trust, and create unity with my team. Over the years I've continued this practice. And in the past few years, as we've been going through all this change with the merger and integration, I knew that it was critically important for me to communicate openly, connect regularly, and both give and receive as much feedback as possible with my team. I've learned through experience that, in situations like this, if you don't communicate all the time, people start to make stuff up— and usually what they make up isn't all that helpful or positive. This integration and massive amount of change we've been through hasn't all been fun or easy, but I think our collective commitment to feedback has helped us not only navigate through the uncertainty, but grow and get better in the process."

"I love it, Robert. Do you mind if I share this story with others? Maybe even use your 'Start, Stop, Continue' technique with some of the leaders and teams I coach?"

Robert nodded.

What Robert was doing with his team was a fairly simple concept, but it took a lot of courage, commitment, and emotional intelligence. It's also a great example of growth mindset, and of how a leader can create a team culture of growth, even during times of great change.

## Feedback Techniques

I did start to share Robert's story after he told it to me, as well as his "Start, Stop, Continue" technique for eliciting and giving feedback. A number of the managers I've mentioned it to over the years have implemented versions of it with their direct reports. I also use it myself to influence and inspire action with teams. I do it in two different ways.

One fairly simple way is as a brainstorming and action-inspiring exercise at the end of a team session, off-site, or retreat. Whether we've spent a half day, a full day, or a number of days together, I often invite the team to spend some time reflecting on what they can Start, Stop, and Continue doing as a team to enhance their teamwork, connection, culture, and overall success and performance. I usually have them break up into smaller groups of four or five people, and each group brainstorms things in all three of these categories. We then have a full-group discussion and write down the best ideas in each category on flip charts or whiteboards. These lists are then typed up and sent out to the team, and someone or a small group of people usually takes on the responsibility for implementing the key changes.

The second way I use the Start, Stop, Continue technique is for individual feedback in a group setting. This one takes quite a bit of skill, maturity, and emotional intelligence from everyone involved, but it can be incredibly powerful and definitely takes the growth mindset of teams to a whole new level. In this case, it's best to do with a small, intact team of 10 people or fewer.

As with the "Appreciation Seat" exercise we talked about in Chapter 2, for this one we go around the table and each person receives in turn feedback from the other team members about what he or she can start, stop, or continue doing in order to be more effective and successful in their role on the team. For this feedback process to work, however, there has to be some trust and safety established—with the team in general and also specifically in the moment as we do the exercise. This is crucial, and is one of my most important roles when I work with teams like this. In some cases we may have already done an exercise like "If You Really Knew Me" as a group, so that can help create a deeper level of connection and safety. But regardless of what has come before, I ask the group if they're willing to do a risky but valuable exercise, and if they'd like to get some helpful, authentic feedback from their team. Even if they seem a little scared, which most people are (at least to some degree), I make sure to check in with the group before we move forward. I also let them know that nothing anyone is going to say is the "truth"; it's just their opinion (as most feedback is, by the way). I also ask if they want their teammates to just be "nice," or if they want genuine feedback with the intention of helping them be the best they can be? Almost everyone says they want it to be real. I also remind them that the purpose of this exercise is for everyone to learn and grow personally, and for them to grow as a team. For the individuals and the team to get the most out of this exercise, it's important that they consciously embrace a growth mindset—which is all about being open to learning and growing, even if it might be uncomfortable.

Once I have set all this up and gotten permission and buy-in from the people in the group, we start with the first person, usually the leader. I often check in with him or her before the session to ask if they're up for doing this exercise and willing to go first, and if their team is mature enough and in a good-enough place (in terms of morale, trust, connection, and collective mental-emotional state) to do it. The more openly the leader is willing to take feedback from their team (in other words, to model growth mindset in real time), the easier and safer it will be for the rest of the team to do so. People then start to offer things to their leader that they can start, stop, or continue doing. We then go around the entire group and give each person a chance to be on the "feedback seat." Most teams I've done this with have found it incredibly valuable—both in terms of the feedback they were able to receive and give, and in terms of the collective bonding and growth it encourages. When we debrief after the exercise, people are amazed that it wasn't as difficult or painful as they expected, and that despite their fears they actually found it refreshing and valuable.

Feedback is such an important instigator of growth. And one of the ways we enhance both our growth mindset and our practical skills is by eliciting and valuing feedback. But feedback can be tricky for a number of reasons. We've all had experiences of both giving and receiving feedback that didn't go well or, in some cases, may even have caused real harm and pain for us and others.

There are four key things to remember when we're giving feedback, if we want it to be well-received:

**Permission.** There has to be implicit or, ideally, explicit permission for us to give someone feedback. Unsolicited feedback, even if it's spot-on and valuable, can be hard to take. Asking someone if they're open to feedback or whether we can give them some, while sometimes awkward, can be helpful and important. This is true even if we're their boss, parent, or mentor, or in any other type of relationship with them where permission for our feedback may seem implied. Making sure that we have permission to give feedback shows that we respect and value the person to whom we're giving it. It also usually makes feedback feel less like judgment and more like help, allowing the person to be more receptive to what we have to say.

**Intention.** It's important for us to check in with ourselves about the intention behind our feedback. In other words, why are we giving them this feedback? Do we genuinely want them to be more successful? Are we annoyed with them and want to let them know why? Are we trying to prove or defend ourselves? Are we trying to control them or the situation? There are all kinds of reasons why we give feedback to others, and sometimes there is more than one. But being real with ourselves about our motivation behind giving feedback can help us determine whether or not it's even going to be helpful. And assuming we decide that it is, making sure our intention is genuine and positive will make it more likely that the person will be receptive to it.

**Skill.** Giving feedback effectively takes skill. Of course, from a growth-mindset perspective, giving feedback is not only important, but also one of many things we can improve upon the more we practice and dedicate ourselves to doing it. Because giving and receiving feedback can be a vulnerable experience for everyone involved, it requires attention, commitment, awareness, and courage to do it well. And even with all those things, it's still not easy. The more willing we are to do it, the more we can develop our skill of giving feedback successfully. And there are, of course, different ways to skillfully give feedback. Oftentimes, especially at work, we may give it directly and explicitly as part of a review or development conversation. But as Melissa Daimler, Senior Vice President of Talent at WeWork and former Head of Learning at Twitter, once told me, "Sometimes the best feedback I've gotten has been when I didn't even realize it was feedback."

**Relationship.** The most important aspect of giving effective feedback is the relationship we have with the person we're giving it to. We can have explicit permission, the most positive intention, and a lot of skill in how we deliver it—but if our relationship isn't strong or it's actively strained, it'll be very difficult for us to give feedback to someone and have them receive it well. I could get the same exact feedback from two different people but react to it differently depending on my relationship with each of them. Let's say, in one case, I know the person cares about me, appreciates me, and believes in me. I'm much more likely to be open to their feedback and to take it positively. But if, in another case, the person is someone I don't know as well or may have some unresolved issues with, it's less likely that I'll be open and take their feedback well. This is all about personal credibility, which we talked about in Chapter 1. Making sure the relationships we have are strong and authentic helps us ensure that we can give feedback effectively when we need to do so.

All four of these things—permission, intention, skill, and relationship—are important for us to remember when giving feedback. And they're also important for us to think about in *receiving* feedback. The other side of the same coin is making sure that we give people permission to give us feedback, check in with and pay attention to what their intention might be, give them feedback about how they're giving it or how we like it to be given, and work to strengthen our relationships with the people around us. The most effective ways to enhance our ability to receive feedback are to ask for it, be open to it, and genuinely consider it when it comes our way. Receiving feedback is essential to our growth and success. And the more willing we are to seek it out and take it in, the further along the continuum of growth mindset we can move.

Even though I know all this, have myself been a seeker of feedback for a long time, and believe deeply in the importance and power of feedback, it can still trigger me into an extreme fixed-mindset place. As Gloria Steinem says, "The truth will set you free, but first it will piss you off." That pretty much sums up how I feel about feedback, especially concerning certain things. In the process of writing this book I've learned even more about my relationship to feedback.

Melanie Bates, my writing coach and personal editor, has been working with me every step of the way on this book, as she did on my previous book. She and I have worked together for almost six years. I've given her explicit permission to give me feedback—on the manuscript, as well as on my business and life. Her intention in her feedback is clear and positive: to support and empower me as a writer. She's skillful in her editing, her coaching, and her feedback. And our relationship is super strong—we know each other well and care about each other very much, and our professional relationship has grown into a trusting and authentic friendship. Yet despite all that, as she was sending me back her edits and feedback on the early drafts of the chapters of this book, I found myself getting angry, defensive, and self-righteous in reaction.

Given what this book is about, of course, the irony of my response has not been lost on me. However, Melanie's feedback and my response to it had me take an even deeper look at my own fixed-mindset triggers, especially when it comes to the vulnerability I feel about my writing. I know at the deepest level that feedback is not only helpful in the process of writing a book—it's essential. I want, need, and couldn't do without feedback, especially from a person as good, talented, and connected to me as Melanie. Nevertheless, I don't usually enjoy getting feedback, especially at first.

This is an example of both emotional intelligence (especially the self-awareness and self-management aspects of it) and growth mindset. The more aware we are of our own triggers and how we react to feedback, the more we can shift ourselves in the direction of growth. This process and awareness sparked some great conversations between me and Melanie, which both enabled me to receive her feedback even better, and inspired me to be more open to feedback generally.

As important as it is for us to be open to feedback— from a growth-mindset perspective—it's also essential for us to be discerning and to consider the source. Another great quote from Dr. Brené Brown that I love is this: "If you're not in the arena getting your butt kicked too, I'm not interested in your feedback."

It's important to make sure the feedback is coming from someone who knows us, cares about us, and has earned the right to give it to us. In today's world, where there's lots of feedback flying around on the Internet, we have to remember that not all of it is useful. Giving and receiving feedback in a healthy, helpful, and credible way is essential for us to learn and grow. And if we have the courage, willingness, and commitment to engage in feedback from a growth-mindset perspective, it can be incredibly valuable for us and the people we work and live with.

### Commitment and Accountability

Making commitments and being held accountable are also essential aspects of growth, success, and our ability to operate with a growth mindset. However, these are things that many of us, myself included, shy away from at times. Commitment and accountability can be hard for a number of reasons; for example, when we commit to something and are held accountable for it we can potentially fail, let people down, or not come through in the way we'd like. These fears, which are normal, and for most of us are fixed-mindset triggers, often hold us back from making explicit commitments. The challenge is that without commitment and accountability, growth and success are more difficult, yet commitment and accountability, in and of themselves, can be uncomfortable and scary.

Commitments and accountability get us to do stuff we want to do but resist or fear doing. From things as small as going to the gym or starting a new hobby, to bigger things like asking for a raise or looking for a new job, if we're willing to make a commitment first to ourselves and then share it with others, and to set up a structure of accountability to hold us to it, we challenge ourselves to push past our perceived limits and use the risk of failure as a way to motivate us to success. This is what growth mindset is all about. And when we have a team of people around us operating with a growth mindset as well, they can support us and we can support them with our individual and collective commitments.

Cindy Elkins from Genentech, whom I talked about in Chapter 2, shared an example of this with me. She said: "I was spending so much time focused on coaching my team and helping them with their personal development plans, I had to ask myself, 'What's on *my* development plan?' I decided to challenge myself and do something I'd wanted to do for a while, which was to try to become a member of the board of directors of a large organization. I did some research and found out that the data was against me, because only 20 percent of board members are women, and it's kind of stagnant at that level. I didn't have any experience with this and didn't know if it would happen, but decided I was going to create this big goal for myself and share it with my team, as well as with my family. I wanted to show my team, and especially my daughters, that I was willing to go for something important that I wanted, even though it might not work out. My team was excited and wanted to see me make it happen. They also wanted to see how I would go about it. It wasn't easy and it took a while, but eventually I was invited onto the board of Weight Watchers, which has been a phenomenal experience. Sometimes I think it's really important for us as leaders to be vulnerable with our teams like this."

Cindy's story is a great example of the power of commitment and accountability. There are lots of ways we can commit and create accountability for things we want to do, learn, or accomplish. In Cindy's case, she chose to share her goal with her team and her family, so she could have their support and encouragement, but also to make her commitment public and to have the people around her hold her to it. In her case, if it hadn't worked out, there wouldn't have been much of an actual consequence—except maybe some embarrassment or disappointment. And from a growth-mindset perspective, it's not really about the outcome anyway; it's more about the learning and the growth that takes place in the process.

Of course the outcome is also important, and sometimes when we make specific commitments there are significant consequences if we don't follow through or produce the desired result. But when we approach our goals with a growth mindset, our ability to learn, grow, adjust, develop, and achieve is actually enhanced through the paradox of focusing on the process and lessening our fixed attachment to the outcome. And the bold act of making a commitment and being held accountable to it has a way of inspiring the power within us and around us to support the fulfillment of our intention. As this famous passage, written by W. H. Murray in 1951 in his book *The Scottish Himalayan Expedition*, reminds us:

> Until one is committed, there is hesitancy, the chance to draw back. Concerning all acts of initiative (and creation), there is one elementary truth that ignorance of which kills countless ideas and splendid plans: that the moment one definitely commits oneself, then Providence moves too. All sorts of things occur to help one that would never otherwise have occurred. A whole stream of events issues from the decision, raising in one's favor all manner of unforeseen incidents and meetings and material assistance, which no man could have dreamt would have come his way. I have learned a deep respect for one of Goethe's

couplets: "Whatever you can do, or dream you can, begin it. Boldness has genius, power, and magic in it."

Even though it can be scary to make commitments and seek accountability for them, when we have the courage to do this, two important things can happen. First, we're more likely to grow, learn, and actually achieve things we weren't sure we could achieve. And second, we continue to train and develop the mental and emotional muscles of commitment and accountability, which are essential aspects of growth mindset.

## Failure

I'm not a huge fan of failure. I don't know many people who are. Failure, however, is one of the most important components of success and is necessary for us to embrace if we're going to operate with a growth mindset. Our fixed mindset wants to solve the same or similar problems over and over again to reinforce our competence. But our growth mindset is about challenging ourselves and developing our skills and talents, which inevitably involves us failing.

I learned a lot about failure playing sports when I was young. Although baseball was my primary sport, I also played basketball all the way through high school. My high school basketball coach, Don Lippi, was one of the best coaches I ever played for, and he taught me a great deal about the importance of failure and growth mindset (although we didn't call it that back in the early '90s). He was all about playing hard and hustling. He rarely got upset with us for making mistakes, but if we didn't hustle he would go ballistic. Basketball didn't come naturally to me, and a lot of the guys on our team at Skyline High School in Oakland, and in our league, were bigger, stronger, faster, and more physically talented than I was. I had to work incredibly hard just to get on the court and keep up with the pace of the game.

In one game during my junior year, we were playing against Oakland Tech at their gym. I was bringing the ball up the court and made a bad pass, which was intercepted by one of the best players on the other team. He got the ball and, with a full head of steam, raced toward the basket and went up for a dunk. I chased him down as fast as I could, and tried to catch him and defend the basket so he couldn't score. Not only did he score, but he dunked on me in such an emphatic way that the ball hit me on the head as we both came crashing down to the floor. I also fouled him, so he would be going to the free-throw line for a potential three-point play. The crowd erupted and the guy who dunked on me got right in my face and taunted me. I was mortified—this is one of the worst things that can happen to you on a basketball court, especially when you're 17 years old and in the other team's gym. As I got up and looked around, the crowd was cheering and laughing at me, and most of my teammates were staring at the floor, unsure of how to react or what to say to me. But when I looked over at Coach Lippi on the bench, he was clapping enthusiastically and pointing at me.

He yelled, "Yes, way to hustle back on defense, Robbins, I love it!"

He meant it, and taught me something very important in that moment. Yes, I still felt disappointed by my bad pass, and I still felt incredibly embarrassed about getting dunked on, taunted, and laughed at. But Coach Lippi's enthusiastically positive response and his appreciation of my hustle made me feel a sense of pride about my courage, tenacity, and heart.

Michael Jordan, arguably the greatest basketball player of all time, famously didn't make the varsity basketball team at his high school when he tried out as a sophomore. But he continued to work hard, and over the course of his incredible professional basketball career he scored 32,292 points (fourth all-time), earned six NBA championships and five NBA MVP titles (tied for first all-time), and made 14 All-Star Game appearances. Jordan said, "I've missed more than 9,000 shots in my career. I've lost almost 300 games. Twenty-six times I've been trusted to take the game winning shot and missed. I've failed over and over and over again in my life. And that is why I succeed."

Failure is simply feedback that something's not working the way we want it to, or that we're not quite there yet—in a particular moment, or in general, depending on what we're doing or where we are in our growth process. Failing is a natural and necessary part of learning and success. As scary and painful as failure can be, the more willing we are to risk it, the more likely we are to develop and achieve. This is a simple truth, but not always an easy practice. Almost every important success story that we've heard that inspires us, as well as most of the success stories in our own lives and careers, involve some amount of failure. It's how we respond to failure—in other words, our mindset—that ultimately makes the biggest difference.

## Personal Growth

As we look at the importance of growth mindset in this chapter, and at the idea of bringing our whole selves to work in this book, what we're really talking about is being able to show up as a full, dynamic, imperfect, and ever-evolving human being in our professional lives. This is no small thing, and there are both many challenges to doing this and enormous potential benefits. So much of what we've been discussing is predicated on our interest in, desire for, and commitment to our own personal growth. Personal-growth work keeps us in a place of growth mindset and, of course, in a place of constant learning. And as the personal and professional worlds continue to come together these days, it seems that personal growth is professional growth, and professional growth is personal growth. There is no real separation.

For us as human beings to be effective and fulfilled in our work, it's important that we engage all aspects of ourselves—body (physical), mind (mental), heart (emotional), and spirit (purpose and our connection to a higher power, however we experience that)—and that we make a commitment to growing and developing all these aspects. While some of these things are quite personal in nature and may, in fact, take place outside of work, they all relate to our work and how we show up professionally; so the more willing we are to focus on them and on our personal growth, the more successful we can be in our work.

In a very basic sense, my work has always been about personal growth and how it connects and relates to our professional lives—how we do our jobs, and how teams and companies can organize themselves and set their culture. This focus has been driven by my interest in and passion for personal growth in my own life. As I've continued to learn and grow more as a person, it has impacted every aspect of my work as well.

In addition to the mindfulness practices I shared in the previous chapter, I want to share some of the things I do and focus on for my own personal growth—both as examples of my "best practices," and to make this as tangible as possible.

**Taking care of my body.** I do the best I can to take care of my body—sleeping well, eating healthily, and exercising regularly. There are so many great techniques for and approaches to doing this; and the information and resources about health, fitness, nutrition, and well-being that we have access to is vast (and at times overwhelming). My approach to this has always been to keep it simple, focus on what works best for me, and remember that taking care of my body creates the foundation for growth, development, success, joy, and fulfillment in my work and personal life. These days I'm focused on getting seven to eight hours of sleep per night, which is a welcome change for me and one that has been helping. I follow an eating plan that involves eating lots of vegetables and protein, and eating every three hours. When I stick to it, it really boosts my energy level and helps me stay lean and fit. For exercise, I have five things I'm doing right now—walking, hiking, yoga, jumping on my rebounder (small trampoline) in my office, and the "7-minute workout" which is a short circuit routine of 12 exercises that you do for 30 seconds each (which I do along with a video to make it super easy). I try to do one or more of these things each day. While these practices are focused on my body and physical well-being, I notice that when I'm doing them consistently (or inconsistently), there is an impact on my mind, heart, and spirit too.

**Working with coaches, counselors, and therapists.** Starting in college, I've worked over the years with some amazing coaches, counselors, and therapists. I'm grateful for all I've learned from these wise, talented, caring individuals. Some of them have focused on specific aspects of my life and growth—working through depression, grief, and change, as well as helping me with my business, marriage, money, and more. In most cases, I've worked with these professionals to help me more deeply understand myself, heal my pain, make peace with my past, change negative patterns, and grow and evolve in new ways. As I've mentioned, currently I'm working with an incredible spiritual counselor named Eleanor, whom I adore. I've also been working with Melanie Bates for the past year or so, as she's been coaching me on this book, my business, and my life in general. Michelle and I have a wonderful couple's counselor named Heidi, whom we've worked with for the past few years. Working with these people now (and others in the past) has helped me to grow mentally, emotionally, and spiritually, and having their support is fundamental not only to my personal growth, but to the process of constantly expanding my growth mindset.

**Reading books, listen to audios, and watch videos.** I like to constantly learn new ideas and be inspired by teachers, writers, business leaders, and people of all kinds. I love books, although I'm not a huge reader—I prefer to listen to audiobooks since I'm such an auditory learner. This has also drawn me to audio programs, and, more recently, to podcasts. Watching TED talks and other inspiring videos is also something I enjoy doing. I sometimes like to listen to or watch something interesting and inspiring while I'm exercising, so I can work my body and my mind at the same time. The things I read, listen to, and watch vary in content and theme, but always focus on some aspect of my growth that I'm interested in at a particular time. Reading/listening/watching helps me expand my mind, for sure, and can also touch my heart and my spirit, which I also appreciate.

**Taking personal development workshops, seminars, and courses.** Workshops, seminars, and courses have had a profound impact on my personal growth and my life over the years. Taking workshops through an organization now called Landmark Worldwide in my twenties helped me move through some of the pain, fear, and challenges associated with the end of my baseball career. I also met Michelle there, and a number of other amazing people. Over the past 20 years, I've taken many powerful workshops through organizations like Challenge Day, the Mankind Project, the Ford Institute, and Peak Potentials; with various authors and teachers; and at conferences, churches, retreat centers, and other places. Nowadays there are also many incredible courses available online, some of which I've also enjoyed—although I still prefer to be in a room with a group of people for a day, a weekend, a week, or other a period of time, doing personal-growth work in community, in person.

In late 2016 I did one of the most powerful personal-development programs I've ever done called the Hoffman Process—a weeklong intensive, focused on "family of origin" healing and changing negative patterns. I found this workshop, and the subsequent courses I've done with the Hoffman Institute, to be incredibly healing and empowering. Participating in these types of programs often helps me heal and grow, on all four levels—physical, mental, emotional, and spiritual—and it also allows me to disconnect from the day-to-day activities of my life and work, so I can tap into a deeper level of myself and connect more clearly to what matters most.

**Participating in a men's group.** I'm grateful to have been a part of a few different men's groups in my life, and have found them to be a very important element of my growth as a man and as a human being. The men's group I'm in now is amazing. There are 10 of us, and we meet every other week. We get real, and support and challenge one another. We love and care about each other too. For me as a man, especially having grown up without my father around or any brothers, being a part of a supportive men's group is something that helps me be a better man, husband, and father. It also helps me be more clear, focused, and confident in my work and how I show up in the world.

I've also been in a few professional "mastermind groups," which had both men and women in them. We met in person or virtually once a month or once a quarter, and supported each other in our work and our lives. I found those groups to be super helpful and empowering.

Most of us understand that, in order to be healthy, it's important for us to take care of our bodies with exercise, good food, hydration, and sleep. Doing this well and over the long term can be challenging, and takes commitment, focus, and dedication. And even if we don't do as good a job of this as we'd like, very few of us dispute its importance. The same is true for our personal growth: for us to be fully alive and engaged in our work and in life, it takes a lifelong commitment to an ongoing process. And as with our physical well-being, how we go about our personal growth will evolve over time.

The great news about this is that with the way things are changing, a holistic approach to personal growth is much better understood and supported these days in the world around us, even at work—through increased awareness, scientific data, and the lessening of taboos. The understanding of emotional intelligence and mindfulness in the business world, which we talked about in the previous chapter, are two examples of this. And there are many more examples that we see in businesses of all types and sizes.

Eric Severson is the Chief People Officer for DaVita Kidney Care and the former Co-Chief Human Resources Officer for Gap Inc. I met Eric when he was working at Gap and had a chance to partner with him and his team several times. He's a leader who is as committed to his personal growth and the growth of the people around him as anyone I've ever known. He's a passionate advocate for growth mindset, and for the past decade has been working to implement this approach into the architecture of how companies help their employees and teams achieve their goals. When I interviewed Eric on my podcast, he said, "There is a science behind a healthy workplace and there are many practices companies can put into place to encourage a healthy environment. Optimizing the mind, body, spirit, and emotional energy allows human beings to perform at their best, because all their domains are being fueled and in balance."

At Gap, he and his team created a powerful employee-wellness program called Performance for Life. The tagline of the program was "Better You, Better Gap." He told me, "The research points out that when people take better care of themselves and feel their employer is interested in their well-being, they are much more likely to perform at a higher level and commit to their work."

I was on a panel at another Wisdom 2.0 event, this one with Eric and also Karen May, VP of People Development at Google. During our panel discussion, Karen said, "At Google we try to offer our employees a wide variety of learning options to support their interests and growth." When I first partnered with Google back in 2010, the seminars I delivered for their employees on emotional intelligence, stress management, and relationship building were part of what they called their "School of Personal Growth."

What companies like Gap and Google, and leaders like Eric and Karen, understand is that supporting the personal growth and well-being of their employees is both good for the employee and good for the company. The same thing could be said about growth mindset in general—it's good for us as individuals and also for our teams and organizations. Growth mindset is a fairly simple concept to understand, but it takes real courage, awareness, and commitment to embrace and embody it. When we do this, however, we not only create the best conditions for us to thrive, but we allow our work to be a catalyst for our growth—which is a key aspect of bringing all of who we are to the work we do.

# PRINCIPLE #5–
# CREATE A
# CHAMPIONSHIP TEAM

Have you ever been on a team where the talent was strong, but the team wasn't very good? On the flip side, have you ever been on a team where not every single member was a rock star, but something about the team just worked? We've all had these types of experiences. It can be difficult to understand what makes one team successful and another one not. I've been fascinated by this phenomenon for many years.

It started for me growing up playing baseball. I played from age 7 until almost 25. I was on some teams where we had remarkable talent, but we didn't perform well as a team. And I was on some other teams where we didn't have the best talent, but we performed at an incredibly high level. I found this to be confusing and exciting at the same time. There seemed to be an "X-factor" in the success of my teams. In sports we call this "chemistry." No one can quite define what that is, but you know when you have it, and you definitely know when you don't have it. And it's not just some touchy-feely thing: it actually has a profound impact on how you perform as an individual and as a team. It may be intangible, but as I learned throughout my years as an athlete, team chemistry is one of the most important factors of success in sports.

I erroneously thought this was a phenomenon specific to sports. But after baseball, when I got into the business world, I noticed it there as well. In business we call it "culture." It's basically the same thing. It's that intangible quality that brings people together or pushes them apart; and it makes a huge difference in how we perform individually and collectively. When I realized this, I became somewhat obsessed with it. I wanted to figure out if this was something that occurred just randomly, or if it was something that could be learned, taught, and deliberately created.

It was this obsession, among others, that prompted me to start researching, speaking, and writing about teamwork and culture 17 years ago when I started my business. And being able to bring our whole selves to work is predicated on the environment around us, the people we partner with, and the teams that we build. In this chapter, the fifth and final principle of the book, we're going to look at the importance of teamwork, at the key components of creating a culture in which people can thrive, and at ways you can influence this with your own team and others with whom you work.

## Teamwork Fundamentals

In all my years of being a part of many teams, and in almost two decades of studying, speaking to, and working with teams of all kinds, there are some key lessons I've learned, which I often share with the teams I work with, and that I want to address up-front before we dive deeper into this discussion:

**We aren't well trained to work in teams.** Most of us didn't receive much helpful or healthy teamwork training growing up. Even if we played team sports, as I did, or were involved in other team-oriented activities, our primary training for work came through school. And, what was "teamwork" called when we were in school? Cheating! We were encouraged to do our own work, and we were graded individually on how we performed on tests, papers, and projects. Group projects in school were few and far between, and my experience of doing them was often frustrating because it was hard to get everyone on the same page and make sure they all did their fair share of the work.

After years of education that often discourages teamwork, many of us find ourselves in the business world being told to work within a team. Yet although some organizations encourage teamwork more than others, we still tend to get evaluated, compensated, and promoted as individuals, so the incentive or motivation to work collaboratively can be undercut.

The paradox of teamwork is that for us to fully show up, engage, be successful, and create meaning and fulfillment in our work, collaborating with others is essential; while at the same time, there are forces within us (like our egos, personal ambitions, and fears) and within our teams and organizations (like competition, territorialism, and scarcity), that can spur us to focus primarily on ourselves. It's important for us to acknowledge this paradox with awareness, ownership, and compassion, and to work through it as best as we can. Teamwork can be challenging, and often involves lots of growth opportunities for us and our colleagues. So the best way to approach it is with a growth mindset, as we discussed in the previous chapter.

**Mechanics vs. Psychology (Above the line/Below the line).** I heard peak-performance expert Tony Robbins speak many years ago, and it had a big impact on my thinking. Tony states that, in almost every circumstance, "80 percent of success is due to psychology—mindset, beliefs, and emotions—and only 20 percent is due to mechanics—the specific steps needed to accomplish a result." Through my own experience in sports and business, as well as my research on performance and success, I have found this to be true—on both the individual and the team levels. The challenge is that we spend so much of our time, energy, and attention focused on the mechanics, that we sometimes forget to address the psychology, which diminishes our ability to be successful.

From a team standpoint, I often describe mechanics as "above the line" (what we do and how we do it) and psychology as "below the line" (how we think and feel, our perspective, and the overall morale and culture of the group). Since the below-the-line stuff is 80 percent of our success as a team, we have to pay more attention to these intangible things if we're going to be the kind of team we want to be.

**First Team/Second Team.** The idea of asking "What's my first team?" and "What's my second team?" was introduced to me through the best-selling book *The Five Dysfunctions of a Team* by Patrick Lencioni, one of the best books out there on teamwork. This concept is particularly important to managers at every level in an organization. If you're an individual contributor, your first (and only) team is usually pretty well defined. Most often it includes your peers—the people who report to the same manager as you. You may have a larger team that your intact team rolls up to, but since you don't really have a second team, your first team is fairly straightforward.

However, when I ask most managers to tell me about their team, they usually talk about their direct reports, or the larger organization that reports up to them if they happen to be a senior leader. This makes sense, especially when we get all the way up to the executive-team level within a company. Most leaders feel a sense of pride, ownership, and commitment to "their team"—since the people who report to them directly or roll up to them are the ones they're responsible for, are tasked with coaching and developing, and are evaluated themselves in large part based on how they perform.

But leaders, leadership teams, and companies function best when they understand that their "first team" is actually the team they're a member of, and their "second team" is the team that reports to them. This may seem counterintuitive, because most leaders are going to spend a majority of their time focused on the team they manage. But for things to operate in the healthiest, most effective way, leadership teams should function as actual teams and support one another as peers and fellow members of the same team, not just as a group of managers who have the same boss. This can be tricky, as we'll get into throughout this chapter, because things can get competitive and priorities can be at odds with our peers, particularly at a senior leadership level. However, understanding that as leaders our peers are our first team and our reports are our second team benefits everyone involved. And any misalignment on a leadership team (especially the higher up in the organization it occurs) creates exponential misalignment in the level or levels below.

**The difference between our role and our job.** This important distinction was first taught to me by Fred Kofman, Vice President of Leadership and Organizational Development at LinkedIn and author of *Conscious Business*. When most of us think about our "job," we think of what we do—engineering, sales, project management, marketing, human resources, operations, design, finance, and so forth. While these descriptions may encapsulate what we do and the title we hold, they're not actually our job. If we're part of a team, we each have a specific role, which is what we do, but our job is to help fulfill the goals, mission, and purpose of the company, whatever they may be. In other words, we're there to do whatever we can to help the team win. The challenge with this is that most of us take pride in our role and we want to do it really well, which is great. However, when we put our role (what we do specifically) over our job (helping the team win), things can get murky—our personal goals become more important to us than the goals of the organization. It takes commitment and courage, but organizations made up of people who understand this simple but important distinction—who realize that everyone on the team has essentially the same job but different roles—have the ability to perform at the highest level and with the most collaborative environment.

**There's an important difference between a championship team and a team of champions.** Given my sports background, I've always thought of teams who operate and perform at their peak level as "championship teams." A championship team doesn't necessarily always win, but they play the game the right way, with passion, and with a commitment to one another as well as to the ultimate result. A championship team is usually greater than the sum of its parts. It's often chemistry and the below-the-line intangibles that separate the good teams from the great ones. Teams of champions, on the other hand, might have great talent and motivated people, but they're often more focused on their own individual success. Championship teams know that talent is important, but they focus on the collective success of the team and the highest vision and goals of the group. With leadership teams I make this same distinction in a slightly different way: between a team of leaders (a group of managers who focus on being the best they can be) and a leadership team (a group of leaders who realize that they're each other's first team, and that the more unified they are, the more it benefits them, each other, and the people who report to them).

Understanding these five fundamental ideas about teamwork gives us the framework to focus on some of the things we can do to enhance the performance and culture of our teams—regardless of the specific role we play. Our ability to bring our whole selves to work has a lot to do with the environment around us and the team to which we belong. So the more we focus on creating a championship team, the easier it becomes for us to show up fully at work. And the more willing we are to bring all of who we are to work, the more influence we can have on our team. These things are intricately and dynamically linked.

## Team Performance

A pioneer in the field of team effectiveness was the late J. Richard Hackman, Professor of Social and Organizational Psychology at Harvard University. Hackman's research focused on what he called "enabling conditions" that allow teams to thrive. Hackman believed that if you created the right conditions, the success of the team would flow from there. If, however, the conditions weren't set up in a way to enable success, it didn't matter how talented the team members were—their success would be limited. I agree with Hackman that conditions are essential to the success of teams. And in my own study and experience of high-performing teams in today's dynamic business world, I've found that there are two important conditions that most effectively enable a culture of engagement, connection, and optimal performance:

**Healthy High Expectations:** High expectations are essential for people to thrive. But they have to be healthy—meaning there is a high standard of excellence, not an insatiable, unhealthy pressure to be perfect. We almost always get what we expect from others; however, if we expect perfection, everyone falls short and people aren't set up to succeed. Healthy high expectations are about setting a high bar and challenging people to be their absolute best. This also has to do with being clear, and holding people accountable in an empowering way.

**High Level of Nurturance:** Nurturance has to do with people feeling cared about and valued—not just for what they do, but for who they are. It also has to do with it being safe to make mistakes, ask for help, speak up, and disagree. In other words, as we discussed in Chapters 1 and 2, this is about people feeling appreciated and their ability to be authentic. Nurturing environments are also filled with a genuine sense of compassion and empathy—people feel cared for and supported.

We often think that in order to have a high bar we can't also be nurturing. Or we think that if we nurture people, we can't also expect a lot from them. Actually, the goal for us as team members and leaders, and teams as a whole, is to be able do both at the same time, and to do so passionately. Bringing our whole selves to work, and creating an environment that supports both high expectations and strong nurturing at the same time, takes courage on everyone's part, and at times goes against conventional wisdom. But being willing to focus on both of these things simultaneously, and encouraging others to do the same, creates the conditions for everyone to thrive.

A great example of this is Hughes Marino, a commercial real estate firm based in San Diego. Jason Hughes, the chairman, CEO, and co-owner of the company, contacted me back in the summer of 2011. He and his team were planning their first firm retreat and he invited me to come and speak.

In our initial phone conversation, Jason said to me, "Mike, I want to support the people on our team to be successful at work and also in life." I was inspired by his commitment to his team and to their growth and development, both in business and in their personal lives. In talking more to Jason and his wife, Shay—Hughes Marino's president, COO, and other co-owner—in preparation for their retreat, I found out a few interesting things about their firm and their approach.

First, they represent only tenants. In commercial real estate, which involves the leasing and buying of office space for companies, it can sometimes be challenging and create conflicts when real estate companies end up on both sides of a particular deal, representing the tenant and the building owner simultaneously. In order to eliminate those potential conflicts, Hughes Marino works only for tenants (companies looking to find office space) and not for building owners who are looking to lease or sell.

Second, commercial real estate is a high-stakes, pressure-filled, commission-based business that often creates an internal culture of negative competition and not much collaboration. Jason and his team at Hughes Marino were committed to creating a team-oriented, family-type atmosphere within the firm.

These two things—coupled with their commitment to both personal and professional growth, and the fact that they were including in the retreat all the spouses and significant others of their 15 employees—had me very excited about speaking to all of them about creating a championship team, at work and at home.

The session I delivered at their retreat seemed to resonate with them, and to inspire them to make further commitments to growth and team culture. Over the past seven years, I've had a chance to work with the Hughes Marino team on an ongoing basis. They've created core values for their firm that include "Embrace the Family Spirit," "Nurture Your Personal and Professional Life," and "Be Authentic, Grateful, and Humble." These values aren't just nice words for them; they are core beliefs and commitments by which they operate as a company. When you walk into their beautiful office in downtown San Diego, you see on the video screen in the middle of the atrium a scrolling slide show of photos of their team members having fun with their families and doing things that are important to them. In addition to their annual company retreats, they've implemented ways for their team members to connect, support one another, learn, grow, share, and embody their core values. They also hold regular events for their clients—some of them they've invited me to speak about creating a winning culture and about the importance of appreciation and authenticity.

Their commitment to nurturing their team and building their culture, coupled with their intense focus on excellence and success, has paid off for them in big ways. They now have more than 100 people on their team, with offices in Los Angeles, Orange County, San Francisco, Silicon Valley, and Seattle, in addition to their headquarters in San Diego. Their business is growing exponentially. And just like other successful companies with strong cultures that I work with, when you walk into a Hughes Marino office, their commitment to both high expectations and high nurturance is on display physically, in the beautiful design and impeccability of the office space and the personal touch of team-member photos, as well as intangibly, via the energy and attitude of their team. When you talk to their employees, there's a passion, enthusiasm, and gratitude for being a part of a company like theirs that is infectious. When we're a part of a team that expects a lot from us in a healthy way, and nurtures us in genuine and generous ways, we can truly thrive—individually and collectively.

## Psychological Safety

Google conducted an in-depth research project between 2012 and 2014 aimed at determining the key factors that consistently produce high-performing teams. They called it "Project Aristotle," and it involved gathering and assessing data from 180 teams across Google, as well as looking at some of the most recent studies in the fields of organizational psychology and team effectiveness. After analyzing the data and research, a number of key findings emerged. According to Project Aristotle, the most significant element of team success is what's known as psychological safety.

Psychological safety is a concept popularized by researcher and Harvard Business School professor Amy Edmondson. According to her research, psychological safety is a shared belief that the team is safe for risk taking. People on teams with psychological safety have a sense of confidence that their team will not embarrass, reject, or punish them for speaking up. The team climate is characterized by an atmosphere of interpersonal trust and mutual respect in which people are comfortable being themselves.

One difference between psychological safety and trust is that psychological safety focuses on a belief about a group norm, while trust focuses on a belief that one person has about another. Another difference is that psychological safety is defined by how group members think they are viewed by others in the group, whereas trust is defined by how one views another. Another way to think about this is that trust is a one-on-one phenomenon, whereas psychological safety is a group phenomenon, so when we're talking about psychological safety, we're talking about group trust.

I've seen the importance of psychological safety up close for many years with the teams and leaders I coach. When a team creates norms and practices, both explicitly and implicitly, that allow their members to be themselves, speak up, make mistakes, and fail (as we've been talking about in different ways throughout the book), they are more likely to collaborate and succeed. All the talent and skill in the world can't make up for a lack of psychological safety.

According to Edmondson's research—which was backed up by the findings of Google's Project Aristotle—there are three things that leaders can do to help create and enhance psychological safety:

- **Frame work as learning problems,
  as opposed to execution problems.**
  Edmondson says, "Make explicit that
  there is enormous uncertainty ahead and
  enormous interdependence. In other words,
  be clear that there are areas that still require
  explanation and that each team member's

input matters. For example, saying things like 'We've never been here before; we can't know what will happen; we've got to have everybody's brains and voices in the game,' helps create this atmosphere."

- **Acknowledge your own fallibility.** Edmondson says, "Make simple statements that encourage peers and subordinates to speak up, such as, 'I may miss something—I need to hear from you.'" Another way to think about this, based on what we talked about in Chapter 1, is lowering the waterline on your iceberg.

- **Model curiosity by asking a lot of questions.** According to Edmonson, asking a lot of questions "actually creates a necessity for voice, because team members need to generate answers." We could also think about this in terms of what we discussed in the previous chapter on growth mindset. The more a leader focuses on curiosity and learning, the easier it becomes for people on the team to speak up, ask questions, and embrace the discomfort of not knowing, all of which are essential for growth and psychological safety.

At the end of the day, so much of psychological safety comes down to the relationship the leader has with his or her team and each individual member.

Stuart Crabb, former Global Head of Learning at Facebook and co-founder of Oxegen Consulting, told me in an interview, "Progressive organizations realize that the manager trumps the brand, every time. None of the perks matter if your manager sucks." He continued, "A company should never pay someone extra to be a manager; it incents people to want to lead for the wrong reasons. Focusing on the larger social community is what's most important." At Facebook they have set things up organizationally in a way that allows people to advance to a very senior level as individual contributors, so they don't become managers simply to progress in their careers or make more money.

Leaders have a responsibility to do everything they can to set the tone for the team, build strong and trusting relationships with team members, and create conditions that are conducive to psychological safety. However, championship teams understand that it's more than just the leader who creates this environment—it's up to the entire team. Psychological safety is a key element to providing a highly nurturing work environment, which makes it safer for people to speak up, take risks, make mistakes, and ultimately bring all of who they are to work. When this happens, in combination with healthy high expectations, our teams can perform at their best, and so can we as individuals.

## Inclusion

Another essential element of creating an environment that is safe, nurturing, and conducive to the success of our teams is inclusion. *Inclusion* means "having respect for and appreciation of differences in ethnicity, gender, age, national origin, disability, sexual orientation, education, and religion." It also means "actively involving everyone's ideas, knowledge, perspectives, approaches, and styles to maximize business success." The groups and organizations that get the importance of diversity and inclusion understand that it's not about political correctness, compliance, or public relations; it's actually about creating the most dynamic, innovative, and supportive working environment for their teams, which allows them to produce the best results.

Katherine Connolly and Boris Groysberg of Harvard Business School conducted a study a few years ago of 24 companies that had earned a reputation for making diversity and inclusion a priority. Some of their key findings were encapsulated by remarks by two executives they interviewed. Brian Moynihan, CEO of Bank of America, said, "When internal diversity and inclusion scores are strong, and employees feel valued, they will serve our customers better, and we'll be better off as an organization." Ajay Banga, CEO of MasterCard, said, "My passion for diversity and inclusion comes from the fact that I myself am diverse. There have been a hundred times when I have felt different from other people in the room or in the business. I have a turban and a full beard, and I run a global company—that's not common." These executives realize that for their companies to be successful in today's global economy, creating an inclusive culture is necessary.

In my own research for this book and the interviews I conducted, this topic of inclusion came up on many occasions and in lots of different ways in the context of bringing our whole selves to work.

One of the most fascinating stories I heard was from Jay Allen, the former Chief Administrative Officer at Charles Schwab. Jay told me about coming out as a gay man in the early '80s at IBM, which was not easy or a common thing to do at that time. Jay said, "In 1983 I was working for IBM in the Bay Area. Only the people who were really close to me at work knew I was gay. It was mostly unspoken."

But when he applied for and got a promotion, it became a bit of an issue. "It was taking a really long time for my promotion to go through and for me to get officially announced in this new role," Jay said. "I was told that I needed to meet with Jesse Henderson, the man who would be my new manager, because he had something he wanted to discuss with me. Jesse—a big, African American, ex–football player—was a pretty imposing figure and a man of few words. When we met, he said, 'I've heard a rumor that you're gay and I want to ask you if that's true?'

"'Yes, it's true, I am gay,' I responded.

"'Okay,' he said, 'we'll have to deal with that. It might cause a problem with your security clearance.'"

Apparently in those days, being gay and in the closet was considered a security risk because it was something that could be used for blackmail.

Jay continued, "I said to Jesse, 'Can I ask you a question? Would you have felt better if I had said no?'

"He seemed a little taken aback by my question, but said, 'No, I wanted you to tell the truth.'

"I think he did want me to tell the truth, but it seemed to me like he wished the truth was that I was not gay. I'm not sure where this came from in my being, but I then said to him, 'Look, here's the deal, you're black and I'm gay, the difference is everybody can look at you and they know you're black. But when people look at me, they don't know if I'm gay. In terms of our ability to do the job, there's no difference. So this really seems irrelevant and unfair to me.'

"When I said this, Jesse paused and it seemed like there was a little shift in him. He said to me, 'Well, we're going to make this work.'

"That was the end of our meeting and that's what prompted me to officially come out at IBM."

Jay went on to tell me that Jesse ended up becoming his mentor and one of the most important people in his career. They became very close, and Jesse gave Jay tons of opportunities to grow and advance in his 14 years at IBM. After that he worked for GE and NBC, among others, before ending up at Charles Schwab where he became Executive Vice President of Human Resources and ultimately Chief Administrative Officer, before retiring in 2015.

Hearing Jay's remarkable story of coming out at work, and a number of others like it, has made me realize that, as sensitive and aware as I try to be about things like this, I have no idea what it would be like to go through that experience myself. It's yet another example of me recognizing more fully my own privilege.

And although society has made a lot of progress since Jay was at IBM in the early 80s, for people in the LGBTQ community there remain issues and challenges to navigate at work that those of us who aren't a part of that community don't have to think about and in many cases don't understand. When I first started thinking about writing this book a few years ago and Googled "Bring Your Whole Self to Work," I found information about the Human Rights Campaign (HRC), America's largest LGBTQ civil rights organization. Since 2002 they have administered an annual report called the Corporate Equality Index (CEI), which looks at how companies cultivate an environment of diversity and inclusion, specifically with respect to members of the LGBTQ community. The HRC also provides resources, support, and guidance for coming out at work. Among other things, they encourage people to "bring their whole selves to work," and organizations to support their people by cultivating an inclusive environment.

Gender diversity and awareness is another essential aspect of inclusion. When I interviewed Donna Morris, Executive Vice President of Customer and Employee Experience at Adobe, she said something interesting I'd never thought about before. "Bringing your whole self to work as a woman can be a challenge. The more senior you become, the more acutely aware you are of the differences. Most of the female colleagues I know have working partners, while many of our male counterparts have spouses who are at home, so they're not having to manage and coordinate the same types of things outside of work that many women in their same roles do. That's a big difference. And while there has definitely been an emergence of stay-at-home dads or partners in recent years, I still think we have a hard time addressing and discussing the additional pressure and challenges women face at work."

There are many layers of complexity when it comes to gender diversity and inclusion. Talking to Donna made me realize that women continue to face the challenge of opportunity, and even when they do get a seat at the table, there are often different expectations, pressures, and life circumstances that can add to the difficulty. Her insights reminded me of the famous line about Fred Astaire, "Sure he was great, but don't forget that Ginger Rogers did everything he did . . . backwards and in high heels."

Issues such as gender, race, sexual orientation, nationality, age, disability, and religion and more can be hard to look at and even harder to talk about, since they touch on things that are both deeply personal and difficult to understand from our various perspectives and world-views. They also touch on issues of privilege, oppression, bias (both conscious and unconscious), and opportunity. These things bring up a lot of pain, strong emotions, and reactions for many of us, for a variety of reasons.

For people of any minority group—which means just about everyone except straight white males—the reality of the group or groups they belong to can raise issues of pride, challenge, identity, and struggle for them, especially at work. Inclusion is about all of us doing what we can to think about, talk about, and be aware of these issues, and about creating an environment that is as open, understanding, supportive, and as safe as possible—which isn't easy and can be understandably messy and uncomfortable.

The term *covering* was coined by sociologist Erving Goffman to describe how even individuals with known stigmatized identities make "a great effort to keep their stigma from looming large." Kenji Yoshino, a constitutional law professor at NYU, further developed this idea and came up with four different categories in which we "cover": (1) Appearance, (2) Affiliation, (3) Advocacy, and (4) Association. In essence, we often do what we can to cover aspects of ourselves that we believe might put us out of the "mainstream" of our environment. Yoshino partnered with Christie Smith, Managing Principal of the Deloitte University Leadership Center for Inclusion, to measure the prevalence of covering at work. They distributed a survey to employees in organizations across 10 different industries. The 3,129 respondents included a mix of ages, genders, races/ethnicities, and orientations. They also came from different levels of seniority within their organizations. Sixty-one percent of respondents reported covering at least one of these four categories at work. According to the study, 83 percent of LGBTQ individuals, 79 percent of blacks, 67 percent of women of color, 66 percent of women, and 63 percent of Hispanics cover. While the researchers found that covering occurred more frequently within groups that have been historically underrepresented, they also found that 45 percent of straight white men reported covering as well.

Issues of diversity and inclusion impact all of us. And while they clearly play a significant role in the lives and careers of women and members of every minority group, it's important that we all be willing to look at and talk about these issues, and do what we can do to create an environment that is as inclusive as possible. For us to do this, it takes everything we've been discussing in this book—authenticity, appreciation, emotional intelligence, growth mindset, teamwork, and the rest. As we discussed in Chapter 1, the paradox of being human is that on the one hand we're all unique—by virtue of how we look, our background, how we think, our skills, our personalities, what we value, our histories, and so forth—yet on the other hand, the further down below the waterline we go on our iceberg, the more we're alike. We're all human beings and we experience the same emotions—love, fear, joy, shame, gratitude, sadness, excitement, anger, and more.

I was reminded of this specifically on a trip to India last year to speak to the leaders and employees at the Bangalore office of my client Nutanix, a cloud-computing software company based in San Jose, California. It was my first trip to India, and I was blown away by the beauty and passion of the people, the vibrancy of the culture, and the energy of Bangalore and the country as a whole. I was also made keenly aware, as I often am when I travel outside of the United States, of my own privilege and how my cultural background shapes (and in many cases limits) how I see the world. It was both humbling and eye-opening— definitely a growth opportunity. And at the same time, as the Nutanix employees and I did the "If You Really Knew Me" exercise together, I found that many of the things that were below the waterlines on the icebergs of the people in India were similar to what's below the waterline on my own iceberg and that of many of the people I know and work with in the U.S. In other words, we're way more alike than different. Being able to understand and appreciate the paradox of our differences and commonalities is fundamental to creating a culture of inclusion. And this type of inclusive environment is foundational to being a championship team and encouraging people to bring all of who they are to work.

## Celebration and Fun

At the Wisdom 2.0 conference in February 2015, when I was on that panel with Dr. Michael Gervais and George Mumford about peak performance, Michael said something else about teamwork that fascinated me. It was just a few weeks after the Seattle Seahawks lost the Super Bowl to the New England Patriots in dramatic fashion. The Seahawks had won the Super Bowl the previous year and were marching down the field to score what looked like the go-ahead touchdown to win back-to-back championships. Unfortunately for Seattle, it didn't turn out that way, as they threw an interception at the goal line just before the clock ran out, and New England hung on to win the game.

Since Michael works closely with Pete Carroll and the Seahawks, he was asked about the Super Bowl loss and how he and the team reacted. "It was awful," he said. "In the locker room after the game we were all stunned and upset. I could see every stage of grief displayed right in front of me. Some guys were angry, some were in denial, others were in tears, it was devastating to lose, and to lose the way we lost, when it looked and felt like we were about to win. But I'm a psychologist, so in addition to my own feelings about the game and the outcome, I started to think about what was happening for all of us—the players, the staff, and the fans who were rooting for the Seahawks to win. There's a difference between loss and actual grief. Nobody died. We lost a game. Yes, it was a big game, but it was just a game. What I realized in that moment was that what we'd actually lost, more than the game, was the ability to celebrate with one another. If the team had scored that final touchdown and we'd won the game, we would've been screaming, hugging, high-fiving, and celebrating passionately with each other in that locker room, and so would've all the fans who were rooting for the Seahawks."

Michael's insight was powerful and poignant. Oftentimes, what we want as much as or more than the accomplishment itself is the permission to celebrate with the important people around us. In our obsession with performance and achievement, we sometimes forget to celebrate along the way, which is essential. Why do we have to wait to win the Super Bowl to allow ourselves the joy of celebration? As a former athlete and lifelong sports fan, I enjoy following the games, teams, and seasons. And as someone who is passionate about teamwork and culture, I find that sports teams are often great case studies in these things. But one of the many differences between sports and business is that in most businesses there's no "championship" at the end of the year—so there aren't always big, built-in collective goals that can focus our attention and effort over a finite amount of time. Because of this, business teams have to create reasons and opportunities to celebrate together and to have fun.

At most of the company conferences and offsites where I speak, I can tell that one of the most valuable things about these events for the people who attend them is the opportunity to come together, spend time with one another outside the office, and have some fun with each other. Conversing over dinner, telling funny stories at the bar, or taking goofy photos during an adventure or teambuilding activity end up being what people enjoy and remember the most from these events. And making things fun on a daily basis in the office is also something championship teams do. In *301 Ways to Have Fun at Work*, Leslie Yerkes and Dave Hemsath write that "organizations that integrate fun into work have lower levels of absenteeism, greater job satisfaction, increased productivity and less downtime."

Creating a positive and fun environment can attract people to our team or company. In a *Forbes* article titled "The Benefits of Fun in the Workplace," Kathy Oden-Hall, Chief Marketing Officer of Paycom, an online payroll- and human-resource-technology provider, stated that "60 percent of 2015 college graduates reported that they would rather work for a company with a 'positive social atmosphere' even if it meant a lower paycheck."

Matthew Luhn knows a thing or two about working in fun and creative environments. He worked on the story team at Pixar Animation Studios for more than 20 years. His story credits include *Toy Story, Finding Nemo, Up,*

*Monsters Inc.*, *Cars*, and many others. He began his career at the age of 19 as the youngest animator on *The Simpsons* TV series. Growing up, he worked for his family's business—a chain of toy stores in the San Francisco Bay Area called Jeffrey's Toys, owned and operated by his parents, as his grandparents before them, and his great-grandparents before them.

When I interviewed Matthew, he told me, "I learned a lot working on *The Simpsons* early in my career, and, of course, being at Pixar for over twenty years. In those environments they didn't set out to create a 'creative culture' per se; they just allowed us to be ourselves, have fun, and create—without too much pressure or stress. Hierarchy kills creativity." Matthew continued, "I think some of the things that my dad taught me as a kid are the key elements in allowing fun and creativity to flow organically in business."

Celebration and fun are essential to creating a positive environment and culture, which help us engage more in our work, connect more to one another, and tap into our creativity. Championship teams know this and do what they can to both directly and indirectly concentrate on these important aspects of teamwork.

The Golden State Warriors have had an incredible run of success over the past few years, winning NBA titles in 2015 and 2017, and setting a record for most wins in a season in 2016. Their head coach, Steve Kerr, has four core values that he, his coaching staff, the team, and the entire organization focus on: joy, mindfulness, compassion, and competition. I'm a lifelong Warriors fan, having grown up in Oakland (where the Warriors play). For most of my life, they were one of the worst teams in the NBA, so to see them having this kind of success is really fun. What's even more exciting to me, however, is the way they play. They really do embody those four values, and I love that joy is the first one, because if you watch the Warriors, they do play the game of basketball with joy. And the fun they have on the court, on the bench, and with each other is not only inspiring to watch, it's also an incredible example of a championship team in action.

## Competition

Let's talk about another one of Steve Kerr's four core values: competition. As a former athlete, and as someone who worked in sales and has quite a strong competitive spirit, I know a few things about competition. I've also studied it and seen it play out in both healthy and unhealthy ways within teams and companies for many years. Competition is part of life, and especially of business. It can be harnessed in a productive way for teams, but it can also be incredibly damaging and detrimental to the culture of a team or company. So, it's important to understand that there are two types of competition: negative and positive.

**Negative competition** is when we compete with others in such a way that we want to win at the expense of the other person or people involved. In other words, our success is predicated on their failure. Negative competition is a zero-sum game, and is based on the adolescent notion that if we win we're "good" and if we lose we're "bad." It's all about being better than or feeling inferior to others—based on outcomes or accomplishments. In a team setting, negative internal competition shuts down trust and psychological safety, and negatively impacts the culture. It usually takes one of three forms:

- One person competing against another person on the team
- One person competing against the entire team
- One team competing against another team within the organization

**Positive competition** is when we compete with others in a way that brings out the best in us and everyone involved. It's about challenging ourselves, pushing those around us, and allowing our commitment and skill, and the motivation of others, to bring the best out of us and tap into our potential. When we compete in a positive way, it benefits us and anyone else involved. Of course, we may "win" or we may "lose" the competition we're engaged in, and there are times when the outcome has a significant impact and is important. But when we compete in this positive way, we aren't rooting for others to fail or obsessed with winning at all costs, and we realize that we aren't "good" or "bad" and that our value as human beings isn't determined by the result. Positive competition is about growth, grit, and taking ourselves and our team to the next level.

A very simple example of this comes from exercise. Working out with another person is a positive, practical strategy for getting in shape, because having a workout partner creates accountability, support, and motivation. Let's say you and I decided to work out together on a regular basis, and we picked a few different activities such as running, biking, and tennis that we'd do a few times a week. And let's imagine we decided to add a little competition to make it more interesting. If we competed against each other in a negative way, I would be obsessed with figuring out how to run faster, bike farther, and beat you at tennis. And if I got really into it, I might find myself feeling stressed before we worked out, and after we got done I'd be either happy or upset depending on how I did in comparison to you on a particular day. I might even find myself taunting you if I "won," or feeling defensive, jealous, or angry if I "lost."

However, if we went about these same activities in a positively competitive way, we could still compete to win in tennis or race each other in running or biking. We wouldn't waste our time and energy attaching too much meaning to the outcome, but instead would realize that by pushing one another past our perceived limitations we would both get a better workout, helping each of us to be as healthy and fit as possible

In a team environment, it's important to pay attention to competition. We all have the capacity for both negative and positive competition. The more aware we are of our own and others' competitive tendencies, the more easily we can talk about and pay attention to them when they manifest themselves. Championship teams embrace competition, and harness its positive power to fuel individual and collective growth and success. And creating a culture of positive competition can bring out the best in us and everyone on the team.

## The Impact of Culture

Chip Conley, founder and former CEO of Joie de Vivre Hospitality and current Strategic Advisor for Hospitality and Leadership at Airbnb, is a business and thought leader who is passionate about company culture. In addition to having started Joie de Vivre at age 26 in 1986, and then making it very successful over the next 24 years with himself as the CEO (before selling it in 2010), Chip is the author of a number of best-selling books, among them *Peak: How Great Companies Get Their Mojo from Maslow,* which shows how legendary psychologist Abraham Maslow's ideas helped his company, and can help other companies as well, to operate at peak level. When I interviewed Chip on my podcast, he told me, "Culture and customer service, especially in the hospitality industry, are one and the same. If you don't have a strong culture, you're not going to have a reputation for service." His interest in and passion for building a strong culture in his company came early.

Chip went on: "There was a book from the 1980s called *The Service Profit Chain,* written by three Harvard Business School professors: James Heskett, Earl Sasser, and Leonard Schlesinger. They were able to show empirically that companies with a strong culture create happier employees, which creates happier and more loyal customers, which creates market-share growth, which creates more profitability, which creates happier investors who are more willing to invest in the culture, so it becomes a virtuous cycle." The book had a profound impact on how Chip thought about culture and business. In naming his company Joie de Vivre, which means "enjoyment of life" in French, he created both a challenge and an opportunity. The challenge was that people couldn't spell or pronounce it, and didn't know what it meant. The opportunity, however, was that it was the company's name and its mission all in one, which made it easy for his employees, customers, and investors to understand once they got it.

"We created something called the 'Joie de Vivre heart,'" Chip continued. "Just imagine a visual icon of a heart with four points on it. At the base of the heart was 'Culture,' and if you did that well, there was an artery on the heart that pumped blood to the second point, which was 'Happy Employees.' Point three on the heart had an artery to it, which was 'Loyal Customers.' And point four was 'A Profitable and Sustainable Business.' So, we could teach our employees, 60 percent of whom spoke English as a second language, about our mission and our culture in their first week on the job. The visual image of a heart is universal and it transcended language. We empowered people to speak up if one of the arteries in the heart was not working well."

## "Service Profit Chain"

Developing Strong Customer Loyalty

3

Building an Enthusiastic Staff

2

Maintaining a Profitable & Sustainable Business

4

Creating a Unique Corporate Culture

1

## Joie de Vivre Heart: Karmic Capitalism

Chip said that one of the things they had to do as they grew, especially once they got past 1,000 employees, was to "democratize culture." He said, "We created cultural ambassadors for all fifty-two of our hotels. The ambassador took on this role, in addition to their regular job, and it couldn't be the general manager—it had to be a mid-level manager or a line-level employee. They were elected by their fellow employees and would be in the role for a year. There were three primary focuses for each of these cultural ambassadors. First, was to figure out how they could grow and evolve the culture of their particular property. They would work with the GM and the head of HR at the hotel to come up with creative ways of doing this that resonated with that site and their unique team. Second, they worked to develop and evolve the recognition program so that it stayed fresh and motivating for everyone. And third, they focused on philanthropic activities that allowed the employees to connect with and contribute directly to the community."

Chip shared an example of such initiatives—an idea that came from one of their cultural ambassadors. "During a downturn in the economy, we were trying to find creative and inexpensive ways to recognize our employees. One of our cultural ambassadors had the idea of inviting one of their regular guests who was currently staying at the hotel to come to their monthly staff meeting and talk for ten minutes about what they enjoy about being there. They asked the guest beforehand if they would call out at least three specific people and publicly recognize them at the meeting. It ended up being a simple but powerful way for us to show recognition to our employees and connect with our most loyal customers. And it didn't cost us anything. We were able to share this idea that came from one of our cultural ambassadors, and scale it to the entire company."

Chip ended our discussion about the importance of culture by saying, "Culture is the ultimate strategic differentiator for a company. My favorite line about culture is, 'It's what happens around here when the boss is not around.' Culture is really the personality of an organization." The investment Chip and his team made in their culture paid off in many ways. Joie de Vivre became the second largest boutique hotel company in the United States. By making a commitment to culture as their foundation, they were able to create happy employees and loyal customers, which led to a profitable and sustainable business.

## Championship Team in Action

Another great example of how teamwork and culture impact results in a significant way is the San Francisco Giants. Over the last eight years I've been honored to have been invited several times to speak to their front-office staff, as well as to some of their players and coaches during spring training. I first partnered with the Giants in the spring of 2010. They had a young team that year, and some talented prospects in their minor league system, so the future looked bright. It seemed like they were a year or two away from being really good, and also like they were starting to develop some real chemistry as a team and as an organization.

They ended up making it into the playoffs on the final day of the 2010 season, but all the experts said they didn't have enough talent to win the World Series. They ended up getting hot that October, playing incredibly well in the playoffs, proving the experts wrong, and winning the World Series for the first time since the team had moved from New York to San Francisco in the late 1950s. It was a huge deal for the entire Bay Area and for Giants fans everywhere. Just as Michael Gervais talked about, it gave everyone permission to celebrate—and we did, big-time.

The Giants ended up winning three World Series championships—in 2010, 2012, and 2014—during a five-season stretch. And not only was that incredibly difficult in itself—they did it as underdogs in just about every post-season matchup they were in during those championship runs. They had good talent, but in most cases they didn't look like the best team on paper. Their ability to play well in big games, fueled by their incredible team culture, is what propelled them to those World Series titles.

They seemed to understand and embody all the essential intangible qualities—that below-the-line stuff that truly drives success and performance. Two particular examples epitomize to me both the success of the Giants during their championship run, and what it means to care about each other and know that they're all in it together.

On the Friday night of the final home series of the season, the Giants give out an internal award called the "Willie Mac Award." It's named after Hall of Famer Willie McCovey, who played for the Giants his entire career, from 1959 to 1980. It's voted on by the team and coaching staff, and is given to the most inspirational player each year. In 2013 the award went to Giants right fielder Hunter Pence. Hunter was an All-Star player who the Giants picked up at the trade deadline the season before. He became the team's inspirational leader in the playoffs in 2012, and his energy and enthusiasm in the clubhouse and dugout, as well as his play on the field, helped lead them to their second championship in three years that previous season. He played really well in 2013, but the team was, unfortunately, not going to the playoffs that year.

I was at the ballpark for that last Friday night home game of the 2013 season, and was excited to see the announcement of the Willie Mac Award, which is always a big deal and a fun ceremony. I was fired up when they announced that it was Hunter Pence, who seemed quite deserving of the award, and I also looked forward to hearing him speak, since he's such a passionate guy. Upon being announced as the winner right before the game, he came out onto the field surrounded by past winners of the award, and stood next to Willie McCovey himself, who was in a wheelchair beside the podium. Hunter got to the microphone, thanked Willie and others for the award, and then said something directly to his teammates that I wasn't prepared for: "I love every minute with you guys. I tell you that every day. I know some of you get uncomfortable when I tell you that I love you. You think it's soft. But I actually think it's the strongest thing we've got."

I was deeply moved by Hunter's courageous and vulnerable expression of love for his teammates. Telling them he loved them in front of 42,000 fans (let alone the multitudes watching it on TV), and the fact that he underscored it by saying that love is the strongest thing they had together, made my heart sing on so many different levels.

Fast forward to the next season (2014): The Giants are back in the World Series, it's game seven, and they're on the road against the Kansas City Royals. With two outs in the bottom of the ninth inning, they're up by one run, but the Royals have the tying run on third base. Giants pitcher Madison Bumgarner gets Royals catcher Salvador Pérez to hit a pop-up into foul ground. Giants third baseman Pablo Sandoval catches it for the third and final out of the game, and they win their third World Series title in five years. As Buster Posey, the Giants' All-Star catcher, comes out to the mound to give Bumgarner a celebratory hug, these two big, strong, tough men from the South— Georgia and North Carolina respectively—embrace each other. And right before the rest of the team comes piling out of the dugout to jump on top of them, you can see Bumgarner lean over and say into Posey's ear, "I love you!" It was one of the most heartwarming things I've ever seen on a baseball field. It moved me to tears and epitomized what a championship team is all about—caring about each other, knowing that they're all in it together, and, ultimately, loving one another.

Creating a championship team takes commitment, courage, and faith. We have to be willing to put our egos, agendas, and personal ambitions aside, at least to some degree, so that we can focus on the bigger goal and vision. A great team epitomizes what we mean by the whole being greater than the sum of its parts. With our work teams, this is about being all in, having each other's backs, and being willing to work through issues, challenges, and conflicts together. It's also about making a commitment to care about each other as human beings. This isn't always easy to do, but it's necessary if we're going to create the kind of success and fulfillment we want. And when we do this, we become part of something bigger than ourselves, and we give meaning and purpose to the work that we do and to our lives—which is what bringing our whole selves to work is truly all about.

# BRINGING IT ALL TOGETHER

Bringing our whole selves to work is about being authentic, utilizing the power of appreciation, focusing on emotional intelligence, embracing a growth mindset, and creating a championship team. These are the five principles we discussed in-depth in this book. In this final chapter, we're going to take a look at how we bring all of this together and put it into action in our personal lives, at work, and with the people around us. In the pages that follow, we'll briefly review the five principles and some key concepts and distinctions of each of them. We'll also discuss specific ways you can put these principles into practice for yourself and your team. As you'll notice, some of the action ideas mentioned in this chapter were discussed previously and some are new. This last chapter is designed as a recap and resource guide for you.

## Principle #1: Be Authentic

Being authentic is the foundation of bringing our whole selves to work. It takes real courage to show up, interact, and communicate with authenticity, especially at work.

Key concepts:

- **Authenticity Continuum:** Authenticity exists on a continuum with Phony on one side, Honest in the middle, and Authentic on the other side.

- **Authenticity Equation:** Honesty – Self-Righteousness + Vulnerability = Authenticity

- **Two Types of Credibility:** Professional credibility is about our education, résumé, background, and title. Personal credibility is about our authenticity, trustworthiness, and ability to connect and relate to people in a genuine way.

## Authenticity Action Ideas:

**Lower Your Waterline.** Look for any opportunity to lower the waterline on your iceberg with the people around you—at work and at home. Be willing to admit your fears, doubts, insecurities, challenges, and whatever else is real for you. This can be done in simple day-to-day interactions. You can also lead and facilitate the "If You Really Knew Me" exercise, which can have a profound impact on the connection of your team members to one another, as well as enhance the empathy and psychological safety of the group. You can refer to pages 39–44 in Chapter 1 for the specific instructions on how to set up, facilitate, and debrief this powerful exercise.

**Ask for Help.** Most of us like helping others, but have a harder time asking for and receiving help. Asking for help shows vulnerability. Many of us fear that if we ask for help we will either get rejected or be judged. But if we have the courage to ask for help, a few important things can happen. First, we might actually get some help, which can lower the stress and pressure on us. Second, we might impact the culture by making it less taboo to ask for help. Third, we would give other people the opportunity to do something most of us love to do: help. If we think of asking for help as a courageous and generous act (which it is), we can have more freedom to ask for it, which will benefit us and everyone around us. It's also important to remember that just because we ask doesn't mean people have to help. We need to make it okay for people to decline. And if we practice asking for help in a gracious way, and we're grateful when we get it, we can create a virtuous cycle of giving and receiving help on our team or in our work environment.

**Check In with Others.** It's important to check in with the people around us, especially in the fast-paced world in which we live and work these days. We can ask "How are you?" and really mean it—not as just a social norm. By checking in with the people around us, we give them an opportunity to lower the waterline on their iceberg a bit and vice versa. Some of the best teams I work with have a simple check-in process they go through at the start of their meetings. It's usually brief, but it allows people to be more present and share something about how they feel, where they're at, and what's going on, which connects the members of the team on a human level and sets the tone for the meeting. Some of the best managers I work with make sure they really check in with the people on their team when they have their one-on-ones—not just go through a list of tasks and goals. Checking in is a simple technique which is about connecting authentically with those around us, especially when we're all busy or stressed out.

**Admit When You Don't Know Things or Make Mistakes.** Although it can sometimes seem counterintuitive, one of the best things we can do to liberate ourselves and build trust and connection with those around us is to admit when we don't know something or make a mistake. Many of us, myself included, have learned how to "save face." This is a nice way of saying we know how to lie in the face of not knowing something or messing something up. While this might be a decent survival skill, especially in business, it creates unnecessary stress and can lead to mistrust in our relationships. The more comfortable we are admitting that we don't know something or that we've made a mistake, the easier it will be for us to learn and make amends. Doing this also allows our co-workers to trust us more deeply, and it creates an environment where not knowing everything and messing things up from time to time is acceptable. This is about remembering that we're human and imperfect, and being willing to model this courageously.

**Address Conflicts Directly and Quickly.** One of the biggest things that gets in the way of authenticity is our avoidance of conflict or potentially difficult conversations. We have a tendency to avoid conflict because it can be scary and uncomfortable. The more willing we are to lean into that discomfort and have those "ten minute, sweaty-palmed conversations," the better our relationships and culture will be. Most real conflicts don't just go away on their own. And they usually don't improve with time if we avoid them. But if we can acknowledge and address them as they come up, we're more likely to resolve them and not give away our power to the fear of conflict. Sometimes we may need some coaching or direct support in both addressing and resolving a particular conflict, which is okay. Dealing with conflict takes courage and is one of the most vulnerable aspects of being human and working in a team environment. And when we're willing to address conflicts directly and quickly, it benefits us and everyone around us.

## Principle #2: Utilize the
## Power of Appreciation

Utilizing the power of appreciation is fundamental to building strong relationships with the people around us and keeping things in a healthy and positive perspective. Bringing our whole selves to work is about being willing to show up fully and be seen, and also about being able to truly see and empower the people we work with. This is exactly what appreciation provides.

Key concepts:

- **The Distinction Between Recognition and Appreciation:** Recognition is about what people do (their results). Appreciation is about who people are (their inherent value).

- **Gratitude:** The foundation of appreciation is gratitude. It's the quality of being thankful; readiness to show appreciation for and to return kindness.

### Appreciation Action Ideas:

**Appreciate People.** As Oprah said, people want to be seen and heard, and to know that who they are matters. Appreciating people is about letting them know that we see them, hear them, and care about them. Look for things to appreciate about people—we almost always find what we look for in others. Create opportunities to express appreciation for the people around you in meetings, conversations, e-mails, and day-to-day interactions. A little bit of appreciation goes a long way, and when you make it part of how you interact and communicate, and how your team operates, it has a positive impact on everyone. You can also do the "Appreciation Seat" exercise with your team. It's a powerful way to express appreciation specifically and to enhance your connection with each other. You can check out pages 62–67 where I walk through how to set up, facilitate, and debrief this activity.

**Ask People What They're Grateful For.** The simple question "What are you grateful for?" is such a great conversation starter. As I mentioned in Chapter 2, I ask this question about once a week on social media and it's on the outgoing message on the voicemail in my office. You could do one or both of these things yourself. It's also a great question to ask in team meetings and one-on-ones, or in any conversation. Gratitude is a generating emotion—it makes us feel better physically, mentally, and emotionally when we think or talk about what we're grateful for. Creating an "Attitude of Gratitude" for yourself and your team, like Cindy Elkins and her team did at Genentech, takes some thought, commitment, and follow-through, for sure. However, doing it can have an impact on both the culture and the performance of your team.

**Write Heartfelt Handwritten Notes of Appreciation.** Expressing appreciation of any kind and in any form can have a positive impact, as long as it's done in a real way and with genuine intention. However, one of the most memorable and profound ways for us to express our appreciation for other people, especially these days, is to write a handwritten, heartfelt note of appreciation. Handwritten notes are becoming a bit of a lost art and practice in our digital world. And while this makes sense for a variety of reasons, when we do take the time to write someone a card in today's environment, it really gets their attention. You could make it a practice to write at least one handwritten note of appreciation each week for someone you work with. Doing this is a simple act that can have a meaningful impact on the people around us.

**Start Meetings with Good Stuff and End with Appreciations.** Some of the best and most positive teams I work with start their meetings with good stuff and/or leave a little time at the end of meetings for some quick appreciations. Meetings can start late, run long, be boring, and not always be the most productive or inspiring use of our time. But taking just a few minutes at the start of the meeting to talk about some good stuff, as Erica Fox did with her remote team at Google, often sets a positive tone for the meeting and gets people more personally connected with one another. Leaving a little time at the end of the meeting for some appreciations—for each other, for what got accomplished, or for what's going on with the team or in the company—is a nice way to wrap up and end on a positive note, especially if the meeting was in any way difficult or things are stressful in general. These are ongoing practices you can use to maintain and enhance the morale and culture of your team.

**When Someone Compliments You, Just Say "Thank You."** You know what you're supposed to say when someone compliments you? Thank you. Then, shut your mouth. If you listen to yourself and other people, what comes after the "thank you" (if that even gets said), is almost always weird and insincere. We often either give a compliment right back or we somehow discount or disagree with it. A compliment is a gift, and our job is to receive it as graciously and gratefully as we possibly can (whether or not we agree with it). We have to get past the social norms we've been taught about receiving compliments and appreciation from others, so that we can open up and really let it in. When we do this, not only are we more able to receive the appreciation, but we actually make it more likely that people will be comfortable giving us compliments more often. I've seen this one thing change the dynamic and culture of teams. It actually creates more psychological safety for the team when we know that we can express appreciation for one another and that it won't turn into a joke or an awkward experience.

## Principle #3: Focus on Emotional Intelligence

Emotional Intelligence (EQ) is one of the most important aspects of our ability to bring our whole selves to work, as well as to be successful both at what we do and in our relationships with others. Remember what Jeff Vijungco from Adobe said: "IQ often gets us our job, but EQ gets us promoted."

Key concepts:

- **The Four Components of Emotional Intelligence:** Self-awareness, self-management, social awareness, and relationship management.

- **Mindfulness:** Being mindful and creating mindfulness practices has become widely accepted and encouraged in today's business world, and is also one of the best ways for us to enhance our capacity for self-awareness and self-management.

- **Listening:** The key to communication is listening. And our ability to be socially aware and to manage our relationships effectively often is predicated on our ability to listen. It's important to be aware of what gets in our way when we listen and to remember the three levels: (1) Listen to what's being said, (2) Make an emotional connection, and (3) Clean out our filter.

## Emotional Intelligence Action Ideas:

**Check In with Yourself.** The first and most important aspect of emotional intelligence is self-awareness. If we aren't aware of ourselves—what we're thinking and how we're feeling in the moment, and more generally our tendencies, trigger points, and motivations—we can't focus on self-management, social awareness, or relationship management. It all starts with us. Being able to check in with ourselves in a healthy way, and on a regular basis, is essential to raising our EQ. It could be something as simple as taking a deep breath, noticing our posture, or asking ourselves "How am I feeling in this moment?" Checking in with ourselves is important for us to incorporate into how we move through our day so that we can be present and fully show up.

**Create or Enhance Your Mindfulness Practices.** Mindfulness practices are specific and habitual ways we can enhance our ability to be mindful and emotionally intelligent. If you don't currently have any mindfulness practices, think of some things you can do that might work for your lifestyle and personality. There are so many tools and resources these days—books, videos, apps, and more—to both teach us and remind us about how we can slow down, meditate, and be more mindful in our lives. I shared some of my own mindfulness practices on pages 101–105; feel free to copy or modify any that resonate with you. And even if you already have a set of mindfulness practices, it's always good to continue to check in with yourself to see if it might be time to change or enhance anything you're doing to make sure it's serving you most effectively in your life right now. It can also be fun and productive to talk about this at work, and even to look at ways you and your team can implement some mindfulness practices that can positively impact the energy and morale of the entire group.

**Write in a Journal.** This is a simple practice, and it's one of the mindfulness practices I recommend, but its impact can be profound. As I mentioned, I've been writing in a journal since I was in college and these days I have two journals—a regular one and a gratitude/self-forgiveness one, both of which I carry around with me in my briefcase. If you already have a journaling practice, that's great. It's just important to remember to do it regularly. I notice a big difference in my life and my work when I'm journaling consistently and when I'm not. And, if this hasn't been a practice for you, it can be fun and easy to pick up a nice journal, and to start sharing some of your thoughts and feelings in it on a regular basis. You can keep it by your bed, on your desk, and/or carry it around with you in your bag like I do. Journaling is a great mindfulness practice and a great way for us to check in with ourselves, be real about our thoughts and feelings, and to be able to share what's going on inside of us in a way that's safe and healthy. It's also a great way to enhance our emotional intelligence.

**Give People Your Undivided Attention When They're Talking.** As we discussed in this chapter on EQ, listening can be challenging, especially in today's world with all our devices and distractions. The truth is, we can't effectively listen to other people in a way that is both empowering to them and helpful to us, if we're not paying attention. As hard as it can be at times, we have to put down our phone, turn away from our computer, and give the person we're talking to our full and undivided attention. If we're not able to do that, it's both disrespectful to them and ineffective for us. If we can create a culture where we give each other our full attention or we're willing to be honest about our inability to do so, it ends up benefitting everyone, as well as enhancing our communication and our relationships. Some of the best and most productive teams I work with have clear norms about phones and laptops at team meetings. While sometimes it might be necessary for these devices to be used in meetings, they usually aren't needed, and just take everyone away from the conversation and from connecting with each other. It's a good idea to discuss this dynamic with your team, and potentially come to some specific agreements about how devices should be used (or not) when you meet as a group.

**Clean Out Your Filter.** The filter we listen through determines the quality of our communication and has a big impact on what we hear and the nature of our relationships with others. If our filter gets clogged up, like the filter in the dryer, it's important that we clean it out. There are really only two ways to do this: (1) address the issue or issues that are clogging up the filter directly with the person or people involved, and be willing to hang in there for as long as it takes until the issue is resolved; or (2), simply choose to let it go and change our perception. Both of these options can be challenging for different reasons. The first one usually involves some of those "sweaty-palmed conversations" that can be scary or uncomfortable. The second one involves us rising above our judgments and self-righteousness, which we often think are "true." In either case, if we're truly committed to resolving the issues and cleaning out the filter, we can do it, and it will benefit us, our communication, and the relationship we have with the other person or people involved.

### Principle #4: Embrace a Growth Mindset

Growth mindset is a powerful perspective that we consciously choose. It's a belief and understanding that we can improve if we're willing to work hard, dedicate ourselves, and practice. Growth mindset is also about looking at everything that we experience as an opportunity to learn and develop, which is essential to bringing our whole selves to work.

Key concepts:

- **Fixed Mindset vs. Growth Mindset:** Fixed mindset is the belief that our talents are innate gifts that we're either born with or not, and that can't be changed. Growth mindset is the belief that our talents can be developed through hard work, learning, good strategies, and input from others.

- **Why is this happening FOR me?:** When something happens we don't like or understand, instead of asking "Why is this happening *to* me?" we can ask, "Why is this happening *for* me?" And that shifts us from victimhood to a place of curiosity, empowerment, and potential growth.

- **Fixed-Mindset Triggers:** Our mindset exists on a continuum from fixed, to mixed, to growth; and is not static. It's important for us to pay attention to certain "triggers"—such as criticism, comparison, and failure—that can snap us from growth mindset to fixed mindset in a hurry.

### Growth-Mindset Action Ideas:

**Get a Coach/Counselor.** Having people in our lives like coaches, counselors, mentors, and others whom we explicitly empower to give us feedback and support us in our journey is a great way both to help us grow and to enhance our growth mindset. Growth is growth, but growth mindset is our attitude or perspective concerning growth. As I mentioned in the chapter on growth mindset, I've had many amazing people in my life who have helped me along the way. I currently have some wonderful coaches, counselors, and mentors who support me in my own growth, healing, and especially my work. If you already have someone (or more than one person) in your life like this, great. If not, finding one or more people to support you is a great way to accelerate your growth and to make sure you are operating with a growth mindset as much as possible.

**Take Personal-Growth Workshops.** Personal-growth workshops are a powerful way to make breakthrough changes in our lives. As I mentioned, I've been taking personal-growth workshops, seminars, and courses for the past 20 years, and I have learned, grown, and changed a great deal because of them. It's also how I met Michelle. There are many good programs out there. I highly recommend the Hoffman Institute and Landmark Worldwide, two organizations that offer personal-growth courses. I also recommend retreat centers like Esalen, 1440 Multiversity, and the Omega Institute. These beautiful places have workshops and retreats every week and weekend throughout the year, all delivered by teachers, authors, and experts of all kinds. If you check out their websites, you'll probably want to sign up for a dozen courses. Make taking personal-growth workshops a regular practice for you and the benefits will be enormous, both personally and professionally.

**Make Commitments to Your Team.** Commitment and accountability are essential to our growth and success. A great way to support your development and actively practice your growth mindset is to make commitments to your manager and/or your team. Let them know what you're up to and working on. Creating a team environment in which we talk openly about our development plans, what we're working on, and how we want to improve not only makes it more likely we will improve, but also brings the team closer together, creates more psychological safety, and fosters a team culture of learning and growth. The people on our team (and in our lives) can be great resources for us, as we can be for them. Making commitments to them, and allowing them to hold us accountable, is extremely important and beneficial.

**Celebrate Failure.** When Samantha, our older daughter, was learning to walk we would cheer for her when she tried to do it but fell down. It was a beautiful example of celebrating failure and knowing that doing so was supporting her ultimate success. At some point, fairly early in life, we tend to stop celebrating failure, and we often try to avoid it or cover it up when it happens, thinking that it's "bad." Failure is essential to learning and success. And embracing and celebrating failure is what growth mindset is all about. What can you do in your personal life, at work, and with your team to celebrate failure? The more willing we are to talk about and celebrate failure, the less power we give to it—and the more likely we are to take risks.

**Use Start, Stop, Continue As a Practice.** These three words—Start, Stop, Continue—denote powerful concepts to think about when making changes—in our personal lives, at work, or as a team. They're also great words to use when we're both giving and receiving feedback. As I talked about on pages 128–134, I use them (and you can too) with teams in two different ways: at the end of meetings or offsites as a way to focus on change, and to give feedback in a one-on-one meeting or even as a group. It takes courage, commitment, and a high level of maturity and emotional intelligence to use these practices, especially the group-feedback one. But embracing feedback and being willing to seek it out, ask for it, and consider it when it comes our way, is one of the best ways we can enhance our growth mindset. And when we're willing to do this with our team, we can grow exponentially and do so together.

## Principle #5: Create a Championship Team

Our ability to bring our whole selves to work is significantly impacted by the people we work with and our work environment. At the same time, when we show up fully we have the ability to impact and inspire those around us. Creating a championship team is both necessary for us to be able to bring all of who we are to the work that we do, and it's often the natural response when we and the people around us fully engage in our work and with each other.

Key concepts:

- **Mechanics vs. Psychology (Above the Line/ Below the Line):** From a team standpoint, mechanics are "above the line" (what we do and how we do it) and psychology is "below the line" (how we think and feel, our perspective, and the collective morale and culture). Since the below-the-line stuff is 80 percent of our success as a team, we have to pay more attention to these intangible things if we're going to be the kind of team we truly want to be.

- **Two Key Conditions That Create High Performance:** (1) Healthy high expectations, and (2) High level of nurturance.

- **Psychological Safety:** This is a sense of confidence that your team will not embarrass, reject, or punish you for speaking up. The team climate is one characterized by interpersonal trust and mutual respect, and in which people are comfortable being themselves and willing to take risks.

## Teamwork Action Ideas:

**Focus on Your Job More Than Your Role.** As we discussed, everyone on the team (and in the company) has the same job—to help the team win. However big or small our team or company may be, remembering that our job is ultimately to do whatever we can to fulfill the mission and accomplish the goals of the company makes things pretty clear. We all have a different role, which is what we as individuals do and focus on each day at work. The more we focus on our job (helping the team win) the more able we are to collaborate with others, let go of petty grievances, and keep things in perspective. Talking to the people on your team about this concept is a good place to start. When everyone gets on the same page about it, it makes it easier for us to support each other and not let our role get in the way of our job.

**Create and Live by Team Values.** Your company probably has stated core values. Your team may or may not have its own particular values. It's important to do whatever you can to have the company's values be alive and present for you and your team every day. It's one of the things that can remind you and your colleagues to focus on your jobs more than your roles. And even if the company's values are clear and present within your team, it's often a good idea to have certain special team values that can help you all operate in the most positive, productive way. If your team already has such values, it's important to make sure you're living by and holding yourself to them. A simple way to create values for your team is to do a brainstorming exercise where you collectively write as many relevant values as possible on one big flip chart or whiteboard, and then have everyone on the team vote by placing colored dots next to the five they like best. Based on the voting and feedback, you can narrow the list down to three to five core values, and then, as a group, articulate what those words specifically mean to your team and how you want to embody them in the work you do together.

**Elect Cultural Ambassadors.** Following the advice Chip Conley shared with me, making someone on your team—maybe you—be accountable for the culture can be a great asset. On the best teams, of course, everyone takes ownership of the culture. But it's incredibly important to have one or more people focused on culture and looking for new, fun, and creative ways to engage everyone and enhance the team chemistry. It's nice when this responsibility gets shared over time as well. It's important to do this in a creative and authentic way, especially based on the specific size, makeup, and dynamic of your team.

**Talk about Your Team Dynamic.** Since 80 percent of our team's success is a psychological or "below the line" phenomenon, we have to spend more time thinking and talking about the team dynamic—how we get along, collaborate, communicate, and interact, and our overall morale. Building in time during the week, team meetings, and daily activities to focus on the health of the team is important. The challenge is that most of our daily activities are focused on mechanics—tasks, results, and so on. It takes commitment, planning, and courage to do this, but it's very important. Setting up regular offsite meetings to discuss larger issues related to the company, the team, the team dynamic, and life in general is essential to the team's culture and well-being. Getting off the treadmill of activity from time to time is necessary. And being willing to have those "sweaty-palmed conversations" about some of the challenging team-dynamic stuff that inevitably comes up, even with the best teams, is crucial to your success.

**Do Fun Things Together.** We spend so much of our time and our life at work that it's important we find ways to have fun together. Doing simple things like going out to lunch together, sharing funny stories from our lives outside of work, and finding activities that we can do together that have nothing to do with work are all things that reduce our stress level, create connection, and make working together more enjoyable. It's easier to win when we have fun working together. Ask the people on your team what would be fun for them, and see if you can set up some of these activities for all of you to do on a regular basis—both at work and when you gather together offsite. It doesn't usually take a lot of money or time to have fun, but the impact and benefits of this on our morale, engagement, and productivity can be huge.

Most of these action ideas are pretty straightforward. Some are probably things you're already doing or have done in the past. Some may be new ideas, or simply ones you haven't tried to practice yourself or with others in the past. My suggestion is to pick a few of the things mentioned in this chapter (or things that were inspired by reading this chapter or any of the previous chapters in the book) and commit yourself to putting them into practice for yourself and to mentioning them to your team. And as you probably noticed while reading this chapter (and throughout the book), many of the things that apply to our work and to our team also apply to our personal lives, our families, and all the people and things outside of work.

There's a Japanese proverb that I love: "Vison without action is a daydream. And action without vision is a nightmare." How we create positive change for ourselves and the people around us is by taking our vision, our ideas, and our inspiration, and putting them together with some specific actions that we commit to and put into practice.

## Keeping Things in Perspective

Arianna Huffington, the co-founder and former editor-in-chief of the Huffington Post, spoke at a Wisdom 2.0 conference a few years ago. She asked us a simple but profound question: "Are you living your résumé or your eulogy?" When we go to a memorial service and listen to people get up and talk about the person who has died, we don't usually hear about their job titles, promotions, awards, or accomplishments. We hear stories about who they were, how they lived, and the impact they had on the people around them. As I write this final section of this book, I'll be heading later today to a memorial service for a 47-year-old friend of ours who passed away suddenly. As I shared in the Introduction, my sister Lori's death, and some of the other significant losses I've experienced in my life, have been painful but important reminders of the impermanence of human life.

Bringing our whole selves to work is about having the courage to be authentic, caring enough to express our appreciation, being aware so that we can focus on our emotional intelligence, having the willingness to embrace a growth mindset, and making a commitment to creating a championship team around us. It's really about choosing to work and live today the way we want people to talk about us in our eulogy, instead of just trying to make our résumé look good.

The concepts and distinctions we've discussed in this book are fairly straightforward, but practicing them isn't always easy. They take courage, commitment, curiosity, openness, faith, and a willingness to be vulnerable, to fail, and to fully show up. This is what being human is all about, and this is what it takes for us not only to bring our whole selves to work, but to bring our whole selves to life!

# RESOURCES

Below you'll find a list of resources from me as well as others (books, workshops, podcasts, events, videos, and more). All these resources are ones that I believe in and recommend strongly. Each will support and empower you on your path of growth, discovery, and bringing your whole self to work.

## From Me

*Be Yourself, Everyone Else Is Already Taken* (book)
*Bring Your Whole Self to Work* (podcast)
   Mike-Robbins.com/Podcast
*Focus on the Good Stuff* (book)
*Meditations* (audios)—Mike-Robbins.com/Meditations
*Nothing Changes Until You Do* (book)
"The Power of Appreciation" (audio)
   Mike-Robbins.com/Resources

## Books

*10% Happier,* by Dan Harris
*Big Magic,* by Elizabeth Gilbert
*Braving the Wilderness,* by Brené Brown
*Conscious Capitalism,* by John Mackey and Raj Sisodia
*Daring Greatly,* by Brené Brown
*Delivering Happiness,* by Tony Hsieh
*Don't Sweat the Small Stuff at Work,* by Richard Carlson

*Drive*, by Daniel Pink
*Emotional Intelligence,* by Daniel Goleman
*Find Your Why*, by Simon Sinek
*The Five Dysfunctions of a Team*, by Patrick Lencioni
*Grit*, by Angela Duckworth
*The Last Lecture*, by Randy Pausch
*Leading with Noble Purpose,* by Lisa Earle McLeod
*Lean In*, by Sheryl Sandberg
*Love Warrior*, by Glennon Doyle
*A Mindful Nation*, by Tim Ryan
*Option B*, by Sheryl Sandberg and Adam Grant
*Peak*, by Chip Conley
*The Power Paradox*, by Dacher Keltner
*Radical Candor*, by Kim Scott
*Rising Strong*, by Brené Brown
*Search Inside Yourself,* by Chade-Meng Tan
*Self-Compassion*, by Kristin Neff
*StandOut 2.0,* by Marcus Buckingham
*Start Something That Matters*, by Blake Mycoskie
*StrengthsFinder 2.0*, by Tom Rath
*Success Intelligence*, by Robert Holden
*The Way We're Working Isn't Working*, by Tony Schwartz
*There's No Good Card for This*, by Kelsey Crowe
*Thrive*, by Arianna Huffington
*Triggers*, by Marshal Goldsmith
*You Win in the Locker Room First,* by Jon Gordon
and Mike Smith

## Workshops

Being the Change (ChallengeDay.org)
The Hoffman Process (HoffmanInstitute.org)
The Landmark Forum (LandmarkWorldWide.com)
The New Warrior Training Adventure
(MankindProject.org)
The Shadow Process (TheFordInstitute.com)

## Podcasts

*10% Happier* with Dan Harris
*Good Life Project* with Jonathan Fields
*HBR IdeaCast*
*The One & Only Podcast* with Mark Shapiro
*Making the Cut with Chris Hill and Shawn Wenner*
*The Marie Forleo Podcast*
*Radical Candor* with Kim Scott
*The School of Greatness* with Lewis Howes
*Sounds True: Insights at the Edge* with Tami Simon
*The Tim Ferriss Show*

## Events/Conferences/Retreat Centers

1440 Multiversity (1440.org)
Conscious Capitalism (ConsciousCapitalism.org)
Esalen Institute (Esalen.org)
Omega Institute (Eomega.org)
Wisdom 2.0 (Wisdom2Summit.com)
WorkHuman (WorkHuman.com)

## Videos/Websites/Blogs

HBR.org (Harvard Business Review website)
*The Mask You Live In* (film), by Jennifer Siebel Newsom
Momastery.com (fantastic, real, and inspirational blog)
*The Shift* (film), by Wayne Dyer
TED.com (any and all videos on this site or app,
    especially by Brené Brown, Simon Sinek, Elizabeth
    Gilbert, and Steve Jobs)

# ACKNOWLEDGMENTS

I feel humbled and grateful when I think of the many wonderful people who helped make this book possible and who support me in my work and life. First and foremost, Michelle Benoit Robbins, you are the love of my life, the muse of my creativity and passion, and such an incredible wife, mother, and partner. Thank you for loving me, supporting me, and doing all that you do so that I can do this work. Samantha Benoit Robbins, thank you for your passion, curiosity, and love. I love seeing you grow, how thoughtful you are, and how deeply you feel. Annarose Benoit Robbins, thank you for your joyful enthusiasm, laughter, and willingness. I love how hungry you are to learn, grow, and challenge yourself.

Lori Robbins, thank you for teaching me and inspiring me in life, through your illness, and in death. I miss you. Rachel Cohen, thanks for being my friend and my sister, and for being there for me always with truth and love.

Melanie Bates, you are so gifted, talented, and full of wisdom. You truly are a book shaman. Thank you for your coaching, your feedback, your editing, and your incredible support and partnership with this book, I could not have done it without you.

Steve Harris and Michele Martin, thank you for believing in me and my work, and supporting me and this book. Judy Wang, thank you for your great research for this book and your passion for the topics, I appreciated working with you on this project. Jessica Woodall-Massey, thank you for your constant support of me, my business, and our family. I am grateful for your hard work, dedication, and tenacity, and for all that you do to make things work in my world.

Reid Tracy, Patty Gift, Sally Mason-Swaab, Marlene Robinson, and the entire Hay House team—thank you for your partnership and support on this book and in general. I'm grateful to be a part of the Hay House family.

Cai Bristol, thank you for your continued support over the past few years and for helping me stay open, clear, healthy, and energetically aligned with my purpose. Eleanor, I'm grateful for your support and the wonderful work we've done together over the past six years. You've helped me change, heal, and bring even more of myself to my work and my life, thank you.

Cindy Elkins, Chip Conley, Stuart Crabb, Eric Severson, Melissa Daimler, Catey McCreary, Donna Morris, Rich Dutra-St. John, Yvonne St. John-Dutra, Marc Lesser, Chade-Meng Tan, Matthew Luhn, Erica Fox, Jay Allen, Jason Hughes, Shay Hughes, George Mumford, Michael Gervais, Tim Ryan, Kelsey Crowe, Aditi Dhagat, Chris Mauger, Soren Gordhamer, Karen May, Don Lippi, and Jeff Vijungco—thank you for your wonderful stories and quotes, and for allowing me to share them in this book.

Dacher Keltner, Michelle Gale, Bob Andrews, Gopi Kallayli, Robert Holden, Jonathan Fields, Gabrielle Bernstein, Michael Bungay Stanier, John O'Leary, Lisa Earle McLeod, Chantal Pierrat, Ann Robie, Joe Greenstein, Tom Kelly, Mark Shapiro, Dan Henkle, Jon Gordon, Jen Glanz, Rachel Macy Stafford, Brett Berson, Nancy Collier, Chris Hill, Tami Simon, Vicki Hoefle, Jennifer Rock, Mike Voss, and all my other guests on the *Bring Your Whole Self to*

*Work* podcast—thank you for opening up and sharing your stories and wisdom.

Brené Brown, Glennon Doyle, Elizabeth Gilbert, Sheryl Sandberg, Simon Sinek, Tony Schwartz, Daniel Pink, Marcus Buckingham, Daniel Goleman, Adam Grant, Tom Rath, Amy Edmondson, Carol Dweck—thank you for your inspiring work, which has had an impact on me personally, on my work, and especially on this book.

To all of our clients, especially the ones who partner with us on a regular basis—Google, Wells Fargo, Gap, Schwab, Genentech, Hughes Marino, Microsoft, Pinterest, eBay, Airbnb, Western Digital, Yum Inc., Adobe, Nutanix, OneMain, Washington Speakers Bureau, and Eagles Talent—thank you for your interest in my work and for trusting me to speak to and work with your people, leaders, and teams. I'm grateful for our partnership.

To the wonderful staff at the Roman Spa in Calistoga, California—thank you for taking such good care of me all the times I came to stay at your property while I was writing this book. I love it there!

I am also grateful to my friends and all the people who support, inspire and challenge me to be myself and bring all of who I am to my work and my life. Thank you!

# ABOUT THE AUTHOR

Mike Robbins is the author of *Focus on the Good Stuff; Be Yourself, Everyone Else Is Already Taken;* and *Nothing Changes Until You Do,* which have been translated into 14 languages. He's a sought-after speaker, consultant, and thought leader who delivers keynotes and seminars around the world. His clients include Google, Wells Fargo, Microsoft, Gap, Adobe, the IRS, Charles Schwab, Airbnb, State Farm, the NBA, eBay, Deloitte, the San Francisco Giants, and many more.

Prior to his current work, Mike was drafted by the New York Yankees out of high school, but chose instead to play baseball at Stanford University, where he pitched in the College World Series. After college, he played baseball professionally in the Kansas City Royals organization until an injury ended his career while he was still in the minor leagues. He then worked in sales and business development for two tech start-ups, before starting his own consulting company in 2001.

He's been a regular contributor to the *Huffington Post* for the past decade, and his work has been featured in *Forbes, Fast Company,* the *Wall Street Journal,* and many other publications. Mike lives in the San Francisco Bay Area with this wife, Michelle, and their two daughters, Samantha and Annarose.

To learn more about Mike and his work, visit Mike-Robbins.com, or connect with him on Facebook (@ MikeRobbinsPage) and Twitter (@MikeDRobbins).

# Hay House Titles of Related Interest

We hope you enjoyed this Hay House book. If you'd like to receive our online catalog featuring additional information on Hay House books and products, or if you'd like to find out more about the Hay Foundation, please contact:

Hay House, Inc., P.O. Box 5100, Carlsbad, CA 92018-5100
(760) 431-7695 or (800) 654-5126
(760) 431-6948 (fax) or (800) 650-5115 (fax)
www.hayhouse.com® • www.hayfoundation.org

———

*Published in Australia by:*
Hay House Australia Pty. Ltd., 18/36 Ralph St., Alexandria NSW 2015
*Phone:* 612-9669-4299 • *Fax:* 612-9669-4144 • www.hayhouse.com.au

*Published in the United Kingdom by:*
Hay House UK, Ltd., Astley House, 33 Notting Hill Gate, London W11 3JQ
*Phone:* 44-20-3675-2450 • *Fax:* 44-20-3675-2451 • www.hayhouse.co.uk

*Published in India by:* Hay House Publishers India,
Muskaan Complex, Plot No. 3, B-2, Vasant Kunj, New Delhi 110 070
*Phone:* 91-11-4176-1620 • *Fax:* 91-11-4176-1630 • www.hayhouse.co.in

———

## Access New Knowledge.
## Anytime. Anywhere.

Learn and evolve at your own pace
with the world's leading experts.

www.hayhouseU.com